# BURIED
# THREADS

## Kaylin McFarren

THREADS SERIES – Book #2
October 2013 Distributed by:
Creative Edge Publishing LLC 8440 NE Alderwood Road, Suite A Portland,
OR 97220

Copyright Author: Kaylin McFarren Cover Artist: Amanda Tomo Yoshida

ISBN 10: 1492120464
ISBN 13: 9781492120469
Library of Congress Control Number: 2013917730
CreateSpace Independent Publishing Platform
North Charleston, South Carolina

Printed in the United States of America 10 9 8 7 6 5 4 3 2 1

## AUTHOR'S NOTE:

I like to describe my books as thrillers or romantic adventures, but they also revolve around family drama. This is by no means an accident. We all have families— good ones, bad ones, absent ones, indifferent ones—and sometimes members we never knew existed. However, for the purpose of my stories, it really doesn't matter. The connection is easy enough to make, and readers will relate despite inherent complexities. You see, I've learned how to turn my family dysfunction into an interesting garden. If you dig deep, you can find the richest literary soil. It is the place where I sow seeds of distrust, cultivate secrets and misdeeds, and grow vines of tension, twisting and turning in all directions. The thorns of betrayal cut more deeply, pain lingers longer, and the senses are left reeling from the poison of deceit. For an author, this is the gift of writing. This is what I hope to achieve.

So let me once again thank my remarkable family for their patience and understanding. My parents had hopes and dreams for their future together and in their own way provided the encouragement that led me to pursue mine. The children I've been blessed with will forever remain my most prideful accomplishments and have grown to become my true and dearest friends. Yet there is one person who has opened my life to endless possibilities and who has taught me to follow my heart...wherever it leads. This is, of course, my darling husband Junki—to whom this book is dedicated. Thank you for loving me, for your tasty late night suppers, shared bottles of wine, and for allowing me to drift away from time to time to dangerous, exotic places.

## BURIED THREADS

Two hungry souls consumed by greed,
Secured by honor, trust, and deed,
Did break the ties bound by a thread;
Succumbed by lust, their hunger fed.

A warrior's heart turned evil green,
Could not abide the troubled scene;
He pulled his sword with great disdain,
And slashed two throats to end his pain.

In foolish haste he'd killed a prince,
Would pay the price, his crime immense;
With no remorse, he took his knife
And joined his cruel, unfaithful wife.

The prince was laid on upturned stone,
Encased in jade to shield his bone;
Then hid within a walled divide,
His secret kept, the truth denied.

The heart of darkness at his side,
Held back the evil blue moon tide;
But greed returned September morn,
Freed the demons, lost and forlorn.

The night will come when all will flee.
Waves will take the dead to sea.
But if two Tridents find the key, A
Shoten monk will set them free.

---Kaylin McFarren

*Some people come into our lives,*
*leave footprints in our hearts,*
*and we are never ever the same.*

# 1

*The mystery begins...*

Kenji Ota didn't fit the description of a bloodthirsty killer. Upon meeting him, it would be difficult to believe he'd gotten away with murdering at least twenty-five men. He was intelligent, intuitive, and physically attractive. His black hair was kept short and neat, and from the professional manner in which he dressed and carried himself, he could have been mistaken for a television announcer or successful business executive. He socialized in mixed circles—with stockbrokers, politicians, and street-smart hoodlums alike—and his charming, larger-than-life personality drew the attention of attractive women everywhere. However, after meeting Mariko Abe, his taste in the fairer sex had been spoiled forever. No one in his mind would ever compare to Kyoto's most beautiful geisha or be foolish enough to keep her away from him.

At 8:45 p.m., he stepped inside RAIN, one of the hottest nightclubs in Japan's Roppongi district with his face hidden behind a katou anime mask. He knew that only the "big" people in Tokyo could gain access to this place, and at the age of twenty-nine, he was already considered one of the largest. His loyalty to his yakuza family, the Zakura-kai, carried great weight and had earned him three rankings within the Japanese syndicate: Kaito Mitsui's bodyguard, his personal advisor, and captain of his own crew of soldiers. Yet his hard-earned promotions were not the result of monies earned, smart business dealings, or his ability to entice new, ambitious recruits. They came as the result of his eight-year incarceration on behalf of his boss for a botched extortion scam.

With renewed interest in the noisy scene before him, Kenji pulled off his mask and tucked it into his black studded belt. He ran his hand across the back of his sweaty neck—the irritating result of another muggy August night. Unlike the devoted men in his crew, he shied away from solid black suits by wearing tight jeans and a loose white shirt most days. And although the police had released him only four days earlier, across his back he carried a red wakizashi—a lethal thirty-one inch sword.

Associates who were below Kenji's rank moved quickly aside and bowed in respect as he passed. On more than one occasion he'd proven himself a deadly adversary with his sweeping blade, the most memorable occurring ten years earlier. Boss Mitsui had called a meeting between Katsu Nagura and all the underbosses in the Zakura-kai to discuss territorial issues. Foolishly, Nagura had challenged their supreme leader, bringing him to his feet.

"You're not even worth killing! You stupid ingrate!" Kaito Mitsui yelled at the top of his lungs.

Dedicated to his mission to protect his boss at any cost, Kenji appeared in front of Nagura in the blink of an eye. He whipped out his sword and slashed the yakuza boss's face twice across both cheeks. Within seconds, four of his men jumped in and were dropped to their knees with gaping wounds and severed arteries. The ones that could stand scrambled to get out of there. The two that couldn't were carried off and deposited in a common grave. Strangely, the whereabouts of these men were of no interest to local officials or members of Nagura's group. Kenji was never confronted for his part in the bloody incident and was left to conduct business as usual in the Zakura-kai with the same unaffected attitude he exhibited tonight.

As he neared the DJ's booth, the bass-infused rock music grew louder. Hundreds of bodies bounced to the techno beat. Dresses shimmered beneath flashing strobe lights, and the surrounding bar was filled three deep with thirsty customers. By Kenji's estimate, it was unusually busy for a Monday night, even with the discounted drinks and rockabilly theme.

While he continued to eye the club's glitzy interior, contemplating owning it one day, two girls crossed the dance floor and headed straight for him. "Ken-chan, come dance with me," the girl in the skimpy red dress called out. She was swaying her hips to the music provocatively and angling a come-hither look. Her friend in a blue micro skirt joined in, matching her move for move. In his book, with their thigh-high stockings and hemlines barely covering their assets, they looked like Sasebo bargirls. But another quick look around convinced him they weren't alone in their meat market attire.

"You promised last time," the girl in red persisted.

Right. Kenji feigned a smile. He knew these girls belonged to Tak, a "family" member who enjoyed cheap whores and spending his money in by-the-hour love hotels.

"He's not interested in you," the other girl said, tugging at his arm. "He promised to dance with me. Right, Kenji?"

He hadn't, of course. He had better things to do and would have remembered if he'd made a promise to anyone...especially these two. He pulled his arm free with little effort. "Sorry, Tak's waiting. Maybe another time." Kenji could hear their annoying little whines as he stepped away.     Hustlers like these were more disappointed in the watered down drinks you didn't buy them than the time you weren't willing to spare.

He edged his way around the crowd and spotted his friend at the back of the room. As usual the acne-scarred rebel was hold-ing court in one of the club's high-back chairs with drinks on the table and two girls seated before him hanging on every word.

As he drew near, Tak's eyes lifted. "Hey, man! Been wait-ing for you. What took you so long?" Unlike most of the people Kenji socialized with, Takashi Bekku lacked proper manners. He was slow at paying tabs unless there was someone at the table he needed to impress. Although he was street smart, his educa-tion had ended at junior high. The knife scars on his arms and cheek came from his father and not from gang members as his girlfriends were led to believe. But despite it all, Kenji Ota valued their friendship and was confident that if worse came to worst, Takashi would be there for him—watching his back all the way.

"Sorry I'm late," Kenji said. "I had some business to take care of." He pulled up an empty chair, and two new girls came over to join them. They giggled, prattled away, and patted his shoulder, but he paid them no mind.

By the look of excitement in Tak's eyes, he knew exactly what Kenji was talking about. Earlier that night, Mitsui-san had ordered a hit on Nobu Kimura. He was a retired detective who had spent half his life trying to bring down the Zakura-kai. The man was clever, considering he was old, half blind, and favored a leg from a childhood injury. But he was also brazen and secretly corrupt. He had raided their clubs, planted wires, and hassled their business associates. He even went so far as to interrupt the boss's birthday party just when his cake arrived. All because

Mitsui refused to drop a dime—hand him a boss on a silver platter to make him look good with his department heads.

Of course it came as no surprise when Kenji got the order to get rid of him. Yet the recollection left him grimacing. He didn't mind taking care of the competition or squirrely guys in the organization, but this was different. Kimura was an outsider, a well-known official people were likely to miss.

Tak was grinning over the top of his drink. "So how'd it go? As good as I'm guessing?"

Kenji glanced away, recalling the white bathroom's blood-splattered walls. He grew anxious and started bouncing his heel under the table. Like chewing on fingernails, he found it hard to sit still and not move when surrounded by people.

"C'mon, gimme the gory details," his friend insisted.

Kenji leaned in and lowered his voice. "I sliced his neck from ear to ear like I'm gonna do yours if you don't shut up."

Tak laughed and slapped his fist into his hand. "Aw, man! Nice. Quick death. Now if it was me, I would've delivered slow torture."

"Yeah, that sounds like you. Anyway, you didn't ask me to come here to discuss Kimura. There must be something else on your mind, right?"

The girl on his left handed him one of the beers from the table. He nodded his thanks and twisted off the cap. After a long pull, he sat back and waited for Tak's answer. "I heard Satoru Yamada hooked up with an American treasure-hunting company and is flying in from Los Angeles tonight. The lead diver showed up three days ago and has been real tight with your sister Yuki ever since. They've been buying gear and going to libraries. Checking out history and treasure hunting shit. No one seems to know much, but I got a good feeling about this one."

Kenji listened closely, thoughtfully nodding. "Anyway, it turns out this guy has been trying to line up a dive boat. Since you got one stored in that marina you own, this could be your chance to pull in some real dough...maybe even throw a few crumbs my way."

Kenji snorted a laugh. "Yeah, right. What else do you know?"

"They're getting together for a meeting on Friday night and Yamada is planning to invite that geisha Mariko Abe to join them. One of my guys saw him checking out rings in Los Angeles a few days ago. Before the night is over, they might be celebrating more than a partnership." Shit. Kenji swallowed hard. He lowered his crossed arms but managed to keep his eyes level, knowing the slightest sign of weakness could undermine his position.

"Is that it?" he asked.

"So far. I'm going to do a little more snooping around to see if there's anything worthwhile to report. Just wanted to give you a head's up."

Ah...now it made sense. The real reason Tak had called and insisted he show up. It wasn't about his sister forming an alliance with Yamada. They'd been friends for years and were always covering for each other. But when it came to his boss, if the American was here to recover something of value, stealing it and handing it over to Mitsui could result in gaining his favor. Maybe even expedite a promotion.

"So where's this meeting going to take place?" Kenji asked. "If it's anywhere near the Tanahashi mansion, you won't make it in there alive. There are hundreds of guards surrounding that place. You'll be cut into tiny pieces if you take one step on their ground."

Tak was quick with a comeback. "No way in hell. You think I'm stupid? My connection at the Garden restaurant said they're due at six thirty."

"Fancy. Yamada must've swindled some rich gaijins out of their money," Kenji said. "So you got any idea what they're after?"

Tak half shrugged. "Not a clue."

"Well, if you hear anything, I'd be interested in knowing."

"Sure, you got it. Anyway, I'm thinking of crashing their party."

Kenji huffed a laugh. "Why would you do that?"

"Firsthand information, of course."

"Well, good luck with that." Kenji stood up to leave.

Tak reached out and grabbed his arm. "Wait a minute! I need your help."

"No way. It doesn't matter how much I hate Yamada, I'm not going anywhere near him. Not without the boss's say-so."

Tak's eyes narrowed. "Whatever I find out could benefit the Zakura-kai," he reminded him.

It was no secret Kenji would do anything for the family: infiltrate investment companies, circulate meth, demand protection money…even destroy their enemies should he be called upon to do so. And even though friendships were short-lived, they were equally important. He didn't want to waste the rest of his life looking over his shoulder. Too many years had been spent that way.

Kenji heaved a sigh. If he didn't go along to keep Takashi Bekku out of trouble, the next execution order he received could have his name written all over it. "All right," he finally said. "What do you want me to do?"

"You'll love it. I picked up a wig and borrowed some women's clothes. I heard they're looking for wait staff, so I thought we'd sneak into the restaurant pretending to be servers."

Kenji unleashed a cynical laugh. "You're kidding, right? Women's clothes? And who do you think is going to wear those?"

Tak's brow furrowed. "You got a better idea?"

"As a matter of fact I do." Kenji thought about Yamada and Mariko, and the promise he had made to himself to never let anyone have her...especially that ridiculous self-serving monk. "I might have to clean out half my bank account before I'm through," he said, "but in the end, it will all be worth it."

The doorbell buzzed again. Kenji laughed and walked to the front door of his apartment with his towel draped over his shoulder and his white shirt unbuttoned. He was getting ready to tell Takashi he wasn't interested in his stupid plan or in hearing more about the container he was in the process of loading. But by the time he'd pulled the knob and begun to swing the door open, he realized he really didn't know who was on the other side and almost slammed the door in the face of a nerdy-looking guy.

"Kenji Ota? I'm here about a plumbing issue. Sorry, am I interrupting?"

What the hell. Kenji looked him up and down. "Yes to the first, no to the second," he said sternly. The guy had brownish hair, which was scattered ambiguously about his head. His face was freckled and he appeared to be middle-aged with neither the build nor the dress of a yakuza gang member. All in all he looked perfectly harmless. Still, Kenji reflected, so had the others.

"I'm in charge of maintenance," the man explained. "My name is Daiichi Asano. As you may know, there have been some concerns about possible water leakage in the building. We're having a terrible time trying to find the source, though, and we're reduced to looking at any suspect blip in our readings, no matter how insignificant. Uh, have you noticed anything leaking in your apartment?"

"I was using the shower earlier," Kenji said. "Would that do it?"

Daiichi sighed. "Ah, yes. I believe it would." He fiddled with the seam in his pants, then seemed to notice himself and swiftly placed his hand in his back pocket.

"Did you want something else?" Kenji said.

"Well…I know this is a bit of a bother, but might I take a look around, just for appearance sake? If I can't tell my boss I gave this an inspection, even a cursory one, he'll have my head."

Kenji hesitated, but decided that he might as well let the man take a look rather than arouse any kind of suspicion, however small. "Sure, help yourself," he said.

Before Daiichi could respond, Kenji immediately walked into the kitchen. He took Kimura's watch from the counter where he had left it and slipped it into his back pocket. When he looked up, Daiichi was peering around the corner, scrutinizing his movements.

"You keep this place pretty neat."

"Well, you know…confirmed bachelor here," he said with forced cheer.

The man nodded and flashed a wry smile, showing he didn't have a clue. He followed Kenji through the kitchen and looked around. Surprisingly, his gaze passed over a steak marinating on the counter and the diamond-inlaid tanto knife Kimura had confiscated from a local hood—the same one Kenji had reclaimed on his sister's behalf and intended to flaunt at their next meeting.

"Getting dinner ready?" Daiichi asked.

"Yeah. I hope you're not planning on joining me."

The man turned away with no comment. He stepped into the living room and didn't seem to find anything of interest. Then he took a quick peek into the bedroom before withdrawing into the hallway.

"Well, I think we're good here," he said, smiling the wide smile of someone who didn't really want to be there.

Kenji nodded and smiled back. He walked toward the entry and waited for Daiichi to follow. But as the inspector passed by the bathroom, he halted. "Oh, mustn't forget!" he said.

Before Kenji could stop him, Daiichi ducked inside and took a look around. Kenji rushed after him, thinking up distractions. By the way the man was staring, it was obviously too late.

"What on earth is this?" he asked.

Wrong question, Kenji thought. The sudden urge to take this little man and put his head through the wall threatened his self-control.

"I don't believe it!" Daiichi said. "Have you been washing clothes in here?"

Kenji had the sense to look at the floor, feigning deference and biting the corner of his lip to hide the smile that was threatening to break out. "Yes," he managed at last. "As a matter of fact, I have. Exactly. God, how embarrassing."

"Mr. Ota, while I doubt that this habit of yours has anything to do with the water leaks, it sure isn't helping to prevent them. We have washing machines in the basement to take care of your laundry needs. Why don't you use them instead of wasting water and doing this in your own home?"

While he was talking, Kenji had been staring at him, but now he glanced back at the pile of clothes in time to notice a tiny thread of blood weaving its way down the drain.

Daiichi's eyes were stretched wide in horror.

Great. Kenji sensed that he was about to say something that would undoubtedly evoke a negative reaction. His faithful wakizashi was still hanging on the back of the bathroom door. It would only take two seconds to grab it. One quick swing and this annoying little creep would be silenced forever.

"Oh that," Kenji said, following his line of vision.

Daiichi tilted his chin. "Exactly. What's been going on here?"

"Relax, Mr. Asano. I work part time as a butcher. I ripped a carcass wide open earlier today and had to rush home to change for a date. Normally I wear an apron when I work…especially when there's a mess to clean up. But as you can tell, I left everything in the wash."

Daiichi's eyes dropped to Kenji's ripped abs and the claw marks tattooed on his chest. His Adam's apple bobbed up and down with his audible swallows. "Right…okay…great. I think we're done here," he said. "But if this happens again, I…well, never mind. Just finish what you need to get done."

"Thank you," Kenji said, smiling. "I always do."

He shut the door behind the maintenance inspector and peered through the keyhole. As soon as Daiichi was out of sight, he leaned against the wall. This time it had been a little too close. His confidence was making him bold and careless. But at least now he had a faithful ally— someone who would vouch for his innocence, if it ever came to that.

Kenji wiped his damp forehead with the towel from his neck. He went into the bedroom and mused over how easy it was to convince simple-minded people of anything. Their naivety wouldn't allow them to see the worst in mankind. He knelt down in front of his closet, opened it, and reached deep inside, grabbing a small box hidden behind his shoes and spare arsenal. It was heavy, and its contents clinked as he pulled it out. He removed its lid and dropped the watch on top of all the others. Then he stood back and looked into the dresser mirror.

"How sad," Kenji said aloud. "People just have too much faith these days."

# 2

Rachel Lyons arrived at the LAX international departure gate just as the plane was boarding for the 11:30 a.m. flight to Tokyo with 15,800 yens in her purse, a heavy Coach duffel bag, and a growing sense of apprehension over Trident Ventures' new assignment. In preparation for her trip, she'd read dozens of books on the Christian crusades and absorbed as much basic Japanese as her brain would allow. She'd forced herself to appreciate the nuances of exotic Asian cuisine—although anyone's interest in eating raw squid when it could so easily be cooked would forever remain a mystery.

During her meetings at the San Palo Archeological Museum, Rachel had learned that her company had been hired by a Buddhist monk and about the obstacles she and her fellow crewmembers would face during their search for the missing green Templar stone, or Heart of Darkness as Dr. Ying had called it. Prehistoric-looking  Goblin sharks and Japanese street gangs were on the top of his "watch your back" list, leaving her cringing and wishing Chase Cohen had stuck around long enough to be fully briefed. With their recent success at recovering the ancient Wanli II shipwreck and the Heart of the Dragon diamond hidden onboard, it seemed she and her new partner were quickly becoming recovery agents for missing hearts in some of the most dangerous places in the world.

"Good morning," came from the petite blond flight attendant in the plane's open doorway. "Do you know where you're seated?"

"I believe so." Rachel extended her boarding pass and was quickly directed to an aisle seat in the twelfth row on the left side of the main cabin.

Great. Few things made her happier on long-distance flights than discovering an empty seat next to her. As she jammed her carry-on bag into the overhead bin, she peeked at the attractive Japanese businessman next to the window, completely absorbed in his newspaper.

"Is this seat taken?" She asked. It was her intention to spread out a few books, healthy snack bars, her laptop, and her research file. She half-expected her well-dressed seatmate to laugh good-naturedly at the pile trapped in her arms. Instead, he remained somber and tilted his head to one side.

"It's all yours." Surprisingly, his words revealed only a hint of an accent, leaving her curious about his background and occupation. As she settled in for the eleven-and-a-half-hour flight, he silently watched, revealing little aside from his tan complexion, trendy haircut, gray pinstriped suit, and polished Gucci shoes. He was definitely a "metrosexual man" by Tokyo standards, at least according to the New York Times article she'd recently read. In any event, the elegant stranger seemed harmless enough.

The cabin flight attendant passed by a second time, checking for secured seat belts and reminding passengers to silence their electronic devices. When the plane finally took off, Rachel arranged her in-flight office and alternated between reading books, munching granola bars, and scanning the materials she'd spent close to three weeks assembling. She fell into a comfortable, relaxed state of mind before glancing to her right. To her dismay, she saw that her handsome neighbor seemed to be exuding all kinds of nervous energy. When not glancing out his window, he was turning his iPad on and off, rocking his heel, tapping his fingers, and flipping through one in-flight magazine after another.

Rachel accepted several complimentary drinks, packets of mini pretzels, and a cold chicken salad from two flight attendants and their rolling carts during the next three-and-a-half hours. Oddly, her plane companion refused every offer, and eventually her curiosity got the better of her.

"Excuse me. Do you mind my asking you something?"

"Not at all," he said.

"I couldn't help noticing that you've been sitting here for hours without even having a drink. Aren't you bored?"

He shrugged nonchalantly. "Not really." "Wow…unbelievable. Personally, I can't sit on a plane without feeding my face. I guess you must travel a lot, huh?"

The gentleman laughed softly. "I guess you could say that. I'm on this flight once a month. After awhile, you just settle into a routine."

"Once a month? That's a lot of traveling, especially with the distance and time difference. Japan is sixteen hours ahead, right?"

"Last I counted."

She was silent for a few seconds, determining an eloquent way to ask her next question. "I hope this isn't intrusive, but what kind of job do you have that brings you to Japan so frequently?"

"I guess you'd call me a recovery agent," he said, "since I locate the misplaced and ensure they reach their rightful home.

Shanghai, Egypt, New York, Paris, Hong Kong…I've traveled the globe on my missions. Even though economic conditions have been affecting everyone, I've got more work than I can keep up with."

Ah…a private investigator. And a mysterious one at that.

"So perhaps we should be introduced?" He thrust out his right hand. "I'm Shinzo."

Without hesitation, she took the proffered hand. "Rachel Lyons." She bristled at the man's touch—the strange sensation it evoked. Although she wanted to draw her hand away quickly, his other hand closed over hers and held it tight. After an endless moment he released his grasp and leaned back in his seat, giving her the space she craved.

How odd.

He pointed at her files and borrowed copies of Emperors of the Han Dynasty and The Knights of Templar. "Looks like you've got some heavy reading to do. We definitely have a lot in common."

She quirked her brows. "We do?"

"In regard to your interest in history. So what is it you do, Miss Lyons?" He flashed a wide, disarming smile.

She hesitated before answering. "I find missing things too… under the sea."

"You're a treasure hunter?" he asked.

Rachel nodded.

"That sounds intriguing."

She opened her file and felt his gaze sharply, as if he had reached out and touched her skin. She sensed that he wanted to delve further into her life, but for the next two hours she studied ocean topography and reports on strange sea creature sightings, and made a point of not sparing him more than the briefest of glances. The lights on the plane were eventually dimmed, and all around her window shades were pulled down.

It had been three long days since Chase left their warm bed in her father's beachside cottage for salvage preparations in Japan. His absence and the anticipation of her trip had left Rachel completely exhausted. As the air thickened and the cabin stilled, her eyelids fought gravity. The gentle swaying and steady hum of the engines lulled her into a deep, dreamless sleep.

Eventually the sound of the breakfast cart jolted her awake. Still groggy, she forced her eyes open and inhaled the enticing aroma of hot coffee, reminding her of freshly ground heaven. However, her calm was short lived. With one look to her side, she realized the file she'd been reading prior to drifting off to sleep had been tucked into the seat pocket in front of her.

*You've got to be kidding me.* Rachel studied Shinzo while he sheepishly sipped his coffee. His concerted effort to avoid eye contact left her wondering if he'd taken advantage of her carelessness by snooping through her confidential papers. Everything she'd been sworn to keep secret might have been exposed to this invasive stranger, endangering not only Trident Ventures' project but also the individual who had risked his life to hire them.

She hesitated before asking, "Did you by chance move my file?"

"Your papers fell," he answered. "By the looks of them, you might want to keep those close to you, Miss Lyons."

His inference was unnerving. Although tempted to ask if he'd found anything of interest, she simply mumbled, "Thank you."

With that, Shinzo turned his view to the window.

Mindful of the cart's proximity, Rachel stood abruptly and pulled down her carry-on. She emptied the seat next to her, zipped her bag shut, and returned it to the overhead bin. Then she resumed her seat and stared straight ahead with her hands clenched in her lap. Buried anxieties surfaced by the second, curbing her appetite. She shook her head, declining breakfast when it arrived in the hands of the blond flight attendant.

"That looks delicious," Shinzo said, lowering his tabletop. Rachel watched as a tray containing a cheese omelet, blueberry yogurt cup, croissant, and strawberry jam was set down before him. The flight attendant returned a second time with coffee, cream, and sugar.

Wonderful. Rachel picked up the in-flight magazine and flipped blindly through its pages. She rocked her heel nervously, anxious for this tortuous ride to be over. Her cheeks warmed at the practically pornographic noise that came from her seatmate as he threw his head back and munched gratifyingly, his eyes closed in contentment. She noticed a spot of jam on the corner of his mouth and looked away determinedly.

"There's nothing better than warm bread and eggs in the morning," he said, recovering from his omelet orgasm.

Rachel glared at the annoying man, willing him to be sucked out the window. But then she'd never know his whole story. "You're not a private investigator, are you, Mr. Shinzo?" she grilled.

He picked up his torn roll and smeared it with more jam. "I never said I was."

"But you inferred as much."

"That was never my intent. If you recall, I never told you what I actually recover."

She shook her head and sarcastically laughed. "Oh my God… you're a treasure hunter, aren't you? I've been sitting next to my competition this whole time."

Shinzo chuckled. "Not quite." "So what do you collect then?"

"I think you'd have a hard time believing me if I told you."

"Try me," she said then inwardly cringed at her insistence.

After another well-chewed mouthful, he looked directly at her and replied in a matter-of-fact tone, "Souls."

# 3

What? Rachel looked at Shinzo warily. There was a sense of unease about the whole situation. Still, he hadn't done anything threatening—at least not yet. She swallowed thickly and forced herself to remain calm. "You're kidding, right?"

"No, not at all," he said.

"You actually collect souls?"

"In a matter of speaking."

No way! Tiny hairs on her arms lifted. He had to be joking.

"It seems to me you have a rational mind," he said. "I knew you'd have a hard time understanding. But not everything can be understood rationally or explained away by science, especially when spirits are involved."

"Spirits? What exactly are you talking about?" This was crazy. "Are you some kind of ghost hunter? Is that what you're trying to tell me?"

He laughed. "Perhaps it would be best if we didn't discuss this right now."

"No please, enlighten me. I'm totally interested." Disturbed was more like it. She glanced to her left to see if anyone was paying attention, but all the nearby passengers were engrossed in their meals, finishing their movies, or filling out customs forms. Obviously they hadn't heard his shocking reveal.

"What do you want to know, Miss Lyons?" he asked. The repeated mention of her name was becoming increasingly annoying. She lowered her voice to ensure her obscurity.

"How do you go about gathering souls? And for what purpose?"

"I'm assigned by my superior to various places around the world. Usually it's where the greatest number of lives has been lost as the result of battles or major disasters. Through meditation and energy transference, I help trapped souls ascend to heaven. You see, we're all descendants of Moses, no matter where we come from. Religious beliefs are simply a matter of interpretation." He spoke quietly, but the words thundered in her ears.

After extracting eight large photographs from a manila envelope, he handed them to her and added, "Perhaps these will explain better."

Rachel examined each one. Within the quarter-inch border, the main focus seemed to be Egyptian pyramids until Shinzo pointed out the recurring anomalies. Glowing white orbs hovered above the massive triangular structures, resembling something from a sci-fi movie.

"I've heard of this before," she said. "Some people claim they're spiritual beings, but it's actually dust reflected on a digital camera lens."

Shinzo was quick to correct her. "These time- stamped photos were taken with a friend's disposable camera while I was praying for tortured souls. You might notice in the last two pictures the orbs become fewer and lighter until they completely disappear."

Rachel shivered, feeling as if she'd just fallen down the rabbit hole. "And you actually make a living out of this?"

"Oh yes. It's all about awareness...not just noticing what's going on around you but what's going on within you as well. People are incredibly grateful, especially when I provide them with insight into their past lives."

Past lives? Curiosity drove Rachel to ask her next question—one she would have been wise to avoid. "So can you tell me something about myself?"

"If you wish." Shinzo pressed his palms together in prayer fashion and closed his eyes tightly. He lowered his head and was quiet for a few seconds before his whole body began gyrating. Rachel anxiously looked around and considered signaling for help, but then his seizure ended and he opened his eyes. He appeared to be calm and collected, as if nothing strange had just happened.

"Your name was Junko and you were twenty-three years old living in Okinawa," he said. "You were walking near the beach with your two young children. It was an early morning, just after dawn on October tenth and the basket of fish you were carrying was heavy in your arms. You heard a rumbling sound in the sky and looked up. Four American carrier planes passed by directly overhead. Minutes later, bombs hit an airfield three miles away and the ground under your feet shook. Smoke filled the sky and you were frightened for your safety. You wanted to run, but one of your daughters was missing. A sneak wave had caught her and pulled her out to sea. You dove in trying to save her, forgetting you couldn't swim. As you struggled to reach the surface, your throat filled with water, making it impossible to breathe. Unfortunately, you drowned...along with your child."

Rachel huffed. "That's horrible. Why would you tell me that?"

"Not all past lives are pleasant ones. However, if we close our eyes and listen to them, they can tell us something about ourselves. Maybe even explain the fears we have and feel the need to overcome."

"Well, to be perfectly honest, that's one story I would have preferred not to hear."

"Actually, I think it explains your anxieties over being a mother and why you believe you lack the ability to protect children. This, of course, is perfectly natural since abandonment issues have come up more than once in your life."

Rachel shifted her weight, distancing herself from him. "What?"

"Your mother and father both deserted you, didn't they? Your desolation left you drowning in guilt, afraid of the water and the happiness you truly deserve. But you needn't fear, Miss Lyons. You've beat the odds, and you'll do so again...while cave diving in Japan."

"How...how could you know that? Who told you? Did you read my papers while I was sleeping, Mr. Shinzo?"

A strange smile came over his face, as though he was enjoying a private joke at her expense. "I'm sorry. I really should have been up front with you. Although at this point you'd probably prefer otherwise, I should tell you...I'm actually your employer."

Yeah, right. Rachel's gaze slid from the strange man to the two flight attendants chatting at the front of the plane. She considered asking one of them for the air marshal, but inquires would serve no purpose other than dragging her into an international incident.

With narrowed eyes and a tilted look in his direction, she said, "I don't know who the hell you are, but if you toss out anymore crazy notions, I'm going to have no choice but to—"

"Hopefully hell has nothing to do with it," Shinzo interrupted. He pulled a card from his pocket and extended it with his two thumbs in Japanese business fashion. His action exposed the brown prayer beads bordering his shirtsleeve. "My real name is Satoru Yamada, but most people call me Shinzo. I believe you've already met my brother."

Rachel's mouth sagged. "You mean you're really a monk? But how's that possible? You're not even wearing a robe, and your hair…"

He simply smiled.

"So you've been sitting here this whole time knowing who I am?" Her face was suddenly warm, recalling her derogatory remarks and murderous thoughts.

He nodded. "Actually my brother Akio went to great lengths to ensure I was seated next to you. It's important to evaluate the people you plan to work with, don't you think?"

Yeah, right. Even the fruitcakes that hire you. She accepted a cup of coffee from the passing attendant and listened quietly as Shinzo expounded on her skepticism, stubbornness, and reluctance to change her mind.

"All in all, you're more intellectual than creative, but you're very passionate too," he assured her. "And you have a beautiful aura, by the way. Very strong."

"You got all that from our conversation?" she asked.

He smiled again. "Your handshake actually. Over the years, I've discovered there are mysteries within the soul, which no assumption can uncover and no guess can disclose. We must trust our instincts to look into another's heart…to know their true passion."

Her brow furrowed as he elaborated, basing the distrust she had exhibited on her father's tragic death, her former boss's unwarranted advances, and her turbulent relationship with Chase Cohen—which in his opinion would ultimately find resolution if she were more honest about her feelings.

"All right, I admit it. I'm extremely impressed," she said. "You've obviously done your homework. But everything you've said from my father's death to my previous job at the foundation could have easily been read in newspapers or discovered by researching my history online."

"True enough. But let me ask you something else, Miss Lyons. Does your father still come to you in your dreams?"

Rachel choked on her coffee. He handed her a napkin, and when her coughing subsided, she managed to squeeze out, "How could you know that?"

"He's always with you, Miss Lyons, watching out for your safety."

She glanced impulsively to her left. Seeing nothing out of the ordinary, she looked back, more perplexed than ever. "Are you telling me you've actually seen him?"

Shinzo angled himself toward her. "No, but he's always there...within your heart and your memories. Remember that and whenever you feel most alone, close your eyes and quiet your mind. Connect with his spirit and you will feel his eternal, infinite love. He is guiding you on your journey, Miss Lyons. That's how I know you were chosen. You see, no one is more protected than you."

She had her doubts about that and even more over her new employer. But she was here on a paid assignment. His religious organization had already supplied a substantial advance and would be footing the entire bill along with a tidy bonus when she and Chase were through. It was time to ignore all the craziness surrounding this nontraditional monk, time to set aside her apprehensions and focus on the task at hand, no matter how many ghosts might be floating around in his crystal ball.

# 4

Rachel waited for her luggage in the Narita customs area with growing exhilaration at seeing Chase on the other side of the distorted glass partition. He was going to be in for quite a shock after discovering the passenger she'd been seated next to was the same Buddhist monk he'd traveled there days earlier to meet. It was odd how that had happened—the miscommunication that had obviously taken place. But she imagined Chase would have a logical explanation, just as he always did when things went awry.

The person in line ahead of her stepped away, and it was now her turn to clear customs. Rachel approached an agent's counter while Shinzo split off to get his passport stamped at the returning residents' desk. As soon as she finished answering the man's questions, she ventured a look at the Japanese agent seated in front of Shinzo. The man's face had miraculously transformed from stoic to joyous, and it suddenly dawned on her that her companion had a remarkable affect on the people around him. According to Dr. Ying, director of the San Palo museum, Mr. Yamada's brother was a bit of a celebrity in Japan. Although she would forever remain a skeptic, as they entered the public greeting area, deep bows, finger pointing, and gasps within the crowd confirmed that the man's notoriety was more apparent than she'd originally believed.

"Miss Lyons!" a woman's voice called out. "Over here!"

Rachel's gaze passed over the top of the buzzing ebony-haired crowd and caught sight of a striking Asian woman standing nearly a foot taller. She had dyed brown hair, a pretty, smiling face, and the slender physique of a top fashion model. Her hand was waving high in the air above the cuffed sleeve of her flowing white shirt.

As Rachel drew closer, maneuvering her way through the noisy horde, she found herself intrigued by the summoning stranger. The young woman wore her hair swept up and held in place by multiple ornate pins, with several long silky strands cascading over her shoulders and down her back. Designer jeans hugged her thin legs and were tucked at the ankle into stylish open- toed boots.

"I'm Yuki Ota, Shinzo's friend. Mr. Cohen asked me to assist you today." She bowed politely, casting her eyes to the ground, but not before revealing something dark and intelligent swirling in their depths.

You don't say. Rachel bit her lip, struggling with her silly inadequacies. She bowed her head in Japanese fashion and issued the appropriate first-time greeting. *"Hajimemashita.* Rachel Lyons *desu."* She watched Yuki from the top of her eyes, hoping for a sign—a raised eyebrow or a nod with a matching response. Instead she received a twisted smile and a handshake, ending any further attempt on Rachel's part to speak the difficult language.

"Did you have a good trip?" Yuki asked.

"Yes, but I have to admit it was one of the longest flights I've ever taken."

"Then you must be tired." Yuki gestured at the Coach duffel bag and black Crossroads suitcase resting at her feet. "Just these two?"

Rachel nodded. She glanced around the crowded room, hoping to see Chase then realized he was nowhere in sight. Disappointment was apparent in her voice. "Where's Mr. Cohen? Didn't he come with you?"

"I'm sorry, Miss Lyons. He's tied up with negotiations and asked me to meet you instead. He'll be joining us at the hotel later tonight."

"But Shinzo…he's right here." Rachel glanced over her shoulder and spotted her companion eight feet away, watching two men take turns in a phone booth.

"I apologize for the confusion," Yuki said. "Mr. Cohen spoke with Shinzo yesterday regarding his delay. I assumed you knew."

Rachel gnawed on the inside of her mouth. It would have been nice if Chase had taken the time to call her as well, instead of leaving her ill prepared. She tried to shield her hurt feelings with a weak smile. "I guess he must have called after I left the house."

As Shinzo approached, Yuki's face brightened. *"Okaerinasai,"* she said. Then with a glance at Rachel she added, "Chase wanted me to thank you for taking care of Miss Lyons."

His mouth hitched in an almost smile. "It was my pleasure. Our exchanges made the trip much shorter and very pleasant."

Rachel sniffed a laugh. "Well, it was far from normal, that's for sure."

"Never settle for normal, Miss Lyons," he told her. "Normal is not natural. Extraordinary is natural, and that's why you're here. To do something extraordinary." His smile spread. The press of the crowd increased as exiting passengers joined them. As if aware of Rachel's growing discomfort, he held out his hand and asked kindly, "Shall we proceed?"

A short, jowly man suddenly appeared before them, his palm extended in similar fashion. "Preeze...this way," he urged.

As they followed him Yuki informed her that he was the driver who'd been hired to accompany them to their hotel. His assistant, a slight man with black-rimmed glasses, had already collected Rachel's luggage and was charging ahead of them toward the closest exit. Outside, the cool, fresh air came as welcome relief from the overheated building. One after the other, they made their way across the street and into the adjacent parking structure. They soon arrived at a silver Toyota van with automated doors that opened at the press of a button.

Before stepping inside and joining Yuki in one of the rear seats, Rachel glimpsed three men in a corner of the parking garage involved in a hushed, animated conversation. Their shiny, tight---fitting suits, pointy-toed shoes, and longish pomaded hair were comically retro when compared to the gray-suited, mild-mannered men in her company.

As she watched the odd trio, they suddenly faced her and openly stared back.

Shinzo tapped her on the shoulder. "Please...get in, Miss Lyons."

"Who are they?" she asked, genuinely interested. He dismissed her question by insisting, "After you."

Then he took a step forward, blocking her view. As instructed, Rachel climbed inside; however, her gaze remained fixed on the three men as the van door slid shut. She couldn't help noticing that they moved in matched procession, climbing into a black Mercedes sedan and pulling out of the parking lot directly behind them.

When they reached the second intersection, Rachel drew a sharp breath. "They're following us," she exclaimed.

Shinzo twisted halfway around in his seat. "I know. They're yakuza...what we call gurentai. They model themselves after American gangsters like Al Capone. They use threats and extortion to control business owners and unions. Years ago, their predecessors carried swords. These were replaced with guns, which have been outlawed in this country since World War Two. At one time, men like the ones behind us protected villages and the unfortunate people living there. Now they're criminals and outcasts, keeping to themselves. But they're not to be taken lightly, Miss Lyons. There are over one hundred thousand members, and unlike gangsters and drug dealers in America, they have no interest in keeping a low profile or being ignored."

"Obviously," Rachel said. "But why are they following us?"

"It's a bit too complicated to go into right now." Rachel flashed Yuki a worried glance. She returned a stern expression in an obvious attempt to silence her, but her warning went unheeded. "But if it has something to do with this project—"

Shinzo turned in his seat. "Rest assured, Miss Lyons, I'll explain soon enough. In the meantime, let's focus on getting you to your hotel and having a nice cup of hot tea."

# 5

*Meanwhile, in the heart of Kyoto...*

With no designs on marriage, Mariko Abe's greatest ambition was to become the most admired, sought after geisha in Japan. After ten years of dedication and hard work, she'd managed to become just that. She not only exemplified grace, beauty, and humility, but also possessed blatant sex appeal and a remarkable complexity of character. However, most of the foreigners she'd encountered had no comprehension or appreciation of her chosen lifestyle. They considered her sad, unappreciated, and old-fashioned in her beliefs. Yet Mariko held great pride in her time-honored, esoteric profession.

She had perfected her ability to entertain men from all corners of the world with witty conversations, elegant dance steps, and sweet songs accompanied by her samisen's flawlessly plucked strings. She spoke five languages fluently, including English, and excelled in traditional tea and sake service. Abiding by her training in subtle seduction, she permitted merely a peek at her slender wrist as she poured drinks for her wealthy and politically connected clientele. As Japanese executives were well aware, less was more in her flower and willow world. Whether spoken aloud or whispered in her tender ears, their secrets were safeguarded behind sliding shojis in the Gion Kobu teahouses she frequented. She had become a trusted advisor and treasured companion and appreciated the monetary rewards earned from her contributions.

Unfortunately, however, Mariko had recently become troubled. This evening, as she leaned close to the tabletop mirror on her bended knees, examining her carefully applied white makeup, black eyeliner, soft pink blush, and red painted lips, she felt no connection to the twenty-two year old gazing back at her. Great effort had been spent styling the beautiful black wig she wore, exposing the back of her slender, sensual neck. Her prized tortoiseshell comb had been added as a seasonal feature, and lavender oil had been applied to her hands and arms, and still she remained numb. Along with a contracted patron attending to her needs came the cruel realization that no matter how successful she might become, her life would never be completely her own.

Years ago, a coming-of-age ceremony would have involved selling her virginity to the highest bidder, bringing honor to the okiya, or lodging house, where she'd resided and trained since the age of fourteen. The wealthy, elderly danna would begin a sexual relationship by smearing egg whites on her thighs, working his way up higher each night. In a week's time, he'd split her kimono and deflower her on an elegant futon bed. But times had changed and the ancient ways were discarded in lieu of modern thinking. Yet earlier that day, one of Mariko's male patrons had met with Oneesan, the Inoue house's highly respected governess and a former geisha herself. They had struck a bargain in regard to Mariko's future and the cost of her living expenses.

"According to the terms of our agreement," Oneesan had told her, "all the debts you've incurred, including the cost of your kimonos, will be paid for in exchange for your loyalty and affection. This will include your furnishings and new apartment. You'll be meeting your danna at the Prince Hotel at nine thirty tonight, so dress appropriately, and above all, don't be late, Mariko-chan."

Although she'd given her permission, much to her dismay Oneesan had turned a blind eye to the matter of suitability. The gentleman she'd struck a bargain with had been a frequent visitor for the past five years and had his share of positive attributes: money, good looks, and affluent relationships. But he was also a known gangster and notorious womanizer. He had to have boasted about his wealth and aspirations to acquire Oneesan's hard-earned approval, for what other reason would her big sister agree?

It was a known fact this man's fortune stemmed from his father's ownership of sixty pachinko parlors— gaming centers run by Koreans and men on the edge of society. However, with resources drying up as a result of the country's economic downturn, the cost of maintaining the lifestyle the Inoue house geishas had become accustomed to was dependent on Mariko's popularity, as well as the maikos she'd mentored. Without the generosity of their dwindling list of patrons, the doors to their okiya—their cherished 400-year-old home—would be permanently closed. The elegant garden surrounding it would be sold off as commercial real estate or turned into another tourist attraction.

"What choice do I have?" Mariko said to herself then banished her selfish thoughts. She slid the closet door open and chose her finest ensemble. With the assistance of a hired male dresser, she was clothed, sculpted, and tightly bound, concealing her shapely figure. She smoothed her hand over the exquisite silk kimono, admiring its delicate, handcrafted detail. Crème-colored cranes were subtly embossed in the textured fabric. Yellow flowers and green leaves swept up from the hem in celebration of the sultry season. The floral brocade obi secured around her middle repeated the popular August theme. Folded and knotted at her back, the contrasting accessory added elegance to her doll-like appearance. The addition of a pearl and emerald brooch she'd been gifted by her deceased father was the finishing touch to her perfectly coifed illusion.

For the past two weeks, Mariko had received numerous invitations, which would now require her patron's approval. However, the union office had prearranged tonight's engagements a month ago, and in her mind they remained exceptions to the rule. She would make a brief stop at a teahouse gathering and greet corporate moguls from Tokyo at a formal dinner party. By allotting herself no more than thirty minutes per visit, she'd make extra money for the okiya and have plenty of time to join her new benefactor—the only living male heir in the Ota family.

Kenji. Her heart skipped a beat at the thought of his dark, piercing eyes, gorgeous black hair, and trim, muscular body. Tonight he would be expecting her to surrender her most prized possession: her virginity. With only a Kama Sutra book and directives from her fellow geishas to guide her, she could merely hope the encounter would entail patience and understanding on his part.

After a deep bow to Oneesan, Mariko slipped on her woven zori slippers and hurried to the Yasaka Shrine. She tossed a few coins, rang the bell, and bowed deeply. After clapping her hands twice, she asked the gods for beauty, guidance, and plenary protection. With downcast eyes and fleeting thoughts of Shinzo, her close, protective friend, she crossed the street and walked past the cascading willow trees lining the Shirakawa Canal to her first appointment. If not for his travels abroad, the monk would have undoubtedly appeared on the doorstep of the okiya, voicing his disapproval over the choice for her danna—especially with the history they'd shared. But sadly, even though he'd made his feelings known and had alluded to their future together, Shinzo's priorities didn't include her.

"Mariko!" Tamayo's shrill voice turned her head. As she approached, Mariko evaluated the sixteen-year-old maiko she'd been charged with directing. A yellow silk chrysanthemum was pinned in her hair. Rows of tiny pink flowers trailed down the right side of her stark white makeup, concealing a sprinkling of adolescent pimples. She was wrapped in a lustrous gold floral kimono and balancing poorly on stilted okobo shoes. Her pursed red lips told Mariko all she needed to know. News of her patron had reached the ears of her imouto-san. Although schooled in silent discontent, the young maiko had been reprimanded on numerous occasions for her forward and outspoken behavior. Her fondness for Kyoto's popular playboy had been rumored in the pleasure quarters—filled with squat wooden bars and blaring disco lounges.

However, her resentment had little effect on Mariko's situation. Even though she could refuse the bargain reached by Oneesan if she were deeply opposed to her selection, there was still the matter of her future— her ability to sustain herself and excel in their ostentatious, secret society.

"Opportunities don't come along like this every day," Oneesan had reminded her. "You're very lucky to have someone so young, attractive…and generous."

Mariko glanced down and swallowed her trepidation. With the aging woman's aching back and liver problems, caused from years of heavy drinking, Oneesan's patience with the other geishas and young apprentices in the house had ceased years ago. Testing her temper with disparaging words would serve no purpose other than aggravating her grievous condition.

Tamayo stepped closer, breaking into Mariko's troubled thoughts. "Why Kenji?" she asked. "Surely there are other men more qualified."

Mariko glared admonishingly. "You're not a schoolgirl. You know the responsibilities of a maiko, the expectations of your calling. Mind your tongue, little sister, or you'll end up in Atami with drunken tourists performing the Gangnam-style horse dance."

The young novice's pout vanished. Her watery eyes met the stony walkway. Understanding her plight, Mariko softened her voice. "I'm on my way to the Komura teahouse. Would you like to join me?"

Tamayo shook her head.

Mariko tried again. "A formal banquet is planned in honor of the Panasonic president. Geishas from all the houses plan to attend. Your company would be welcomed..."

The young girl lifted her chin. "I have a gaming lesson with Okaasan." She paused and bowed deeply. "I apologize for my rudeness." The corners of her lips lifted in a plastic smile. "Please accept my best wishes for your happiness." With a quick nod shared between them, she turned and continued on her way.

Mariko pushed aside her disconcert and increased her pace along the bank of the Kamo River. Soon she reached the first ochaya on her list. Upon entering the 300-year-old teahouse, she removed her shoes and was directed by a maid to a room on the second floor. As she slid the door open, her eyes met five Japanese men and one striking foreigner seated on green zabutons along the sides of a large rectangle table. Three geishas were kneeling behind them, whispering softly in their ears. Mariko bowed and stepped inside before lowering herself onto the woven tatami mats. In appropriate manner, she remained closest to the door, greeting her fellow entertainers, the dignified silver-haired host at the far end of the table, and the other businessmen in attendance.

"Mariko-san!" one of the women exclaimed. "We've all been waiting for your arrival. Please tell us about your poor friend."

"Excuse me," Mariko said softly. "What are you talking about?" Evidenced by her choice of language, the woman had been focusing her attention on the handsome blond American in their midst. His light blue eyes lit on Mariko's face and remained fixed there in a curious stare. "You don't know?" The middle-aged geisha paused briefly to allow a grinning guest the opportunity to refill her sake cup. After completing their toast, she continued her mischievous assault. "Shinzo Yamada has been traveling the world searching for a rich bride but came back empty---handed."

"Actually, he had more important matters to attend to," Mariko insisted, leaving everyone laughing. She saw no humor or reason for the unkind remark. At least not until the door slid open again.

What is he doing here? Kenji Ota stepped forward in a tailored linen suit. A wink in her direction confirmed his involvement in the poorly executed prank. It wouldn't be the first time his irreverent behavior gave her pause, nor would it be the last, according to the look on his self- satisfied face.

"Nothing wrong with having the finer things in life...especially when someone else is willing to pay for them. Eh, Mariko?"

She smiled demurely and nodded, hiding her humiliation and disappointment. Then she moved quickly aside, providing her danna a place at the table. She accepted a warm ceramic bottle from the well-seasoned hostess and elegantly poured, just as her station prescribed.

When everyone was finally served, Kenji lifted his filled cup and yelled, "Kanpai!"

Most of the guests followed suit, tossing back the searing liquid with reckless abandonment. Mariko watched in amazement over the next two hours as Kenji and his four drunken companions guzzled ten bottles of sake and ordered another round. The stranger introduced as Chase Cohen watched silently, maybe even in a little shock from Kenji's fool hearted display.

With each drink, Kenji claimed they were celebrating everyone's good fortune, although Mariko had no idea what this entailed. Cohen had sipped barely six ounces of the plum wine he'd been served, while their silent host refused any at all. Meanwhile Mariko continued to drink warm tea, allowing all the others to believe she was participating in their riotous merrymaking.

The night progressed, and soon it was time for her to perform two choreographed dances. Moving into position, she kneeled and spread the ends of her obi and kimono until perfectly placed. Then she extracted her colorful fan. As the samisen played, she rose and moved methodically with grace, confidence, and precision, capturing the attention of her jovial audience.

Upon completing the second dance, she bowed politely in response to their applause and returned to her place behind Kenji. He hiccupped, and a cockeyed smile spread across his face. His nose and cheeks were red from the alcohol he'd consumed. Then he started to giggle like a silly schoolgirl.

From his ill manners, no one would have suspected this was the great Kenji Ota—protected by the yakuza and respected by all levels of Japanese society. As the sake continued to flow, Mariko grew increasingly tired of his ungoverned behavior and at his insistence that she remain. She had already missed two of her other appointments, irking her more than she was willing to admit.

"What's so funny?" she finally asked.

Kenji giggled a few more times. "Hiroshi's son," he slurred. "He gave up a sword to keep his freedom instead of using it to ensure it."

"What are you talking about?" their host snapped. "He surrendered nothing."

Kenji smirked. "Is that what he told you? What a brave little soul you've raised. He stole a tanto and a crooked cop took it from him," he slurred. "And I carried it away with me. We were like frogs in a pond, jumping over one another. But no one could get over that hair of yours."

"My hair?" their host asked, instinctively touching his bristled silver hair. Finding it completely in place, he frowned at Kenji's rude antics.

"Oh yeah." Kenji chuckled. "It defies gravity." Then he began laughing uncontrollably, bringing his legs to his chest, rolling onto his back and burying his face in his knees. Hiroshi Mori glared at his ill-mannered guest. Not knowing what else to do, Mariko grabbed hold of the sake bottle.

"Okay, I think you've had enough," she said.

The bottle was instantly yanked back. Kenji stared coolly, but Mariko realized he wasn't really focused on her. His attention had slipped to the faces of the other geishas, silently watching in disbelief.

"Mine," he said possessively of the still half full bottle. He clutched it even tighter against his chest.

"Come on, Kenji-san," Mariko said. She grasped the warm brew, tugging it away slowly, not wanting to alarm him or evoke his undue anger. His eyebrows knitted together, as if wondering why the bottle was moving out of his hands.

With the libation now absent from his grip, he blinked several times. "Where'd it go?" He looked around him, but the teahouse hostess and her staff had taken the precaution of removing every bottle from the table.

"Someone should put him to bed before he hurts himself," Cohen suggested.

Mariko resented the outsider's interference. He had no understanding of their culture or the manner in which she was expected to behave, and yet the sincerity in his sea-blue eyes compelled her to agree.

"He needs to go to the hotel where he's staying for the night," she said.

"I can take him," Cohen volunteered. Then he turned to the men seated around him. "Why don't you guys go ahead? I'll catch up with you tomorrow."

"I need to come with you," Mariko insisted. "He may be difficult and I don't want anything bad to happen—"

"Don't worry, ma'am," he interrupted." I've had to deal with a few drunks in my lifetime. I won't have any problem handling him."

The other geishas exchanged troubled looks. With secrets impossible to keep in the Hanamachi district, they were fully aware of Mariko's awkward situation. She was responsible for her foolish danna's well being, just as he was for hers, and it now appeared she was being left to completely manage on her own. The disloyal men in Kenji's group were already halfway through the open doorway. As the result of her danna's rude and thoughtless behavior, Mori-san had no intention of offering Mariko assistance or his American guest a helping hand.

Cohen smiled sweetly. "I'll tell ya what. Just help me get to where we're goin' and I'll make sure your friend arrives safely."

Mariko joined him, slipping her hands under Kenji's arms and helping to pull him upright onto his unstable feet. With one of Kenji's arms looped around Cohen's neck and with the elderly maid's assistance, they managed to claim their shoes at the bottom of the narrow wooden staircase.

"Not tired," Kenji mumbled over and over again.

"It's after ten. Time to get some rest," Cohen assured him. "We've had a long day negotiating fuel charges, rental fees, and diving permits. Got an even longer one tomorrow."

"*Gaijin wa dete ike,*" he mumbled under his breath. "*Mezawari da!*"

Mariko was appalled at Kenji's obscene retort, the lack of respect he held for others...especially naive foreigners. She glimpsed Cohen's mystified expression and choked her anger with a smile.

"He said he doesn't know how he would've managed tonight without your help," she lied.

After climbing out of a green MK taxi and entering the hotel lobby, Cohen waited with Kenji braced against the wall while Mariko obtained the key to his room. Without saying a word, they entered one of the elevators and ascended to the eighteenth floor. Once the door to his room was unlocked, Mariko moved aside, allowing Cohen space to march his business associate across the room and deposit him on the bed. Although he appeared slightly more sober, Kenji clung to the American's arm.

"Come on, pal. Let go," Cohen said. He tried to pry Kenji's fingers free from his shirtsleeve, but her danna seemed to be lost in a trance—staring up at him with dull, emotionless eyes.

Mariko shared Cohen's apparent dismay. "Ken-chan, let go of him," she urged softly.

"Why?" he asked, tilting his head to one side. Another smile came to his lips, but more sly than silly this time. "You like him better than me, don't you?" His insistence in speaking English was obviously for Chase's benefit and not her own.

"Of course not," she said. She slipped her hands around Cohen's arm and tried to separate him from Kenji's grip then realized too late he could have easily done the same. Beneath the starched white fabric covering his biceps, Cohen had been hiding his impressive strength.

"Don't pay him any mind," he told her. "That's just the liquor talking."

Mariko's look of surprise had little to do with Kenji. She glanced away, hoping to hide the effect of Chase's maleness and his close proximity. Unfortunately, Kenji didn't miss her discomfort or the opportunity to address it.

"What an interesting pair you two make," he scoffed. A warm blush rose in Mariko's cheeks. She looked down and exhaled a deep breath. Then she lifted her eyes and addressed Kenji as sweetly as she could. "Cohen-san came here to help you, and now I believe it is time for him to leave."

"Is that right?" Kenji snapped. He grabbed her wrist and pulled her close. She could smell the alcohol oozing from his pores, see the spit collecting at the corners of his mouth.

Sensing a defensive action about to take place, Mariko shot Cohen a warning glance, mentally urging him to stay back.

"I say who comes and goes," Kenji told her. "Is that understood?" They were now nose to nose. The sake on his breath was an instant reminder of his drunken state. She shivered involuntarily. There was something suggestive lurking in his dark eyes. An animalistic quality she'd never experienced before. His voice was husky when he spoke again. "I'm your danna, the only man in your life...and I want you...now!"

Mariko couldn't move, couldn't speak. He brought their lips together hard and demanding in an unexpected kiss. She gasped in his mouth, shocked by his aggressive behavior. Heat rose from her neck, and she became keenly aware of Cohen's presence in the room. From the look of his clenched jaw, it was clear he didn't approve of the coarse exchange.

Kenji stepped back, releasing her from his hold. Then he collapsed, landing on the bed with a great flop.

The lines in Cohen's brow softened at seeing his weakened state.

"It's okay," Mariko said. "I'll take care of him now. Can you find your way back to your hotel?"

The gentle stranger paused before nodding. "Are you sure you'll be all right here?" he asked.

"I'm fine, really. You'll have to hurry to catch your train, if you hope to get back to Tokyo tonight."

He reached the door then turned back to face her. "Have Kenji call me in the morning...after he's feeling better."

"Of course," she said, more calmly than she felt. She lowered her eyes and bowed politely.

"I sure wish my girlfriend Rachel was here tonight. She would've loved meeting you."

Mariko smiled softly and nodded. "Oyasuminasi. Sleep well, Cohen-san." As soon as the door closed, she returned to Kenji's side. He was staring down at the bed sheet and by the look on his sickly pale face he wasn't feeling well at all.

"Why are you being so nice to him?" he grumbled. "He's nothing to you."

"Perhaps, but he's only shown kindness—"

Kenji suddenly shoved himself away from the bed and ran out of the room. Mariko ran after him but stopped at the bathroom door when she heard the retching sounds inside. She winced and waited for him to stop heaving his guts out.

After a full minute, the bathroom became silent. She cracked the door open and peeked inside. Kenji had a death grip on the toilet seat. Her protective guardian, self- assured danna, was panting and covered in sweat. She slowly walked over and gently rested a hand on his shoulder, startling him. Upon seeing it was Mariko, he relaxed and rested his forehead on his arm.

"Are you okay?" she asked and only got a nod in reply. "Come with me. I don't think you want to sleep in the bathroom." She helped Kenji to his feet and guided him back to bed before allowing him to collapse facedown. Anticipating a second round, she located an empty wastebasket in the adjacent living room and came back to discover he'd rolled off the bed and run into the bathroom to throw up again.

She winced every time she heard him heave and set the basket on the carpeted floor before going to collect his tired body from the cold tile floor. Before depositing him carefully on the bed, she helped him remove his linen trousers and white shirt. Although she was aware of his yakuza connections, she was ill prepared for the lavish black, red, and yellow tattoo covering his back. Intricate in its design, the fierce openmouthed dragon clutched a gold ball with the kanji character for strength in its claw—the well-known symbol used by Zakura-kai gang members.

Mariko sighed aloud then instinctively covered her mouth. Fortunately Kenji was oblivious to her reaction. With his body spent, he'd fallen asleep in a matter of minutes. She hesitated before placing a gentle kiss on his forehead. Then she returned to the bathroom to remove her elegant wig and lavish kimono. After erasing her makeup with a soapy washcloth, she lightly misted her uncoiled hair with water and gently brushed each section with the wire hairbrush she had thoughtfully packed in her bag. Although it took extra time, the natural wave she'd fought since childhood gradually lessened and a smooth, glossy sheen was restored to her long ebony hair. She retired to the living room in her white cotton undergarment and curled up under a light blanket on the cream velour couch. Relief washed over her. Tonight she would remain wholesome and virtuous— untouched by the man who would become her first, exclusive lover. However, as she drifted off to sleep, another man invaded her thoughts: the stranger with the shaggy blond hair and electric-blue eyes.

Chase Cohen. He had demonstrated true chivalry— reaching for her hand to assist her from the taxi, moving aside to let her pass. Throughout the evening, his kind eyes had watched her, sympathetic to her plight. He'd accidentally brushed up against her while moving through the hallway with Kenji then offered a gentle smile, releasing a flock of butterflies in her stomach.

Mariko sighed. Although she knew it was nothing more than passing infatuation, from now on it would be necessary to safeguard her emotions and lower her eyes in his presence. After all, Kenji was her danna, her master. The man who had agreed to pay twenty thousand dollars for each of her seasonal kimonos, provide her housing, and address all of her needs. Even though he was a prideful and possessive man with a worrisome past, she had resigned herself to her fate. There would be no looking back, no shameful regrets…not unless she was willing to negate their agreement and destroy the reputation she valued more than life itself.

# 6

As they arrived at the beautiful New Otani hotel in downtown Tokyo, dozens of questions were flooding Rachel's mind. Who are these members of the yakuza? What do they want? Why won't Shinzo explain anything? She managed to remain quiet with the knowledge that Chase would soon be arriving to fill her in and hopefully put her mind at ease.

After exiting the van, she and Yuki were escorted by a female receptionist to the coffee shop in the elegant hotel lobby, while Shinzo attended to a waiting call. With their drink orders taken, the clerical worker returned to his duties, leaving the women seated in the middle of the chic, ultramodern room. Rachel's quick glance at the low tables surrounding them confirmed that each one was filled with Japanese executives smoking, reading newspapers, or engrossed in deep conversations. She spotted two women a short distance away, perfectly coifed from head to toe. At the bar, a slip of a girl sipped a Coke and studiously read a book as she listened to music from an earpiece, tapping her foot to a steady beat.

Yuki leaned forward and kept her voice low. "You must remember that you're not in the United States, Miss Lyons. It's important not to pry into personal matters."

Rachel was taken back. "Excuse me?"

"Shinzo has reasons for not answering your questions. When he's prepared to do so, he will."

Really? Yuki's impertinence came as a surprise. Obviously she wasn't a stereotypical Japanese woman: shy, meek, or demure, as one might expect.

"Let me ask you something, Miss Ota," Rachel said. "Just how did you come to know Chase? He never mentioned your name or said anything about you being involved in our business."

"I'm a certified dive instructor, avid climber, and endurance runner. For the past four years, I've been embroiled in archeological digs in Jerusalem, Brazil, and North Africa. While living in China, I worked as a researcher for the Shandong Archaeology Institute. As a practitioner of martial arts, I'm trained to remain calm in the face of adversity and danger. I'm also very familiar with weaponry and all aspects of this project." She took a sip from her water glass then continued, "So you needn't worry, Miss Lyons. With your ship Stargazer currently under repair and your crew incapable of joining you, I'm the most qualified dive technician you'll find in Japan."

Yuki's attempt to sell herself left a bad taste in Rachel's mouth. Not from her extensive list of qualifications or the condescending tone in her voice, but from the fact that this hubristic woman seemed to know more about her company's problems than she did.

"Ah, here's our tea," Yuki announced.

Rachel gazed at the delicate white teacups and saucers being set before them by a prim, neatly dressed woman. She added tiny silver spoons and tubes of granulated sugar to their table along with a plate of English shortbread cookies. As she poured from a porcelain teapot, Rachel picked up one of the sugarcoated temptations. It reminded her of the one she'd sampled at a Rotary luncheon in San Palo, during a time when her main focus centered on prospective clients and dispersing foundation grant money. Funny how that now seemed a lifetime ago...so foreign to her new, reinvented self.

After doctoring the dark brew with a splash of cream, Rachel lifted her cup to her lips, hoping the mellow bitterness would revive her. But then she felt the weight of Yuki's hand on her arm.

"I hope I didn't come off sounding arrogant. That's really not who I am."

Although Rachel surrendered a smile, resentment had already taken root. She couldn't imagine what Chase was thinking by involving this woman—an intellectual model, claiming to be the most gifted person on earth.

Yuki withdrew her hand. "I suppose I was feeling a little intimidated after everything Cohen-san said about you." She took ownership of her matching teacup, already filled to the brim. After a quick swallow, she sat back in her seat and lifted her eyes to a scene playing out just beyond Rachel's shoulder. A quick glance confirmed Shinzo was still on the phone, shaking his head and exchanging indecipherable words.

"What kinds of things?" Rachel asked Yuki.

"That you're stunning to look at, intelligent, and very patient...especially when it comes to him."

How convenient. She nibbled a cookie and tried to imagine why Chase would be compelled to sell her attributes to this mysterious woman.

"So..." Yuki said after a few minutes of awkward silence. When Rachel didn't respond, she launched into everlasting chatter, ending with a prying question. "How'd you get into this business anyway?"

Rachel sighed, seeing no relief in sight. "It's kind of a long story." She stole another look in Shinzo's direction. He was still on the phone, which made her wonder who he was talking to.

Perhaps it was Chase.

Yuki lowered her cup. "It appears we have a few more minutes."

Right. In a matter of speaking, their roles had been reversed. It was now Rachel's turn to qualify her involvement. "After receiving a grant, I studied marine biology. I worked for a university in Southern California for five years and met Chase after he came to work for my father. He left town for a while, and when we met up again, we discovered a shared interest in finding lost treasure. One thing led to another, and now we're partners in a salvage company."

Yuki hummed her understanding. "You know, I have to be honest. If you were in a police lineup, I never would have picked you out as a treasure hunter."

Rachel chuckled. "The same goes for me, Miss Ota. And yet somehow you've managed to make a career out of it." She snatched her cup and took a quick swallow, burning her tongue in the process.

"Is it all right?" Yuki asked.

"What?"

"The tea. It's oolong. Not particularly to my liking, but some people enjoy it."

"It's fine." I'm fine, Rachel told herself.

"Oh good. I know this is a bit off the subject, but I have to tell you how lucky you are, Miss Lyons. I know it's not appropriate to talk this way...especially with him being my boss and all... but I'm not going to lie to you. Every time Mr. Cohen shows up at the hotel, in restaurants, or in meetings, I find myself completely captivated. You're definitely one of the prettiest and smartest ladies on the planet, and I know in his mind no one could ever compete. I just don't want you to take offense if you see me staring at him from time to time. It's just that I've never seen anyone with such beautiful eyes or met a more insightful, caring man... aside from Shinzo, of course."

Egad! Is she kidding?

Yuki delivered a sweet smile. "Anyway, like I told Cohen-san, most of the women in this country don't get the education men do. Schools simply don't provide it. Young women are still in the mindset that they need to find husbands with great careers and nothing more." She closed her eyes for a moment as if searching for her next thought. "When this project is finished, Miss Lyons, I want to use my degree to teach a new generation and give them hope. I think the more value you add to your life and to other people's lives, the more successful you become. Don't you agree?"

Rachel forced a smile. "Of course." What the hell? Weirdness had found a new home. In the seat directly across from her. She blew out a breath and glanced up in time to see Shinzo rapidly approaching with an angry frown on his face.

"What is it?" Yuki asked first.

"I apologize for leaving both of you. There's an urgent matter I need to look into involving a close friend. Yuki, after you finish your tea, please show Miss Lyons to her room so she can freshen up. The luggage has already been taken care of. We'll meet for dinner in forty minutes. I hope sushi is agreeable with everyone."

Rachel watched Yuki nod before doing the same. "Perfect," Shinzo added. "Our driver will meet you in the lobby."

After he disappeared through the hotel's main entrance, Rachel turned back to Yuki. "What do you think happened?"

She nipped her bottom lip, as if contemplating an acceptable answer. "He must have found out about Mariko's new boyfriend."

"Mariko?"

"A woman he's fond of."

"Wow… that must have been rough." "Even more so with my brother involved."

A question mark must have registered on Rachel's face, as Yuki was quick in clarifying her words. "I'm sorry to say this, but Kenji's a demanding jerk with good looks and too much time on his hands. I suspected he was interested in Mariko Abe months ago, and with members of his yakuza gang sticking their noses into everything—" "Yakuza? You mean he's connected to those men who were following us?"

She paused before nodding.

Rachel couldn't help herself. "What do they want from us?"

"Something they'll never have." "Which is?"

Yuki smiled. "My, my. You're very persistent, Miss Lyons. If you can manage to be patient a little longer, I promise you'll know soon enough."

"But surely you can tell me something. If they wanted what we're after, they would've hired their own divers, right?"

"Not with the danger involved."

Danger? "What kind of danger?"

"Sharks, for one."

When it came to this subject, Rachel was on top of her game. "Goblins, right? Don't you find it strange that they're not living in their normal environment? From what I've read, they stay below 250 meters. So why would they be circling Shinzo's boat at fifty feet down?"

Yuki motioned her head toward the female receptionist, silently listening at the end of their table. The woman handed Rachel her room key and launched into a lengthy explanation about the spa, continental breakfast, and services included with her stay. Then she presented her with a handwritten note.

Rachel glimpsed Yuki's downcast face before reading it silently to herself.

*Honey, sorry I missed you. I'm catching a train from Kyoto tonight and won't be back until after eleven. Get some rest. I'll try my best not to wake you. Love, Chase*

What? She couldn't believe her eyes. "When did Mr. Cohen call?" she asked the receptionist.

"Ten minutes ago."

"But I was right here."

"I'm sorry, Miss Lyons. You seemed to be occupied."

"Occupied?" Rachel shook her head,   exasperated. "Did he leave a number? Somewhere I could reach him?"

"No, I'm sorry. He didn't."

"Great," she grumbled.

The receptionist stared down at the carpet like an admonished child. "Is there anything else I can do for you?" she asked.

"No. Thank you." Rachel watched the woman trudge back to her desk. "I can't believe it. Chase isn't coming back until late tonight."

Yuki angled a scrutinizing look. "Then I suppose it will be up to Shinzo and me to entertain you."

Answer all my questions is more like it. Aside from dependable equipment from a reliable company, Rachel's only request had been for accurate, detailed information. If she acted on the natural instincts Shinzo had claimed she possessed, she'd be on the phone right now, making arrangements to catch the first flight home. But then her partner and occasional lover would be left alone with Yuki Ota to solve the mystery of the missing Templar stone. As Rachel speculated about the brilliant woman seated across from her—with striking looks and an obvious crush—she realized if she had any feelings for Chase at all, it wouldn't be the smartest move she had ever made.

# 7

Rachel sat on a red floor pillow in the Yoshikawa restaurant's private tatami room next to Yuki and across from Shinzo, finishing off her last bite of crab sushi. Although she was anxious to hear a full explanation, she'd already made up her mind this was one mess she and Chase would be wise to avoid...especially after seeing two black Mercedes Benz cars parked conspicuously across the street.

"Okay, we've talked about Japanese food, the restaurant owner, and the sweltering heat outside," Rachel said. "Now do you think it might be possible to discuss Trident Ventures' assignment and why mobsters are involved?"

"Yakuza," Shinzo corrected gently.

Rachel shrugged a shoulder. "Whatever."

Shinzo and Yuki exchanged guarded looks. "It's a bit complicated," he reminded Rachel.

"So you've said."

"I'm not exactly sure what you need to know, Miss Lyons."

Really? "Why don't you just start by telling me why we're being followed?"

Shinzo looked down, as if calculating where to begin. When his eyes lifted, he began his lengthy explanation. "About forty-five years ago, Yuki's father, Sachio Ota, and my father were best friends. They wanted to go into business after graduating from college, but they were short on funds and the banks wouldn't loan them money. So despite my father's protests, Sachio borrowed fifty thousand dollars from Kaito Mitsui, the head of one of the most feared yakuza families in Japan. They opened a photography studio, made good incomes, and had loyal customers. But over time, the interest on the loan became so high they were going to be forced to close and sacrifice everything. Meanwhile, Mitsui was opening up pachinko parlors and involving most of the business owners in town in his protection racket. Sachio saw an opportunity to make some extra money, so he went to work for the Zakura-kai. Before long, he became a full-fledged member, acquiring pachinko parlors of his own."

Shinzo took another sip from his cup. "Then one night, while I was studying in the back room at the studio, I witnessed an argument between my father and Sachio. Voices got loud and fists started swinging. An oil lamp got knocked over and the whole place exploded in flames. But Sachio wasn't about to leave without Mitsui's money. Not when his life depended on it. He tried to ransack the safe while my father carried me out. Minutes later, the ceiling collapsed. Everything was burning. My father ran back in to save his friend and...unfortunately, only one man walked away."

Yuki remained silent, her face grim throughout the story.

"Ota-san became a father to me that night. He encouraged my studies and psychic abilities. With his help, I graduated from Naropa University in Boulder, Colorado, and joined one of the largest Buddhist orders in Japan. But while I was away, fighting broke out between yakuza families. Ota-san was killed and his son Kenji took over for him." Shinzo glanced at Yuki. "When I look back now, I realize he had good reason for hating me. His father was always putting him down and rubbing my accomplishments in his face. So to answer your question, Miss Lyons, the men who have been following us report directly to Kenji Ota. A man who would like nothing better than to see me dead."

Rachel was speechless. She should have been infuriated by Shinzo's disturbing explanation. Instead, she only stared at him, perplexed. Just like the last time he'd confided in her.

"I know it sounds bad, but it's important to understand you're not at risk here. This is strictly a private matter between two grown men."

"Not exactly," Yuki corrected. "Prince Ngami's sword was found before the storm hit. It's buried inside the yacht that sank. If my brother finds out it's still there, he'll do whatever it takes to own it."

"I don't understand," Rachel said. "I thought we were hired to recover a priceless stone."

"You were, Miss Lyons," she said. "*Ryokushoku no shinzo*, which translated into English means Green Heart. It was embedded in the scabbard of a sword created by Gor Ny d Masamune and gifted from Prince Dai Ngami's mother to her son on his twenty-first birthday. She believed that with the love of his people and the world's greatest sword, he would hold the heart of his nation in his hands. But after his death, Japan mourned his loss, and it became known as Kurai Kokoro...the Heart of Darkness. And just for the record...this katana is more valuable than the missing Honjo Masamune. The twenty-carat emerald heart alone is worth over twenty million dollars."

Rachel shook her head, recalling the hours she'd wasted in the library studying the Crusades and Knights Templar. Dr. Ying would definitely hear about this when she got home. "Where did this sword actually come from?" she asked. "A museum heist?"

"Prince Ngami's tomb," Shinzo answered. "The Kokoro was laid by his side to protect him in the afterlife. But there's something else you should know. It was part of a collection...one of three extraordinary swords of varying lengths, from long to short. Each one held a valuable stone in its scabbard, honoring the prince's valor, wisdom, and benevolence. The wakizashi was his second sword, decorated with a multifaceted round ruby, and the shortest sword was a tanto knife, containing a single flawless diamond."

"So...getting back to your story," Rachel said, trying to make sense of it all, "if Kokoro was in the ship that sank, where are the other swords? Are they missing as well?"

"Not exactly," Shinzo said. "You see...all three were involved in an ancient Lothario drama. General Maeda was a cruel, vicious leader of the imperial army. After a massive border raid against hostile invaders, word reached his wife that he was killed. A month later, Maeda returned from the dead and found his wife in bed with Prince Ngami. Blinded by his rage, he used the prince's wakizashi to murder both of them and his knife to kill himself. After learning of his daughter and son-in-law's deaths and witnessing the bloody aftermath, the village's Shinto priest went absolutely crazy. He conjured up demons from the underworld and used them to drive their souls into the swords before burying them with their ashes in unconsecrated ground. Yuki believes she's solved the mystery of their whereabouts; however, in order to set their souls free, the swords must be brought together and purified in the Shoten temple."

"Are you telling me you're only in this to save their souls?"

"Actually, to save mine," Yuki answered. "On March eleventh, the air stilled and the skies turned gray. An earthquake and tsunami came next. When I was finally able to return to my apartment in Higashimatsushima, it was gone. I later learned that eight thousand people died and lost their homes that day.

Millions had no water, power, or heat. It was the worst nightmare ever experienced in Japan…unlike anything you could ever imagine. And it was all because of me."

"You? It was a natural disaster. How could you believe any of that was your fault?"

"Because it happened twenty minutes after I entered the tomb and took Kokoro."

Rachel cringed inwardly. She glanced to her right to confirm the truth in Yuki's declaration, but Shinzo was sitting quietly with his eyes closed, as if he hadn't heard a single word. She looked back at Yuki's frowning face and tried her best to alleviate her blame. "No matter what anyone believes, that doesn't make you responsible."

Yuki lifted her downcast eyes. "You would have believed it if you were there."

"Perhaps," Rachel conceded. "But to be honest, I can't imagine what would compel you to rob a grave in the first place." She brought her knees up beneath her, preparing to stand.

"Please." Yuki urged Rachel to remain seated before presenting her case. "Mitsui believes that Shinzo inherited his father's debt. With the accrued interest, it was going to be impossible for him to pay it back. I wanted to do whatever I could to help and remembered a story I read while conducting research in China. It was about a dishonored prince buried on Kuchinoerabu Island in the Sea of Japan four hundred years ago. The entire center of this circular landmass had sunk into the sea during a tremendous volcanic explosion, and although the eruption created multiple craters and destroyed the entire village of Shindake, Prince Ngami's crypt remained miraculously intact forty feet under the ocean. I was convinced that if I found it and presented a gift from Ngami's tomb to Mitsui on Shinzo's behalf, all the hatred he's had to endure would finally come to an end."

Rachel released a humorless laugh. "Well, I have to admit... I'm impressed. I've never heard of anyone going to such lengths to protect a friend."

"Shinzo is more than a friend, Miss Lyons. He's my guardian angel." She suddenly rose to her feet and turned around. Without hesitating, she loosened her shirt and allowed it to slide down to her wrists. The sight before Rachel drew an audible gasp. Yuki's bare back was completely covered in tattoos: colorful koi, a female pirate with a knife clenched between her teeth, a scale--- covered serpent twisting around her midsection. Although remarkable in their scope and complexity, Rachel was keenly aware of the condemnation associated with inked skin, especially on eastern women. Tattoos represented political rebellion and were telltale markings identifying the underbelly of Japanese society. Even in the modern world, they were banned from public baths, prevented employment, and drew unwanted attention from the police.

After a brief moment, Yuki covered herself and resumed her seat on the floor, but Rachel couldn't help but stare after being stunned by the disreputable display. She glanced at Shinzo to gauge his reaction and discovered his eyes down and his attention absorbed in his tea.

"When I was young," Yuki explained, "a fight over drugs landed me in reform school. After I got out, I had an affair with a member of my brother's gang. For two years, I worked as a bar hostess and ended up being raped by a girlfriend's father. Then, when I finally found someone who loved and understood me, he was killed by a rival gang member."

Rachel silently studied Yuki's calm demeanor, overwhelmed by her outlandish claims.

"Two days after my twentieth birthday, Shinzo found me half dead in a love hotel. But it wasn't the first time I tried to kill myself." She took off her wide brass bracelet and held out her wrist for Rachel's inspection. It was scarred by what appeared to be numerous suicide attempts. "I was still acting out at twenty-three and had my body tattooed to prove how tough I was to all my yakuza friends. Fortunately, when I was at the lowest point in life, Shinzo found me again. He introduced me to his sensei, a famous sword master in Tokyo. This remarkable man offered me the use of his martial arts school and a place to stay. On a daily basis, he trained with me and eventually restored the pride I'd lost in myself. After two years, he passed away from a massive heart attack and I moved to the States to follow the passion in learning he'd unleashed in me."

Shinzo smiled softly. "If you remember, I told you it was complicated."

"Yeah...you're not kidding," Rachel retorted. She swallowed her disapproval as well as she could. "So this is about rescuing souls and repaying a debt. And nothing more?"

"Exactly," he said. "So what do you think, Miss Lyons? Can we count on your help?" With the orange glow from a burning candle directly behind his head, Shinzo looked as holy as a Michelangelo Jesus. Refusing him was going to be a difficult task.

"To be honest," she began, "you've both given me a lot to think about. I can't even imagine what Chase is going to say after he hears all this."

Shinzo's eyes turned to Yuki. "You didn't tell her?"

"Tell me what?" Rachel asked. "You've got gangsters, Goblin sharks, and man-eating eels tangled up in this mess. Don't tell me you've got a contract on your head too?" The mere fact that Yuki was intentionally avoiding eye contact should have been fair warning, but Rachel was determined to know every secret. "Well," she persisted, "what is it you're not telling me?"

At last Yuki lifted her eyes to bravely meet Rachel's. "I thought you knew," she said. "Mr. Cohen has already agreed."

# 8

After closing the door to the hotel suite and quietly stepping into the living room, Chase spotted Rachel perched on the edge of the sofa, staring mindlessly at a late night television show. Her narrowed eyes, tight lips, and flushed cheeks were clear indications her temper had been percolating for hours. He slipped off his shoes and swallowed hard. After the night he'd just been through, the last thing he needed was another argument.

"You don't have to stay," he half whispered, heading toward the bedroom.

She whirled around at that. He mentally cursed himself, having forgotten how sharp her hearing was and how easily she could be provoked.

She jumped to her feet and propped her hands on her hips. "Whaddaya mean, don't have to stay?"

"Oh, just ignore me," he said. "It was just a passing thought. I didn't even realize I said it out loud." No matter what he might say, Chase knew nothing would suffice. Not in Rachel's present state of mind.

She crossed her arms and gave him one of her glares to let him know she knew he was lying. "You don't have a clue what a partnership means, do you?" she said. She bit her lip and looked down at her feet to prevent an onset of tears. "I don't understand it. We came here to do this together. Then I show up and you're traipsing off to who knows where, making plans without a thought about our safety or my feelings in this matter. If you're not happy with our arrangement, then let's end it now. Find the life you want…without me," she choked.

Chase hated it when she cried—when she doubted the depth of his feelings. He grabbed her chin gently and forced her to look up at him. "Honey, there's no way that's going to happen." He used his thumb to wipe away a single tear that escaped despite her best effort to block it. "I said I'd never leave you again. I wouldn't have made that promise if I didn't intend to keep it."

Rachel's hazel eyes were shining with unshed tears. She was obviously overwrought and tired from the trip, although she'd be the last to admit it. Lately her emotions were up and down like a roller coaster, completely unpredictable, leaving him stumped and at times mildly amused.

Chase pulled her in for a hug, and her arms came up around his waist as she burrowed her head into his chest. He let her go after a minute, and she reluctantly looked up, wiping her eyes on the sleeve of her cotton yukata. He threaded his fingers through her long, auburn hair and rested his forehead against hers. He smiled at the sight of her dressed in Japanese fashion, courtesy of the hotel's free amenities.

"I love you, baby. Try to remember that, okay?" he murmured into her hair before kissing her brow.

She squeezed her eyes shut and took a deep, shuddering breath.

"It's late," he told her. "Let's get some sleep and figure everything out in the morning. If for some reason you're not happy with the arrangements I've made in the light of day or feel the risks aren't worth taking, then I promise we'll head back home as soon as possible. We'll write this whole thing off as a bad idea."

The corners of her lips curled slightly. "Okay."

He scooped her up to carry her to bed and paused momentarily, reminded by how nicely she fit into his arms—how incredibly light she felt. It wasn't as if he wasn't strong enough to carry another person, it was just...Rachel was so small. Rationally, he knew she was short. Even the six-inch heels she wore occasionally did nothing to help her compete with him for height. But she had such a huge, charismatic personality, and her physical size didn't really register when she was ordering people about. She liked being the authority figure, and he was happy to accommodate her...within reason, of course. But now, wiped out and utterly depleted of life, love, and laughter, she just felt tiny and fragile in every sense of the word.

His chest tightened as he glanced down at her closed eyes and beautiful face. She was like an angel who'd been dropped into his life. He couldn't imagine a single day without her filling his thoughts, his heart...his soul. Then as if knowing she was being watched, she cracked an eyelid before burrowing into his neck. Her breath was light against his skin.

"I missed you," she whispered. As he held her above the bed, he debated briefly if he should strip her clothes off and wrap her in his arms.

No. Set her down and let her sleep. There would be plenty of time to make love, to erase all the doubts from her mind. He gently lowered her onto the mattress, her hair pooling as he did so.

Rachel protested slightly, her arms actively clinging to his neck for a moment. With her eyes laden with sleep, she leaned up and pressed a kiss to his nose before dropping her arms from him and curling up on the bed. Chase wondered in amusement whether she'd actually been aiming for his mouth. Chuckling, he reached down and drew up the covers. He brushed trailing hair from her face affectionately before leaning over and placing a kiss on her forehead. Then he closed the bedroom door behind him, hoping she would sleep for a good long time. After sharing the news he'd received from her brother, there was no telling how miserable she'd be in the morning.

He pulled off his shirt and laid it neatly along with his slacks across the beige chair in the living room. After dropping onto the couch, he eyed the sealed packet he'd received after returning to the hotel. He contemplated going back into the bedroom to lie down beside her to make sure she was doing all right, but then he firmly dismissed the thought in lieu of her brother's last message.

With his cell phone in hand, Chase double-checked the time before placing a call to the States. After three rings, a man's voice came on the line. "Good morning, Trident Ventures... Devon Lyons speaking."

"Devon, it's Chase. Rachel is sleeping right now. I'll let her know about Stargazer's mechanical problems and your inability to come here in the morning. We'll just plan on seeing you when we get back. In the meantime, why don't you explain what's in this express envelope you sent to Rachel?"

"Hey...hope everything's goin' okay over there. I just thought you should know I got a call from Dad's attorney right after you left. With Rachel preparing for the trip, there wasn't time to let her in on the latest development, and to be honest, I didn't want to be the bearer of bad news."

"What news?"

"Well, it turns out Sam spent some time in Japan some years back. He hooked up with a woman right after our mom left and ended up with a kid over there. I wasn't sure about the facts until I saw the postcards and stack of money he'd squirreled away in a cigar box. To tell you the truth, I honestly don't know how he kept it a secret for so long."

Chase raked his fingers through the side of his hair. "Geez, your dad had his share of secrets, but that's a whopper."

"I know. I can almost guarantee Rachel won't believe any of it. But I'm hoping you'll be able to convince her to give the ten thousand dollars I deposited into your account to his daughter as he intended."

Chase huffed. "I don't know, man. That's a lot of money. There's no way of knowing how she's going to react after finding out she has a Japanese half sister."

A soft noise on Chase's right caught his ear. He assumed it was Rachel shifting her position on the bed in the next room, but after hearing more muffled sounds, he looked around and saw her standing in the open doorway with a ghastly expression on her face.

"Let me get back to you tomorrow," Chase said, bringing his call to an abrupt end. He set down the phone and stood slowly. "Rachel...I'm sorry, did I wake you?"

She didn't scream, she didn't cry, she didn't throw a tantrum or anything against the wall. She just stood there for what seemed like an eternity, deathly silent.

Chase needed to hear her voice; she had to react so he could. But that wasn't going to be the case. She simply remained quiet with her gaze angled at the floor. He was sure he could see tiny droplets fall from her face and wanted desperately to hold her in that moment, to turn back the clock and change everything her father had ever done to her. It was a strange feeling, but somehow he felt he'd let her down instead of Sam.

Eventually she craned her head up and her eyes met his. There was something there he didn't recognize, just couldn't name. It wasn't hurt or anger. It was just this vacuole of space, gazing back at him with piercing hazel- green eyes.

"Honey, say something." His voice was barely a whisper.

A glimmer flashed briefly in her eyes, an emotion looking suspiciously like anger. She forced it down with an audible gulp. "What do you want me to say, Chase?" she croaked. "That he disappointed me again?"

"Rachel..." He uttered her name gently, shushing as she became more agitated.

"Do you want me to cry over him never being there for me? Watching my mother walk away and out of our lives? Leaving me with bills and a mountain of guilt over the last words I spoke? Do you want me to yell and curse my father's name to the high heavens...wishing he were never part of my life? That's easy, because as far as I'm concerned, he can rot in hell."

"Honey, please calm down. It's going to be all right." "Why?" Her voice cracked as she stepped toward him. "Why would he do this? All I wanted was for him to care...to love me for who I am."

"I...I don't know how to explain what he did...or the reason," Chase stammered. "I just know he wanted you to be..."

"What? Happy?" She huffed. "Why is it just when I come to terms with who he was and trick myself into believing he actually cared, he leaves me another mess to clean up? Another reason for me to hate him?"

"Rachel, your dad was human. He made mistakes…" Chase dragged off. He attempted to approach her with the envelope he'd been given, but in typical Rachel fashion, she wasn't having any part of it. She stepped back beyond his reach, shaking her head and mumbling something about not wanting to know.

"Maybe if you just took a look," he said, "it might explain everything."

An ominous smile crept across her face. "Oh…so you want me to say it's okay. Read his note or whatever's in that envelope and say it's all right, Dad. I forgive you." She let out a bitter laugh and turned away. "You know what? Fuck this, I'm going."

"Going where?" he yelled, exasperated, following her to the bedroom door.

"Back to San Palo. I don't need any more bullshit in my life."

Chase caught her arm, pulling her back around. "Rachel, we're here for a job. There are people depending on us. We'll find a way to figure this out, I promise."

Like a light switch, she shut down all together— staring off into space with a blank look on her face. Not knowing what else to do, he lifted her chin. "Honey, I didn't do this. I'm not your father."

She backed up, beyond his reach. "But you did, Chase. You had a daughter too. One I knew nothing about. Remember? I've tried my best to understand…to develop a relationship with her. But now…with this…I feel like every man in my life has cheated on me. Don't you understand?"

Silence filled the room again, disappointed and heavy. In that moment Chase knew there was no reaching her, no rational thinking. If he pushed further, there would be nothing left in their relationship to salvage. For the past six months, he'd been fighting for the woman he loved, a chance to be trusted and believed in again. But it seemed that every room in her heart was closed to him, no matter how many windows he tried to open.

"I'm tired," she said, sounding defeated. She shut the bedroom door behind her, cutting off any further discussion.

Chase pinched the bridge of his nose and closed his eyes, absorbing the stillness. He dropped onto the couch, debating on what to do next. From the grave, Sam Lyons had opened a wound in his daughter's life, and by the look of contempt in her eyes it was going to take a miracle to heal it.

# 9

Kenji Ota awoke with a start. The moment he opened his eyes, a throbbing pain tore through his brain unlike anything he'd ever experienced. He let out a groan and buried his head deep in the pillow. With concerted effort, he lifted a heavy eyelid and peered out. Somehow he'd been deposited in an enormous bed complete with a white down comforter and a collection of tossed embroidered pillows. But how he'd managed to arrive in this particular spot remained a mystery. Slowly he lifted his head, shielding his eyes against the window's bright light, and tried his best to assess his elegant surroundings. By the sound of the humming air conditioner and the looks of the contemporary mahogany furnishings and silk wall coverings, he'd managed to find his way back to his overpriced hotel room.

With the inside of his mouth like a cotton swab, he found it difficult to swallow. He threw back his covers and discovered he'd been stripped down to his blue silk boxers. His gaze moved to the foot of his bed where a valet rack stood decked out like a designer scarecrow in his Armani suit.

How odd. Tidiness had never been one of his strong points or one of his priorities. He must have spent the night with a neat freak. But no matter how hard he tried he could only recall fragments of the previous night. There was no recollection of seducing anyone…not even the homely maid. And from the size of the hard-on he was currently wearing, he was long overdue.

I need to cut back on drinking. Kenji had made that pledge a hundred times before. But whenever sake was poured, he had never managed to keep it. He slid off the mattress and stole into the neighboring bathroom to empty his bladder. One look in the mirror confirmed he looked as worn as he felt. He turned on the faucet in the bathtub. As soon as it was filled with hot water, he pulled off his underwear and climbed inside. Twenty minutes later, he wrapped a towel around his washboard middle, raked his fingers through his damp black hair, and walked through the open doorway. That's when he heard it—a strange sound coming from the adjoining room. Cautiously he crossed the carpeted floor and peered around the corner.

Someone was curled up on the couch! The dim light on the end table cast an ethereal glow over a woman's face. He edged closer, and it suddenly dawned on him who had taken up residence in his suite. Mariko Abe, his newly appointed charge. But what was she doing here? He pulled back the thin wool blanket covering her body. The small ties securing her cotton undergarment had come loose during the night, exposing a breathtaking sight: porcelain skin, round breasts, perky pink nipples, and a flat, firm stomach begging to be touched. Although the mound between her legs was sheathed in pink silk, the transparent fabric left little to the imagination.

Kenji studied her serene expression and long black hair fanned out over the pillow. He released a deep sigh. Mariko's lips were moist and naturally red. Her cheeks had a tint of blush, making her even more beautiful against her pale complexion. Thick, dark lashes bordered her eyes, the most alluring part of her face. As if sensing his presence, they opened a fraction and her lips slowly curled.

"Kenji..." she murmured before realizing her bareness. Her eyes widened in sudden alarm. She threw an arm across her breasts and held the edge of one firmly to shield them from his invasive eyes. A foolish gesture, as far as he was concerned.

He pulled her hand free and shushed whatever protests might be forthcoming. Then he scooped her into his arms and carried her back to his bed. He reached down and stroked her cheek. It was warm and soft to the touch. With trained expertise, he ran a finger along the edge of her chin before tracing her neck and throat. He stopped at the valley between her tantalizing breasts and contemplated which mound to approach first. Deciding to go for the left, he lowered himself onto the edge of the mattress and gently touched her nipple before kneading it with his thumb. He lowered his head to the other one and licked and sucked before pulling it gently with his teeth. Her taste was addictive. He could feel the growing ache in his loins as his craving increased.

Kenji pushed himself upright and walked toward the end of the bed, directly facing her feet. He spread them apart, dropped his towel, and climbed between her knees. Already she smelled of arousal, the first hint of love nectar glistening between her pink folds. He groaned and lowered his head to taste her. Mariko cried out and began writhing on the bed. He held her hips to keep her still. The scent and taste of her combined as he kissed and tongued her, slow and lingering.

Mmmm... He found another addictive taste, so much sweeter than he had expected. She shuddered with sensation at the scrape of his fresh beard against her inner thighs. He pinned her firmly to the bed and traced her clit with the flat of his tongue, pressing against the pliable flesh, before plunging his tongue inside her again. She moaned and twisted in his grip, then grabbed for his hair and pulled it.

"None of that," he said gently and trapped her wrists against the bed as he bent to tease her again with lips and tongue. God, she was so wet; her slick moisture was sliding down between her buttocks and onto the sheets. Avoiding the center of her pleasure, he dipped long fingers inside her, pushing them slowly in and out. As he did so, he lay alongside her to kiss her mouth, letting her taste herself on his lips and tongue. Her eyes were shut, her cheeks flushed, and she was breathing heavily. She kissed him back, all of her shyness gone, replaced with desperate need.

Kenji felt a thrill of power. In the bedroom, bringing a woman to this state with his lips and tongue was his favorite act. He could bring or deny release, and after years of practice, he knew he was good. His skill was mostly in self-restraint—the ability to watch a woman writhe and not take her. To drive her to begging in breathless gasps and not take her. To taste and smell her body's need and not take her…until he was good and ready.

"Don't be afraid," he whispered across her skin. "Trust me. I want you to enjoy this." It would be her first experience, and from what he'd been told, it could prove painful. He had to make sure she was completely relaxed and mentally prepared to experience the adventure he was about to share. His fingers slid in and out over and over again, until he could feel her muscles clench. He smiled when an uncontrolled spasm followed.

Oh yes…it was time. He licked his lips in hungry anticipation and lifted her hips up so that her buttocks were supported on his lap. With the bend in her legs resting on the hook of his arms, he positioned himself directly before her and took a deep breath. He had been endowed since birth, and it wasn't unusual for women to gasp in surprise at his unusual size. For a brief moment he found himself wondering if Mariko would be able to take him completely inside. His length resting on her groin reached clear to her navel, and his girth could easily equal four of his fingers pressed together. He hoped he wouldn't hurt her but knew it would undoubtedly be unavoidable.

Taking his cock in his hand, he rubbed the head against her, smearing her own wetness around her entrance and over her flushed, sensitive bud. He leaned into her, pushing her open with the thick width of his cock. Even though a gasp escaped her lips, Mariko offered no resistance.

"Kenji?" her voice questioned. He plunged into her without answers. Her body arched, her head flew back. She opened her mouth to scream, but he wasn't about to let that happen. He covered her mouth with his own and pushed himself farther, making her arch even more. With her neck now within reach, he took his leave to trail his tongue along its edge, leaving her whimpering. He could taste the salt in her trailing tears and was puzzled by her reaction. Was it because of the pain or the fact that he'd stolen her innocence? He had no idea, and at that moment it mattered little to him. Despite her oneesan's and Mitsui's reluctant consent, Mariko Abe belonged solely to him. Yet there was still the matter of breaking through her barrier, which was harder than he'd expected. He was pushing again, slowly but surely, and eventually she was able to accept his immense size. Who would have thought being squeezed by a virgin's tight muscles could be actually painful for a man?

Fuck! She was so damn tight, but that didn't deter him. With clenched teeth, he withdrew and tried again. He had to make her relax. His mouth trailed to her left breast and he suckled her nipple. He could feel her tremble beneath him. Relax. Goddamn it…relax. His right hand moved to her lower region to find her sensitive bud. Mariko gasped the moment he touched it. He circled, stroked, and tugged. Then with one final push, he was fully invested. He placed his hands on either side of her head and raised himself up. He gazed down into her eyes, filled with bewilderment, betrayal, and shame.

"It's all right. It's perfectly natural…a man and a woman making love. Now relax and breathe with me," he told her. She followed his instructions, taking long, deep breaths. Then he slid himself out a bit before thrusting again and assuming a slow, steady motion. Once he felt she had adjusted to his tempo, he began rocking faster. She gasped again and kept throwing her head back. Her hands clenched the bed sheets. She bit her bottom lip to suppress a moan. He smiled, knowing that despite her fears and anxieties she was catching on fast and enjoying this wild new sensation. He thrust even harder, in and out, faster and faster, consumed with his relentless pursuit. Her inner muscles clenched a second time and spasms soon followed. With her eyes squeezed shut, her whole body shook. He almost came, but he held on with determined fortitude.

Returning his hands to her breasts, he began massaging and teasing her swollen nipples. He was still deep inside her, hard and ready to go. But he remained still, giving her time to gather her thoughts. After a few moments, she looked up at him with hunger, lust, and confusion, and he knew she wanted more. With their eyes locked and their lips sealed in silence, he resumed his fine-tuned rhythm. Beneath him, Mariko's skin flushed. In the midst of their lovemaking, her hands found their way to his shoulders. Her legs came together, holding him even tighter. With every concentrated push, she dug her nails into his skin—his muscles, his shoulders, and his chest. She bit her lips together, sheathing her moans.

He leaned down and whispered in her ear, "Scream." Then he bit the flesh on her neck. A cry escaped her lips as she clung to him for dear life. He drove his hard shaft deeper and deeper into her with each steadfast stroke. "Say my name!" he demanded as he rammed into her harder than ever, shaking her whole body on impact.

"Kenjiii..." she managed breathlessly.

"Louder! Say it louder! I want to hear you say it again! Say my name, Mariko! Say my name! Tell me who you belong to."

"Kenji Ota!" she screamed.

A groan slipped from his open mouth. "Again! Say it again!" he shouted as he relentlessly pounded into her.

"Kenji Ota! Oh God...Kenjiii..."

"I said I want to hear it every time I slam into you! Shout my name!"

"Kenji! Kenji! Kenjiii...!" she cried out, tears streaming.

His heart swelled, knowing he was the master of her universe. As if riding a thoroughbred into the homestretch, he moved fast and furious, slapping his thighs against hers. "This is mine," he said. "Mine...mine...and no one else's." He felt it again—a third time—Mariko's muscles fluttering and tightening. She cried out as she drove her nails into his shoulder blades. He threw back his head and a howl tore from his chest. Tremors racked his body as he spilled his warm seed inside of her. A final shiver traveled over his skin, leaving him spent and elated at the same time. He dropped his head onto Mariko's chest, completely spent.

After a brief moment, he pushed himself upright and looked down at her blotchy red face. Her eyes were closed and her breathing was ragged. He peeled away from her and climbed off the bed before scooping her up into his arms. With her head resting against his chest, he carried her into the bathroom. Then he slowly lowered her into the tub. She winced as he slid in behind her. With a soapy washcloth held in one hand, he moved her long mane aside and began gently scrubbing her upper back.

"Did I hurt you?" he asked.

"No," she said, obviously lying, obviously shielding the pain he'd inflicted.

"Are you sure?'

She nodded.

Ah, so sweet. That was why he'd chosen her—his obedient lover, high-minded socialite, and ultimate weapon for revenge. Nothing would destroy Shinzo Yamada more than knowing Mariko's innocence had been taken. Than realizing the woman he cherished more than life itself had been placed in his enemy's hands. The corner of Kenji's mouth hitched in amusement. Under the terms of their contract, Mariko had no choice but to depend on his generosity. Manipulating her to do his bidding would prove effortless and far more rewarding than utilizing his crew's strong-arm tactics.

At the dinner party on Friday night—that's when he'd set his plan in motion. Using the guise of partnering on their diving expedition, he'd draw them all together — his sister Yuki, the Americans, and the monk who'd stolen his father's affections. He'd present the conditions for using the dive boat they'd reserved. And should they attempt to dump him and search for another supplier, he'd make sure no one in Japan would lend them a hand.

As for the price they would ultimately pay for Shinzo's debt and his years of humiliation...why, it would be for the treasure they were after, of course. The Kokoro—the world's greatest sword, foretold in ancient Japanese legends. In the meantime, he'd spend every waking moment in this luxurious hotel room ordering overpriced food and pleasuring himself with his beautiful charge. Driving Mariko to the peak of ecstasy and down again, over and over again, until she was left hungry and begging mercilessly for her release.

# 10

Chase cracked his eyelids, hoping for a calm morning and slice of neutral territory in the muted hotel room. However, after tossing the blanket aside and gathering his clothes, he couldn't help noticing that the envelope he'd left sitting on the coffee table was gone. Sometime during the night, Rachel's curiosity must have gotten the better of her.

Carefully he made his way into the bathroom. After brushing his teeth, he gazed into the adjoining room and saw Rachel already dressed in maroon skinny jeans and a snug Rolling Stones T-shirt. She was frowning, propped on the edge of her bed slipping on a pair of black Doc Martens. Like an old, noncommunicative couple, they met at the sink: Chase shaving in his H&M jeans, Rachel brushing her auburn locks back into a long ponytail. He glimpsed her tense expression in the mirror and splashed warm water on his face a few times. Her act of defiance by stretching Mick Jagger's red tongue across her chest in their conservative setting came off as scandalous and childish—so unlike the mature, levelheaded woman he knew.

After using a hand towel to wipe off the few spots of shaving cream he'd missed, he leaned toward her and forced a crooked smile. "Nice T-shirt."

Without looking up, she replied with a snide remark, "Really? You bought it for me."

He chuckled. "Wow! I've got great taste, don't I?" He could have sworn he saw a smile on her face. But as quickly as it appeared, it vanished. He considered another approach, a safer subject to deflate her dour mood. "Did you get any rest last night?"

"Enough," she said. The fine lines under her eyes told him otherwise. She leaned into her reflection long enough to apply black mascara and pink gloss over her luscious lips. The sight set his heart pounding. Before she could get away, he grabbed her and pulled her tight against his chest. She gasped as his mouth covered hers. After a long, exploring kiss, he released her and picked up his white polo shirt.

"As soon as I throw this on, we'll go downstairs and find something to eat," he said. "Then maybe we can sneak away and see some of the city while we're still here."

She brushed past him and returned to the bedroom to collect her purse and the large envelope her brother had sent. Without another word or backward glance, she swept out the door and headed straight for the elevator. Caught completely off guard, Chase ran after her, hopping on one foot then the other until he managed to get both shoes on. He arrived just as the elevator doors opened. Two Japanese businessmen moved aside, allowing them access, and Chase assumed his position next to Rachel along the wall. As the elevator traveled down from the nineteenth floor to the lobby, the men in their company remained absolutely silent. When he chanced a look in their direction, they smiled and nodded, as if understanding his plight.

When the doors opened, Rachel made a beeline for the restaurant at the far end of the long corridor. "I don't know about you, but I'm starving," she tossed back.

Oh, so now we're speaking again. After living with Rachel for six months, he knew a hot meal was the fastest way to improve her disposition. With the way things were shaping up, the sooner she ate, the better—for both of them.

A pretty young hostess greeted them at the restaurant's reception desk. She collected two menus and escorted them through the dining room to a quiet table isolated from the other hotel guests. With their water glasses filled and their food orders taken, Rachel opened the envelope she'd hijacked. There was a stack of returned postcards and a receipt from a bank deposit. The photograph she extracted and placed on the table resembled the geisha Chase had recently met. But then all young Japanese girls looked alike to him... especially in black T-shirts and jeans.

As if reading his mind, Rachel's eyes widened. "You know who she is, don't you?"

"Why would you say that?"

"I can see it in your eyes."

He gave a noncommittal shrug. "You know I could be way off."

"Come on...just tell me what you know."

He released a short sigh and tried to soften the truth. "On my last trip to Kyoto, I did meet someone...a geisha who entertained our group. She spoke English, poured sake, and danced for us. But we didn't share anything personal."

Rachel listened to Chase's full account with a wooden expression.

"As far as her being your sister," he said at last, "I haven't got a clue."

She picked up the photograph and pursed her lips while studying it more intensely. As if she couldn't resist knowing, she glanced up and asked, "What was her name?"

Chase paused before answering. "If I remember right, it was Mari...no, Mariko. Mariko Abe."

"You're kidding." Rachel tilted her head. "How can that be? It couldn't possibly be the same woman."

He took a chance and covered her hand with his own. "Do you know her?"

"I know of her. Last night before going to dinner with Shinzo Yamada, Yuki said something about Mariko being his former girlfriend."

Chase laughed softly. "Well, after Kenji's behavior yesterday, she probably wishes she still was."

Rachel looked up sharply and pulled her hand free. "I don't understand. Why would you pick him to work with us? Especially with his mob connections?"

"I called around," Chase said truthfully. "His company has fully equipped dive boats and all the gear we'll need. I've been told by my contacts that he's the only one willing to work with us."

"Well, I still find it all extremely odd, don't you? Think about it...the likelihood of our company being contracted for this job and you meeting the same woman who's supposed to be my sister." Rachel shook her head. "It's all a bit too coincidental, if you ask me. She'd have to know something about my mother and me. How else would my father have explained his absence to her?"

Chase thought hard about the woman he'd met. There hadn't been anything maligning or malicious about her. At least as far as he could tell. In fact, she came across as an incredibly honest and likeable person.

"Rachel, I haven't always been the best judge of character," he said, "but after talking to your brother and meeting her, I got the distinct impression Mariko doesn't know anything about you...let alone the money your father intended her to have."

"Yeah...and what about that? When my father died, I was expected to pay off his debts and cover his cosigned loans. Now I find out he's tucked away ten-thousand dollars in cash for some love child in Kyoto who went by the name of Aiko."

Chase didn't know what to make of it either. Sam had been his mentor, the father he never knew. Although vindicated years earlier, he still felt the sting of responsibility for the faulty dive gear that had resulted in his death.

Rachel's eyes narrowed. "Hmmm...Aiko. Sounds an awful lot like Mariko, doesn't it? Maybe she changed her name to avoid the stigma of being an illegitimate child."

Chase hesitated before shrugging.

"Yuki might be able to tell me something," she persisted. "The postcards are written in Japanese, along with the letters my dad wrote...or had someone write for him. The concierge told me that according to the address, this girl came from the Gion district. You know...the place where all the geishas live. That's two hours and forty-five minutes away by bullet train. If it's the same house Mariko lives in, then I'll know for sure it's her."

Chase looked deep into Rachel's hazel eyes, gauging her harried state of mind. "If you can wait until Friday night, there's a strong possibility your answer will come to you," he said.

"What do you mean?"

"Kenji Ota is joining us for dinner at a Tokyo restaurant. Since they live together, Mariko will probably be with him. Anyway, I could ask him if you'd like."

She hesitated a moment before answering. "Yeah, actually that sounds like a good idea. But I don't know how Shinzo's going to feel about seeing her again."

Chase nodded in agreement. According to the monk's lengthy story, her presence could prove to be extremely awkward. Still, there was no better way to know the truth in Sam's story.

"What about Yuki?" Rachel asked. "Should we tell her Mariko's coming?"

"We're supposed to meet up with her later this afternoon. I'll make sure she knows."

Their menu order arrived on a large tray, providing a timely distraction. As soon as the waitress stepped away, Chase picked up his fork and shoveled a good portion of the tomato, red pepper, and cheese omelet into his mouth. After another sizable bite, he washed it down with a swig of fresh-squeezed orange juice and noticed that Rachel was staring down at her plate of untouched food.

"Something wrong?" he asked. "I hope you're not letting all this affect you."

"I don't know. Suddenly I don't feel so hungry anymore."

"Ah, come on...just one bite. You'll feel better after you get something solid in your stomach."

When she didn't answer, he dragged his chair next to the one she was seated on and rested there with his chin propped on his left elbow.

"Go away," she whispered, shrinking into her seat. "You're being ridiculous."

Although he had no intention of embarrassing her, it was clearly too late. Like a bee to the honey, their server headed straight for them.

"Is everything all right?" she asked. "Can I bring you something else?"

Rachel grimaced. She picked up her turkey club sandwich and gave Chase a "thanks a lot" look. "How about a new boyfriend?" she asked.

Confusion registered on the poor woman's face.

"She's just kidding," Chase assured her.

The waitress smiled and nodded; however, her feet remained firmly planted. She continued to watch Rachel's food expectantly, as if her job depended on her complete satisfaction.

With obvious reluctance, Rachel took a large bite. "Hmmm... tastes good," she mumbled.

Chase watched the retreating waitress before moving his chair back into place. He picked up his fork and kept an eye on Rachel as she continued eating. Within ten minutes, they had both finished their meals.

Rachel closed her eyes and groaned. "I hope everyone's happy now."

He couldn't help but smile. There was something innately cute about her—the defiant little girl tucked inside a woman's body. He leaned across the table to brush a tendril of hair away from her face. "Still love me?" he asked.

Rachel smirked. "I don't know...maybe."

He chuckled and glanced to his left and grew instantly somber. The same man with the thin black tie and sharkskin suit he'd seen in the hotel lobby when he'd arrived from the airport a few days earlier was watching them from across the room. Although he was doing nothing more than drinking coffee, there was something sinister about the guy. Chase tried to ignore him by chatting with Rachel, waiting for her to finish her tea. The moment she did, the man stood up and approached their table.

"Are you Mr. Cohen?" he asked in perfect English.

"Who wants to know?" Chase answered.

"The name's Takashi Bekku. My boss, Kaito Mitsui, wants to speak to you. I need you and your friend to come with me."

He put a hand under Chase's arm, trying to force him to his feet, but Chase jerked his shoulder back and remained seated. He reached for Rachel's hand and held it, reminding her to remain calm. By the look on her face, she was as offended as he was by the man's abrasive behavior.

"Why does Mr. Mitsui want to see us?" Chase demanded.

Takashi leaned down and lowered his voice. "Mitsui-san's daughter-in-law is waiting outside in the car. You need to come... now."

Rachel appeared to be as mystified as Chase. "His daughter-in-law?" she asked.

Impatience narrowed Takashi's eyes. "Yuki Ota," he growled.

Chase helped Rachel out of the back seat of the car. They trailed after Yuki as she headed toward an ultramodern shopping mall minus the usual stores. It seemed the only product sold here was pleasure. In both directions were bars, hostess clubs, pachinko parlors, and Turkish-style baths. It was a postmodern red light district complete with air conditioning, piped-in music, and automated doormen.

Yuki looked back at Chase and sternly directed, "Don't speak unless asked to do so. You're not here to challenge anyone, so keep your eyes low. And Rachel, remember...Mitsui-san doesn't like Caucasians, hates Americans, and deplores women. You're here strictly to listen. Understand?"

Chase and Rachel exchanged a silent look before proceeding down the narrow alley leading to the back of the building, where Takashi knocked on the club's rear entrance. While they waited for an answer, Chase tapped Yuki on the shoulder. "Guess you forgot to mention your husband was the boss's son," he said.

"Deceased," she corrected.

"But if he isn't alive, then why—"

"You don't walk away from the family unless they decide to let you go."

The door slowly opened. A guy as big as a mountain eyed them suspiciously before permitting them access. One after the other, they ascended the stairs. The first thing they passed was a darkened room, but they didn't go in. By all appearances this was where the regulars hung out, made out, played cards, and smoked. They continued through the beaded curtains and ended up in the center of the building—the playroom, Yuki called it. They were directly above one of the gaming centers, but the loud, relentless whir and clang from the vertical pinball machines on the ground floor was softened by a koto and flute playing the theme song from The Godfather on the club's sound system. A constant hum came from tattoo-covered men slugging down beers. A group of men and women were seated on bar stools, watching a tattoo artist create his masterpiece on a young Japanese girl's back.

Yuki kept her voice low while walking, providing additional instructions and information. They stepped through sliding doors and passed another bar before arriving at their final destination. Mitsui-san, a squat older man, sat toward the back of the room at a table surrounded by bowing chimipras, yes men who responded to every request he made with an unvarying hail of *"Hai! Hai!"* Two women, one in a short black cocktail dress, the other in a schoolgirl's pleated plaid skirt and white blouse flanked him. With every gruff word he spoke, they covered their mouths and giggled childishly, adding to the surreal scene.

Yuki pressed her forefinger to her lips, reminding Rachel and Chase to remain silent. At the same time, Takashi stepped forward and bowed his head in respect. Mitsui-san immediately took notice and stopped talking. Without a word spoken, Takashi formally presented an artfully wrapped object to the older man. It was no bigger than a roll of candy, yet he set it down on the table ceremoniously with both hands. The old man stared at the offering then at Takashi's heavily bandaged left pinkie. The moment remained tense until he nodded. With his face relaxing slightly, Mitsui ordered one of his minions to remove the offering. It didn't take a great deal of imagination to know what was inside. The severed last joint of Takashi's finger. Glancing around, Chase realized this act of appeasement had been repeated over and over again by several other men in the room. He realized that the reason they'd been brought here was to witness the loyalty of these men—to understand that the yakuza would go to any length to prove their devotion to their leader. As he looked around at the black, hollow eyes staring back at him, the thought unnerved him.

"Cohen-san." The sound of his name turned his head. The old man in the corner beckoned him closer and motioned for Rachel to join him. Yuki knelt before the old man on the other side of Chase and Rachel. As they sat waiting, Yuki explained that she would be translating the message the kumicho wished to share. But she fell silent after he erupted with rapid-fire dialogue and was reminded with a stern look and nudge of his head to do exactly as she was told.

"You should never have come to Japan," she said in lieu of his low, hoarse words. "The boat that sank in Kabira Bay was used without my consent. It belongs to me along with everything on board. The fact that Sensei Yamada brought you here to rescue my property is really quite amazing when you think about it." He snorted. "Who would ever believe a monk capable of stealing?"

Chase glanced at Rachel. Her troubled expression told him how close she was to surrendering—to giving up and going home.

"I must ask you, Mr. Cohen," Yuki said, as stoic as the men around her, "do you have any idea what you were hired to bring up or how much it's worth?"

He looked calmly at Mitsui. "Mr. Yamada asked me to find out if the ship was worth retrieving. That's all."

"He didn't give you more details or ask that you find something specific?"

"No, sir," Chase answered in all honesty, since Yuki had actually been the one to fill him in.

Mitsui's eyes narrowed. "I'm puzzled why he would do me this service. It's so unlike him. He gave you no reason at all?" He studied Chase's face and body, looking for any sign of deception—a nervous twitch, shifting eyes, clenched hands—just as Yuki had warned.

Somehow, despite the mobster's scrutiny, Chase managed to remain still. "I'm strictly here to do a job, sir. Perhaps if you speak to him yourself…"

Mitsui grumbled under his breath. He rattled away at length in Japanese with only the sound of Chase's name recognizable. Eventually he crossed his arms and glowered in a bullish manner.

"It's unfortunate that you were brought here under false pretenses," Yuki translated, "but sometimes opportunities arrive when you least expect them." Mitsui reached for a mandarin orange from a filled fruit bowl and peeled it carefully before continuing his dissemination. "I'm a very generous man, Mr. Cohen. My generosity is not always appreciated or understood. Like the day after the earthquake, when forty-five trucks filled with diapers, ramen, batteries, flashlights, drinks, and other essentials were sent to the Tohoku region. Members of the Sumiyoshi-kai and Yamaguichi-gumi even offered refuge and sent supplies, but the minds of the Japanese will never change. They believe we're untouchable…that we have ulterior motives for everything we do. That's far from the truth. We look after people who need us and take care of everyone who works for us, which under the circumstances may include both of you."

Rachel rocked back on her heels. "It's great that you help people…very noble, in fact. But no one needs to offer us a job, Mr. Mitsui. We're fully capable of taking care of ourselves."

Surprise flashed across the old man's face, magnified by Yuki's look of alarm. He silently waited while Rachel's words were translated then he guffawed and raised his hand, quieting the grumbling men in the room.

"Miss Lyons, you are either strong willed or incredibly foolish," Yuki said. "In any regard, I will listen to what you have to say after you understand the position you've placed yourselves in and the reason why you should leave as soon as possible."

Rachel's cheeks flushed. Chase could tell she was biting her lip to control her temper. But just as instructed, she remained quiet for the balance of their meeting. Ten minutes later, after Mitsui finished providing gory details of gangland killings, the side effects of radiation poisoning from the failed nuclear plants, and a history of accidents from faulty dive equipment, Yuki asked a final question on his behalf. "Now do you understand why it's necessary to leave?"

They both silently nodded.

"Wonderful. To ensure your safety and protection while you're visiting for the next day or two, I have asked several of my men to accompany you to your hotel and then to the airport. So please call upon them if you need any assistance with your luggage." The old man smiled confidently and popped the remaining slice of orange into his mouth. Then he turned his full attention to Rachel.

"Do you still have any questions to ask?" he said in perfect English.

Rachel huffed loudly. "Well, actually," she said bitingly, "I thought you should know we plan to stick around and tour Japan for at least a week. Is that a problem?"

# 11

After Rachel and Chase returned to their hotel room, Rachel dropped onto the bed completely exhausted. She was thankful to be away from all the negative energy and to have a quiet moment to regroup.

"You've always been incredibly brave, and I'm proud of you," Chase said, coming out of the bathroom. "But baby, you need to be careful with those guys."

"I know," she said, pushing herself upright. "I just couldn't help myself. Mitsui's a total asshole."

Chase sat down on the edge of the bed. "He's also full of it... pumping me for information the whole time. He didn't know anything about the sunken yacht or what she was carrying. And he's supposed to own it?"

"I know. I picked up on that too. Right after his job offer. No wonder Shinzo wanted us to keep his plan a secret. And here I thought Kenji Ota was going to be our biggest problem."

"He still might be. I have to depend on him for our boat and equipment. And right now I don't know how that's going to work...especially with Mitsui involved."

Rachel looked up. "Chase, I'm sorry for getting upset with you earlier and for saying all those stupid things. I love your daughter like she was my own, you know that. There's no doubt in my mind you're doing the best you can for our business."

"That includes you too, Miss Lyons."

Rachel smiled. "I guess I forget sometimes what it's like to depend on someone."

Chase reached out and wrapped his arms around her, pulling her close. "Just don't forget how much I love you. Okay?"

She sighed happily. "I won't."

As he leaned down to kiss her, Rachel instinctively jerked back, suddenly feeling nauseous. She put her hand to mouth, pushed him away, and ran to the bathroom. After throwing up several times, she laid her cheek on the edge of the stool and waited for the pain in her stomach to subside.

Chase knelt down next to her and rested a calming hand on her back. "Are you okay?"

"I dunno." She shrugged. "I've been feeling sick for the past two days."

"Really? Do you think it might be—"

"It's something I ate," she interrupted. "I'm sure of it. With the water and change of diet, it was bound to happen."

Chase helped her back to her feet and handed her a wet washcloth. He stood against the wall watching while she refreshed herself. Then he scooped her up and brought her back to the bed.

"All this concern really isn't necessary," she assured him. "It's probably just the food from this morning. I'll be all right, really. I just need a little time to recoup."

"Of course, take all the time you need. Only thing we've got going on today is dinner with Shinzo. But if you're not up to facing him, I can make an excuse."

"It's all right, honest. I can handle it," she said, sounding more confident than she felt.

"What about the dive on Friday? Do you think you'll be up for that too?"

Rachel shook her head. "Don't worry about me. I'll be fine."

"Well, that's good news at least. I know you were mad when you told Mitsui we weren't leaving, but I wasn't sure if you really meant it."

Rachel closed her eyes and swallowed hard. Things couldn't get any worse, could they? As soon as the thought pierced her brain, she was reminded of the yakuza boss's directive. As long as they were in Japan, they'd be forced to tolerate his men and follow his rules.

She offered a weak smile and nodded. No one, not even an overbearing kingpin, was going to send her packing with her tail between her legs. Not if she had anything to say about it.

"So I take it that's a yes?" Chase asked.

After a few cleansing breaths, she slid off the bed. She had been compliant for far too long. It wasn't in her nature to play second string...or the sad, wounded female. Even though her father remained a constant disappointment, she could be thankful for the strong backbone she'd inherited from him.

"As a matter of fact, that's a definite yes. Now if I could just take a hot bath and a long nap before dinner..."

Chase smiled. "Wait here while I get the tub ready." Five minutes later he returned and took her hand, pulling her behind him. "Come with me, beautiful."

Steam filled the bathroom, proof that hot water had been drawn. Chase had even taken the time to place a small wooden chair in the middle of the open shower. She stood motionless, allowing him to remove her robe before leading her to the stool. He stepped out of his jeans and tossed them on the sink counter.

Her breath caught as he moved to her side. His body was tall, tan, and smooth, and extremely firm and muscular—a tantalizing feast for her eyes to enjoy.

"According to a book I read on the plane, Japanese baths are suppose to clean more than your body," he explained. His voice was deep and soft, sending a shiver down her spine. "They calm your spirit too. I'll show you how, if you'd like." He leaned down and brushed her mouth with his, sending her heart fluttering. Her gaze dropped to the evidence of his aroused desire. A whisper of a smile touched her lips. She dropped onto the stool and waited while he retrieved the handheld nozzle and porous sea sponge. She remained perfectly still as he circled behind her, cascading hot water over her shoulders and back with the sprayer. The heat felt amazing, but it was his hands, rubbing her gently with the fragrant lavender soap, his fingers kneading her skin, that took her to another place. She closed her eyes, savoring the exquisite feeling of a man—her man—demonstrating the extent of his love.

As minutes ebbed away, he seemed to be totally engrossed in the task of washing her. The sponge continued to slide over her skin, tenderly massaging her. He urged her to raise her arms above her head, and she complied most willingly. His touch against her neck, down her arms, and over her breasts was both erotic and soothing. His hands pushed on her hips, imploring her to slide back on the stool to allow him better access to her buttocks. He continued scrubbing, and the sensation was unlike anything she'd ever known.

When he moved to the front of her, she caught his hands. "I don't expect you to do this, you know."

"I want to," he said. "Touching you makes me happy, and that's all I want for you."

How could any woman not relish being treated with such kindness...such gentle, tender care? She watched the lines in his face relax, leaving no doubt that he was thoroughly enjoying himself. He encouraged her to stand, and with one foot he shoved the stool aside to address her hips. She closed her eyes again as his hands slid over her stomach. He traced her ribs and tense muscles with his soapy fingers, and although she knew he was as aroused as she was, he took his own sweet time cleaning every inch of her. Instinctively she pushed her hips forward, savoring the exquisite touch of his tight fist between her legs and against the skin of her inner thighs.

She let out a deep breath and met his concentrated gaze. "Do I get a turn?"

"Hmmm…maybe later," he replied without looking up. "When I'm done here, I want you to relax in the tub while I clean myself." He leaned down and cupped her breast before kissing her mouth with the same thoroughness he'd shown while washing her.

She longed to touch every part of his body and please him as much as he had her. "Why not now?" she asked.

"This is about you, baby. But if you'd like, we could do this tomorrow."

"Really?" She smiled as he turned her around and finished scrubbing her back.

"Sure, why not." He helped her into the tub and then stepped into the shower. After a few minutes, he turned off the faucet and set the sponge and wand aside.

"Come here," she said, drawing up her knees to make room for him.

Chase settled into the hot water with a soft sigh. He stretched out his long legs and laid his head against the back edge of the tub, allowing the same peace and tranquility that consumed her to fill his idle soul.

He remained quiet for an endless time with her legs over his and her feet resting on his thighs, watching her through narrow, smiling eyes. She wanted to remember this picture...to cherish it for all eternity.

"I should probably get dressed," she said finally. She drew up her knees and climbed out, reaching for a thick white towel. She felt his gaze on her as she rubbed it over her wet skin, and before she knew it, he was at her side drying off too. With towels wrapped around both of them, he took her hand and tugged her toward the bedroom.

"I thought you were hungry," she said, grinning.

"I am." He eased her onto the mattress and watched her face as he knelt before her. "So how about you, Rachel? Are you hungry?"

Her wide smile was answer enough. He took possession of one of her breasts, drawing it into his mouth. Then he moved to her stomach and began tracing his tongue against her skin. Her muscles tightened and rippled beneath his exploring hand and mouth. She let out a soft sigh and pulled him closer. He lowered his head to kiss her again and moved his hand to the damp heat between her thighs.

"While we were living apart, I dreamed about you all the time," he murmured. "I never thought I'd have you back in my life...loving me in spite of my flaws."

She arched her back slightly and smiled again. "Your only flaw was waiting so long to make love to me."

Chase laughed softly, but his eyes were bright with emotion. He kissed her neck and branded her there before kissing his way to her breasts again. He moved to her belly and kissed it once more before whispering in her ear, "Spread your legs for me, baby."

She complied, eager for his attention...his beguiling touch. As he held her thighs in place, he bent toward her, blowing hot breaths across her groin. She gripped the bed sheet with both hands, writhing beneath him. If he kept licking and sucking her, Rachel knew she'd come quickly, and more than anything, she wanted to feel him deep inside her. She exhaled a hot breath and reached for his closest hand.

"My turn," she insisted.

Chase's lopsided grin became decidedly more devious as he sank to his knees on the mattress and crawled up next to her. He laid his head back on the pillow. His eyes met hers again when she took ownership of his body, mounting him.

"Go ahead, baby," he told her." Have your way with me."

Rachel planted small kisses at the base of his throat. She moved up his neck to the sensitive spot just below his ear and down his jaw. He moaned softly. She made her way to his lips and kissed him with fervor. His hands gripped both sides of her waist as he kissed her back, plunging his tongue into her mouth. She felt his erection against her thigh and was aroused by her own power. With her hands pressed against his shoulders for support, she pushed herself upright and straddled his hips.

She lowered her chin and looked deep into his crystal blue eyes. "Let's see how long you can last."

"I love a challenge," he said, smiling.

Rachel reached under herself and grabbed his hard cock. She guided it slowly inside her. He groaned as she shifted back and forth, grinding her pubis against his. With her hands braced on his chest, she lifted her hips up, easing him out of her. Then she slid down again, grinding herself against him even harder. As she slid back and forth on top of him, gradually increasing her speed, she felt the rush of wet heat and his hands slip from her waist to her ass.

"Not fair," he murmured. His fingertips squeezed, digging into her flesh. She gasped and clenched her buttocks. The combination of pain and pleasure was thrilling, heightening every sensation. With each thrust, he bucked his hips to meet her over and over again, leaving her moaning softly. She bit her lip in concentration, determined to hide the control he had over her—to beat him at this tantalizing game.

"Oh baby," Chase rasped. "Oh...oh baby, don't stop..." They were both bouncing up and down now, furiously pounding away. The padded headboard was thumping the bedroom wall like a distant drum.

Damn! He's good at this. So good. She moved her hands to his muscular pecs to maintain her balance. With one look at his scrunched-up face, his eyes squeezed shut and his teeth clenched, she knew he was close.

Suddenly a series of rapid knocks sounded at the door, jolting Rachel. Oh shit! Had the neighbors complained? She pressed Chase's shoulders firmly into the bed then glanced over her shoulder to verify they were alone.

"What? What is it?" Chase looked up at her dazed and confused.

After a few seconds, a man's voice in the hallway broke the silence. "Mr. Cohen, are you there?" The timing couldn't have been worse.

"You've got to be kidding me," Chase bellowed.

"Hello...Mr. Cohen?" the voice called out again.

Rachel rolled off of Chase and onto the mattress. His eyes fell to her pouty lips as he shifted to hover over her.

"Maybe he'll go away if we're quiet."

"It's all right," she said, lacking any sincerity in her words. "Go check. It might be important."

Chase blew out a frustrated huff and climbed off the bed. There was another series of knocks on the door. Rachel dropped an arm across her eyes, burying her anxiety.

"Just a minute!" Chase called out. With a towel secured around his middle, he disappeared through the bedroom door. From where she was lying, Rachel could hear the entry door open and Chase's voice in the next room.

"What is it?" he snapped, sounding angrier than she believed possible.

"I'm sorry to disturb you, sir, but there's a gentleman down-stairs who insists that you've got a car waiting. I would have called your room first, but I couldn't help noticing the block on your phone."

"There's a reason for that, you know," Chase said.

"I'm fully aware, sir, and I do apologize. Normally I wouldn't think of troubling one of our guests, but in this instance, I was at a loss as to what I should do. You see…Mr. Mitsui's personal driver is parked downstairs, blocking the front entry. Apparently he's been asked to take you on a tour of Tokyo today. I told him that we hadn't received word of any prior arrangement and that you were planning to relax for the rest of the day. But this man insisted that you had personally spoken with Mr. Mitsui and wanted to see as much of the city as possible before returning home."

"That's the emergency?"

Rachel imaged Chase's slack jaw at that moment. She slipped off the bed and pulled on a bathrobe then hurried into the next room to join him. The short clerk from the front desk was stand-ing in the hallway. His eyes dropped to the floor at the sight of her; a rosy blush filled his cheeks.

Chase looked at Rachel and caught her smiling. "What a clever man," she told him, "calling my bluff like that. Well, you know what? We have a free afternoon. Why not take advantage of his generosity? Besides, it might be interesting to find out what that old man is really up to."

Chase sniffed a humorless laugh. He leaned down and whispered words that only she could hear. "Not screwing his girlfriend, that's for sure."

Rachel walked hand in hand with Chase toward the hotel's front entrance dressed in tan cotton slacks and a white short sleeve shirt. Approaching the black Toyota Century, she was surprised to find an attractive middle- aged woman waiting and a black-suited driver behind the wheel.

"This is Eiji," the woman told them. The driver glanced in the rearview mirror before nodding. "My name is Tomo Satoko," the woman continued.   "I'm a professional tour guide and have been asked to show you some of the highlights of Tokyo today."

After closing their car door and slipping back into the front seat, she handed them brochures from the sites they were scheduled to visit and talked about Japanese culture in general. Over the course of five hours, she took them to the Meiji Shinto Shrine, dedicated to Emperor Meiji and his consort, and then to the Akasaka Palace, which had immaculate grounds and gardens. They made a quick stop at the House of Parliament before strolling through the Imperial Palace East Garden, epic in its beauty. All the while Tomo expounded on the history of each building, site, temple, and shrine, and allowed extra time to take photos. She picked out an interesting local restaurant where a delicious meal of chilled wheat noodles was served with soup, boiled eggs, and shredded vegetable toppings. They drove through the famous Ginza district and visited the Nakamise shopping arcade, crammed with tiny food and souvenir shops. Chase had three pairs of chopsticks engraved with their names and picked out a cartoon anime mask for his daughter. Before returning to the hotel, they witnessed a water festival and ceremony with a dragon dance.

"Wow! That's amazing," Chase said numerous times throughout the day. Rachel had to admit the places they visited were magical in every regard. She found herself fast becoming a learned traveler, hungry for knowledge.

"We have to come back here with Allie," he said. "As much as she loves pirates, dragons, and castles, she'd be crazy about this place."

Rachel smiled at the thought of Chase's seven-year-old daughter dancing around in the pink floral yukata she had bought in Nishiki market. The inquisitive youngster would have been thrilled to make this trip, but not under the present circumstances...and especially not in the back seat of a mobster's car.

Throughout the day, Rachel kept wondering what the catch was and why Mitsui had been so accommodating. Perhaps this had been his way to earn their trust or demonstrate his benevolence. Yet whatever the reason, for one day she had managed to put aside her animosity and skepticism and simply enjoy the beauty and culture of Japan.

Returning to the hotel, they gathered their belongings and thanked Tomo and Eiji before sending them on their way. Chase carried their gift bags and camera upstairs while Rachel headed toward the lobby restaurant for a cup of strong European coffee. When he joined her again, she was still watching the constant flow of visitors in sports jackets and summer dresses, while keeping her eyes peeled for dark-suited men with unguarded, intrusive stares.

"So what do you think of him now?" Chase asked in regard to Kaito Mitsui.

"I have to admit the old guy provided a nice distraction, but that doesn't change who he is or how he makes his money."

"You're absolutely right. I almost felt guilty enjoying myself today. Then I remembered the promise we made to each other before coming here. When our business ceases to be fun and profitable, we give it up and just travel the world."

"Well, maybe we should rethink that agreement when it comes to this trip. To tell you the truth, I don't know how much pleasure we're going to get out of this after hearing what we're up against."

Chase nodded thoughtfully then glanced up in time to see Shinzo entering the hotel lobby. "Looks like our dinner host just arrived." Both watched the unlikely monk approach their table neatly dressed in a purple shirt and tapered gray slacks.

"Did you have an opportunity to rest?" he asked them.

Rachel glanced at Chase. "Well, actually we toured the city thanks to Mr. Mitsui. It probably wasn't a great idea now that I think about it. I'm afraid we might have compromised everyone's position, and believe me, that was never our intent."

"Caution is natural, Rachel-san. But fear isn't. Sometimes it becomes a difficult balancing act. While caution tells you to look both ways before crossing the street, fear keeps you trapped on the curb. But in life, we all have journeys to make," he said, smiling. "Which is why we're having a special meal tonight. This will be an opportunity for you to grow trust while heightening your senses. I believe you'll find it a valuable tool. Shall we go?"

Rachel rose from her seat and followed Chase and Shinzo through the side exit of the hotel. Passing the doorman, she glanced up and spotted two men from Mitsui's group huddled on the street corner smoking. When they spotted her, they immediately crushed their cigarettes under their heels and rushed to their car. Just as the yakuza boss had promised, as long as they were in Japan, they'd never be alone or have a moment's peace.

# 12

The restaurant host blindfolded Rachel and Chase in order for them to take part in Kurayami Gohan—an eat-in-the-dark dinner. Although it presented a tremendous challenge, she was intrigued by this interesting diversion. With chopsticks in hand, she picked up a piece of cooked tofu and took her first bite. After a few thoughtful chews, she turned to where Shinzo was sitting.

"Is this a sponge?" she asked. Shinzo burst into laughter. Realizing the silliness of her comment, she dropped her guard and laughed along.

"I guess you need an explanation," he said lightheartedly. "This type of dining began in Europe at a restaurant here the food was served in rooms without light in order to heighten the diner's sense of taste. Dark dining is based on the theory that flavors are intensified when people can't see what they're eating. A monk from the Asakusa temple created this concept as part of his eight-week mindfulness meditation class and generously allowed us to take part this evening. So please try to be open-minded. I believe both of you will gain something from this experience."

Rachel swallowed her last mouthful before asking, "Why aren't you participating, Shinzo?"

"I'm your sensei tonight, Miss Lyons…here to teach a new approach and way of thinking."

Buddhist enlightenment wasn't on her bucket list or of any particular interest,  and managing chopsticks without seeing was proving to be a difficult task. After dropping a chestnut three times, she gave up and brought the dish closer to scoop the mysterious item into her mouth.

Mmmm…it was smooth and somewhat soft and the taste was slightly sweet. She had to admit it was more enjoyable than she had anticipated.

"Are we going to meditate after this?" Chase asked. He leaned toward Rachel and whispered softly in her ear, "I can think of a better use for a blindfold."

A small laugh escaped her lips.

"Actually, it's part of this exercise," Shinzo said. "Clearing your mind as well as your palate…giving you the chance to enjoy food in the here and now."

"Well, I don't know what that soft, chewy thing was," Chase said, "but it sure tasted good. Maybe we could get some more of that?"

"Just enjoy what you have,  Cohen-san. You're going to try all kinds of delicacies tonight."

Delicacies? Rachel's mental alarm sounded. "Shinzo, you're not going to make us eat something weird, are you? There were people eating grilled baby octopi at one of the temples we visited today. Tentacles, head, and all. They're not serving anything like that, I hope."

"No, Miss Lyons. The chef has prepared a special menu just for us. It comprises five courses that include mostly vegetable dishes. Part of the fun is guessing what you're eating, but I assure you there's nothing too extreme. Not in your case."

"Oh, thank goodness," she said with a sigh.

"Although meditation and food are not directly connected," Shinzo continued, "they both share many of the same principles and are meant to awaken and enhance mental functionality within each of us. I think people often take for granted everything we do, and many times the simple act of eating is overlooked. By engaging in this practice, we can take the time to enjoy it for what it is."

Rachel placed something crunchy, sweet, and sour in her mouth. She rolled it over on her tongue and kept chewing. The sound of happy humming came from the chair beside her. Apparently Chase was having the time of his life.

"So what do you think you're eating?" Shinzo asked.

Rachel wrinkled her nose. "It's got to be an onion of some sort or maybe—"

"I think it's a pickle," Chase cut in. "One of those daikon radishes."

After a slight pause, affirmation came from their teacher. "You're right, Cohen-san. Very good! And what about the other item in your bowl?"

"Okay, the texture of this one's a little strange," Chase said. "I'm not big on soft, spongy, or squishy, but it tastes…pretty good."

"I'm afraid that's a hard one. Not many people get it right. Do you have any ideas, Miss Lyons?"

"I can taste the vinegar, and it feels like there might be a smooth skin, but I honestly haven't got a clue."

"Try again," he encouraged her. "Move it around in your mouth slowly and think about the grainy texture as well as the taste."

A few seconds later, she had the answer. "Is it kabocha squash?"

"Close," he said. "That's eggplant. Quite a surprise, isn't it? We're used to downing our food fast so we can get on to the next thing. This little experiment shows us how enjoyable it is to eat everything slowly and to really think about what we put in our bodies. I hope when you're both finished here tonight and have a chance to think about it, you'll agree."

Near the end of the meal, before dessert was served, another plate arrived. "So...Cohen-san," Shinzo said, "you guessed the radish, squash soup, and ahi tuna correctly, but let's see if either of you can tell the difference between two rice balls. One was made using an electric rice cooker and the other was made using a traditional Japanese pot, which makes stickier rice. Take off your blindfolds and tell me what you both think."

For Rachel, this was her only opportunity for a right answer. With the rice balls sitting there on the plate before her eyes, it had to be a no-brainer. But after staring at them for several minutes and taking a few bites, she realized telling them apart was virtually impossible.

Chase followed her example, studying them carefully and sampling each one. He shrugged and then ventured, "The one on the left?"

A gentle smile spread over Shinzo's face. "The reason neither one of you could tell the difference is because you can see the rice balls and they look exactly alike, which made you form a biased opinion. If you'd been blindfolded, you wouldn't have thought they were the same at all and would have probably gotten the answer right."

Rachel tilted her chin. "And the point of all this was?"

"That's easy," Chase said. "Don't always believe what's right in front of your eyes."

"Hmmm…" Rachel's lips lifted in dry amusement. "It's that instinct thing again, isn't it?"

Shinzo smiled back, adding warmth to the aura around him. "Exactly, Miss Lyons. But don't let any of this trouble you. Just focus on your inner voice. Concentrate on what's important, and all the doubts in your life will disappear."

If it was only that simple, Rachel thought.

"So where's Yuki?" Chase asked, obviously trying to change the subject. "I was under the impression she was joining us tonight."

"I left a message," Shinzo said, "but I haven't heard back from her. I imagine she has plenty to do before your trip and our final dinner meeting on Friday night."

"Of course," Chase said. "Plus she's probably done this before, right?"

"A number of times, and fairly well, I might add. She has the mindset of a female warrior. Always prepared for the unexpected. You're both in good hands with her, I assure you. I've never met anyone with such strong capabilities and instincts who still hungers for knowledge and acceptance." Shinzo chuckled softly. "It's as if she has two separate personalities. But don't we all at times?"

Chase smiled softly. "I suppose we do."

Shinzo rose to visit the restroom. While he was gone, Chase bent forward on his crossed arms and turned to Rachel. "Tomorrow we'll be able to laugh about this."

A wry smile tugged at the corners of her mouth. "Guess we'll have to ask Yuki about that, won't we?"

Chase remained subdued as he walked behind Shinzo and Rachel on their way to the idling taxi the restaurant manager had called for them. When they were only ten feet away, a black car with dark tinted windows darted from out of nowhere, swerving around the green and white MK cab. It was headed straight toward them in an obvious attempt to run them over.

"Car!" Rachel screamed. She threw a protective arm around Shinzo's waist, drawing him over the curb and out of harm's way. Chase was right behind them, tumbling onto the ground. They had avoided being hit thanks to Rachel's quick, decisive actions; however, this didn't dismiss the fact that someone was out to get them. Exactly who was a mystery, as the car was long gone by the time they stood and dusted themselves off.

Shinzo's look of appreciation spoke for itself. But despite his apparent relief that none of them had been hurt, he made a surprising claim. "I knew you were one of the chosen, Miss Lyons. Although you'd be the last to admit it, you've just proven it in more ways than one."

# 13

There it was…that damn sound again. Kenji could hear it beneath Mariko's pulsing skin—beneath the heated air lingering above their bodies like a thick, invisible mist. He could hear it beneath the soft sounds stifled in her throat, where whimpers and gasps drew forth like a fountain on a steel rim. He could hear it beneath his own swimming mind, beyond the surface of his lust and willful intent. That damned annoying sound. It was low and sweet. Tucked inside Mariko's voice, hidden beneath the crack of her smile. It came from deep within her chest, curling behind the rib cage where her naive heart lay—soft and fleeting like a hummingbird's wings.

"Oooo…"

He kissed the middle of her back and heard it again in her muffled whine. That damned infuriating noise. Her face was half-buried in her pillow and his was tucked under her stomach, bringing her to the perfect height. Two of his fingers were jammed inside her, pumping away with earnest intent. After a few minutes, he felt her tremble. He smelled the pungent aroma of her arousal as he inhaled her very essence. It was an intoxicating, heady potion, capable of driving any man to the brink.

"Haaaa..." She stiffened beneath him for a brief, breathless moment. Then her entire body shook with the force of her orgasm. Kenji smiled at his success. Now it was his turn. He used his knee to gently push her legs farther apart and inserted a third finger, stretching her pussy wide enough to accommodate him. Then he went back to work, building her hunger and ensuring her juices were sufficiently flowing. When she was ready, he settled himself between her thighs and gripped her waist in both hands. He eased forward, entering her from behind. His hips rocked back and forth as he made her take more and more of him. Nothing gave him more pleasure at that moment than the thought of filling her up and nibbling her exposed neck in the process.

Mariko groaned and dug her nails into the mattress. He gripped her tighter and started to move again, determined to give her all of himself. When he was fully divested, he rolled his hips around, teasing her relentlessly—leaving her crying out for him to stop. Then he halted and remained motionless for an eternal moment. When he started to withdraw, Mariko reached one hand around her back and gripped his butt cheek, holding him in place.

"Do you want me or not?" he asked sarcastically.

Mariko answered in a near whisper. "Yes."

"Yes, what?"

"Yes, please." It was exactly what he wanted to hear. The master was back in charge. In no time at all, he was bouncing against her and she was meeting him with each driving thrust. He had done well in teaching and cultivating her sexual need. A few more nefarious sessions and she might even become a temptress—a wanton creature capable of drawing heat with an enamoring smile and simple brush of her leg. He smiled at the possibilities, at the pleasure he would gain by cruelly denying her.

"Mmmm..." Kenji hummed aloud. He was much happier now. He could concentrate on this—on anything but that infuriating noise.

"Aaahhh..." escaped from Mariko's lips.

Magic. I'm making magic. There was nothing better than fucking a woman and doing it well.

"I need to...to know." Mariko wasn't whimpering. Not gasping or moaning or making that damn sound. But still he wanted to gag her. Have her be quiet until he was through.

"Kenjiii..."

Oh hell. "What is it?" he hissed.

"Will I be living here?"

Huh? "Living where?" Kenji rocked his hips back and forth, driving himself even deeper into her, hoping Mariko would stop the annoying noises in her little wet voice. Her arched back came with a gentle groan, making him smile again. He resumed his steady rhythm and felt his control weakening. It wouldn't be long now.

Come on, Mariko. Come on. I know it's in there.

"Here!" she suddenly gasped. "Here, in this hotel."

What? Damn it all to hell. This was turning into more work than he had imagined. At that moment, just to keep her quiet, he'd tell her whatever she wanted to hear...just until he could touch heaven again. "I suppose so," he said. "For a while."

"But Kenji...aah!" Mariko's alabaster knuckles tightened on the clutched sheets as he rammed into her hard.

"Mariko, stop talking," he ordered.

"B---but…"

He could hear the tremble in her soft lips. Imagine the tears in her soft brown eyes.

"But I thought…I need t---to know," she persisted. "Everyone…will be asking…about my home."

Kenji heard her voice trail away and was grateful for his endurance. With her insistent pleas and interruptions, she could curb any man's appetite…except his. He increased his tempo, madly pumping away—willing her to call out his name as she'd done so many times before. "Mmmm…yes…yes. Come on, Mariko. Tell me it feels good. Give it to me…give it all to me."

"I have to…ahhhh!!"A scream tore from her mouth as spasms racked her body. Kenji quickened his pace, slamming into her over and over again. He was flying high, enjoying the ride…never wanting to land. But her constricting muscles were holding him tight, milking and draining every ounce from him—splitting him into a million pieces. Leaving his body jerking with uncontrollable spasms. He moaned and collapsed, empty, against her back.

After a few minutes, he pulled out and she rolled over onto her back. A single tear slid down her cheek, dampening the pillow.

"What is it?" His voice felt puckered as he spoke against her abdomen, as if addressing a young child.

Her exquisite eyes were like honey at the bottom of a pot, changing with her moods from soft brown to gold. A dusky blush now filled her cheeks, making her appear even more young and desirable. "Please, Kenji. I need to go to my apartment for clothes and stop by the okiya. Oneesan will be worried about me. I still have obligations…" Mariko grimaced and shook her head. "I mean appointments to honor, if it's all right with you."

Kenji sat upright and shook his head.

There was another wince and disparaging glimmer in her eyes. He could see through this woman as if she were cellophane. She was looking for any reason to escape—to meet with Oneesan and break their agreement.

"I wouldn't expect you to take me there," she said. "I could call for a taxi. You should...could stay here and rest awhile longer."

Like forever? A chuckle broke through his deep throat, and his ire was momentarily forgotten. "What's wrong, Mariko? Haven't I treated you well?"

"You've been very kind and most...attentive. But I have responsibilities and people who are expecting to hear from me. Surely you understand that as well?"

There was that sound beneath her voice...an incredulous lilt in her words Kenji could no longer stand. His voice fell to a careless hush. "From this day on, I don't want you to do anything without my consent. That includes all your engagements and whom you choose to see. Whatever needs you have, I'll provide for. I've already arranged for a personal assistant to handle your correspondence and a driver to take you wherever you need to go... provided I agree. I prefer to dress you myself and will enlist the services of my personal kimono designer to keep you fashionably dressed. I understand you enjoy running in your free time, so you can expect a membership at a private club and a handpicked qualified trainer. As for your diet, I enjoy eating out but prefer healthy meals in my home...where you'll be living. I travel on business, and while I'm away, my associates have been instructed to look after you. And should there be anything I've overlooked or haven't explained thoroughly, you merely need to ask."

Mariko lowered her eyes and appeared to be digesting his words. When she looked up at him, her eyes were brimming with tears. "What about dancing? Is that forbidden too?"

"Shhh, Mariko," he said, cradling her face. "Don't be foolish. I would never take that away from you. In fact, I went to a great deal of trouble to buy you makeup, hair ornaments, and a beautiful blue and pink kimono for the dinner party tomorrow night. I want you to wear them for me and perform the kouta dance for our friends."

She pulled her face away. "You're serious? But Shinzo and the Americans will be there. It's...it's forbidden. It wouldn't be right."

Kenji could see the shock in her wide eyes, but it had no effect on him. Although embarrassing Shinzo was just a small part of his plan, it would prove incredibly rewarding. The swords would come next, along with the power they possessed. He would own them despite Shinzo's ridiculous claims...the same ones his sister had been foolish enough to share. Together with his geisha at his side, Kenji would turn the Nikkei market into his personal bank account and Japan into the most feared country in the world.

The thought was uplifting in more ways than one. He leaned down and gave Mariko's thigh a wet lick then shifted into a kneeling position. His swollen member immediately sprang to attention. Ah, the effectiveness of those tiny blue pills—ever present on my nightstand. Despite her silent protests, he grabbed her legs and spread them wide apart. After one glance at his downturned expression, she dropped back against the mattress, defeated. He braced one hand on her thigh and used the other to guide his cock, entering her with one push. Then he resumed his onslaught—unleashing years of resentment against his father and her self-serving boyfriend, Shinzo Yamada.

"Kenji, please...not again. Aahh!" Her cry was short, thick, and pointless. He felt her heels dig into the small of his back and her hot, sweaty body tighten around him. This was his mission, his true purpose in life. Fucking her to death. He chuckled under his breath at the depraved thought.

"We can't keep doing this. We can't stay...in this hotel forever." Mariko's breathy words were ignored. She turned her face away and closed her eyes.

He responded by brushing his lips over her neck, kissing red, tender spots along the way. "Relax," he whispered in her ear. "We're leaving tomorrow. Now be still and enjoy the pleasure I'm giving you."

She gasped with his unpredictable thrusts, varying with intensity. Gentle and slow, then rough and fast— breaking her resistance along with her will. The bed sang with the chant of squeaking springs and crushing sheets, urging him on. Miraculously, Mariko remained silent until she finally came with a high, raspy cry. Kenji's body fed on the clench of her climax, and after a short moment of riding out the smoldering heat, he too came with a hot, jolting burst.

Sticky, sweaty, and bone sore, he closed his eyes and draped a possessive arm and leg over her amazing body. But much to his chagrin, he was awakened moments later by an irritating sound.

Where is it coming from? He remained perfectly still, listening to the silence in the warm room, Mariko's soft, even breathing, the beating in his chest as he lazed about like a satisfied, overfed animal. He felt her fingers resting in his hair and knew before long she would try to convince him again. If given the chance, she would try to break down his defenses. He rose up on his elbow and stared down at her face. No words or sounds came forth. He suddenly realized a new, unfamiliar noise had taken up residence. A noise he despised more than the sound of her disappointed sighs. It was the rhythm of contentment reverberating in his chest, threatening to strangle his bitter resolve.

He had to stop its advance quickly. Turn a deaf ear to his heart. He couldn't afford the luxury of wishful possibilities or subject himself to love's mindless foolery.

Taking great pains not to awaken her, Kenji extracted himself from Mariko's warm body. He took the silk bedspread from the closet and relocated to the living room couch. Curling up into a ball, he pulled the coverlet over his ears. He longed for the silence of his loneliness, the sanity of his miserable life. A time when he didn't ache from his mistreatment of Mariko and wish to hell he could be the danna she truly deserved.

Kenji slept deeper and longer than he had in years, but he wasn't particularly excited about waking up today...all right, he was. He wanted to see how his charge was doing. Her long hair was probably down, spread across her pillow in a tangled, uncombed mess. She would be achy, hungry, and extremely tired. As he cracked the bedroom door open, he smiled, recalling the many reasons why.

"Good morning," he said.

Mariko opened her eyes and found him standing over her. "Uh, good morning," she mumbled. She lowered her dark lashes and turned away, avoiding his probing stare.

"Are you okay?" He sat on the edge of the bed and leaned in to kiss her forehead.

She winced at his touch. "I'm fine, thanks... now please get off the bed so I can get up." He could hear the vexation in her voice—so unexpected, coming from his perfect geisha.

"What's wrong, Mariko?" he asked. "You don't like me anymore?"

"No…now stop being a pervert and let me get up." She flattened her hands on his chest to push him away, but he didn't budge.

"Pervert?" he said with amusement. "Is that what you think of me now?"

"Please?" she asked again.

Kenji came to his feet reluctantly. Was this the same woman he'd spent half the night with? The same sexual creature that had moaned and whimpered with every climax-inducing touch?

"Thank you!" she snapped. He watched her run into the bathroom, wondering if she was embarrassed by her nudity in the light of day. From where he stood, he could hear the water running in the sink. She was most likely washing her face with the running tap, cooling her hot cheeks. But why was she acting so strange?

A knock sounded on the door in the next room. "Yes? What is it?" Kenji called out.

"Room service," the man's voice announced. Kenji walked to the door and opened it wide, allowing the rolling cart access. As soon as the bill was signed, the young man slipped it into his folder and asked if he needed anything else. Kenji glanced around the room. Then he picked up Mariko's pink underwear from the floor and smiled, waving them in the air.

"I've got everything I need right here," he said. He closed the door behind the waiter and began lifting the silver domes. Perfect. The smell of fresh bacon pulled him closer. He picked up a piece and began chewing away while surveying his preordered breakfast. Each dish was more appealing than the last: sweet egg omelet, grilled fish, stewed soy potatoes, miso soup, steaming white rice, assorted pickles, fresh orange juice, and two cups of green tea. He pulled up two chairs, straightened the white tablecloth, and removed the unnecessary items. Then he transferred a rosebud vase to the table and sat down, laying a napkin across his bare lap.

A few minutes later, Mariko came out of the bathroom looking elegant and somewhat annoyed. Her hair was twisted and pinned behind her head, and she was wearing the blue silk blouse and tan linen slacks he had bought for her. She sat down across from him, picked up her cup of tea, and mumbled something under her breath.

"Should we try this again?" Kenji ventured. "Good morning, Mariko-chan."

She looked up and said, "Good morning," then offered a weak smile.

"About that…thing earlier, that was nothing."

"Thing?" she asked.

"Yeah…you know. Performing the kouta dance. I didn't really mean it."

"You didn't? Then why did you ask me…no, make that insist I do it? I'm here for you, Kenji. I'll do whatever you want…aside from humiliating myself."

The strength in her words surprised him. "That was never my intention, Mariko. I simply wanted that fool to know what he has lost."

"That's your reason?"

He half shrugged. "Not many people can say they have exclusive rights to the most beautiful woman in the world."

She tilted her chin and stared at him. "You can be exasperating, you know."

"I know, but I'm hoping you'll change me."

"That would take a lifetime."

His lips spread into a slow smile. "That's exactly what I'm hoping for."

Mariko sniffed a laugh and shook her head.

"So, am I forgiven?" he asked.

She pursed her lips, as if pondering an answer. "Maybe."

"Maybe? That's the best you can do?"

"At the moment."

"In that case, I'll have to find some way to make it up to you." Kenji's cell phone suddenly rang. He lifted it to his ear. "Hello… yes…uh… what? I'm sorry, but I can't go now. I'll be there tomorrow. No…evening.   Probably, yes…I will. Bye." He shut off his phone and sighed. "Looks like I'll be going to Thailand…right after dinner."

Mariko's sunny smile vanished. "Why? I thought you were going to help me move."

"It can't be avoided. I'll have some of my guys pitch in."

"Is it that important?" Mariko asked.

"Takashi is shipping containers again," Kenji answered grimly. "Real stupid move on his part. I'm hoping to get there before he shows up this time."

Mariko set her chopsticks down and fell back in her chair. "What's inside? Why do you have to go there to stop him?"

"I really can't go into this. Not yet. It wouldn't be safe for you to know, and I'm not going to take a chance on anything happening to you. Especially now."

"Why?  I don't understand."

"Because of the way I feel about you."

Mariko hesitated before asking, "Which is?"

"Not something I want to discuss."

She stared down at her untouched plate and said nothing. Disappointment was evident in her face and body.

Kenji knew it was the wrong thing to do. It could even be dangerous, especially not knowing who Takashi was partnering with. But the thought of leaving Mariko behind tore at his heart. "Well…would you want to go with me?" he asked.

"Are you serious?"

He looked down and nodded.

"Yes!" she said with a glowing smile. "I would!"

"Great. I hear the food's good. Maybe we could even see a kickboxing match…"

Mariko covered her mouth and giggled softly.

Kenji couldn't help but smile. She was so cute, almost child-like at times…and surprisingly resilient. He wanted to do something special for this remarkable woman, and the idea of seeing her in a sexy full-length dress brought a pleasing image to mind. "I think we need to go shopping today. Maybe pick up some things from Gucci and a few pairs of Manolo Blahnik heels. I don't want to be embarrassed taking you to expensive restaurants and clubs."

"Really?" she asked.

Kenji glanced at her sheepishly. "Yeah."

She jumped up from her chair, circled the table, and threw her arms around his neck. "I can't believe it! I've always wanted to go to Thailand," she gushed. "Thank you so much."

"Okay, okay. Sit down and eat before you get all skinny and ugly."

"Ugly?"

He cocked a silly smile and picked up his fork. Taking a bite of his omelet, he was pleasantly surprised. "Wow, this is really good."

Mariko draped the white napkin across her lap. She picked up her chopsticks and lifted her rice bowl from the table. Then she looked up at him with smiling eyes. "I hope you intend to put on some clothes before we go," she mumbled.

Kenji leaned back with his teacup in hand, admiring the stirring picture before him. In less than two days they would be in Bangkok. He would make plans to take her to the finest establishments and demonstrate the positive influence she had on his table manners and bedroom etiquette. In Chang Mai, they'd ride on elephants through the jungles and visit a village farm where handlers dove into snake-filled ponds for coins from tourists. He would pamper her—splurging on spa treatments and ordering custom-made clothes from the best tailors in town. In the evening, as the sun set on the horizon, they would lounge on the beach in Phuket, drinking Gray Goose martinis and Mai Tai cocktails with fancy paper umbrellas.

"Are you going to eat that?" Mariko asked, pointing her chopsticks at his last piece of miso fish.

Kenji shook his head. "It's all yours." Then he smiled openly, picturing the surprise on Takashi's face when he opened his expensive container and realized his stolen merchandise was roaming the countryside like free-range cattle while he and his beautiful geisha spent the whole afternoon rolling around in bed, making love at the Conrad hotel.

# 14

The phone on the glass nightstand vibrated, waking Kenji from a sound sleep. He picked it up and read the short text from Tak informing him that an urgent meeting had been called. Mitsui-san wanted to see both of them as soon as possible. Kenji glanced at Mariko, snoring softly by his side. He pulled the sheet over her shoulders and swung his legs over the side of the bed. Sweating from the humidity in the air, he went to the window to pull back the drapes. Sure enough, Tak was waiting in the parking lot. The engine of his red Kaido racer spewed gray mist into the air.

Kenji's eyes narrowed. What are they doing here? There was a black Mercedes parked across the street, one building down in front of the Hanamori department store. The headlights were off, but he could see the tail of smoke coming from the exhaust pipe. He squinted, trying to see the men inside, but it was no use. His body tensed, responding to an unknown situation. He tried to convince himself it was nothing—maybe just some of his men staying later than usual. But aside from the make of the car, there was nothing familiar about it, and it's unusual location left him doubting his assumption. He glanced back at the clock on the nightstand and saw it was only ten after four. The fact that his boss wanted to see him at this ungodly hour made absolutely no sense. He wondered if the text had actually come from Takashi or if someone else was in possession of his phone.

What am I afraid of? Kenji shivered and knew it wasn't from the cool air blowing from the air conditioner. It was his body warning him of possible danger—a familiar surge of adrenalin setting his teeth and nerves on edge.

Mariko let out a soft moan and he looked back at her. It occurred to him as he watched her sleeping that he shouldn't have brought her here to this hotel. He shouldn't have made her stay as long as they had. His place outside the city was closer to his office and protected by his men. It wasn't like him to act foolish or put anyone's life at risk...especially Mariko's.

With soft footsteps he went to the closet, moved his bag aside, and ran his hand along the top shelf until he found his red wakizashi. It was right next to his matching katana and the diamond-sheathed tanto knife he'd hidden from view. After a glance back at Mariko, he tiptoed out of the bedroom with his weapon of choice and clothes in hand. He pulled on his jeans and a white shirt in the next room then slipped quietly out the door and into the elevator. Downstairs in the main foyer, the freshly waxed floor shimmered in the glow of crystals on the enormous chandelier and refracted against the hotel's glass windows and automated front doors.

He walked across the slick surface barefooted then stopped to glance around. Oddly, no one was in the lobby, at the reception counter, or manning the concierge desk. The silence of the empty room was disconcerting. He looked in all directions—at the crystal wall lights, into the dark-paneled hallways, closed coffee lounge, and jewelry shop. Nothing seemed out of place. A fresh floral centerpiece with fragrant roses and lilies had been added to the enormous round entry table the night before. But there were no hotel guests or unfamiliar people milling about. Off to his left, a security guard passed by the open corridor and waved a hand in Kenji's direction, leaving him doubting his nagging concerns.

Stupid. He didn't know why he was acting paranoid...so friggin' amateur. He supposed it was the lack of sleep after so many late-night fuck sessions with his beautiful geisha upstairs. But now that she was initiating them and professing her love, how could he resist?

Ah...Mariko. He could still picture her beautiful eyes following him throughout the room. Still feel her lips on his cheek and her fingers in his hair, smiling every time their eyes connected. The corners of his mouth curled just from the thought of her. After a quick meeting with Mitsui-san, he'd be back in her arms again. Kneeling between those silky white thighs. Kissing those sweet, pouty lips.

Kenji looped his red wakizashi around his neck and glanced around the lobby once more. Then he walked stealthily toward the front door. As soon as he ventured outside, he noticed the Mercedes was gone.

Where the hell did they go? After a half dozen more steps, he halted at the front corner of the hotel. He rolled his eyes but remained still, relying on his peripheral vision to search his surroundings. In the parking lot on the side of the building exhaust continued to billow from the back of Takashi's sports car. The driver's seat was empty and there was no movement on the street. A shiver rolled through Kenji's entire being. Something wasn't right. He glanced up the street in the opposite direction and instinctively touched the hilt of his wakizashi. A footstep as light as a whisper caught his ear, spinning him around. He came face to face with a katou anime mask and, above it, a katana raised high in the air.

Kenji flinched involuntarily at the threat. He jumped back and pulled his own sword to ward off the assailant's deadly blow. With a flash of steel, his little finger was lopped off. He dropped his wakizashi, dazed. His heart slammed against his sternum and froze.

Mariko! The fear of losing her filled his thoughts, blocking his quick reflexes. In a desperate attempt to save himself, he reached for his weapon and looked up. A resounding swish filled the air. With the effectiveness of a guillotine, the razor-sharp blade sliced through the air, cutting skin and bone—severing Kenji's head from his body. In the final seconds of his life, his emotions ranged from pain and confusion to grief and fear. A woman's scream came from the lobby. Feet were running in all directions. Wheels squealed in the parking lot. A high- pitched siren passed by. But Kenji's departing soul was watching only one thing: his assassin's stoic brown eyes staring back at him through the anime mask in the passing red car.

# 15

Chase thought he heard a knock on the door. He forced his eyes open to look at the clock on the nightstand. It was only 7:15 a.m. and Rachel was fast asleep in the bed beside him. After a restless night, the last thing she needed was to be woken up at this hour.

Another series of knocks sounded, followed by a voice. "Mr. Cohen, it's Yuki! I need to speak to you right away."

Rachel rolled over and opened her sleepy eyes. "What's going on?" she croaked.

"Yuki's waiting in the hallway." Chase scrambled off the bed and snagged his jeans from the floor.

"What is she doing here?" Rachel sat up slowly and gathered the bed sheets tight against her chest.

"I won't know until I talk to her. Stay here and I'll find out what she wants."

"Maybe she came to return the anime mask you left in Mitsui's car." A faint smile flittered across her face.

"Somehow I don't think so." He stole into the next room, looked down, and zipped up his pants before opening the door.

Yuki rushed inside. From the look of her red-rimmed eyes, he knew something bad had happened—something that could potentially affect them all. As he thought of Rachel, anxiously waiting for him in the next room, he wasn't sure he'd be willing to risk his own life let alone the possibility of losing her.

"It's Kenji," Yuki said, her voice quavering.

"What about him?"

"He...he's dead."

Chase's breath caught. "What? How?"

Yuki's voice fell to a whisper. "The police called me a few hours ago. He was killed in front of his hotel."

"Geez, Yuki. I'm sorry. Did they catch the guy who shot him?"

"No, not yet. And he wasn't gunned down. He was...beheaded with a sword."

"Are you kidding me? He was decapitated? That's..." He broke off, searching for the right word. "Barbaric."

The welled-up tears in Yuki's eyes spilled over, running down her cheeks. Not knowing what else to do, Chase put his arm around her shoulder and she responded by burying her face in his chest and sobbing.

"Shhh...shhh...it's okay. Everything's going to be all right," he said, trying his best to console her. "The police will investigate and find out who did this horrible thing."

"No, they won't," she sniffled. "Not with the yakuza involved. There's no reliable witness, and even if there was, no one wants to go up against a gang leader...especially Kaito Mitsui."

Chase's brow furrowed. "He was behind this? Do you know that for certain?"

"Kenji formed an alliance with the Mori group," Yuki said sadly. "His popularity is growing, and he poses a threat to Mitsui's political aspirations. There were a dozen reasons for the Zakura-kai to dispose of him." She lowered her eyes. "Since my brother considered himself your partner, I just thought you should know."

Her tears were falling again, breaking down his tough facade. Not realizing his good intentions could be misconstrued, Chase lifted her face with his thumb. "Thank you for telling me, Yuki," he said. "I know how difficult this must be right now…"

She closed her eyes and leaned toward him, as if expecting a kiss.

Rachel materialized in the open doorway with a robe cinched around her middle, looking particularly annoyed and confused. "I'm sorry to interrupt," she said, "but it's seven in the morning. Is there something I need to know?"

Yuki pressed a firm hand against Chase's chest to distance herself, embarrassed by her unguarded emotions.

"It's all right, Rachel. Go back to bed," Chase urged. "We'll talk about this later."

"No…tell me now. What is it?"

"Yuki's brother was brutally murdered a few hours ago."

"Oh my God…" Rachel's eyes turned to Yuki. "That's awful. Is there anything I can do?"

The young woman shook her head. "No. But I thank you for asking."

Worry darkened Rachel's brow. "What about Mariko? Is she all right? Does she know?"

Yuki lowered her voice. "I was told she left the hotel right after it happened. No one's seen or heard from her since."

Chase remembered the dinner party Kenji had volunteered to host. "Under the circumstances, I think we should cancel our plans for tomorrow and just—"

"Please," Yuki said, "no matter what, we can't let this affect anything. Especially the small margin of time we have for planning our trip. I spoke to Shinzo before coming here, and he thought it might be a good idea to go to the restaurant as planned…just in case Mariko decides to show up."

Chase glanced at Rachel. Her face was drawn and haggard from sleeplessness, but at the same time filled with care and concern. In his heart, he wished he didn't have to ask Yuki the questions on his mind, but after learning about Kenji, he felt he had no choice. "What about the yakuza? Are we in danger too?"

"They're going to follow us no matter what we do, but I'm confident they won't be diving or posing an immediate threat. My only concern," she told them, "is when all is said and done, how do I kill as many of them as possible and get away with it?"

Her slow, unemotional smile lifted the hairs on Chase's neck. As she moved toward the door and made plans with Rachel to join them the following day, he was left wondering if this mysterious woman, now ingratiated in their lives, was verbalizing her wishful thinking or truly delivering a solemn promise.

# 16

Rachel craned her neck to see all the way to the top of the lit metal structure reminiscent of the Eiffel Tower picture she'd seen in a magazine. With the extra time they'd been allowed, she was grateful to have a chance to travel up the elevator, ascending to over one thousand feet. Her breath caught as she stepped close to the railing in her five-inch heels to take in the heart-pounding view of the metropolis, stretching out to the horizons in every direction. She'd had no idea how immense Tokyo was until she'd experienced it as an excited tourist.

Once back on the ground, she walked past the black-suited gang members leaning against their black cars and made a point of not acknowledging any of them. Lifting the edge of her long beige dress, she stepped through the gated entry and into another world. The paved walkway led to a winding, water-filled garden surrounding the restaurant—a beautiful respite from the humid, hectic city. Eventually she entered the main building along with Chase, Yuki, and Shinzo and traveled down several polished marble hallways before arriving at a private dining room. Behind the sliding shoji screen, a two-step platform led to a low mahogany table preset with folded napkins, crystal glasses, and dishware. Four padded chairs had been strategically placed around it to take advantage of varying views of the Japanese gardens. Rachel slipped off her shoes and walked across the woven mats to take her place at the table. As she knelt down in her full-length halter dress, she was delighted to discover that a drop floor had been created under the table to provide diners with a place to tuck their feet.

Yuki smiled softly. "I thought you'd be happy about that."

Rachel scrunched her eyebrows together and tipped her head to the side. "You sure you're all right being here? I mean... with everything that's happened."

"Yes, Miss Lyons. There's no point in dwelling on something I can't change."

Chase seated himself next to Rachel and whispered in her ear, "We need to treat this as business as usual, just as Yuki has asked."

"I know, but it feels a little cold with us being here. Sorta like we're celebrating Kenji's death."

Shinzo sat down across from them. "This restaurant specializes in tofu," he said.

"Tofu?" Rachel asked. "You mean that white, flavorless stuff?"

Chase patted her hand. "Let's wait and see. Okay?"

"I think you'll be pleasantly surprised," Shinzo added. "This restaurant has a fine reputation and renowned chef in the kitchen."

Soon artfully designed dishes began arriving, seasoned with sweet soy, herbs, and fragrant spices. The two-hour experience changed Rachel's opinion and had her closing her eyes to savor every morsel. Cold sake was provided in view of the warm summer season, and Shinzo was quick to remind Chase and Rachel about the custom of pouring for one another.

"Addressing the needs of others makes for a nice social exchange," he said.

Rachel extended her arm and smiled while Chase filled her small cup to the rim a second time. "I never thought I'd like sake, but this is delicious," she said.

"And dangerous too," Chase teased. "Be careful. Even the strongest can fall."

Dessert came in the form of green tea ice cream decorated with cherries and fresh mint leaves.

"When we eat," Shinzo told them, "we're inspired. Food in Japan is not just for the stomach but for the eyes as well." The shoji door slid open again. A new guest entered the room with small, deliberate steps, bringing them all to their feet.

"*Konbanwa*, Miss Lyons. May I present my card?" The young woman standing before Rachel had a creamy complexion and looked like a living, breathing doll. She was dressed in an elaborate turquoise and pink kimono with an embossed ivory obi cinching her waist. Silk rose petals and glittering accessories adorned her elegant up do, piled high into tucked and pinned rolls. A few loose strands of ebony hair trailed down her left cheek, adding drama to her flawless beauty. Yet above all her features, her enormous almond-shaped eyes were perhaps the most striking. They were sable-brown in color, matching her glamorous makeup, and were framed by long, thick eyelashes.

Rachel smiled cautiously and accepted the small red and black postage stamp from her outstretched palms. The young woman bowed in appreciation before lifting her eyes—so controlled, passive, and demure. As if she would break into a million pieces with any sudden movement.

"That's her name sticker," Yuki explained in a quiet voice. "Japanese businessmen collect those like baseball cards and keep them in their wallets for good luck. Mariko's just happens to be one of the most popular."

Mariko. Rachel tucked the tiny memorabilia into her gold sequin bag. As the geisha moved around the outer perimeter of the room, she found herself studying her more closely—pondering her true identity. Was this Aiko? The half sister her father had secretly hidden away? Her mind filling with questions, she bent toward Yuki, keenly aware of the young woman's occasional glances.

"Why isn't she wearing white makeup like other geishas?" Rachel asked.

"She recently reached senior status and acquired a sponsor. It's no longer necessary in her profession."

As Rachel watched, Mariko approached Chase, and the corners of her mouth instantly lifted. "Ah, Cohen-san. I'm so happy to see you again."

He glimpsed Rachel and smiled, as if seeking her approval. "The feeling's mutual, Mariko-san," he said.

The geisha giggled softly, raising her left hand to her mouth, and barely brushed her fingers against her lips. She continued her progress, stepping close to Shinzo— his eyes wide open in amazement. With a nod of her head, his face reddened almost as bright as the wine in his glass.

"Mariko," he said in a small, gentle voice. "You're...you're really here. What a nice surprise."

"Ah, Shinzo-chan," she answered sweetly. "I'm happy to see you too." Her aloof manner gave the impression that they had an amiable relationship but nothing more. "Would you like me to dance?" she asked and waited politely for his response.

"Yes, of course," he said, obviously shielding his disappointment. "That would be wonderful." Then he directed the rest of them, as if speaking to children, "Turn your chairs around and be seated. Mariko would like to perform for us."

The elderly woman who had quietly slipped into the room was now sitting near the rear wall, resting her fingers on her samisen. Mariko assumed her dance position before them, bending a knee slightly and gripping the ends of her long kimono sleeves with both hands. With a nod of her head, the old woman began plucking the three-string lute and singing a haunting song.

Although the alluring geisha barely moved from her spot, each gesture was slow and controlled, conveying the words of the song through her actions. Yuki translated the artistic verse, hinting at dreams and emotions. "Waiting anxiously for you, unable to sleep, but falling into a doze. Are those words of love floating to my pillow, or is this too a dream? My eyes open and here is my tear-drenched sleeve. Perhaps it was a sudden rain."

Matching the musician's lyrics, Mariko pretended to rub her eyes. She ran a fisted hand along her cheek. Her palm turned up, as if checking for rain. However, as she continued, Rachel couldn't help noticing that her dancing was filled with sexual overtones. She smoothed her hands down her thighs, wrapped her arms around her middle, and rocked from side to side, as if longing for her absent lover. She pulled a fan from her obi belt, opened it wide, and cast an alluring look at Shinzo over its scalloped edge. Then, as she neared the end of her performance, she turned away and allowed her kimono to slip from her shoulder, exposing her bare porcelain skin—something a true geisha would never do.

Rachel felt Yuki's eyes on her face. But she found it nearly impossible to pull her gaze away from the spectacle. When she did, she caught Chase watching Mariko's departure with obvious curiosity and a spark of twisted amusement.

Shinzo leaned his head to one side. "Don't let any of this trouble you, Miss Lyons," he said. "Mariko was honoring Kenji's memory. Although he's no longer with us, I assure you his presence was sorely felt."

She swallowed hard and considered the monk's sad predicament. "I imagine it was," she said.

He gave a forced fake smile and nodded. "In this world, all lust is grief."

# 17

"Now that we're alone, let's get started," Yuki said, unrolling her charts and spreading her photos across the table. By all appearances, she was one of the prettiest, toughest, and most organized treasure hunters Chase had ever met. Although she'd been hired as a dive technician, the young female warrior had taken on Shinzo's project as her own. And Chase had no problem with that. This was her home. She knew the language, the lay of the land, the complex assignment better than anyone. However, Trident Ventures' commitment would depend in large part on Yuki's ability to get Rachel on board, and right now his partner was hedging.

"So this is where it's all happening," Rachel said, peering down at the map.

"You're looking at Kagoshima Prefecture, which governs Kuchinoerabu Island," Yuki said. "It's located on the southwest tip of Kyushu and is surrounded by the Yellow Sea. Once we arrive in Fukuoka, we'll be traveling to a fishing village on the westernmost tip of the island."

"How long will it take us to get there?" Chase asked.

"Five hours by bullet train. But it's less expensive and takes only two hours by air."

"Well, that's a no-brainer."

"If we're all in agreement then, I'll book our flight for tomorrow morning."

Rachel glanced at Shinzo, sitting quietly in the corner with his prayer beads pressed between his palms. "What time will we need to be at the airport?" she asked Yuki.

"Since our departure is at 8:45am, I suggest leaving the hotel two hours earlier to avoid rush hour. If everything goes according to plan, we should be on the water by noon. And one more thing…in addition to the extra tanks and leased equipment, I took the liberty of including three Bluefish jet scooters. They're small and easy to carry, and since time is crucial, they'll move us through the water fast."

Chase nodded his approval. "What about rooms for the night?" he asked.

"Accommodations have been arranged for us at the Takamatsu hot spring resort. Since we're supposed to be tourists on vacation, I suggest wearing comfortable clothes and bringing whatever cameras you packed. There will be fewer questions that way."

Rachel leaned down to take a closer look at Yuki's collection. The photographs included an underwater cave entrance, stone pillars, and various angles of an Egyptian- style ruin. She glanced back at Chase. "Looks like we're dealing with a Kofun tomb," she said. "They were initially built in valleys and elevated basins for elite rulers such as Yamato priest-kings, clan chieftains, warrior kings, and generals. But this one appears to have been tunneled out and constructed inside of a mountain. Like someone was afraid a ghost would get out."

Chase's brow pinched at her creepy assumption. "How far down are we going?" he asked Yuki.

"Sixty feet. But the elevation changes dramatically once we get inside." She traced her finger along lines on the sketched treasure map. "As you can see right here, a stone moon door is located at the cave's main entrance. Next to it is a carved marble lion. When the statue is turned, a hidden latch releases, opening the portal. We'll be exiting through an interior pond and dropping our gear right here." She pointed at a spot on a secondary map. "The rest of the way is on foot. Once we're inside the cavern, there are four concrete columns supporting the infrastructure and twenty-four uneven rock-cut steps to reach three staggered platforms and the real entrance to the tomb. At this point, we'll be hiking through tunnels before arriving at a split path. After turning right, we'll arrive at a tiled staircase that leads to Prince Ngami's tomb."

A slightly pained expression flitted across Rachel's face, but she made no verbal complaints.

"This is the part where it gets tricky," Yuki continued. "We have to squeeze through a cracked wall in the annex room to reach his inner bedchamber." She flipped the page and pointed at the center of a diagram. "The prince's mummified body is resting right here on a raised stone platform next to a bag of rocks I used as a counterweight to take the sword. Ancient tomb designers were real big on booby traps to keep raiders away...just like in the movies. I found out the hard way when a flying arrow nicked my shoulder. So whatever you do, stay close and don't touch anything unless I tell you it's safe."

Chase huffed a breath. He couldn't help wondering what his crew back in the States would make of this Japanese Lara Croft and her crazy tomb-raiding scheme. He glimpsed Rachel's knitted brow and was amazed that she hadn't voiced any objections. By the look in Yuki's eyes, she was equally surprised.

"Where are General Maeda and his wife buried?" Rachel asked.

Yuki thoughtfully thumbed through her hair before picking up a piece of paper. "When I translated the scrolls, I came across a short riddle, which gives me a pretty good idea where to look." She looked down and read, "They lie beneath him in stature and worth, for all eternity buried in earth." Her eyes lifted off the page. "They're either under his burial tumulus or in the ground very close to it."

Rachel eyed her suspiciously. "Why didn't you look for them and take all three swords when you had the chance?"

"I was more focused on getting in and out of there as quickly as possible."

"Why's that?"

"It's not a place you want to stick around in any longer than necessary."

"I bet," Rachel quipped.

Chase disregarded her remark. "After we find the other two swords," he asked Yuki, "is there anything else worth taking?"

"You'll find bronze mirrors, Sue pottery, and jade and jasper necklaces on the floor in the inner chamber. But the iron weapons and armor have to stay."

Rachel eyes were wide with disbelief. "So we've been reduced to grave robbing?"

Chase bristled. "Whatever we take might come in handy for negotiating our safe return."

"Wonderful," she grumbled. "Yuki, I have to tell you…I'm a little confused here. If you did all of this on your own before, why do you need us now?"

Yuki lowered her eyes and swallowed hard before answering. "I didn't go alone, Miss Lyons. Mitsui's nephew stole the key to his uncle's yacht after he heard about my plans. He insisted that I join him. Everything went wrong on our way back."

"So it was his boat. That explains why he's so interested in what's going on. Doesn't he have a valid claim for what's on board too?"

"After it sank, Mitsui issued a recovery reward, but no one responded. He announced to the press that all he wanted was the title to his yacht so he could sign it over to the boat's rescuer and eventual new owner. Still no one came forward. With Chase telling him you're here to investigate the possibility of bringing it up, Mitsui honestly believes Shinzo is doing him this huge favor as a way to pay back his debt. He has no idea about the swords or why his nephew and I were on board in the first place. His vent in regard to the boat's contents was done strictly to test both of you and to find out what your true motives were in coming here."

"And his nephew?" Chase asked.

"He didn't make it out alive."

"Why's that?"

"I didn't know about the Templars until we were on our way back to the boat. The only thing I could figure out is my blood must've drawn them or the guts from the fish the sharks were feeding on. Before I knew it, they were swarming. Kazumi tried to keep them away, but they shredded his arm in seconds flat. I honestly thought we were both going to die. Then a shark came out of nowhere and chased them all away. I managed to get Kazumi back to the boat, but he was in bad shape by then."

Rachel drew her head into her shoulders like the bellows of an accordion. "What the hell are Templars?"

"They're flesh---ripping eels."

"Are you nuts?" Rachel snapped. "Why would anyone subject themselves to that?"

"I know it sounds scary, but I assure you I'll be more than ready this time."

"Indiana Jones, man-eating sharks, and now Templars?" Rachel rhetorically asked. She shot Chase a "what the fuck have you gotten me into" look. "No wonder the stone's worth two million dollars. No one in their right mind would touch it."

Yuki's shoulders drooped and she lowered her head. "I guess that means you're out then."

Rachel nodded. "I'm sorry, but this is absolutely insane. Even if we manage to recover Kokoro, get in and out of the tomb with the other two swords, and avoid being eaten alive, how are we going to keep from running into your yakuza friends and being chopped into tiny bits? Oh, wait...silly me. We'll all have swords, so we can battle our way out."

"Miss Lyons!" the monk's authoritative voice boomed from behind.

Rachel's jaw slackened, stunned by his sudden outburst. As she turned to face him, Shinzo rose to his feet.

"Please, I beg of you," he implored. "Have faith in her...just as she has in you."

# 18

Mariko wiped off her makeup. She put her hair in a messy bun. With a heavy sigh, she gazed into the bathroom mirror and wilted at the sight of her sad, ruinous state. Nearby, on the white tile countertop, her cell phone was ringing—a chronic, annoying sound. From the three voice messages she'd already heard, she knew Oneesan was desperate to find her. But in Mariko's mind, there was no going back, no returning to the life she'd once known. For some strange reason, she belonged here—in Kenji's empty apartment. It was her last connection to him. The place they were planning to call home.

Mariko closed her eyes, recalling the morning she had learned about Kenji's odious death. When the police had finished questioning her at the hotel and allowed her the privacy to grieve, she'd closed the door and curled up in a ball in the corner of the room. She stayed there for hours, seemingly trapped in a bottomless pit—a black hole with no possible way out. In her heart she knew Kenji's lust for her would have turned to love. Through his words and promises, he had given her hope. But he was gone too soon, and like so many sole survivors before her,

Mariko was beginning to understand the power and commitment of revenge.

With an exhaled breath, she opened her eyes and turned off the bathroom light. She walked into the living room to appraise her surroundings. Although sparse in personal effects and wall decorations, Kenji's apartment was spacious in comparison to her studio space. He had comfortable, contemporary furniture as well as enough food to last for a week. With no nosey neighbors to bother her and friends not knowing her whereabouts, she'd found the perfect place to hide out. But the silence had become grating and she needed something to occupy her mind. She dropped onto the couch and reached for Kenji's overnight bag.

It was the same satchel that had provided keys and the address to his apartment on the quiet suburban street. The same one containing assassin tools: knives, handcuffs, rope, wire, garbage bags, plastic cinches, and electrical duct tape. There was also enough lethal poison stored inside to kill an army of men or possibly just a yakuza boss and his traitorous right-hand man. Mariko picked up one of the orange prescription bottles and studied the name on the label. Tetrodotoxin.

Oddly, it was the same name that had been mentioned by a respected psychiatrist at a dinner party four months ago. The slight man with thick black-rimmed glasses had told a story about a former patient killing his bedridden wife with a potent neurotoxin derived from tiger blowfish. At the time, Mariko had been the most interested person in the room, but she never realized until now the value of that information.

She picked up Kenji's cell phone and began dialing. It only took two calls to locate Dr. Suzuki's number. When he answered, Mariko couldn't believe her good fortune or the childish excitement he expressed at hearing her voice. "I had no idea you enjoyed that story so much," he gushed. "Most of the women I've met leave the room before I even finish it."

"To be honest," Mariko said, "I'm not usually interested in personal tragedies. But you told it so well, along with all the side effects that poor woman suffered. I couldn't help but be impressed by your knowledge. In fact, if you don't mind, I was wondering if you would tell me about them once more."

"The side effects?" he asked.

"Oh yes. I'm intrigued with how toxins affect the body." Mariko pushed the button on the recorder and waited. It took only a brief moment for the good doctor to take the bait.

"Now, mind you, this is from my memory," he said. "According to my patient, he slipped two milligrams of poison into his wife's miso soup. Within twenty minutes, she complained of numbness in her lips and tongue. The next symptom was paraesthesia in her face and extremities, followed by a headache, epigastric pain, nausea, diarrhea, vomiting, and difficulty in walking. The second stage of the intoxication was paralysis, where even sitting was difficult for her. The third stage was respiratory distress. Speech was affected next, and the victim in this case exhibited dyspnea, cyanosis, hypotension, convulsions, mental impairment, and eventually cardiac arrhythmia. Although the man's wife was completely paralyzed, she remained conscious for three hours...long enough for him to tell her what he had done."

"It must have been terrible knowing there was no antidote," Mariko said. She could almost see the doctor nodding his head in agreement.

"Retelling this story reminds me of another case involving a man who killed his racehorse then filed a claim through his insurance company. No one would have suspected if he hadn't—"

"I'm sorry, Doctor," she cut in. "I just realized I have an appointment. And as you know, I don't like keeping my guests waiting."

"Oh...of course, of course. No problem at all. I will look forward to hearing from you again, Mariko."

Not in this lifetime. She turned off the recorder at the end of the call. Suzuki had provided more information than she would require, but hearing the misery she was capable of causing made the doctor's explanation worthwhile. She curled her legs underneath her on the soft leather sofa and picked up Kenji's black journal. He'd been surprisingly diligent in keeping detailed notes involving all his past crimes. Although murder was a common denominator, the victims in each case were primarily rival gang members who had offended, disappointed, or threatened Kaito Mitsui. And the list was uncomfortably long, spanning more than a decade. She ran her fingernail along handwritten entries purely out of morbid curiosity. Every individual was given a date and death sentence with Mitsui's specific instructions.

Why had Kenji kept it...this black, incriminating diary? Evidence of the heinous life he'd been forced to lead? Perhaps it was another weapon, carefully compiled blackmail against his yakuza boss. But if it posed a real threat even after Kenji's death, why leave it with his girlfriend along with a phone message incriminating Takashi Bekku as his murderer? It was a puzzle that kept Mariko guessing. That made it impossible for her to close her eyes and disregard his hand-scripted notes.

Then she saw it. The name nearly jumped off the page. It was a nightmare of epic proportion. A reality so inconceivable, she had to reread the listing several times and still doubted her eyes. Kaito Mitsui was a vicious monster with far-reaching tentacles—much farther than anyone could have imagined. He had not only ordered the death of over sixty men during his reign, he had arranged the demise of her father with Takashi Bekku's assistance. The only saving grace in Mariko's life was the fact that Kenji Ota wasn't involved.

Tower alarms sounded in the air, blasting a midnight warning. Still dressed in Kenji's oversized shirt, Mariko crawled off the bed half asleep. She jerked the beige curtain back and looked outside. A woman dressed in white was standing across the street under a lamppost screaming, "He's coming...now!"

Mariko slid the window open wider and leaned out, looking in both directions. As far as she could tell, there wasn't any reason for alarm or panic. But she wasn't taking any chances. After pulling on her pants, she picked up Kenji's red katana and headed for the front door. She took the elevator downstairs and crossed the street. Strangely, the woman was nowhere to be seen.

Above her in the large condominium, people were crying out and waving their arms frantically. Not knowing what else to do, Mariko ran back to the safety of Kenji's apartment, fully intending to call the police. Unfortunately, the front door of the apartment building had locked behind her. The key was still inside.

She looked back across the street. The filled complex had grown incredibly quiet. No one was anywhere to be seen. Driven by curiosity, she wandered back across the street and found the main entry door ajar. She pushed it open and was shocked to discover the lit courtyard was actually the center of a broken-down building. Bats flew out of dark corners and circled the sky like demons in the night. All the residents living there had boarded up their windows and locked themselves inside.

The sound of a man's deep, ominous voice came from a short distance behind her. "I'm here for you," he said.

Mariko panicked. She charged up the first flight of stairs and banged on one door after another, begging for someone to let her in. She looked through an open section in a window just as someone rushed into their bathroom. She knocked again, pleading, telling them she had a weapon for protection. When the door finally opened, it was Tamayo, the young maiko from the Inoue house. Anxiously she urged Mariko inside then locked the door behind her.

"The demon is afraid of water," Tamayo told her. "Hide in the bathroom."

"What demon? Where?"

"Hurry!" she yelled. "I'll be in the bathroom at the end of the hallway."

Mariko did as she was told, closing the door behind her. She turned on the water and let it trickle into the sink. With nothing but white tile surrounding her, she sat nervously in the bathtub for almost an hour. In the next room, she could hear the sound of furniture crashing and glass shattering on the floor. She wondered what was happening and why. Then as fast as it had begun, it ended. There was no sound. No indication that Tamayo was even in the apartment. Mariko drew a deep, calming breath. She convinced herself that it was now safe to come out. But as she looked down at her hands, she suddenly realized the weapon she'd been carrying was gone. Instantly a sense of helplessness washed over. She felt trapped and isolated. Completely cut off from the world.

After awhile, she grew brave again and slowly opened the door. Broken dishes and shattered glass covered the floor. The living room appeared to have been ransacked. In the next room, chairs had been toppled over. Papers and trash were spewed everywhere. Afraid to exit, Mariko shut the door quickly. But in that brief moment, something had managed to slip inside.

Her breath caught. She wanted to scream, but her throat seized up. Across from her, black wings were slowly spreading from the sides of a horned devil with glowing red eyes. It tilted its head and lifted its nose, searching the air for traces of her scent. Mariko's instincts told her the creature was blind and dependent on sound. Any sudden movement posed a threat. She spotted the katana barely five feet away, peeking out from under the shower curtain. But it would be a struggle to pick it up. Every breath, every heartbeat, brought the creature closer.

With her back pressed against the wall, she slid slowly to the floor into a squatting position and picked up the bar of soap from the edge of the tub. The devil narrowed its eyes and cocked its head with each muffled sound. She remained perfectly still, holding her breath, until she felt the moment was right. After mentally counting to five, she tossed the soap away. When the creature snapped its head in the same direction, Mariko reached out and snatched the weapon from the floor. She jumped to her feet and immediately began swinging wildly, attempting to slice the creature with every pass. Then miraculously, before her eyes, the demonic villain transformed.

It became Kenji—her sad, troubled lover—marred by a bleeding slash across his cheek. She stared at him, completely perplexed.

To her amazement, he spoke to her in a soft, caring voice. "Why would you try to kill me when I only wanted to love you?"

She stared at him, stunned beyond belief. The hurt in his brown eyes was awful to see. "I didn't know..." she whispered.

"That it was me or that I loved you?" She swallowed hard. "Both."

"I treated you badly, didn't I? Our time ended much too soon." He reached for her hand and pulled her close. Mariko could feel the heat of his body against her cheek. She wanted to stay in his arms forever. But time was fleeing. She could sense his need to go.

He walked her past the noisy chaos outside and stopped when they reached the threadbare awning, dangling from a bent metal brace. Then he stepped away and shook his head, pointing to the sky above them. Mariko gazed up at the heavens. She saw the dark clouds part and felt the first raindrops on her face. With her eyes squeezed shut, she relished the sensation of water dancing on her skin and trailing down her face. After a few minutes, she lowered her chin and lifted her eyelids, and realized Kenji was gone. People were stripping the boards from their windows. They were opening their doors and coming outside. Their lighthearted voices could be heard singing and celebrating—rejoicing in the evil creature's death.

Mariko stood alone for the longest time with the rain falling around her. She was lost and confused. The only thing she felt for certain was gratitude for being alive. For having known Kenji and the love he was capable of giving. She glanced back at the enormous building as she walked away and found herself wondering why she'd allowed herself to be trapped in such a wicked, hellish place.

Then she awoke and looked around her. There were white feathers floating in the air around her: landing on her hair, scattered across the bed, spewing out from Kenji's torn pillow. The deadly tanto knife was clutched in her hand.

What does it all mean? She laid the weapon aside and got up to look out the bedroom window. In the glass pane, she could have sworn she saw a flash of light and the face of the devil. But she blinked and it was gone. She found herself wondering what Shinzo would make of her dream. Would he tell her that Kenji was the demon who'd been sent from hell to destroy her life? Would he interpret the falling white feathers as signs of an angel hovering nearby—perhaps sent on a mission to protect her from harm? Or maybe he would believe, as she did, that Kenji was trapped between the afterworld and the underworld, waiting for his assassin's death to set him free.

There was a sudden knock at the door. Mariko scurried off the bed, sending feathers flying. She made her way to the front entry and nervously waited. Another series of knocks came, followed by a man's anxious voice.

"It's me, Shinzo."

Mariko shook her head, disbelieving her ears. How is it possible? What is he doing here? She ran back into the bedroom and slipped the knife between the mattresses as far as she could reach, next to the red katana she'd already hidden there. Then she returned to the living room and began nibbling her thumbnail. The adjacent window was too high to climb through and the only way in or out of the fifth-floor apartment was the front door.

"I know you're in there," Shinzo said sweetly.

Mariko realized she had no choice but to answer. "How did you know where to find me?"

"Oneesan sent me," he answered. "She thought you might be here."

"Go away," she demanded. "I want to be alone."

"Open the door, Mariko. I can't talk to you standing out here in the hallway in the middle of the night. We're making a lot of noise. Someone will come along and complain. Please let me in. I'm not going anywhere...not without seeing you first."

She opened the door slightly and he walked in past her. They stood in the center of the room facing each other. Mariko didn't know what to say; it was all so awkward, her standing there barely covered by Kenji's white shirt. She had no makeup on and her face was shiny with cream. Her hair was completely disheveled. But he didn't seem to notice. He was dressed in the same clothes he had worn earlier in the evening, but his shirt looked crumpled now and his tie was loose at the throat.

They remained silent for an endless moment before he finally spoke. "I needed to see you...alone. I had to know you were all right." He looked directly into her eyes. They were kind and sincere—so inviting as he put his arms around her. She stopped thinking and banished the image of Kenji that flashed unbidden in her mind.

Shinzo held her close and she leaned her face against his chest. His linen jacket rubbed against her skin through the shirt's thin cotton fabric.

Kenji's shirt. She pushed Shinzo away. "He was my danna, my master," she said quietly. "Now he's gone and I have nothing."

"I'm sorry...I truly am," Shinzo said, suddenly less brash. "But if you think you have nothing to be grateful for, check your pulse, Mariko."

"Why are you here?" she snapped. "I don't need your advice or a stupid lecture right now."

He lowered his eyes. "Forgive me. You're absolutely right. I have no right to judge anyone. I know I should have respected your privacy, but I'm asking you to let me stay a few minutes. That's all."

She paused before answering, "Okay. But no longer."

He walked over to the sofa and motioned for her to join him. They sat down next to each other and she immediately reached for a pillow to cover her legs. The room was bathed in a soft amber light from the lamps on either side of the sofa. The drapes were drawn and they were alone, apart from the rest of the world's prying eyes.

"What did you want to tell me?" she asked, still amazed at his timing—at the troubled thoughts still lingering in her head.

"I was worried about you. I know you're upset. You had to be incredibly confused to even come here." He shook his head and glanced away. "This matter with Kenji...it's wrong, Mariko. He had no right to involve you. To do everything in his power to keep us apart."

She could smell sake on his breath and feel the heat radiating from his body. It was so unlike Shinzo to drink heavily, to come here uninvited. So why was he doing it now?

Mariko recounted her night—her mindless, flirtatious behavior. Was it my dance? Is that why he's here? She lowered her eyes. Her gaze fell on his lap and she looked away quickly as if caught at some lewd, forbidden thing.

He leaned over and enveloped her in his arms, and before she knew it, they were kissing. She yielded, the upper part of her body pressed against him, her arm around his back, her lips trembling, her tongue searching his. His right hand slipped down her waist, caressed her thigh, her belly, through the shirt. Mariko had to force herself not to grab his hand and guide it where she wanted it to stroke her. She strained against him, hoping he would find her.

He led her to the bed and she lay on top of the sheet, mindlessly waiting for him. He undressed quickly, dropping his clothes half on the bed, half on the floor, until he stood above her naked, his sculpted chest and smooth stomach so perfectly toned. She slipped the shirt off her shoulders and slid it off from beneath her. He lay down next to her and softly touched her cheek. She ran her hands over his chest, across his belly, looking so tan, so exposed. She was moved by the vulnerability of his nakedness. But when he entered her, he was hard and sure. He filled her, leaving her gasping with joy to feel all that power inside her. They made love for a long time and then lay together silently. After a few minutes, she rolled over to the nightstand and checked her phone.

"Expecting a call?" he asked.

She stared at the empty screen before setting it down. Then he climbed under the sheet and tried to draw her to him. "What are you doing?" she asked, sitting up.

"I'm going to sleep. It's three in the morning. We have to be up in a few hours. Come, get some rest."

"You have to go," she said in a panic. "You can't stay here. I can't have another man in Kenji's apartment...in his bed."

"Don't be foolish, Mariko. I'm not going to leave you alone in this place. And please don't worry," he said more softly, "it's all right. I'll make sure no one sees me leave. I wouldn't embarrass you like that." Then he turned over. He fell asleep almost immediately, while she lay there wide awake, trying to move as far away from him on the bed as possible. Trying not to touch him or to let herself think about what had just transpired. He'd seduced her...or had it been the other way around? She closed her eyes, puzzling over the dilemma then realized it really didn't matter. Not now. She just wanted to get through this night—wanted it to be morning, afternoon, a hundred years from now.

I'll figure this out tomorrow, she told herself, staring up at the ceiling. In the light of day, the whole experience would seem as if it never happened. Just as it never should have...or ever would again.

# 19

It was barely 11:30 a.m. in the remote village in Kyushu and already hot as hell. Rachel's cotton T-shirt was sticking to her back within five minutes of walking from the taxi to the marina. She wore matching blue hiking shorts and sneakers and had a backpack slung over one shoulder. With Chase at her side, she headed around to the other side of the bay where Yuki had planned to meet one of her buddies, the owner of the Scuba---Do diving shop.

The building was painted bright pink with a blue and white striped awning, resembling an octopus perched on the water's edge. Rows of dive tanks lined the side of the building. Dozens of wetsuits, buoyancy vests, and regulators hung from long bamboo poles, drying in the blazing sun. Rachel stepped inside, hoping to avoid the heat. She glanced around feeling as if she'd just entered an overstocked Sea World gift shop—Japanese style. Even with the glass doors braced wide open, the stinky smell of dried fish permeated the air. There were souvenir T-shirts, swim trunks, hanging mobiles, magnets, paperweights, packages of dried squid, rice crackers, key holders, miniature kites, and pink, blue, and gold plastic fish filling every shelf and rack from floor to ceiling. The upper walls were covered with a collection of resin-coated fish, enormous turtle shells, spider crabs, and jagged, teeth-lined jaws from area sharks, including one from a nasty-looking Goblin priced at 390,000 yen, or a little over four thousand US dollars.

Crazy. Only in Japan would something so hideous be worth so much.

Rachel looked around at the people shopping. There was no sign of Yuki anywhere. She wove around stacked cases of ramen noodles, fishing rods, Pokémon toys, and inflatable life jackets. Ahead of her, at the end of the last aisle, Chase halted and peered into a white refrigerator. He glanced back, smiling.

"They have red bean ice cream bars. Do you want one?"

She wrinkled her nose. "I don't think so." It sounded terrible, but that didn't stop him from dropping a few coins on the cash register counter and popping a vegetable Popsicle in his mouth.

As customers edged by, she stood off to the side, trying to avoid blocking traffic.

"Sure you don't want a bite?" he asked. "It tastes great." Rachel shook her head. She scanned the room a final time and relaxed after spotting Yuki. She was heading toward the side door with a large bag of ice and six dangling water bottles.

"Found her!" Rachel announced. Chase finished off his last bite and dropped the stick into a waste bin before hurrying to catch up with his new employee.

"Let me get that for you," he said. After capturing Yuki's load, he walked outside toward the end of the dock where their boat was tied up.

"My friend's out back," she told Rachel. "He speaks pretty good English. Why don't you come along?" She led the way to a small warehouse littered with dive gear in tangled disarray. Long air hoses from dive regulators were piled high on the workbench before a shirtless, sweaty man like a nest of snakes, leaving Rachel worrying about the condition of the equipment they had rented.

"Hi, Goro. This is Miss Lyons. She's visiting from America," Yuki said. "Thanks for loading our boat. I see Captain Aoki's already on board."

The shaggy-haired man could have passed for twenty if not for his leathery skin and the major bags under his eyes. "Eigo?" he asked, squinting.

Yuki nodded. "Hai."

He twisted his lips, obviously not happy with her choice of language.

"How's business?" she asked.

"I hate work here," Goro said. "People no care. Hoses leak. Divers leave BC hooked up. Drop heavy tanks. Complain we have bad stuff." He looked at Rachel, eyebrows knitted with anger. "It not true."

"How soon can we leave?" Yuki asked.

"Five minutes. Captain getting fuel. Then ready go."

"What about those men I told you about? Have you seen any of them?"

Goro shook his head. "Tourists, fishermen, boaters. No yakuza."

"What is the wreck site like?"

"Cloudy. Hard to find. But you know where look. No too many divers today but lots fish."

"Great. Did you put the extra tanks on the boat as I asked?"

"Yes. And Bluefish too."

"All right, we should be back around five. Call me on my cell phone if anything changes."

"Okeydokey." He accompanied them to the front of his shop and waited while they walked toward the boat and climbed inside. As they pulled away from the fuel station, he stood on the tiny wharf waving before disappearing from view.

Yuki joined Rachel near the gun rail. "Don't worry," she told her, "Goro is smarter than he sounds. Despite all his complaining, I haven't heard of anyone drowning while using his gear. At least not yet."

As Yuki walked away, an ambiguous smile flitted across her face, giving Rachel pause and another reason to check her gauges.

As they headed across the water toward Kanmon Strait, Rachel didn't think it could get any hotter, but it did. While Chase nursed a bottle of semi cold water, she ventured downstairs on a self-guided tour. The fiberglass day boat was equipped with a toilet—commonly referred to as the head—and a small galley manned by a cook preparing lunch for them. In the mid-cabin was a salon where divers could relax on upholstered benches and dine at an expandable wood table. At the rear was an uncovered sun deck as well as a shaded area, although it served little purpose today. She noticed the diving air compressor, designed to handle a large crew, and made a mental note of the oxygen first aid tank mounted against the wall. When she arrived at the bridge upstairs, she peeked inside and was happy to see a GPS, VHF radio, and depth finder, along with a state-of-the-art instrument panel.

"*Ohayo*," came from the man behind the wheel. His smile lit up his wizened face.

She smiled back and returned his greeting. "*Ohayo.*"

"I guess you must be Rachel," he said, adjusting his worn straw hat.

"You know English," she said, pleasantly surprised.

"Most people do. It's a school requirement here. Some of us just take it more serious than others."

"Well, I'm glad you did. How long have you been at this, Captain?"

"Going on five years. I was hired by Mr. Ota to keep his boat running, but it seems I'll be working with Yuki from now on."

"I know. I heard about that. It must have come as quite a shock...his death and all."

He showed no emotion on his face, simply stared straight ahead with his jaw set.

Rachel used the silence to take in the beauty of the steep cliffs dropping to the sea. "You sure have a great job here. Who wouldn't want to do this every day?"

Only his mouth smiled. "It pays the bills."

By the looks of the LED graphic speed control, they were cruising at twenty-eight miles per hour at 3,200 RPMs and throwing a nice wake behind them. Although she considered asking more in-depth questions, the dark mood on the bridge brought a safer one. "So, how long until we drop anchor?"

"Fifteen minutes," Yuki answered from above. Her bare feet and long, athletic legs were descending the steps leading to the upper deck. A black form-fitting bathing suit soon followed along with her braided ponytail and exposed tattooed back. In the light of day, the fearsome designs appeared more vibrant and detailed than Rachel remembered.

"If you and Chase would like to join me in the galley," she said, "I thought I'd take the extra time to review our first dive." Rachel readily agreed. Within minutes, everyone was sipping cold tea, looking down at Yuki's detailed drawing.

"The motor yacht sank near the mouth of the inlet," she explained. "By my best estimate, it's no more than fifty feet down, but the sonar will give us a more accurate read. The floor plan is laid out much like this one, but there are two double-bed cabins and one king-bed master on the lower level. That's where Kokoro was left...under the master bed."

Chase leaned back in his seat and crossed his arms. "I have to tell you...something's been bothering me all morning. If this sword is so easy to find, why has it been sitting at the bottom of the ocean for almost two years? There's gotta be something you're not telling us."

Yuki's eyes brushed the tabletop. She blew out a breath then lowered her voice. "Kazumi's still there...trapped inside. I didn't have the courage to go down alone, and no one was willing to help me."

"Oh God," Rachel moaned. "Surely the Japanese Coast Guard is trained to recover bodies! Didn't you notify them?"

"They were told to stay away."

"By who?" she asked.

"Mitsui. He didn't want his nephew's body disturbed."

"But what about a funeral?" Rachel asked. "His mother and father?"

"None of them got along. They haven't spoken in years. Mitsui said Kazumi deserved to be there...rotting away after taking his boat without his permission. He didn't know about Kokoro or the tomb we found. If he had, nothing would've kept him from hiring divers and stealing everything they could get their hands on."

Chase's eyes narrowed. "How did he react when he found out you were involved?"

"He still doesn't know. Kazumi promised me he would never find out." Yuki's gaze met Rachel's. "If he had any suspicion, even now, there's every reason to believe I wouldn't be here."

Rachel placed her hand on Chase's cheek and looked up at him lovingly. "Well, we've come this far. We might as well go all the way, right?"

Threading his arm around her neck and shoulders, he drew her close. He dipped his head and pressed his lips against her forehead. "Baby, I want you next to me the whole time," he said. "And Yuki, if those goddamn Templars or Goblins or anything else comes after us, sword or no sword, I'm grabbing Rachel and we're out of there. Understand?"

She nodded, her solemn face softened by a smile. "Of course. Safety should always come first."

# 20

Rachel stood at the back of the boat, looking out at the vast expanse of gently rolling waves. It was going to be a long day with enormous challenges, but she had mentally prepared herself to make the best of it. She pulled on her dry suit, designed to fit her neck snuggly to a point of near strangulation. The BC dive vest and tank came next. She adjusted her full face mask, making sure it was secure, and checked the earphone and speaker built into it for communication with her fellow divers. Last were her fins and weight belt, adding twenty pounds to her gear.

With a dive knife strapped to her leg and a spear gun in hand, Rachel glanced at Chase and smiled. "Here goes nothing." She stepped off the dive platform and descended rapidly into the murky sea. Seconds later, Chase followed and arrived protectively at her side. Yuki was last in the water but quickly assumed the lead. Together they traveled beyond the anchor line and above the moving ocean floor, swimming through thick green and brown sediment and algae. Rachel waved her hand before her, estimating her vision at about two feet—more challenging than she'd originally anticipated.

By sticking with Yuki's plan, once they reached the boat, they would swim along the deck, around the bow, down the hull, and back to the stern. The door leading to the salon would give them the easiest access to the stairwell and lower cabins. Then it would be a matter of locating the master suite and reinforced storage compartment.

At twenty feet under the surface, the visibility significantly improved just in time to experience a remarkable sight. An enormous Echizen jellyfish was drifting with the currents in the water. It had to be five feet in diameter and close to four hundred pounds in total mass. Rachel had read about the anomaly of these sea creatures and the serious problems jellyfish invasions were creating for rural fishermen. But never in her life had she imagined seeing one this size or this close. As they swam deeper, reaching forty feet, Rachel watched two stingrays take flight, darting from their hiding places and disappearing into the gloom. She motioned to Chase, but his attention was on Yuki, pointing to the ghostly boat barely visible straight ahead. The mast and crow's nest were tipped to one side and rigging lines were draped in the silt and sand. Rachel remembered Yuki's friend still trapped inside and grimaced at the thought. A nasty encounter with a man's decomposed body would give anyone nightmares. Worse than being challenged by great whites or the elusive Goblin sharks they had yet to see.

As they drew closer to their target, Rachel saw that it was teeming with life. Spotted and striped fish of every size and color drifted in the rigging and darted through portholes. A fresh blanket of coral covered the hull: red, blue, and orange. It amazed Rachel how quickly the ocean residents had moved in and staked their claim in every enclave and on every smooth surface. For a mindless moment, she stared in wonder, transfixed by the aquarium circling around her. She nearly forgot the purpose of being there until Chase tapped her arm and pointed at his watch, gently reminding her time was running out. One after the other, they entered the boat with Yuki directing the way. It was pitch black inside, and if not for the diving lights they were wearing, it would have been impossible to find their way in or out of the cavernous space. Their pathway was littered with rotting debris. Wires hung from the ceiling and pieces of metal jutted from surfaces, making it essential to move slowly. The last thing they needed during their exploration was snared gear and damaged hoses.

"Almost there," Chase said, obviously to comfort Rachel, although Yuki nodded back. However, it quickly became clear that the deeper into the narrow interior they went, the greater the risk of being trapped inside. Yuki pointed a spotlight into the black, allowing them to see the passageway leading to the winding lower staircase just beyond the salon and galley. From the view in Rachel's mask, the tangled path to reach it seemed to stretch on forever.

"Watch your tanks going down," Yuki said. With her spotlight guiding the way, they held the metal rail and descended to the next floor. But at the foot of the stairs, their access was impeded by something large and bulky. An air compressor had broken loose, leaving a two-foot margin open at the ceiling.

"I'll go," Chase said. He unsnapped his vest and with the tank still attached slid it off and held it out before him. Then he swam up and over, clearing the heavily damaged compressor. Rachel was next. She copied what Chase had done, and although grateful for her training as a marine biologist, her anxiety rose to a new level as she squeezed through the tight space. She looked back from the other side. Yuki was doing the same. As soon as she was clear and had secured her vest, she resumed the lead position ahead of them.

The movement of their fins lifted sediment, clouding the water and making it difficult to make out exposed wires, broken dishware, and jagged pieces of wood. Yuki signaled to keep going, and somehow they managed to find their way to the corridor leading to the lower level and the crew's quarters. As they entered, fish scurried from their hiding places and disappeared into new ones.

"Here it is!" Yuki called. She pulled on the partially open door at the end of the hallway, but it was jammed and showed no sign of budging. Chase tried his hand as well, exerting all of his strength to get it open. Still it held tight. He disappeared for a few seconds and returned with a bent piece of metal. Using it as a pry bar, he shoved hard to the right and the door eventually gave way, allowing Yuki and Rachel to venture inside. The super storm had completely demolished the suite. Every built-in piece of furniture and wall-mounted luxury item had busted loose and was completely demolished. Floating refuse that had shifted as the boat sank now littered the sole of the boat up to three feet high in places.

Chase joined the women, blindly digging through layers of rotting boards, rusty nails, metal strips, and muck. After a few minutes, Rachel stopped long enough to check her pressure gauge and was surprised to see she still had one thousand psi remaining. Plenty of air to get back to the surface if they could just find what they were looking for.

Five more minutes slipped away. Then Rachel's hand closed around something solid. It was smooth and hard and felt like a piece of metal, possibly the hilt of the sword. With both hands wrapped around it, she pulled upward with all her might. The hidden relic sprang free, but she couldn't see it or move it any further. When the cloud finally cleared and she could see once more, Rachel realized she was holding a watch on a skeletal arm.

"Ahhhhh!" she screamed, dropping it and scrambling away as fast as she could. The protruding limb fell back on the pile, lifting a gray cloud of sediment in its wake. Rachel stared back like a scared child cowering in the corner, gasping desperately for air.

"Oh shit," came from Chase after unearthing more remains. He turned and crossed the space to reach Rachel. "Take it easy... take it easy. Breathe slowly, baby. It's going to be okay. At least we know where to find Kazumi now."

Rachel's gaze fell on Yuki, still busy digging away on the opposite side of the cabin. Surprisingly, the discovery of Kazumi's body seemed to have had no effect on her at all. She glanced back over her shoulder at Chase and Rachel, as if wondering why they weren't working with the same blind obsession before continuing her search. Seconds later, her determination paid off. She lifted the sword out of the muck, stirring the sediment and silt once more.

"I've got it! I have Kokora!" She held the wrapped weapon high above her head. Apparently, in the midst of her thievery, she'd had the foresight to protect it in heavy-gauge plastic to keep the metal blade from oxidizing.

"Okay. Let's go," Chase said. Yuki swam out of the compartmented cabin and headed straight for the staircase. With Rachel and Chase following a short distance behind, she disappeared from view over the top of the air compressor. While still focusing on their safe return, Rachel cleared the narrow passage and waited for Chase. He was in the midst of unfastening his vest to join her when the light on his wrist suddenly went out. The space around him was thrown into complete darkness.

"Chase?" Rachel called out. "Are you all right?" It was eerie, cold, and silent—almost as if he'd been thrust into a grave and covered over.

# 21

"I'm okay. Don't worry," Chase shouted into his mask. "Direct your light toward me. After I climb over and get on the other side, stay close to me." He located the opening and squeezed through, pushing his tank and vest ahead of him. As soon as he was clear, he fastened up and breathed a sigh of relief. They swam up the stairs and entered the galley. He remembered it was another ten feet to the salon and rear deck. Then it would be a straight shot to the open sea.

"Keep to the middle," he told her. They moved slowly in the murky water, brushing against a tangled web of lines and jagged metal. Finally the walls of the cabin opened up into the next compartment. That's when the regulator in his diving mask sputtered, giving him a few short bursts of air before quitting.

*Shit!* Precious seconds passed. The store of oxygen in his system diminished. He was getting dizzy and his vision was blurring. Turning to Rachel, he squeezed out one word. "Air."

She gave him the alternate hose from her tank and a spare mask she had the foresight to pack. *Stay calm*, he told himself, praying she had enough air left for both of them. Together they moved slowly through the compartment. They reached the outside deck and Chase halted to check the gauge on Rachel's tank. It was rapidly approaching the red zone. At only forty feet, it should have lasted for at least two hours, not one. They had to move quickly or neither of them would make it out alive. With their fins moving at a rapid pace, they headed toward the surface. They had barely reached the halfway mark when something large and fast passed by. A few seconds later, it sliced through the water again. Without even seeing it, Chase knew exactly what they were dealing with. He'd encountered plenty of sharks at sea. They were territorial, unforgiving creatures, and he'd witnessed what they could do to living prey.

His heart raced as he mimicked Rachel, remaining calm and perfectly still. The shark passed by a third time, adding weight to the underwater current. Then it miraculously disappeared. Chase knew at that moment if they didn't act quickly, there was no chance of escaping. With Rachel at his side, they rose through the water, maintaining a steady, controlled ascent. A quick glance behind him brought welcome relief. Although his greatest fear was being followed and viciously attacked, the creature kept its distance.

*Thank God.*

They swam toward the vessel's dark looming hull, making safety stops along the way. Rachel grabbed the anchor chain and began pulling herself up hand over hand as he followed behind. When he finally broke the surface, Chase laid his head back in the water and gazed up at the sky, amazed by its intense blue color.

Rachel was at his side in an instant. "That was close. Are you all right?"

"I am now." He lifted his head from the water and stared up at the dive boat. "Where is she?"

"Back on board, I assume."

*Of course.* If he didn't know better, he was apt to believe she'd intentionally left them down there as a way to dispose of them and keep the sword for herself. With his anger building, Chase followed Rachel as she swam toward the stern. He assisted her on the ladder then climbed up and stepped past her. As soon as his feet hit the deck, he rushed over to Yuki in the lounge chair and jerked the bottle of water out of her hands.

"What are you doing?" he yelled.

"I've been sitting here...waiting for you to come back."

"We almost drowned down there! Where the hell were you? You were supposed to guide us back and instead you're up here... sunning yourself?"

"I don't understand what the problem is. All you had to do was follow me. When I left, you were both fine." Her brow wrinkled. "What do you mean 'drowned'?"

"Besides sharing space with a shark, my air quit and my damn light went out."

"A shark? It couldn't have been a Goblin. They stay below 100 meters...at least their young do. It had to be a white."

"Who the fuck cares?" Chase raked his fingers through his hair with short, agitated strokes and paced back and forth like a caged tiger. Then he halted and whirled around. "What kind of fucking equipment did you get us anyway?"

Yuki shook her head in confusion. "What are you talking about? There shouldn't have been anything wrong with your gear."

Chase picked up his gauge and held it out to her. "Look for yourself. It's empty."

After a few seconds, her eyes met his. "It's split right at the fitting...see. No wonder you ran out of air. You must have scraped against something in the passageway. Probably sliced it on a piece of metal."

Chase wasn't having any part of it. He'd come too close to dying and wasn't about to let that happen again. "You don't think I know what the hell I'm doing? I didn't run into anything. Just check the damn gear!"

"But...but I did. I checked everything—" Her words broke off when Chase started shaking his head.

"Obviously not well enough. You were hired to do a job just like the rest of us. If I can't depend on you, then I don't know why the fuck you're here."

Yuki snapped her mouth shut. Humiliation was written all over her face.

"I'm taking over from now on," he growled. "After lunch, get me up to speed with everything I need to know for our dive tomorrow...and give me the goddamn sword."

Her mouth worked before she finally choked out the words, "I'm sorry. I'll check everything again and give you the complete file. But as far as Kokora...I don't understand why you feel the need to—"

"Just deal with it!" He strolled over to the gun rail and stared out at the sea. He glanced back at Rachel, standing at the stern with a towel wrapped around her shoulders. From the look in her hooded eyes he could tell she wasn't pleased with the way he had behaved, and she was probably right. He'd most likely over-reacted. But close calls and bad judgment brought out the worst in him. Always had and always would.

He rolled his eyes and heaved a breath. After lunch he'd take Yuki aside and apologize for his rude outburst—make everything right with the world. But for the time being, he'd hang onto his anger and frustration...and the sliver of insanity that had brought him here in the first place.

# 22

In one of the Inoue okiya's finest rooms, Kaito Mitsui sat cross-legged on a long tatami mat beside Takashi Bekku. Sweet bean desserts had been placed before them on hand-painted plates. Tamayo was kneeling to the left of both men while Oneesan sat authoritatively behind them. With a gold-lacquered tea bowl, bamboo whisk, and long-handled scoop positioned before her, Mariko began preparations for the special green tea Mitsui had requested.

"I inquired about you a few days ago," he said. "I understand you recently returned from a trip." It was more of a question than a statement, but the geisha kept her eyes down and simply nodded. She scooped a small portion of green tea powder into the bowl of water and stirred gently with the splayed whisk, determined to make it taste just right.

"I'm glad you're back," he continued. "I'm sure Oneesan is too. This beautiful okiya wouldn't be the same without you."

Mariko politely nodded again.

"We're delighted that you decided to stop by today," Oneesan said, her hands pressed neatly in her lap. "You are always welcome here, Mitsui-san. Why, Mariko just told me this morning how much she was looking forward to your visit."

Mitsui tilted his head. "Is that right? Somehow I thought otherwise."

"Oh no. Why would you believe such a thing? She's incredibly happy you're here. Aren't you, Mariko?"

The geisha erected a smile. "Of course I am," she said.

"In that case, I would like to have a private moment to speak with you. That is if Oneesan and Tamayo don't mind."

The elderly woman lifted a brow before reluctantly agreeing. Then Mariko lowered her head. "As you wish, Mitsui-san."

Oneesan and Tamayo pressed their hands on their knees and bowed low at the waist. Before standing, the maiko leaned close and whispered, "I'll be in the next room if you need me."

Mariko nodded. As beads of sweat collected in her scalp, she glanced down at the clay teacups sitting before her. She considered the two carloads of gang members keeping guard in front of the okiya...the stoic look on their faces as she walked by. Soon they would discover what she had done, but thoughts of her father and Kenji were foremost in her mind. She was determined to follow through with her plan, no matter what consequences might follow.

"So...now that we have a chance to talk," Mitsui said, "I would like to form a bond between us and clear up any misunderstandings. You are a beautiful geisha without a danna to look after you. At present, it appears your future rests solely in running this okiya. Such a sad dilemma indeed. I would hate to think of you wasting away with no future prospects." He lowered his eyes briefly, forging genuine concern. "Let me propose an offer," he said. "One I would strongly suggest you accept. In order to guarantee your safety and the kind of life you richly deserve, why not allow me to become your new danna? Every need would be provided for and I would ensure your oneesan had enough money to retire in Europe, if she chooses to do so."

Mariko looked up at him from the edge of her eyes. "I don't understand why you would take so much interest in me, Mitsui-san. I'm just a simple geisha with little to offer."

"Not so, Mariko-chan." He chuckled. "You have much to offer. Especially to a man like me."

She stifled her laugh with one hand in trained maiko fashion. The thought of this overweight, deplorable man exploring her sexuality brought a warm blush to her cheeks.

"You are so charming, Mariko...so sweet and enchanting. If given the chance, we could create wonderful memories together."

It took tremendous effort to meet his eyes. To hide the disgust she carried inside "Ah, Mitsui-san. I've only just lost my patron. You offer a wonderful opportunity, but I'm afraid it will require time and careful consideration on my part."

"Of course. I completely understand," he said, grinning like a silly old fool. "Just don't wait too long. I don't have many good years left."

Fewer than you know. Mariko smiled demurely. She placed the filled cups before each of her guests. Then she slid back in place and patiently waited for them to drink the frothy tea.

Mitsui cast an admonishing glare at Takashi. "There's something else you should know," he told Mariko. "I came here with an explanation that should dispel any rumors or concerns in regard to Kenji Ota. You see, Takashi made a stupid mistake two nights ago when he misplaced his car keys and cell phone. It's my belief that his drunkenness may have contributed greatly to your danna's death. Although he attempted to make amends for his thoughtless behavior, I brought him here today to apologize to you as well."

Her eyes fell to Takashi's left hand where the first joint on his pinky finger was missing. As she contemplated the extent of his offering, he braced his hands on the floor before her and lowered his head to the mat. For several seconds he remained there before finally speaking.

"I'm sorry, Mariko-san. I don't know how it happened or why anyone would have deliberately taken—"

Mitsui slapped his back full force, bringing Takashi's head abruptly upright. He yelled a guttural insult, causing his minion to bow repeatedly like an overwound department store dummy. "Forgive me. Forgive me," Takashi brayed.

Mariko stared at both men, gnawing on the inside of her mouth. This new development put a crimp in her vengeful plan. But there was still the matter of her father and all the others she'd read about. After a thoughtful silence, she bowed deeply. Then she held her sleeve and waved her hand gracefully, directing them to the waiting tea. "Please," she urged.

Without another word, they picked up their cups and drank deeply. They hummed satisfaction in unison after finishing their last swallows. Then, with rushed disregard, they tossed the desserts into their mouths and pushed themselves upright.

"I will be looking forward to your call," Mitsui reminded her.

Mariko walked both men to the main entrance of the okiya with Oneesan and Tamayo at her side. They bowed deeply as Mitsui-san and Takashi Bekku climbed into the back seats of their matching cars and drove away.

"Good---bye forever," Mariko said under her breath.

A quick glance at her watch confirmed it was 4:25p.m. and only one hour until preparations would begin for the dinner hour. In the meantime, there was plenty to occupy her mind and to enjoy about this beautiful summer day. In just twenty minutes, the effects of her poison-lined teacups would be felt, and neither man would know the sweet taste of revenge she had enjoyed at their luxurious expense.

# 23

"What are you talking about?" Mariko asked, believing she'd misunderstood.

"Mitsui-san called after you left the okiya tonight," Oneesan said. "He told me to remind you about the funeral tomorrow."

Mariko's cell phone slipped from her hand. With just eight gut-wrenching words, her governess had delivered her worse nightmare. If Kaito Mitsui and Takashi Bekku were still alive, something had gone terribly wrong. If it wasn't blowfish poison in the bottle, then what was the substance she'd used?

The phone rang a second time. She picked it up and recognized the number immediately. After a moment's hesitation, she answered. "Hello, Shinzo. What do you want?"

"Are you upset with me?" he asked. "When I left this morning, you hardly said two words."

"There wasn't anything left to say."

"It's because of Kenji, isn't it? I only wanted to comfort you and then everything..." He sighed on the phone. "I'm sorry it got so out of hand."

Mariko remained silent, wishing all the mistakes she'd made in the last twenty-four hours would go away.

"I don't mean to sound uncaring…you obviously have a lot on your mind. But Oneesan shouldn't have agreed with Kenji's proposal. It was a terrible mistake. You should have refused, Mariko."

She stifled a laugh and shook her head ruefully. "My mistake is that I trusted you, Shinzo…that I let my guard down. My mistake is that I believed you four months ago when you said you cared."

"But I do care," Shinzo tried to assure her. "The way I left you…it was wrong. I know that now. Mariko, please…you have to believe me."

She dashed the bitter tears from her eyes. In just four days, her life had been drastically altered. She wasn't the same woman he'd known—not the same geisha willing to accept whatever fate had in store. With concentrated effort, she kept her voice low, hard-bitten, and pitiless.

"You could have done something to prevent this, you know. An hour and a half after I talked to you, I called again. They told me at the temple office you had left the country and would be gone for months. It turned out you were too busy doing other things. Saving dead souls while mine was in jeopardy. Maybe you could have protected me…protected Kenji with your God-given gift. But instead he lost his life. He died a horrible death with his head rolling around on the ground while you were sound asleep in your bed."

"I'm sorry, but you have to understand. I didn't want to believe you were with him. I knew my feelings, just as I thought you did. I wasn't prepared to commit when we last spoke. I wanted to make a difference first, earn extra money so we could have a good life together. But then…it was too late."

177

"Yes, Shinzo. You were too late. Just like now. Please don't call or talk to me again. There's nothing left for us to say."

"But let me try to explain. Let me—"

"No. Don't do it. Please don't."

"Mariko, listen," he begged. "You say he lost his life as if it were something you could possess when the truth is you don't have a life. You are life. The one consciousness that pervades the entire universe and takes temporary form to experience itself as a stone or blade of grass, as an animal or a human being. And when it's gone, that spark of existence, what's left behind, is what matters...the positive difference we made in being here. I ask you to search your heart," he told her. "If you can honestly say Kenji did this, then he deserves your tears and prayers of salvation from everyone who loved him."

In her mind's eye, she could see him taking her hands into his reluctantly and delivering his profound message—clever, insightful words changing absolutely nothing. She was convinced that no one, not even her best friend, could take the burden of her heartache away.

"I have to go," she said. Then, as quickly as she ended the call, she dismissed him from her life.

The hour was late and Mariko was growing tired. She looked at the short sword resting on the coffee table before her. There was still the matter of Mitsui and his ridiculous offer to consider. He wouldn't be easy to refuse, and unfortunately she wasn't skilled enough in martial arts or weaponry to end his harassment. Tomorrow she would call Oneesan and insist on an acceptable solution.

*It's the least I can do,* Mariko told herself. She pushed herself upright, intending to go to bed, when her cell phone rang again. With hesitation, she picked it up. She had no interest in hearing from Shinzo again...in listening to his sermon about the importance of love and forgiveness. But then she glanced at the receiver and realized it was an unfamiliar area code. Very few people knew her private number—only those she had chosen to give it to.

"You need to pay attention," the raspy voice said on the other end of the line.

"What...who is this?" Mariko asked. She had gotten two of these calls earlier in the evening from different numbers. At first, she hadn't thought too much of it. Just a wrong number, she had assumed. The second came from the same area code. But this one was from a different place altogether. Not anywhere near her hometown in Osaka.

"You can't...stay there." Static filled the pause between words. The caller could be a woman, but it was hard to tell. It sounded almost as if the voice had gone through an electronic filter. Or perhaps the caller was a heavy smoker. Maybe it wasn't a person at all.

"What are you talking about?" Now Mariko was definitely frightened. "Tell me who you are or I'll... I'll..." She tried to think of a good threat, but the prankster was quick to respond.

"Leave now. Do you hear me? You don't belong there." It was spoken at the same volume. A soft, quiet, eerie volume that when heard could pick up the hairs on the back of your neck.

"Stop it! Just leave me alone. If I hear from you again, I'll call the police!" Terrified, Mariko slammed the phone down on the table and burst into tears. She buried her head in the toss pillow and screamed. Who is this freak...this depraved lunatic? Is it a childish prank?

The phone rang, causing Mariko to breathe faster. She stared at it until it grew silent. Fifteen seconds later, it rang again. She let out a soft scream and backed away from it, grasping the pillow with both hands. A fourth series of rings followed. By this time Mariko was pushed up against the wall next to Kenji's living room window.

"Why are you doing this to me? Please...please stop," she begged. The phone mercilessly rang, ignoring her pleas. She slid to the floor and hugged Kenji's pillow close. Then the ringing stopped. A foreboding silence fell for what seemed an eternity. Then the peace was broken when a small pebble struck the window, causing her to lurch around to face it. Holding the pillow before her in self-defense she approached the window slowly, her breathing fast and heavy. Craning her neck she cautiously peeked down at the street. A familiar woman in a conservative gray kimono stood in the middle of the road staring up at her.

Mariko threw the pillow angrily on the sofa and slid the window open wide. "Oneesan!" she called out. "You nearly gave me a heart attack! What are you doing here?"

"I tried to call you a dozen times but your phone has been busy. I want to know why you're staying in Kenji Ota's apartment when you have a perfectly good home to go to." The elderly woman's voice sounded strained and far away.

"Are you all right, Oneesan? You sound sick."

She hacked a few times and replied, "Yes. But it's just a cold."

"Okay...well, come inside. It's late. You're definitely not helping it by standing out there."

"I can't," she said. "The security gate is locked and I'm tired of waiting. If someone doesn't open the door in the next two minutes, I'm going home."

Mariko slammed the window shut. She crossed the living room floor and bent to slip on her tennis shoes. As she straightened, she heard three quick knocks on Kenji's door. She was startled at first but then reasoned that one of the tenants had heard Oneesan calling out and had let her in through the gate and to the elevator.

"One moment," Mariko yelled. She glanced down at her stained white T-shirt and denim cut-offs and realized she wasn't dressed appropriately—not for entertaining guests, especially not Oneesan. But with no forewarning, there simply wasn't enough time to change. She ran her fingers through her hair, fixing it as best she could. Then she slowly opened the door, expecting a reprimand for her unkempt appearance and poor manners.

"I know what you must think..." Mariko stopped midsentence. The entryway was empty. Oddly, the hallway showed no sign of activity in either direction. All the apartment doors lining the hallway were closed. The strip of exterior hall lights was shut off. The only source of illumination came from the red emergency sign above the fire escape door. It filled the corridor with a strange, unearthly glow and gave Mariko hesitance in further investigating.

"Oneesan, where are you?" The silence sent a shiver of cold fear through her veins. She paused and took a deep breath before leaving the safety of Kenji's apartment and approaching the exit door, barely ten feet away.

"Oneesan?" There was still no answer. She stood on her tiptoes, trying to see through the small meshed window in the metal door, but it was no use. Hesitantly she cracked the door open and looked down the narrow flight of concrete steps. From where she stood, Mariko could see a body crumpled at the bottom of the stairwell in a tight fetal position.

"Oneesan!" she screamed. She hurried down the steps, fearing the worst. "Are you hurt? Should I call someone?" Her eyes adjusted slowly to the dim neon lighting and the sight before them made her gag and gasp for air. The person she was standing over was Hiroshi Mori—the old man Kenji had been partying with four nights ago. He was lying in an inhuman position with one arm snapped back behind the silver wig covering his head. Pools of blood surrounded his gray kimono and were spreading across the ground. His black eyes bulged in terror.

Mariko turned away. Bile rose in her throat. She tried not to vomit as she stood bent over with one hand pressed against her stomach and the other over her mouth. After a few seconds, the sensation passed, leaving her dizzy and light-headed.

Was it possible that Mori-san had come here disguised as Oneesan, pretending to have a cold to hide his voice? Had he tricked her into letting him in with the intention of harming her? She kept her eyes closed, wishing with all her might that this was a bad dream...another nightmare she'd wake up from. But when she opened her eyes, it became real. All too real.

Behind her, a deep voice spoke, breathing heavily in her ear. "Be quiet, angel. You'll wake the dead."

Mariko's heart skipped a beat. Her legs weakened beneath her. Everything faded to black as she dropped into the murderer's waiting arms.

"Are you all right?" a young woman's echoing voice asked. Mariko's eyes flew open and she sat bolt upright on the bed, gulping breaths of air as if she'd been drowning. She focused her eyes on Tamayo's for only a few seconds before she pulled her into an almost crushing embrace.

"Oh, Tamayo," she murmured into her hair, still not fully awake.

The maiko rubbed Mariko's back soothingly. "It's okay," she said. "I'm here. Everything is going to be fine."

After a moment, Mariko loosened her grip on Tamayo's arms and eased back against the headboard. Her breathing was slowly returning to normal. She swallowed thickly, realizing a look of uncomfortable vulnerability must have been covering her face.

"What...what are you doing here?" Mariko asked. "How did you get in?"

"My friend Daiichi works in the building," Tamayo answered. "One of the neighbors heard a commotion in the hallway and called the manager. Daiichi rushed upstairs and found you lying in the hallway just outside the doorway. After realizing who you were, he unlocked the door to the apartment and carried you into the bedroom. Then he called the okiya. It's a good thing I answered the phone. Oneesan would have been very upset."

Mariko took a ragged breath as she pressed the palms of her hands into her eyes. She raked her right hand through her hair, moist with sweat. "I'm sorry," she said, her voice barely a whisper. "Just seeing you here..."

"It's okay," Tamayo replied. "Can you tell me what happened? Did someone hurt you?" she asked tentatively.

Mariko took a quick assessment then looked back at Tamayo. "No, not really. But Mori-san..." Her voice cracked. "I saw him in the exit outside. Someone pushed him down the stairs. It was...so horrible. He's all bloody and his body is mangled and...twisted.".

Tamayo's eyes were wide. "Really? Oh my goodness. Is he still there?"

"I don't know. Maybe we should call the police. Someone's apt to see him."

The young maiko stepped toward the phone.

"There were these strange calls," Mariko added, staring into space, "and the next thing I knew...he was just there. Wait a minute." He eyes swung back to Tamayo. "So was someone else. You said I was found in the hallway?"

Tamayo nodded.

"He must have carried me there." Ohhh... She shivered at the thought and wrapped her arms around herself and squeezed tight. "Why would he do that? Why would a killer leave me where someone could find me?"

The maiko shook her head. Her face was filled with concern. "I don't know what to think. But I wouldn't be staying here if I were you."

A knock came at the door. It was cracked opened, allowing a voice to travel. "Hello...it's me, Daiichi."

"We're in here," Tamayo answered.

A freckle-faced man with messy brown hair leaned in the open doorway. "Hi, Mariko-san. We met a few years ago." He seemed rather shy and uncomfortable about being there. "I'm glad you're okay. Is there anything you need?"

"She's fine," Tamayo answered for her. "But there's a dead body outside. Look down the stairs in the emergency exit... please. Then call the police."

He vanished from view and was out of the apartment for less than a minute before he returned scratching his head. "I...uh... don't know what you're talking about. There's no one down there."

"Are you sure?" Tamayo asked. "Mariko saw Mori--san."

"I'm telling you...there's nobody there."

"What about the blood?" Mariko asked. "There was so much of it."

"I don't know if you fell and hit your head or what," he said, "but maybe you should call a doctor."

"I'm telling you Hiroshi Mori was there!" Mariko insisted. "I saw him as clearly as I'm seeing you."

"Well, he must have stood up and walked away...and cleaned up after himself too."

Mariko pressed her hand against her forehead, thoroughly confused. After all the prank phone calls, was her imagination simply playing tricks on her? She hesitated before turning to Tamayo to offer a suggestion. "Maybe if you called Hiroshi's wife..."

Tamayo gaped at her. "Oh, no...that wouldn't be appropriate."

Mariko suddenly felt stupid. "Sorry," she mumbled. "That was a silly thing to ask. In fact, I don't even know what you would say. Mrs. Mori...we think your husband might be dead?"

"I know," Tamayo said shyly.

Mariko sighed. "Thank you for being here," she said in earnest. "You should go back home and get some rest. I'm fine, honestly."

The maiko's face became serious. She seemed disappointed at not being able to help. After scooting off the edge of the bed, she walked toward the door. Then she swiftly turned around.

"You're not all right," she said in a firm tone, defying Mariko to say otherwise. "So you can stop saying so because you're not fooling anyone. And we can both try to pretend Kenji wasn't murdered and that you're living here at his request. But that's pointless because we both know it's not true."

Mariko's eyes dropped to her hands, still clenched in her lap.

"If you're going to stay here and have nightmares," Tamayo said resolutely, "then I'll help by making sure they don't return." She approached the bed and reached out her hand. "Give me your keys."

"What?" Mariko asked in nervous surprise.

"Your keys."

Mariko swallowed hard. "Why do you want them?"

"Because whether you intend to stay here or move back into your apartment, I don't think you should be alone. So I'm going home to pack a bag and move in with you."

"Inouye oneesan would never allow that to happen."

"I think you could convince her to change her mind…if you wanted to."

Mariko regarded Tamayo warily before hesitantly complying. She reached for her keys on the nightstand and held them out. "Are you sure about this?" she asked. "What about your training and your preparations to become a full-fledged geisha?"

"Don't worry, I'll manage," Tamayo said. "With everything that's happened, it's more important for us to be together," she added with a soft smile. She took Mariko's hand and threaded her fingers through hers. "We're okiya sisters but we can be friends too. Right?"

Mariko smiled softly. "Of course." She wasn't sure about having a roommate…especially this young maiko. But there was something remarkable about her kindness and unselfish concern. She was so different than Mariko had originally thought. And to be honest, it wouldn't hurt to have someone around—someone to share company with and to help keep the demons away.

# 24

"I got our bags," Chase told Yuki, standing before the reception counter. Rachel rested her tired legs on a velvet settee a few feet away while admiring their stunning surroundings. In every corner and on every wall and surface in the traditional hot spring resort, kiln-fired pots, gold silk screens, massive woodcarvings, and exquisite watercolors were on display. It was as if Yuki had made arrangements for a private tour through a museum instead of an overnight stay. Rachel picked up a brochure and glanced at its pictures and detailed description. In addition to a beautiful setting and remarkable décor, there were forty guest rooms with private baths and toilets. Every amenity and need had been addressed. However, at that moment, Rachel's only concern was how quickly she could climb into bed and inhume thoughts of Mitsui and his band of threatening outlaws.

As soon as Chase finished checking in, each of them received a key, terrycloth slippers, and a folded cotton robe. They were escorted across polished wooden floors, over an indoor stream, past a gift shop, karaoke bar, and two international restaurants.

They took an elevator to the next floor and eventually arrived at a hallway filled with doors leading to individual suites.

"I suggest visiting the bathhouse," Yuki told them, standing outside their room. "It will help you relax, and when you return to your room, you'll find a kaiseki meal waiting."

*"Kaiseki?"* Chase asked.

"It's a dinner with lots of small local dishes…each one representing the season."

Chase and Rachel exchanged a tired smile.

"It's included with your stay," Yuki reminded them.

"Oh sure," Chase said. "Sounds great."

"If you need anything else…" she said in an obligatory voice or a sad voice or a tired voice—it was hard for Rachel to tell.

"I'm sure we'll be fine," he said reassuringly.

"In that case, I'll see you in the morning."

*"Oyasuminasi,"* Rachel said, bringing a smile to Yuki's face.

*"Oyasuminasi,"* Yuki repeated, adding a quick bow. As soon as Chase closed the door, a woman in her forties knocked and entered the room. She was dressed in traditional geisha fashion and insisted on helping them unpack their duffel bags. Then she asked with a mix of Japanese and sign language if she could assist Rachel with putting on her summer kimono.

"I think I can figure it out," Rachel told her, not knowing if she was truly understood. As it turned out, that was apparently the case, as the woman unfurled the robe and held it out before her, waiting for Rachel to undress. Chase turned around to give them privacy and then was offered the same assistance.

As soon as they were both tightly wrapped and belted, the woman stepped toward the window shoji and slid it open, exposing a concealed private garden complete with a water feature and tiny stone walkway. She pointed out the large-screen television in the corner, two floor chairs in the center of the room, and the table stationed between them, where two cups of cold green tea and a bowl of rice crackers had already been delivered. Yet as far as Rachel could tell, there wasn't a bed or folded cot anywhere, only the tatami-covered floor.

"I'm sorry, but where are we supposed to sleep?" she asked, thoroughly confused. The woman smiled and bowed deeply before leaving them for the night.

"I read about these places," Chase told her. "It's like magic. They change the sitting room into a dining room and then into a bedroom. Sleeping on a futon is supposed to be good for your back."

"I could care less about my back," Rachel moaned. "I just want to go to sleep. I haven't had a decent night's rest in four days."

He took Rachel's hand and tugged her behind him. "Come on, honey. Let's go have a hot bath. We'll have a light dinner then I'll put you to bed."

They padded down the long hallway in their assigned slippers and followed all the signs leading to the bathhouse. After taking the elevator to the lower level, they split up, going in opposite directions toward the men and women's changing rooms. Once inside, Rachel discovered a long row of low plastic stools, wooden buckets, and wall-mounted showerheads and was relieved that she understood how they were actually used. She also encountered two elderly Asian women in the dressing room who were walking around completely naked from the centrally located lockers to the exterior hot spring pool. Although their bodies were slack and sagging, modesty appeared to be the least of their concerns.

Rachel removed her yukata, folded it neatly, and placed it in her locker. Then with little more than a washrag to conceal the top of her legs, she exited through the glass sliding door leading to the steamy environment outside. The green ferns, stacked boulders, and cascading waterfall transformed the open space into a world within itself. She took her time, easing herself into the thermal pool and onto a submerged concrete ledge. The tiny, round-faced women were sitting deep in the water with their chins resting on the surface. Each one acknowledged her with a gentle smile and slow nod. Then they closed their eyes and laid their heads back, retreating to another place.

Rachel settled against a smooth rock and extended her legs. She floated her arms and let her head drop back to gaze up at the heavens. Millions of tiny stars shimmered against the fathomless field of night sky, leaving her feeling insignificant, as if the scope of her problems was minute. As she watched the brightest star, her eyes grew heavy. She closed them, allowing the calm to envelope her inner spirit—to transport her to a serene nonexistence. A place of absolute peace she never wanted to leave.

Although the women stepped quietly out of the water around her, their sudden movements broke the stillness and brought Rachel back to the present. She blew a deep breath into the steaming air and enjoyed her quiet space a few minutes longer. Then with reluctance, she followed them back into the dressing room. She lowered herself onto a stool and soaped up and showered before drying off and reclaiming her cotton robe. With it cinched tightly around her, she wiggled her toes into her slippers and headed toward the exit, anticipating the comfort of her waiting bed.

A white-uniformed attendant was waiting outside. "Miss Lyons?" she asked.

"Yes? What is it?"

"Please come." With no other words spoken, she beckoned her onward. Rachel mentally hesitated before ultimately surrendering. In the next room, two thin mattresses had been laid on the floor and were covered with two white sheets. The woman moved her hands in a circular motion, indicating she was a masseuse.

"For me?" Rachel asked.

The woman nodded eagerly before stepping behind the white curtain. Not prepared to argue the point, Rachel removed her garment and hung it over a chair. After sliding between the sheets facedown, she heard a sound and turned her head in time to see a familiar pair of feet. Her eyes continued to travel upward, meeting an impossible, cockeyed smile.

"Let me guess," she told Chase. "This was included."

"It appears so. Couples massage. Don't you love it?"

"No." Rachel cringed inside. This wasn't a honeymoon vacation or an opportunity to bond. And although she valued their time together, the added service was by far the last thing she needed or wanted. "Can't we just skip the massage and go to bed?" she whimpered.

"Go with the flow, honey. We're here to do a job, but we're also getting a chance to experience Asian culture up close. Just relax and pretend I'm not here." He smiled and dropped his robe.

Rachel turned her face away, fearing the curtains would part at any moment. With Chase lying beside her and a strange woman rubbing his bare ass, how the hell was she supposed to relax?

Ah...this is just what I need, Chase thought. Two white-smocked therapists stepped into the room. Only the backs of Rachel and Chase's heads were visible above the sheets. From the way he was positioned, he could barely see her face, and when she opened her eyes, it felt invasive and kind of creepy to stare. So he only peeked at her once in a while.

For some reason, he was having a hard time relaxing, and when the small-framed woman kneading his shoulders tried to manipulate his limbs, he felt rude by not offering his assistance. She moved his arm one way, and he moved it along with her. However, his effort took it farther than he expected and his hand landed between her legs. Instinctively he closed his fingers, which resulted in him grabbing her crotch.

She jumped back and gasped.

"Oh shit. I'm sorry," Chase mumbled, thoroughly embarrassed.

Rachel lifted her head briefly. From the question mark in her eyes, she seemed to be wondering what was going on.

"Hey..." he cooed then rolled his eyes when she looked away.

Great. It was like being caught with another woman. He tried even harder to relax and go limp, but by then the only thought registering was that the young masseuse probably thought he was a pervert, trying to feel her up. He didn't know how to prove that he wasn't other than to avoid touching her altogether, which suddenly felt like a lot of pressure since he hadn't meant to do it in the first place.

When the ordeal was finally over and they were wrapped up in their robes again, they stumbled out the doorway with their hair greasy from massage oil. The cool air from the air vent in the hallway felt nice and was a relief from the cramped, heat-filled room.

"Never again," he said.

"Never again," she agreed.

When they reached their room, Chase opened the door and found a meal fit for royalty spread out on the table. There were twelve handmade pottery dishes containing artfully designed food just begging to be devoured.

"So skipping the massage, tell me what you thought of the spa," he said, sliding into his chair. Without waiting for Rachel, he picked up his chopsticks and dove into his bowl of rice.

"It was amazing," she said. "I've never experienced anything like that in my life. I'm thinking maybe we could do some work in my back yard when we get home...maybe even design a water feature like that."

"If we did, you'd never get out of it."

Rachel smiled as she slid into her seat. She stretched her legs out under the table and eyed their unbelievable spread. Although she ate only a few bites from each dish, she was genuinely enjoying herself, while Chase scarfed down as much food as his stomach would hold. When he was nearly finished, their room attendant returned bringing crystal stemware and a bucket of chilled yellow label champagne. She uncorked it with a white folded napkin and poured generous servings in each glass, adding bubbles to their delicious eight-course meal.

"I'm glad we're doing this together," Chase said. "Here's to more adventures." He lifted his glass in a mock salute, but Rachel didn't share his toast. She set her glass down and glanced at the empty dinner dishes. Then she looked across the table at Chase.

"Do you think they give expensive champagne to everyone?" she asked. "That's pretty extravagant considering this place rents for three hundred dollars a night."

Chase lowered his crystal flute. He was having such a good time that it hadn't dawned on him how naive he'd been until that very moment. He considered the spacious room, gourmet food, VIP treatment, and logic in Rachel's assessment.

"That's what she told me," he mumbled, then realized the absurdity of his spoken words. Who was footing this bill? He rose and was looking around for the phone to call Yuki when the attendant suddenly returned. She was followed closely by a young assistant carrying a large tray and by another woman who began opening hidden compartments in the back wall. They'd obviously come to clear their meal and prepare the room for the night.

"Excuse me," Chase tried, hoping one of them would understand. "Do any of you know who gave the bottle of champagne to us?"

The youngest member in the trio smiled broadly. "Why, the owner," she said in perfect English. "He paid for all of your expenses and asked that you be treated as his personal guest."

Chase swallowed hard. "Can I ask who this gentleman is?"

She bowed her head slightly. "Mr. Kaito Mitsui. He owns all the resorts in this area."

"Mitsui? All of them?" His voice rose.

"Oh yes," she assured him. "He stopped by earlier this evening but was called away on business. He told me to ask you before you both leave tomorrow if you enjoyed your stay and wanted me to remind Miss Lyons to let him know if she needed any help with her future plans."

Rachel's mouth dropped. She stared at the young woman in utter disbelief. At that moment, Chase wanted to pack their bags and get the hell out of there. But by his best estimate, they had less than six hours to sleep before heading back to the marina and resuming their search for the underwater cave. Taking into account Rachel's present state of mind, he had to bite his tongue, smile, and bury his anger. Nothing would be gained by proving how incapable he was at finding another place to stay or what a poor job he was doing at keeping his partner safe.

# 25

Rachel awoke to the sound of a man and woman fighting and throwing things around. A door slammed, and she looked outside the window to see what was going on. A young Asian girl was running across a field. She ducked down in the tall grass, and seconds later, a man walked out of the shed carrying a nunchaku—a crude farm implement used for separating rice from straw. He appeared to be looking for the girl, and Rachel began worrying for her safety. She was considering calling out for someone when the girl suddenly stood up and the man turned around. They both stared up at her as if they had heard her thoughts through the closed window. Their black hollow eyes, ghostly white skin and stony expressions chilled Rachel to the bone. She knew in an instant these zombie-like creatures were searching for souls of the living. Everyone in the inn, including Chase, was in danger.

Rachel took a step back and watched them as they approached. Not knowing what else to do, she ran downstairs to lock the main entrance. Then she returned upstairs and found Chase still fast asleep. Moments later, she heard a scraping sound inside the walls, like a family of rats crawling around. She shook Chase's shoulder, trying to wake him, but he wouldn't stir. Then the noises shifted to the wall directly behind their bed.

"Stop it!" she yelled. The wall suddenly grew still. Then a beetle crawled out of a small hole near the baseboard and scurried across the wooden floor. It was followed by a dozen more. Rachel shivered and awoke to see the dark shadow of a man standing outside the shoji- covered window. She blinked and he was gone. Frightened by what she had seen, Rachel shook Chase's shoulder repeatedly to rouse him, but it was useless. He was sleeping so soundly that nothing was going to wake him. She was afraid of letting down her guard and falling asleep again. But after a few minutes, her body gave out and her weary eyes closed. Strangely, her dream resumed where it had left off, but this time the girl had transformed into a sleek black leopard that sent the gardeners at the front of the inn running. She could hear women screaming on the lower level and knew the creature was now inside the building, rapidly approaching the stairs leading to their room.

With her heart racing, Rachel rolled over and whispered in Chase's ear, "A wild animal is coming. Wake up. It's going to attack us."

He grumbled in a loud voice, "What are you talking about?"

"Shhh..." she said. "Don't let it hear you." She tried to listen to determine how far away the creature was, but the hallway had grown completely quiet. Stay strong, she told herself. Everything will be fine. The door to their room burst open and Rachel reached for the table lamp. The shadow of a man spread across the floor and her eyes lifted to the image of her father standing outside in the hallway. A small smile slipped over his lips.

"Dad? Is that you?" she asked, trying to overcome the near heart attack he'd given her.

"I'm sorry," he said insincerely, shrugging his shoulders. "I didn't mean to disturb you, but there's someone I want you to meet."

"Who?" she asked curiously. She rose to her feet and stepped closer to see him more clearly. His peppered hair was grayer than she remembered, but his eyes were the same. Blue and green with brown in the center, the exact reflection of her own.

Sam didn't answer. Instead, he held out his hand to seemingly nothing and the snarling leopard magically appeared. As he turned and walked away, it came in through the open doorway. With each padded footstep, the animal grew smaller and smaller until it arrived before Rachel the size of a kitten. She reached down and picked it up by the nape of its neck and stared into its golden-brown eyes. It was so cute that she was tempted to fold it in her arms and nuzzle her cheek against its soft fur. But just as she brought it close, the animal lifted a paw and swung its claws at her face. It missed, and Rachel immediately let go, dropping it three feet to the ground. It looked up at her and purred as if satisfied with its effort. Then it sashayed back through the open door. Rachel crossed the room and peeked outside. The hallway was completely empty. Stunned and fascinated, she stood frozen for a moment before closing the door slowly and setting the lock.

She woke from the strange, disorienting dream and couldn't fall back to sleep again. Not with the sensation of someone having invaded her life and her father allowing it to happen.

# 26

B y early afternoon, the chartered boat was anchored in the drop zone as indicated on their map. Everything they would need was packed in their waterproof bags and secured to straps on their BC vests. Yuki took a spear gun from the boat rack and handed a second one to Chase. She tucked her "secret weapons" into her pocket, signaled OK, and tumbled over the side. Rachel and Chase held their masks, leaned back, and rolled into the water behind her. With their jet scooters propelling them through the ocean, they remained in close proximity of their leader. All the while, Rachel kept reminding herself of Shinzo's warning to trust her instincts and be prepared for the unexpected.

They were traveling east toward a submerged ravine and the entrance to the Seku Island cave and had barely reached thirty feet down when, out of nowhere, a menacing-looking creature charged from the shadowy depths, coming to within ten feet of her. It passed by a second time, cutting between her and Chase. The agitated twelve-foot-long white circled around, deliberately separating her from the other divers. During all her years as a marine biologist, Rachel had never experienced anything like this.

Yuki lifted her spear gun and prepared to fire just as the shark snuck by a third time. It passed inches away from Rachel's left hand, but there was no time to be scared or to panic. There was only time to stare after it and plot its next move. With her headset tuned in, Rachel listened to Yuki urging her to remain calm and still.

"From the look of its notched tail, this guy has seen plenty of action," Yuki said. And it was obviously looking for more. However, on its fourth approach, the shark did something totally unexpected, something that would remain with Rachel forever. It turned on its side so that its doll eyes were looking directly into hers, and a strange exchange took place. Although it lasted only a few seconds, it was as if the shark was seeing directly into her soul. Then like a ghost in the night, it vanished back into the blackness, leaving the three of them moving their fins slowly in place.

Chase was the first to speak. "That was crazy. Rachel, are you okay?"

She blinked several times, trying to comprehend what had just happened.

"Rachel?" he asked again.

She drew a ragged breath before signaling OK. Then, like horses shaking themselves off, they dismissed the whole experience and began moving through the water again—focused on their destination and the urgency of their mission.

Rachel felt a vibration in the current around her. Concerned about the shark returning, she increased her speed and joined Yuki in the lead. A fast-moving fin, then another one, and another one suddenly broke the murky water in front of them. They were surrounded by a pod of dolphins numbering into the hundreds. The beautiful, streamlined creatures swam in all directions, flipping and turning in an acrobatic show. If Rachel hadn't seen it for herself, she wouldn't have believed it possible. The phenomenon lasted for close to twenty minutes, leaving her with the belief that some type of migration was taking place. But even at that, it was an odd time of the year for a diaspora of this magnitude to take place.

Chase gave the signal to hurry, breaking into her engrossed thoughts. She adjusted the speed on her jet scooter and followed Yuki to a depth of sixty feet. They entered the mouth of the cave one after another and dropped another ten feet into the black hole, knowing full well hungry Templar eels could appear at any moment.

"Stay clear of the alcoves," Yuki warned. As if on cue, the head of a monster materialized out of the darkness. The giant, thick, leathery-skinned eel slowly uncoiled itself from its nest, apparently intrigued by all their commotion. It nonchalantly skirted around them, setting up a subtle barrier. Chase swam away in a flurry, running Yuki into a jagged, protruding boulder. She righted herself quickly and pulled a packet of chum from her pocket. In an obvious attempt to distract the eel, she dispersed it in the water, allowing Chase and Rachel ample time to escape. But as she finned away, Rachel happened to glance back and realized this wasn't the best plan in retrospect. The serpent was now slithering between Yuki's legs and frisking her thoroughly for more sushi. Meanwhile, she was emptying her pockets in a whirling dervish frenzy. Fish bits flew everywhere as she hastened to rid herself of the eel's tasty meal. After it finally headed off in a hasty retreat, Rachel signal to Yuki that it was now safe and got a shaky reply as their brave leader scoured her wetsuit for collision injuries and debilitating bite marks.

Rachel climbed out of the water and glimpsed the spooky cave walls surrounding them. "Ah...saved the best for last," she said to no one in particular. After leaving her dive gear in a neat pile, she finished pulling on her stretchy Wave Walker Zip shoes and arrived at Chase's side in her snug-fitting blue swimsuit. Yuki adjusted the small tourniquet she'd created from a torn T-shirt, stemming further blood loss from the gash in her thigh.

At seeing the damaged he'd caused, Chase inwardly cringed. "I'm sorry. Is there anything I can do to help?"

Yuki dismissed his concern with a directive. "Just try to keep your eyes peeled for anything."

Chase shot her a mock salute before maneuvering between the enormous stalagmites covering the ceiling and floor. He unclipped the flashlight he'd carried from the boat and extended it before him. Its far-reaching beam bounced off the sculpted interior, revealing strange markings on the walls and a thin, winding stream leading the way.

As he pressed on, he could hear the sound of an unseen waterfall echoing off the cavernous walls, assuring him that they were nearing an important target on his pocketed map. Rachel followed a short distance behind him with Yuki pulling up the rear. They matched his steady pace with rubber-soled aqua shoes gripping the uneven, slippery floor and stopped only long enough for Rachel to snap a few photos. When they reached a bend in the first cavern, Yuki pointed out the first landmark—a glistening mound of limestone resembling a statute.

"There's the Buddha I told you about," she said.   "Got it," Chase tossed back. The trail narrowed and doubled back and the stream widened, picking up speed across the smooth bedrock. As if mimicking its blind pursuit, pores opened in Chase's skin, adding fresh beads of sweat to his bare chest and down the middle of his back. He could almost see the steam rising from the ground, adding weight to the stifling air around them. After two more turns, they arrived at a huge toppled slab of stone serving as a natural bridge across the now raging stream. Chase tested its soundness and crossed over first. Upon reaching the other side, he waved Rachel on. She followed his carefully laid steps and was only midway across when a colony of bats blasted out of a hidden wall crevice and began circling and charging her from all sides.

"Ahhhh!" she yelled, dropping to her knees. She swung her arms wildly, trying to keep them from latching onto her. Yuki acted quickly, setting off a high-pitched alarm from the pressurized canister she'd thoughtfully packed. The swarm vanished as quickly as it came.

"Are you okay?" Chase called out anxiously.

Rachel righted herself and wiped off her hands. "I'm fine," she said, sounding slightly embarrassed. Up ahead, the water converged and dropped ten feet into a circular pool. Chase pulled out the map and checked it with his light a second time. Just as Yuki had indicated, a chiseled staircase rose from the rear wall, mirroring the scene stretched out before him.

"Take it easy," Yuki instructed. "We've got a long way to go."

Because every step was a few inches too steep, Chase moved slowly and carefully. He had to bury his fascination with the imposing structure, as he'd almost lost his life by being ignorant of his surroundings. Six months ago, while searching for the Wanli II, his carelessness had left him tangled in a discarded fishing net. If not for his knife, he would have drowned. Then, before his mission was over, he faced angry sharks and fought a bloody battle with pirates under the ocean. There was no chance he'd risk that again. Not with a priceless sword hanging on his back.

With each yard he ascended, Chase noticed that nothing seemed out of the ordinary. Save for the monolith, he was climbing hundreds of feet underground. Kokoro rocked to and fro in its scabbard as he rose to the uppermost platform. His head was now level with the foundations of the pillars that lined the top of the tower.

"Wow!" Chase yelled as he looked over the edge, surprised to see the bluish glow of flickering sconces bouncing off the dark granite. Obviously someone had been caring for the tomb, but there wasn't even a footprint on the dust-covered floor to attest to Yuki's previous visit let alone evidence that anyone else had been there. He scanned his surroundings once he arrived at the top of the uppermost platform. It was square, as were the lower slabs. Four tall granite columns stood resolute at each corner, adorned with the same uniform symbols he'd seen etched in the walls near the cave entrance. He caught Kokoro by its lever and extracted the weapon halfway from its scabbard. He smiled at his own memory, seeing that the sword bore the same patterns on its intricately etched metal blade.

After slinging Kokoro over his back, Chase turned his gaze to the middle of the platform. A cylindrical dais protruded from the stone with something inlaid into its surface. He cast a wary glance around, searching for any sort of trap or hazard. Once he was satisfied that the coast was clear, he slowly approached the dais. Atop the round protrusion was a system of rusted gears under two thin levers, one pointing toward him and the other pointing to the far left corner of the stone chamber. He placed a hand on the clock-like gear system and found every part completely seized. It was to be expected, but he thought that surely the people who had buried the prince would have realized metal would rust in a moist underground cavern and would have used something else.

"You all right up there?" Rachel called.

"Yeah. But I think you might wanna come up here and take a peek at this," he called back. "It's not any kind of treasure, but it's really...something!"

"That's not saying much." "Will you just get on up here?"

"Fine, fine. I'm right behind Yuki."

Chase waited for them to climb the enormous staircase, listening to the sound of their footsteps growing steadily closer. Once Yuki stepped aside and Rachel reached the uppermost platform, he watched her eyes traverse the columns surrounding them. Just as he expected, her expression mirrored his initial reaction.

"This is amazing," she said quietly. "How did you light it up?"

"I didn't. It was already like this when I got here," he replied. "Yuki, what do you make of this?"

"It's the Ryukyuan...an ancient tribal colony that lives in the nearby mountains. No one ever sees them, but some of the anointed ones have been known to frequent tombs. Once a month they add a mixture of propylene glycol and poi to the clay wall pots to keep them from going out."

"First the Egyptian influence and now this," Rachel quipped.

"Maybe, but that's not what I wanted to show you."

Rachel followed Chase's gaze to the cylindrical protrusion. Moments later, a booming sound echoed from below. She looked over the edge and around the entirety of the cavern, her brow furrowed all the while. "I don't want to alarm you," she said, "but we must have triggered something by climbing up here. There doesn't seem to be another door or room that leads out of here."

Chase stared down at the dais. "Then we better hope this thing opens another path or a doorway out."

Rachel laid her hand on his arm. "Let's not forget about the swords, okay?"

"Okay. We'll find the swords then get the hell out of here." Chase dusted off the clock-like system. "But I don't think we'll make any headway until we find the answer to this little puzzle."

"Let me take care of that, Cohen-san," Yuki said. "The last thing we need is to set off a booby trap."

He smirked at Yuki. He found it almost humorous that she could be cockier when immersed in her element. After they were free of dust and cobwebs, she attempted to turn the iron hands on the clock, but to no avail. Chase felt a pang of worry. There were no visible paths or means of entering the tomb, aside from the possibility of the puzzle opening one. And if the entire mechanism was as seized as the levers that operated it, they had no way to return to the surface. Something sparked in his mind as that thought ran through his brain. Whenever a gear on Stargazer stiffened, a little grease and oil was almost always the best answer. How was this any different?

Chase rummaged through his bag for the suntan oil Rachel had given him fits for packing. As he had told her at the time, "You never know when you'll need it."

"Got any ideas?" Yuki asked. "Try this," he answered.

Yuki glanced at him, then at the orange tube in his hands. "That just might work." She unscrewed it then immediately poured the entire contents on top of the dais. Chase watched the thick liquid trickle down between the teeth of each gear as well as the single pin that held both levers in place.

"Go ahead and use all of it," he sighed mockingly. "Do you wanna get out of the mess we're in or not?" she chided, waiting impatiently for the oil to settle between the thin cluster of gears and spindles. It was certainly a large amount for such a small area by comparison. If this didn't work, Chase had no solution to offer. After a few minutes, Yuki tried the small lever. It didn't budge at all. Once her patience was spent, Chase grabbed the longer lever with both hands and applied all the pressure he could muster. To his surprise, it creaked loose and turned clockwise.

"Yes!" Rachel cheered, giving Chase a playful shove. "Good job. Now we just have to figure out what the symbols mean and what time to set it to."

"Assuming it's a clock," Yuki said.

Chase snorted. "What else can it be? Just look at the damn thing! Now I need you to think. Is there any time of day that would have any relevance to the prince or this place?"

Yuki ran a hand over her mouth and chin in contemplation. The puzzle could have been set to any random time, and as far as Chase knew, Yuki wasn't a mathematician. But her scientific mind seemed to be toying with a plethora of theories as she circled the dais, squinting at the clock from every possible angle. Rachel stood back wearing a similar contemplative expression. She had an anxious look on her face, as if she couldn't wait to get her hands on the device, while he felt increasingly dimwitted as clueless seconds crawled by. Thankfully Yuki broke the silence with her voiced thoughts.

"Okay...let me go over what I do know. Prince Dai Ngami was the first son in his family. Although he didn't live up to his family's expectations, he was the third in line to rule the province. His wife had two sons, and the number twenty-one seems to have relevance, with him receiving the sword on his twenty-first birthday and the blue moon occurring on August twenty-first. There's also the matter of him being caught with his mistress at..." Yuki stopped midsentence. She turned the minute lever straight up then did the same with the shorter hour lever. "Midnight!" A slow smile spread across her face, but after a few seconds, when nothing happened, she stepped back, her expression cross. "Maybe not."

Chase frowned at the clock. If anyone was going to get the answer, it would have most likely been Yuki. He had virtually no ideas left, but then Rachel stepped forward to test her theory. She bent down, inspecting every centimeter of the clock's inner workings. The cluster of gears beneath the levers shrouded most of the system, partially blocking something that made her eyes widen. Beneath the levers, the pin that held them bore some sort of hinge—presumably allowing vertical movement.

"Yuki, what was the point of creating this type of temple?" Rachel asked.

"Well, in ancient times, the towers were used as observatories because they were the closest distance to the stars. Why do you ask?"

Rachel grinned in response. She dove into Chase's bag again, this time retrieving the rope he had carefully packed. With obvious excitement, she wedged the loop of the rope underneath the parallel levers.

"Hold on, what are you doing?" Chase asked as if she were about to eliminate their only access, which was entirely possible.

"I think I found the real reason for this tower," she replied. Before Chase could respond, she jerked the rope backward and was rewarded with a click before the slack loosened. The dial shifted to the right toward an ancient symbol resembling a planet, and remarkably, her idea proved correct. The sun reached its peak in the sky at high noon, even in medieval times. With both levers now pointed directly toward the ceiling, the gears whirred to life. A resounding bang followed and the tower beneath them shuddered, as if struck by a wrecking ball. The muffled sound of much larger cogs spinning filled the cavern, echoing across the high ceiling. The floor beneath them shook, and Chase felt the platform descend at a crawl as the sound of grinding stone filled the room.

"Oh my God! What did you do, Rachel?"

"Hopefully the right thing," she answered.

All three of them turned in time to see the top of the staircase rising above them, signaling that the tower itself was moving. Chase peeked over the edge and realized the platform they were standing on was slowly sinking into the slab below, revealing its hollow casting. The structure shook once, and the two platforms leveled out before sinking again. In the span of a minute, the triadic structure virtually fell into itself, inverting the entire tower even farther underground. The firelight on the walls did nothing to illuminate the stone pit that they now stood in, forcing them to depend on their dive lights.

Then, before any of them could say a word, the interior of the platform in front of them crumbled, kicking up a small cloud of dust. A small section of the granite fell, revealing a narrow stone passageway large enough for them to pass through.

Chase's jaw hung slightly; his eyes were wide in awe. "You never fail to amaze me," he said.

"I wasn't sure that would actually work." Rachel's eyes fell on the dais between them.

"Seems you're a lot smarter than you think."

"Actually, both of you figured out most of it," she said meekly.

He shook his head and snorted a laugh. "Baby, when are you going to learn how to accept a compliment?" Before she could answer, he took the lead once again. After ducking to squeeze through the entrance of the new pathway, he called back from the dark tunnel, "Well...you coming or what?"

"Right behind you," Yuki echoed back. Both women bowed their heads under the low ceiling, following their lights. As they drew near, Yuki's muffled comment reached Chase's sensitive ears. "Don't worry, he means well."

He chuckled softly. After the events of the past few days, that was exactly what he needed: laughter. The lighthearted banter between the women continued as they walked, and it was enough to allow him a rare moment of relaxation. He sighed at the mention of Shinzo's sacerdotal beliefs and heard Rachel do the same.

They were now a few hundred feet underground. The deeper they traveled, the narrower the tunnel grew. But its confined dimensions and drastic drop in temperature didn't bother Chase. It was the foul smell wafting through his nose that had become oppressive— the stench of something old and moist. He figured it was simply the natural aroma of the ancient caverns, dripping with the occasional trickle of water.

They walked in silence, their footsteps the only sound echoing down the stone passage. Chase continued to lead the way, unable to walk side by side with Rachel or Yuki due to the constricting walls. As he glanced back, he couldn't help noticing that Yuki's limp had worsened and her pace was governed by extreme care. He knew far too well how much pain a deep cut could cause. Fortunately for Yuki, her makeshift bandage wasn't bleeding through, despite being dampened from the dripping water.

After several silent minutes, Chase's thoughts became free to wander, mulling over accounts of the Asian woman's tainted life and the harrowing episode she had secretly shared regarding her deceased husband. He couldn't fathom how traumatizing it must have been being forced to watch him being brutally murdered right before her eyes. Yet here she was...reasonably sane. Determined to fulfill her mission by locating the two remaining swords in Prince Ngami's tomb. Had Yuki been so numbed by the horror she'd witnessed at a young age that her own brother's death paled in comparison? Perhaps that was why she appeared distracted at times— so uninvolved and secretive. And here he was...acting like a hard ass. Jumping down her throat over the faulty equipment, confiscating the sword, and reminding her that he was in change. He wouldn't blame her for hating him, now that he thought about it. She'd demonstrated her leadership ability whenever possible—at least for the most part.

Chase angled a look back over his shoulder and noticed that Yuki's expression had shifted from bleak to practically glowing with excitement.

"Look!" she yelled. "There's the end of the tunnel!" Ahead of them, the passage split in two directions, each branching off toward another vast expanse of darkness. To the right, liquid had pooled on the rock- embedded floor and was trailing down a slope into the dark unknown. If memory served him, this was the path on Yuki's map—the one she had pointed out to them.

She smiled and reached into her pack.

"Do you smell that?" she asked. "Crude shale kerosene...I'm sure of it. The tomb guardians use it to light their way." After withdrawing a box of matches, she struck one and dropped it on the ground, immediately igniting the fluid. She motioned them all back as a tongue of flame lashed out before traveling down the long line. Judging by the last tunnel, Chase expected to find another vast cavern illuminated in front of them. Instead, a tall hallway came into view with flames erupting from alcoves carved into the bedrock, ascending clear to the ceiling. The floor was made of sandstone tiles, chipped and eroded with age. At the other end of the long hallway was a doorless threshold. Their destination was clear, but Chase knew getting there wasn't going to be as easy as it seemed.

Unsurprisingly enough, it didn't take more than a second for his dread to be confirmed. As soon as the flames hit the long niche in the wall, chaos erupted in the hall. Five slits in the stone revealed enormous swinging scimitar-like blades suspended from thick lengths of rope secured to the ceiling. The horizontal guillotines swung in interchanging intervals, preventing them from making a straight run through to the other side.

Chase shot a sidelong glance at Rachel, who he expected to be wearing a look of pure horror. Instead, her green-blue hazel eyes had erupted with their signature flame. An insane grin spread across her face, followed by crazy laugher. "Didn't I say Indiana Jones?"

Yuki appeared to be stumped. "This wasn't here before," she claimed. "It's either been added or one of us triggered another trap."

"So how the hell do we deal with those?" Chase asked. "I'm not looking to get a clean shave and I sure doubt you are."

Yuki's eyes were transfixed on the swinging blades at the end of the hall. "Cohen-san, do you know how long I've been waiting for something like this to come along? To be able to atone for my mistakes?"

Chase cocked an eyebrow. "Hold on, just what are you talking about? You're starting to creep me out."

"Good. Now turn your fear into energy because you're going to need it." She pointed to the expanse of floor in front of them and spewed out quick instructions. "We don't have a lot of time, so listen carefully. We have about twenty feet of safe passage, right? Wrong. Notice how the floor has changed from stone to tiles. Unless the temple creators had a mind for making raiders' deaths more luxurious, I think we're looking at another trap. Check this out." She pointed left to a closer portion of wall, forcing Chase and Rachel to notice the pinholes in the stone. "That's a classic booby trap...a wall of poisoned projectiles. I can guarantee that ninety percent of these tiles will trigger its firing mechanism. In fact, look at the floor." Their eyes traversed the seemingly uniform tiles. "Only someone with keen vision and experience in this stuff would catch the trail of tiles set just a little lower in the stone all the way down the hall."

"That's impossible. We'll never make it!" Chase bellowed.

"Look," Yuki said, pointing above their heads. Chase's eyes widened at the plume of black smoke coming from the ceiling. It was thickening by the second and would eventually engulf the entire cavern. "I don't know what I was thinking. I shouldn't have lit that trail. "

"You've got to be kidding me," Chase groaned. "We've got no choice...other than going back the way we came."

"Oh no!" Rachel yelped. She motioned at the slab of stone that was slowly closing the passageway behind them. "What are we going to do now?"

Chase grit his teeth. If they didn't move fast, they were all going to suffocate in a matter of minutes. "You're right," he told Yuki. "You fucked up big time. Now screw your head back on and get us the hell out of here!"

# 27

"We can't afford to make a wrong move," Yuki warned them. "I'll mark where you need to step. Jump to the tiles where I leave flat stone markers and only when I tell you to."

With every word she spoke, Rachel's apprehension grew into a crippling fear. Her legs quivered and her shoulders followed suit. Her gaze shifted from Chase to the closing door forty feet away, searching for an alternative solution.

Yuki evidently saw the fear in her face as she called out, "Turn it into adrenaline or we'll all die. Now follow my lead!" Rachel kept her eyes on Yuki as she tucked her arms to her sides and leaped to a shallow tile of sandstone almost a yard away. As planned, she laid a stone down and continued on, providing the only safe path. She moved slowly but surely while approaching the enormous swinging blades.

Rachel took a long breath and gathered whatever courage she could harness. With Chase's steady gaze behind her and his constant words of encouragement, she jumped to the first marker, almost falling forward and onto one of the many triggers Yuki had pointed out. She quickly regained her balance and leaped to every designated tile as instructed. Then, with barely three feet to go, she stopped in her tracks. Both feet were confined to one small piece of beige stone. She stood frozen, looking for the next square tile—contemplating her best life-saving move. Had Yuki forgot to mark the trail to the end, or was that her intention? Was she planning to deliberately leave them behind?

"Rachel!" Chase called out. He coughed repeatedly from the black smoke pouring from the ceiling above him. The door behind him was now halfway closed. "Make a move! Now!" he yelled.

She faced forward and saw that Yuki had cleared the first blade guarding the tomb's open doorway. With an unintelligible cry, she followed her lead. She leaped past the first blade, just barely avoiding the giant silver edge. But less than a yard separated each swinging guillotine, forcing her to confine her body to a single tile.

Rachel knew that for the time being, Chase was a sitting duck. The smoke was getting thicker, and seeing would soon be impossible. From the sound of his coughing, he was choking on the putrid air. His time was slipping away quickly and depended on her and Yuki's success in clearing the obstacles. At Yuki's call, Rachel's head snapped up to find her already between the second and third blade, signaling for her to jump yet again. She wasted no time in complying and kept her eyes forward, unwilling to look at the blade hurtling toward her from the right. In hindsight, she realized it was a big mistake. Midway through her jump, she felt the cold steel scrape against her back. She cried out in agony before landing haphazardly on the next stone-marked tile.

Chase shrieked her name in terror as she wavered on trembling legs. She felt warm blood trickle down her back and knew she'd been seriously cut.

"Rachel!" Chase blasted again before breaking into a coughing fit. "Are you okay?"

"Keep moving!" she yelled back. "Don't worry about me." Even from where she stood, she could see his sky-blue eyes, wide and fearful for her well being. Nonetheless, she turned around and found her moment, bypassing the third blade and landing safely on the other side. She watched helplessly from the edge as Chase did everything he could to focus, gritting his teeth in the effort.

"Chase! Jump now!" Yuki and Rachel yelled in chorus. At their call, he leaped forward, allowing himself more than enough room to land. He did the same with the next blade, while Rachel stood at the safe end of the hallway, urging him on.

"Just one more jump," she called out. His reaction was instantaneous. He didn't wait for Yuki's signal or watch for the approaching swing of the final guillotine. Instead, he dove forward, his eyes darting to the swinging razor edge a mere yard from his face, closing in too fast to avoid.

"Oh my God! Chase!" Rachel screamed. "Watch out!"

The world slowed to a crawl as Chase watched the final moment of his life flash before him. This was it. Everything he knew, every dream he ever hoped for was about to disappear in a swift slice of cold steel. Coming here was all for nothing. All the hard work he had put into diving, staking claims, finding treasure, making a name for himself...none of it mattered. Only the thought of Rachel's fearful face registered in his brain and the memory of his young daughter kissing him goodbye an hour before he boarded his flight for Japan. What had he done to deserve dying like this, in the worst possible way imaginable? Was this really the end? His last view before dying?

It couldn't be, not like this. He wasn't about to call it quits. He was Chase Cohen, captain of the Stargazer, treasure hunter extraordinaire, Rachel Lyons's partner, soul mate, and husband...if she'd have him, that is. He had more reasons to live than anyone, even if he were crippled by his effort.

"No!" With a cry of defiant outrage, Chase reached over his shoulder and snatched Kokoro from its scabbard in midair. Before the guillotine reached him, he brought the steel of the sword between the blade's razor edge and his face. Sparks flew as the two collided, throwing Chase through the air and into the wall, knocking the wind from his lungs and leaving him crumpled on the ground. When he looked up, the giant blade rested only inches away, miraculously frozen in place. He thought of Kokoro's demise and his broken promise to Shinzo—all for the sake of his life. But then he looked back at Rachel gasping and Yuki standing apart, and a remarkable sight took shape. The Asian warrior, hero to their cause, was holding the Heart of Darkness sword in both hands...sliding it back into its scabbard and peering at him over its perfect, unscarred edge.

The stone slab closed with a trembling thud, sending a slight quake through the cavern floor and trapping the nauseating odor in the air. The flickering wall sconces now cast an eerie blue glow, illuminating their immediate surroundings. Chase got back on his feet and edged his way past the blade to join Rachel. Her trembling hands were rummaging through her black nylon bag, searching for the roll of gauze and tape she'd packed earlier that day.

"Here...let me help you," he said. She turned around, revealing a long cut. Chase allowed himself a short sigh of relief once he saw that the wound wasn't as deep as he feared. However, it was enough to draw a steady flow of crimson. He tore strips of tape with his teeth and quelled the bleeding with a layer of gauze. Then he glimpsed the blood-soaked cloth on Yuki's leg. "Do you mind if I have a look at that?" he asked her.

She offered the sword back, but he declined, believing she'd more than earned the right to protect it. After slinging it over her shoulder, she moved closer and knelt down to remove her makeshift bandage. Chase dropped down beside her, trying to shake off the light- headed feeling—the strange sense of not really being himself.

"I'm not great at apologizing, but I meant it," he said as he doubled up the gauze to cover the gash in her thigh. "Don't worry…it happens," she said, making light of her injury. "I'm just glad you're okay."

"Seems you have a magic sword there."

"In Japan, they believe a man's spirit is ingrained in his weapon." She reached up and reverently touched Kokoro's handle. "Masamune and Prince Ngami's are definitely in this one."

Chase couldn't take his eyes off the remarkable woman in front of him. The passion she carried for the sword was evident in her eyes and parting with it would require incredible willpower. Combined with her fiery personality, there was no doubt in his mind Yuki Ota could excel in whatever she set out to accomplish.

"It's my fault, you know," she said. "I made a terrible mistake taking Kokoro, and now you're both here risking your lives. I don't know what Shinzo was thinking by bringing you here."

"It doesn't really matter at this point," Chase told her. "You've proved your worth in more ways than one. So let's just get this job done and—"

Chase stopped short with the feel of Rachel's hand on his shoulder. "I don't know if anyone has considered this besides me," she said, "but exactly how are we planning to get out of here? Because obviously it's not the way we came."

As he looked back at the sealed door and silent blade, he realized she was right. Within a fraction of a second, his life would have been over, and now all of their lives were at stake. Not since his gut-wrenching battle to save Rachel's father did he feel so weak and vulnerable. He'd always been confident in his ability to take huge risks and laugh in the face of death, but he realized when it came to protecting the ones he cared about most, he'd grown reckless and irresponsible. When would he ever learn? Could he even go on with his passion for recovering treasure and defining the unknown after this? Even if he was alone the next time, the memories would always be there.

He turned to Rachel. "Why did you come with me? You should have stayed away...kept your distance while you had the chance. But of course you didn't. And now look what I've gotten you into." Chase couldn't look at her anymore. He shut his eyes and turned away.

"How can you say that? I admit it hasn't been easy over the past four years. But despite everything we've been through, I've hung in there. I signed onto this partnership for better or worse, and overcoming our differences has proven to be a test of wills. If our relationship survives this, and I sincerely hope it does, I'll be the happiest woman on the planet. But right now we need to focus on getting the hell out of here."

Chase had no idea how Rachel had such an effect on him, to make his emotions run high at every turn. Perhaps it wasn't her specifically. Perhaps it had simply been too long since he allowed his feelings to overflow like this. It would certainly explain the past three days more clearly. Rachel had become his confidant, his closest friend. His trusted lover with no demands or expectations. Even if her feelings didn't run as deep as his, he needed her. He couldn't be alone right now, not at this point in his life.

Yuki's sharp intake of breath echoed through the room. Chase immediately turned and saw the source of her concern. Near the crack in the wall, she had discovered what appeared to be small chunks of bone and a shattered skull surrounded by tattered clothing. Just a few feet away, in the opposite corner, there was another skull—this one neatly sliced in two. He saw that Rachel had also noticed what Yuki was staring at and was looking on in equal disbelief. He crossed the cavern with carefully laid steps. As he bent down for a closer inspection, he heard a sound that chilled him to the bone. A woman's voice, whispering in his ear. "Get out." And then an even more desperate warning. "Run!"

He turned to Yuki, who had obviously heard it too. Both she and Rachel moved quickly toward the only exit in the chamber. With equal determination, they squirmed and squeezed their way through the crack in the wall, entering the tomb's inner chamber. As soon as they were safely inside, the floor of the outer chamber began to tremble and groan. A very faint humming drone began to resonate in Chase's ears. The ground he stood on was now shaking so badly that he was convinced an earthquake had started and the walls were going to collapse any minute. He stuck his right leg through the crack first. With his head and one arm now inside, he pushed against the wall, trying to force his way through. If he didn't know better, he would have thought the space was shrinking right before his eyes. He struggled and struggled, angling his shoulder and flattening his body the best he could, almost frantic to squeeze through. Rachel dropped her flashlight and grabbed his arm. She tugged with both hands. Yuki joined in and Chase moaned from the sheer agony of being pulled so hard. He looked up at Rachel and could see complete terror in her eyes. Then he felt it. A cold hand wrapping its fingers around his ankle, gripping tighter and tighter. Tugging him in the opposite direction.

"Something is holding my leg! Something is holding my leg! Pull harder!" he screamed.

Using all their strength, both women yanked at the same time and pulled him through, falling to the ground in a heap. As his left foot cleared the opening, he looked back and gasped. Rachel's dropped flashlight had reflected on something resembling a hand. At least it bore the same shape, minus any discernable fingers. It vanished into the dark, and all the while, the droning noise grew louder and louder. The glow in the outer chamber intensified, turning blood red in a matter of seconds and illuminating the crack they had crawled through.

He closed his eyes, covered his ears, and yelled at the top of his lungs, "What the hell are you?" Instantly the light faded to darkness. The droning hum stopped and the rotten stench in the air faded. The only sounds he could hear were his pounding heart and the heavy breathing of the women huddled around him.

# 28

When Rachel turned, the first thing she saw was a shimmering, futuristic-looking mummy. She drew a slow, calming breath before edging closer to the stone slab. The strange armor-like suit covering Prince Dai Ngami's body was made of rectangular pieces of green jade, joined by silver wires threaded through small holes drilled near the corners of each piece. His feet, hands, and head were sealed in what appeared to be ivory. Matching plaques were used to hide his eyes and plugs to fill his ears and nose. By all appearances, it seemed every orifice in his body had been addressed.

Badly in need of a distraction, Rachel looked down at the collection of artifacts surrounding him. They were items she would have never imagined being stored in a tomb: a horse saddle, leather straps, metal ornaments, mirrors, and other trappings, along with crude pottery made of bronze. She knelt down and reached into one of the bronze pots, withdrawing a handful of curved jadeite stones. Then she looked up at Yuki, who seemed to be keeping a watchful eye. "What are these?" Rachel asked.

"They're magatama." Yuki took one of the jewels from Rachel's palm and rolled it between her fingers, studying it more closely. "Each stone is a tama and is part of tamashi...the spirit. They're beautiful to look at but are filled with bad karma. Some of the priests from the local village practiced an ancient voodoo magic known as *ushi no koku mairi* and often used them for casting spells. I suggest you put them back."

She dropped the one she held back into Rachel's hand just as a gust of cold air passed by. It was immediately followed by a disgusting odor that brought the thought of rotting meat to mind. The torches on the four walls surrounding them flickered wildly and glowed even brighter. Rachel stood and looked around for Chase. He was standing toward the back of the chamber, smoothing his hands over the rock wall.

"There's something here," he said. "I can feel a draft. I think there might be a room on the other side." He pushed against a rectangular stone, triggering a hidden blowpipe and sending a small dart flying at lightning speed. "Ow! That hurt!" He pulled the dart from the side of his neck and examined what had hit him before tossing it to the ground.

"I told you they were everywhere," Yuki said.

For a moment Chase looked crestfallen. Then he glanced back at Rachel with a crooked smile. "Well, I guess that's one less dart we have to worry about."

Rachel flashed a quick smile. Moments later, another chill hit the air. "Chase? Did you feel that?" she asked.

As he turned to face her, a black cloud of soot rose from the floor in the center of the tomb. It assumed a dark silhouette, almost human in shape. Yuki quickly picked up a mirror from the ground and began chanting strange words—some foreign language Rachel didn't recognize or could ever hope to understand. She stood before Rachel and Chase with the glass reflecting outward, blocking the apparition from coming closer. It slowed as if it had legs and seemed to take a step back. Then a light began to emanate from the adjoining chamber. It wasn't red as it had been previously, but a white light, almost too bright to look at. The ghostly figure appeared to be struggling against it, but fruitlessly—it was literally being dragged back through the crack in the wall, letting loose a deafening scream in protest. When the light seemed to envelope the evil creature the screaming wail was silenced and the light retreated back into the cave with its prisoner as quickly as it had appeared.

Yuki readjusted the sword on her back, while Rachel and Chase stared in stunned disbelief. "Try not to be distracted," Yuki warned. "They're here. I can feel them. The swords are buried in the floor or somewhere near the altar. Look for any loose stones or unusual markings." Chase blew out a deep breath and moved gingerly toward the prince's body. As he ran his palm over the surface surrounding him, Rachel joined him and began inspecting the bottom of the raised platform. After a few minutes, her fingers found a loose tile.

"I think there's something here," she said. With sheer determination, she lifted the heavy slate and set it aside. Chase squatted down beside her and helped her remove another section, exposing a chiseled-out two foot square cubicle. Inside they found a primitive clay pot and scattered magatama stones, much like the ones Rachel had found in the bronze pot.

Chase motioned for the Asian warrior to join them. "Look at that," he told her. Pressed into the interior wall was a distinct impression of a short sword...now missing. Yuki masked her disappointment with a trite response. "We don't know for certain if the tanto we're looking for is the same weapon that was stored there."

Rachel came to her feet. "Well, someone's ashes are definitely inside, and I have a sneaking feeling it's the general's wife. If her father practiced voodoo like you said, don't you think it's possible he buried her with the tanto to protect herself?"

"Of course. But there's no way of knowing for sure. And there's still the wakizashi to think about. So, if you don't mind, I suggest we keep looking."

Chase resumed his position behind the prince and began studying the walls and floors more carefully. "Am I seeing things or are those footprints in the dust?" he asked.

Rachel took a few steps closer. "I see them too. They're going in both directions…as if someone was circling around this room." As her eyes followed the faint trail, a whirring noise filled her ears. It started out small and seemed to grow in volume. She looked around anxiously, dreading the aftermath of a mislaid step. "Where's that sound coming from?" she asked.

The ground began shaking slightly. She took a step back and noticed a widening crack before her. Without warning, the floor beneath her suddenly split apart, dropping her onto a pile of bones in an eight-foot deep pit.

"Ahhhh!" Rachel screamed. She scrambled to get off the skeletal remains and flattened her back against the dirt wall. Directly across from her was another wall covered with drilled holes.

Chase was instantly there, reaching down for her hand. She raised her arm high over her head, but something within her compelled her to move. *Now!* Rachel jumped back as razor-sharp spikes suddenly came bursting out of the holes. She dropped to the ground and waited. Then she looked up and realized she'd barely missed getting hit by all of them.

"Holy shit!" came from Chase. Yuki looked equally shocked. "Are you all right?" he called down to her. Rachel wanted to curl into a ball and whimper, but she had no desire to stick around. With her knees still shaking, she managed to stand and slide along the wall, avoiding the knifelike spear tips. She made a grab for Chase's wrists with both hands, and he dragged her out of the unmarked grave and into his comforting arms.

"Look!" Yuki shouted. "Under the spears, right there. I think it's a sword. Can you see it?"

The middle section of the wall had crumbled away, exposing a small hidden channel. Inside was an exposed black butt cap. Chase released Rachel and lowered himself to his knees then onto his belly. He stretched his arm until his fingers gripped the very end of the sword. Then he began withdrawing it slowly between the spears. As soon as it was halfway out, he grabbed the handle firmly and drew back onto his knees. He remained still for several seconds until he was sure it was safe to stand. When he did, Yuki was there to take the weapon from his hands. She wiped it off on her shirt and extracted the sword from its scabbard. Then she ran her fingertips across the steel, examining it thoroughly.

The corners of her lips curled. "It's the missing wakizashi sword. Look! There's a ruby on the scabbard, just like the legend said."

Rachel stared in disbelief. The second sword was as beautiful as the first. When unsheathed, it appeared to be remarkably flawless and its edge as sharp as the day it was made. The brilliant ruby shimmered in the light with the same intensity as the demon light they had encountered, reminding Rachel of the growing threat surrounding them.

Chase smiled and wrapped his arms around her. "Let's finish up and find a way out of here…quick." She looked up at him and smiled nervously. Without wasting another minute, he released her and joined Yuki in her search for the last sword.

As soon as his back was turned, Rachel shivered with the feeling of being observed. It was as if the dead were standing in the corners watching them. While Yuki held a torch near the hole and Chase prodded the loose dirt with a stick he'd found, Rachel's mental impression grew. It became so strong that it personified itself into a specific entity she imagined abstractly as a young Asian woman about twenty years of age with dark, deep-set eyes. They were so black in fact that they bled into and around her sockets like cast shadows. Yet the skin on her face was pale—almost to the point of pure white.

Rachel couldn't call this an actual conscious image. It was an instinct, a heart-racing impression that no one else could see or understand...not even Chase. It was beyond logic and reason—something she couldn't possibly explain even if she tried. This entity was composed from a feeling rather than visual imagination. At the same time the vision appeared a stream of thoughts entered her head. It was as if the entity was communicating with her telepathically. Telling her something important—something essential they all needed to know.

Suddenly the thoughts in her mind became real, jarring her consciousness, manifesting themselves into loud, blaring words. She covered her ears and squeezed her eyes shut and screamed at the top of her lungs, "Take the swords and leave now, before he kills all of you!"

# 29

Rachel covered her mouth to stifle her scream. Her eyes were wide with alarm. She saw Chase staring back at her, shock evident in his enormous blue eyes.

"Who are you talking about?" he demanded.

"There was someone here."

"Where?" He stood up and looked around. "I don't see anything."

She couldn't shake the feeling that another person was among them—an oppressed, invisible presence that no one could see or hear. No one except her. "There's a spirit of a dead woman in this room. She's been showing me things, horrible visions of people dying, decapitated bodies, and blood splattered walls. There's evil spirits haunting this place. We need to get out while we still can."

The woman's voice was back, speaking softly in Rachel's ear…directing her toward the prince and telling her it was the only way out. While Chase stood back watching, Rachel moved around the raised platform, running her hand along its stone edge. Then she stopped and took a half step back as she felt a tiny crack in the invisible seam.

"It's here," she said. She pressed harder, and the sound of a click hit the air. The catch in the hidden door released, separating it from the wall by mere inches.

Yuki looked up at her openmouthed then glanced around the chamber in wild suspicion. "How did you find that? Who showed you?"

"You wouldn't believe it if I told you," Rachel answered.

Yuki's attention returned to the hole in the ground. She was hanging over its edge, barely holding on. Reaching down to retrieve something. When she finally eased back, Rachel spotted the glittering stone between her fingers. She watched as Yuki took a small pouch out of her fanny pack before returning to the hole again. She was picking up stone after stone, tucking them away as quickly as possible. It seemed she had a hidden agenda in coming here all along—a secret she'd kept to herself. With Chase's attention now fixed on the opening in the wall, Rachel realized he didn't have a clue as to what was going on.

"Is that what this was all about?" Rachel snapped. "Stealing jewels from a grave?"

Yuki disregarded her and continued scrounging for every stone she could get her hands on.

"What's going on here?" Chase directed his words at Rachel. He spotted Yuki frantically digging away and walked over to where she was working. Without saying a word, he leaned down to pick up one of the stones she had inadvertently dropped and brought the torch close to his hand. The gem shimmered in the flickering light.

"What's this?" he asked Yuki. "You never said anything about diamonds."

"The priest dumped them all over General Maeda's body. They're worth millions!"

"Why would anyone do that?" Chase asked. He looked back at Rachel as if expecting an answer, and strangely, she had one.

"They were given to the general's wife as a gift. But her father cursed them along with their souls."

Chase stared at Rachel in disbelief. Then he turned back to Yuki and pitched the stone into the grave. "We're leaving. Now!"

She swung her eyes up at him. "I can't. Not yet. You and Rachel go on ahead. I'll catch up as soon as I—"

"No!" he shouted. "I'm not leaving anyone behind. Grab your stuff and let's go."

"But what about the last sword? It might still be in here."

"Really? And how long were you planning to stay? Until you could steal everything you could get your hands on?" Chase was standing over her frowning. She begrudgingly accepted his outstretched hand, and he pulled her back onto her feet. Rachel stood back watching as he crossed the chamber quickly and pried the door open, using his shoulder for leverage. When there was enough room for all of them to fit through, he motioned for both women to join him.

The air suddenly grew cold. The droning sound was back. Rachel looked around and saw a dark cloud seeping from the cornerstone in the room, growing larger with every passing second. A man's black-hooded image was in her mind, becoming sharper with each passing second. Could this be the unholy priest? The twisted soul who could conjure up demons? Somehow she knew he was connected to the approaching evil and that he had no intention of letting anyone leave.

As if sensing her fear, the woman's voice was back, whispering loudly in Rachel's ear. "It's gone...gone. Hurry...hurry. He's coming. He's coming." Rachel repeated the frightening words faster and faster. She screamed in unison with the voice, "He's here!"

Chase picked up the wakizashi sword and led the way as they passed through the doorway and scrambled into the dark tunnel. Even with the light from the wall torches still lit behind them and his flashlight blazing the way, the spiraling portal was disorienting. Fear seemed to be affecting all of them. If Chase wasn't tripping on something or banging his head, then it was Rachel and Yuki. They'd made enough turns while climbing steadily upward that the light from below should have been left far behind. But instead it seemed to be getting closer and brighter, lighting the tunnel below in a sickly red light. They finally reached a long, straight section, but as they neared its end, the passageway split off in two directions.

"That way!" Rachel yelled, pointing left. "Go that way!"

They picked up speed and managed to distance themselves from the light below. Yet they couldn't outrun the overpowering stench and the droning sound that had grown louder and more high-pitched, like a copper teakettle approaching its boiling point. Chase and Rachel reached the far end of the tunnel at the same time and discovered the dirt-layered incline was the only means of escape. Rachel looked back at Yuki. Although her face was clothed in near darkness, the tip of Kokoro's gleaming black scabbard could still be seen above her shoulder.

"Is everyone okay?" Chase asked.

"Yes," Rachel answered for both of them. While they took a short breather, she pressed the built-in light on her watch to check the time and was shocked to discover they'd been gone for three hours. The boat captain had undoubtedly given up on them by now. He'd be back at the dock eating his warm supper, as Rachel's growling stomach longed to be doing.

"We have to get going," she told Chase. "It will be dark out-side soon. Since we have no map to go by, there's no way of know-ing where we'll end up."

"What about your spirit guide?" Yuki snipped. "Don't tell me she bailed on us now?"

Rachel ignored her sarcasm. "I have no idea what that was about. I just know we need to get out of here as quickly as possible."

Chase crouched down slightly. "Okay…here goes." He sprang toward the dirt slope with the sword in his hand and began drag-ging himself upward. Rachel and Yuki followed suit, duplicat-ing his efforts. It wasn't so steep that they couldn't transverse it, but for every two feet they gained, they slid back a foot, mak-ing the climb even harder. The light from below was beginning to encroach on them again and the droning had become even louder and more high-pitched.

They finally reached what appeared to be the top of the mound. However, an old wooden trapdoor rested above them, barring their way. Chase explored options on how to open it. First he tried pressing the door with both arms high over his head. The door held fast, as if something heavy was holding it down. He searched the edges of the wood casement for a hole or some type of opening as a start for digging them out. But there was nothing visible under his flashlight. Then Rachel and Yuki joined him in pushing with all their might. It was useless. Nothing was going to budge it. Finally they screamed for help while pounding on the trapdoor. As if drawn by their pleas, the light below came after them like a magnet. It seemed to be just around the corner from the straight section of the tunnel. Then it swerved and rushed upward, heading straight for them. It flickered wildly and glowed with blinding intensity.

"Cover your eyes!" Rachel screamed. The light flew by them, exploding into a million glittering pieces, vanishing into the fine cracks above them.

From the halls of hell beneath them came a gurgling, almost demonic sound. It was storming through the winding tunnel... coming closer by the second. Yuki and Chase were pressed against the packed dirt wall with their faces turned away and their eyes closed tight in fear. But something inside Rachel kept her strong and alert. She stood just beneath the wood hatch with her teeth clenched and her gaze fixed downward in defiance. The gurgling sound transformed into a primal scream and flew up the tunnel right past her. The air was searing hot and putrid as it swirled and followed after the entity. The tiny hairs on Rachel's arms stood on end as the woman's tortured scream tore through her body. Then the dark, semisolid mass followed in pursuit, blasting through the trapdoor like an invisible missile. Shards of wood rained down on them as the final rays of daylight flooded in, exposing their shocked, dirt-covered faces.

Almost as if reading each other's minds they shot through the exit: Chase first, then reaching back to help Rachel and Yuki. They stood up on a field of dry grass, brushing off their bathing suits and grimy skin. Then they lifted their eyes and just stared at each other, as if waiting for someone to make a move.

A man dressed in a white hooded garment came around the corner from the crumpling remains of an ancient walled fortress. Although his head was down, Rachel sensed something vaguely familiar about him: the confident stride and compact stature, the air of peace and harmony he naturally emitted.

The stranger flipped his hood back, and Rachel knew his face instantly. "Hello, Shinzo. How did you find us?" she said, never so thrilled to see anyone in her life. However, her broad smile waned at the sight of his jaded brown eyes. She followed his line of vision and realized he was staring at Yuki and the two swords in her hands. The mission he'd sent them on had been all for nothing. They'd failed miserably, and it was Rachel's fault. At least for the most part.

"If it's about the tanto knife, I can explain," she tried. "You see, I heard this woman's voice and she told me it wasn't there and I—"

"No," he said, cutting her off. "There's no need. Goals are like the stars. They're always there. Defeat is like the clouds. They're temporary and move on. Be proud of yourself, Rachel-san. You surpassed what you set out to accomplish."

Her mouth sagged. "I did?"

"Since it wasn't possible for the trapped spirits to cross over water, you delivered them through the passageway. As the result of your inner strength and God-given intuition, you've fulfilled your obligation threefold."

"But what about the tanto?" Yuki asked.

"If Rachel says it's not there, then I believe her, and finding it becomes another matter altogether. There's only one person who can disclose its true whereabouts. The person who has it. Unfortunately, at this point, there's no telling who that might be."

"So what do we do now?" Chase asked Shinzo, concern evident in his voice.

"You've done all you can, I assure you. Take Rachel back to your hotel in Tokyo and get some rest. You've got a long flight home tomorrow. As for me, it's time to join members of my congregation who have been patiently waiting for my return."

"What about the swords we found?" Chase asked. "Should we take them with us?"

"I appreciate your concern, but I prefer to keep them with me this evening to pray over. I will meet all of you in Tokyo tomorrow morning. We can only hope the tanto will miraculously turn up by then." He nodded at a taxi parked a short distance away. "Miss Lyons, there's a car waiting to take you to the inn to freshen up. Yuki will help arrange transportation back to the airport."

He held out taxi fare, and when Yuki reached for it, he held her hand for an extended moment. Rachel's eyes searched Yuki's and saw something unreadable in her face. She thought she saw her smirk, just a little. But if she did, she hid it well.

"What about you?" Rachel asked him. "How will you get home?"

"Please don't worry. I'm meeting with my superiors at Tochoji temple later tonight. Then I have a train to catch. I'll be back before you know it."

As Rachel watched Shinzo walk away, she could almost see his anguish, like a dark cloud hovering above him, and by the gloom on Yuki's face, she was feeling its thunder.

"I don't understand," Rachel said. "Surely there's something we can do. I feel like we're leaving Japan without finishing our job."

Yuki's eyes were down. She seemed to be deep in thought—contemplating a solution no one had thought of yet. "There's someone I need to call," she finally said. "A man who might have the answer to this mystery. Shinzo may have given up, but I haven't." She smiled, but it wasn't true. It didn't reach her eyes and instead fell flat after a few seconds. "The meter's running," she said. "We should get going."

Rachel's hand instinctively reached for Chase's. Her stomach churned, and she chewed anxiously on her lip. She couldn't help noticing no mention was made of their harrowing escape or the fact that Yuki's fanny pack was now carrying diamonds.

# 30

ariko took a deep breath and decided it was time to be brave and ignore the whispers of her troubled heart. She looked down into the casket for a full thirty seconds and tried to convince herself that Kenji was simply sleeping and would wake up any moment now. But his unnatural complexion and posed hands vanquished the notion. As prescribed by the Buddhist faith, his body had been reassembled and washed thoroughly prior to dressing. He had on a white kimono crossed right over left in proper funeral manner and wore white leather sandals, which seemed odd, since there was no reason to believe he'd actually owned a pair. Rose-colored prayer beads lay over his hands, and above them were six coins for traversing the River of Three Crossings. Beside them were a pack of Marlboro cigarettes and a roll of his favorite breath mints to enjoy on his journey.

Two hundred members of the Zakura-kai were in attendance. They solemnly and systematically passed by the small assembly of mourners: Kaito Mitsui, two of his henchmen, Kenji's mother,

Nikki Ota, and Mariko Abe. His sister Yuki was conspicuously absent along with his best friend, Takashi Bekku.

"I'm sorry for your loss," each of them murmured as they left envelopes of condolence money in the red lacquered dish. With a concerted effort, Mariko lifted her eyes to take in the sea of faces and the scene playing out before them. Everyone was talking quietly among themselves and stilled suddenly to listen to shared comments and prayers. There were so many flower arrangements filling the temple that it looked like a botanical garden. A photograph of a smiling Kenji leaned on a wood easel at the side of his coffin—perhaps a reminder to all as to who was lying inside.

Throughout the funeral, lavender incense burned on the altar and was accompanied by sutra chants from the local priest. Kenji was given a new Buddhist name written in elegant Kanji to prevent his untimely return. Then, at the end of the funeral service, as each guest passed by a final time, they placed flowers in the coffin around Kenji's head and shoulders as a tribute to the assassin they'd grown to fear and admire.

Mitsui leaned forward so Mariko could hear his soft words. "A car is waiting outside. I think it would be best if you sat next to Kenji's mother."

As instructed, Mariko slid into the back seat of the second stretch limo. She stared at her hands resting on top of her black kimono during the ten-minute ride to the crematorium. With her stomach tied up in knots, she stared through the tinted window at the majestic red maple trees lining the mountain road. She wondered what Kenji would have thought of the beautiful scenery and if the hills would have been similar in Thailand.

Even now, with the fan cranked on high, the air in the car was sweltering. Mariko could feel perspiration collecting on the back of her neck and at the base of her spine and couldn't imagine how Mitsui and Nikki Ota were coping. Throughout the ride, in their black attire, they remained stoic. Not a single word passed between them. Once they arrived, the driver assisted with their doors, placing a gloved hand above their heads to prevent them from hitting the top of the door panel. Everyone who had attended the funeral service moved like wooden soldiers toward the stone building's massive double doors. With one glimpse to her right, Mariko couldn't help noticing the army of dark-suited, white-tied men exiting their matching Lexus and Mercedes Benz cars. Just as remarkable were the forty police officers lined up to observe the same gang members, as they had done throughout the funeral.

Once inside, four bodyguards were escorted to a waiting area while Mariko and her solemn faction entered an adjacent room. As she stood by bidding her final farewell, Kenji's elm coffin was closed and placed on a rolling metal tray. The geisha stared in disbelief as the automated door on the redbrick oven slowly lifted.

This isn't real...this isn't real, she kept telling herself. The heat in the room dramatically increased as Kenji's body was rolled into the glowing red flames. The end of the wood coffin ignited immediately. Mitsui tapped Mariko on the shoulder and encouraged her to leave as the door slowly lowered and the coffin became fully engulfed. They walked side by side into the waiting area to join his entourage drinking green tea and observing mourners with oversized portraits of their departed loved ones.

Two excruciating hours later, an attendant in a white smock appeared and escorted their small group into a private, sterile room. A metal gurney was rolled in once again. But this time, it was carrying Kenji's fully intact skeleton, leaving

Mariko gasping beneath her hand. Mitsui held out a pair of long chopsticks and urged her to take part in the surreal ritual of picking up hollowed-out bones and transferring them to the marble urn.

"The feet are always first," Mitsui explained to her. "The bones of the head are last. This ensures the proper order. We wouldn't want Kenji going to heaven upside down." If not for the stern expression on his face, Mariko would have viewed the mob boss's words as an attempt at crude humor.

Beside her, Nikki took her chopsticks in hand and appeared unaffected as she delivered bone after bone. One of Kenji's associates was next, followed by the attendant. As soon as Mitsui was finished, he moved away from the others, allowing Mariko room to step forward. She had no interest in taking part, but after a backward glance at Nikki's stern expression, she swallowed hard and picked up a small section of Kenji's lower leg. She watched in strange fascination as the attendant crushed it with a pestle before adding it to the urn.

The process continued over and over, seeming to take forever. When nearly every bone was disposed of, the attendant cleared his throat. "Ota-san was a healthy man," he said, assuming the role of his physician. "It's most evident by the density and color of his bones. I don't know if you realize this, but they have to be fired at over twelve hundred degrees to come out so perfectly preserved." He lifted a severed bone from the neck area. "Ah...the hyoid. Unfortunately, this bone has been badly damaged. It usually looks like a heart."

The man took great care in covering the crushed remains with a black velvet cloth. He tucked it neatly into the jar and added the top of Kenji's skull. Then the urn was paired with its matching lid and formally presented to Nikki. The large black-and-white portrait one of the men had been carrying was handed to Mariko while Mitsui rejoined his whispering men outside, standing at relaxed attention next to their cars. In a dreamlike daze, she shambled forward through the crematorium's doors, walking toward the waiting limo. As she settled into her seat, she stared at the gray marble jar in Nikki's lap, completely mystified as to how a man as large and imposing as Kenji Ota could actually fit inside.

Outside their window, Mitsui bowed deeply and apologized for his need to address other matters. Nikki and Mariko were ultimately left in each other's company. They remained silent, avoiding eye contact at all cost as they traveled down the long, winding road. After ten minutes, Mariko lifted her eyes from the black carpet and considered offering sympathetic words, but Nikki's head was turned away and her eyes were shielded behind dark sunglasses. It seemed the middle-aged woman preferred her solitude over Mariko's company, which was not unexpected, especially with the horrible circumstances surrounding her son's death.

The limo driver adjusted his rearview mirror and watched them from the front seat. A few more minutes slipped by then Nikki turned to Mariko and asked, "Anywhere in particular you want to go?"

Mariko was startled at first at hearing her deep, sultry voice. She considered the woman's question and realized delivering her to her deceased son's apartment wouldn't be appropriate or fully understood. "I'm not sure," she managed. "I haven't thought that far…"

"Then keep me company while you decide," Nikki said, before instructing the driver to take them to Shirakaba.

"The bar?" he asked, his eyes large in the mirror.

"That's right. I need a drink." She sniffed and added, "Make that several."

Mariko offered a weak smile. The legendary, hard-to- find gem he was taking them to was in a residential area on the side of Yoshida Hill. She'd been invited there by a friend years earlier for a cherry blossom party and was met by a local mix of cigarette-smoking intellectuals and young bohemian types.

"Stay here," Nikki told the driver as he pulled up outside. "We'll be back in twenty minutes." She set the urn on the seat beside her and waited for him to open the door. "Keep an eye on my son, would you?"

The driver nodded and kept his eyes down as both ladies climbed out of the car. Nikki took Mariko by the hand and walked her into the dimly lit bar. She sat down in a booth directly across from her, ordered two martinis, and then tapped a cigarette on the table before lighting it. "My son wasn't an easy man to love," she said with all sincerity. "I know you had feelings for him despite how he misbehaved. Unfortunately, the only person my sympathy goes out to is you, Mariko."

The geisha wasn't sure how to react, or if this woman was genuine in her cruel assessment. "I'm surprised you feel that way, Mrs. Ota," she replied. "I understand you weren't close, but I thought since you were his mother..."

"That I would be all choked up? Sobbing uncontrollably? Screaming for justice and death to the villain who did this?" She took a drag from her cigarette and blew a stream of smoke to the side. "My son's murder was inevitable. It might have been less brutal if he wasn't involved with Mitsui, but he earned his share of enemies all by himself."

Really? Mariko swallowed hard before defending Kenji. "I knew him for five years before he became my danna," she said softly. "He was kind to everyone in the Inoue household, had a pleasant manner and nice singing voice. He earned my oneesan's favor and had great plans for the future and, sadly, his share of flaws. But he still—"

"Flaws?" Nikki burst into a fit of laughter—loud, coarse, hard laughter, so utterly unlike any sound Mariko had ever heard issue from a woman's mouth. "Oh, that's what killing is...a character flaw. My goodness, Mariko, you are either the most forgiving or unbelievably naive person I've ever met. Aside from my daughter, that is. To this day, she wants to believe her absent father actually cared about her." Nikki shook her head. "At least my son understood how it worked. His father watched him grow from a street hoodlum to a gang leader and encouraged him to follow right along in his footsteps. There may not have been any love lost between them, but at least they were realists."

"I don't understand," Mariko said. "Kenji and Yuki had different fathers?"

"Of course. How could you not know?"

"No one ever said anything. And from what I've heard, Yuki was close to her brother."

"Oh my goodness, Mariko. You honestly believe that? She knew about the funeral and didn't have the decency to show up. She didn't even bother to call. If she cared so much about him, then where was she today?"

Mariko had no answer. She sat quietly, staring at the martini the waiter was placing before her.

"Ah...perfect," Nikki cooed. "Just what I needed." She wasted no time throwing back half of her drink. Then she picked up her lit cigarette from the ashtray. "Those two had the strangest love-hate relationship. When Yuki was growing up, she wouldn't think anything of stealing from him. But try stealing from her and you'd be lucky to walk away in one piece. You know now that I think about it, she might even have been the one who killed him.

That would be a sad scenario for a mother, don't you think?" She took another long drag from her cigarette. Then she tilted her head back and let it out slowly through her red, pursed lips.

Mariko was appalled. "That's...disturbing, Mrs. Ota. I can't imagine why you would say such a thing."

"With my children's history, it would make complete sense. Did you know Yuki's husband was murdered in her apartment after he almost beat her to death?"

Mariko drew a quick breath. "No...I didn't."

"My son claimed he wasn't there at the time and didn't know anything about it. But that's what love is in this family...maniacal and cold blooded...with no respect for human life." She picked up her martini glass and studied Mariko over the top of it.

"But that's not true. He cared about people. He cared about me."

"Really? Well, perhaps I misspoke then." She finished off her drink and set her glass down on the table. "So you actually loved my son," she said, matter-of-factly.

Mariko glanced down and nodded slowly.

"Unbelievable," Nikki said. "How in the world did that come about?" Her delicate hand toyed with the pink conch shell necklace resting at the hollow of her throat.

"On the first Friday of every month, he came to Gion for business. We often spent time together at the okiya and various teahouses. Over time, we developed a friendship, which grew into much more. I know he had his moments and could be difficult and extremely unpredictable, but given time, I believe Kenji would have settled down and become a fine—"

A hiss was nearly wrenched out of Mrs. Ota's mouth as her thin lips curled into a vicious sneer. The mere mention of her son's name sparked a frown to bloom upon her sharp features, her eyes narrowing slightly. She explained that she hadn't spoken to him in over three weeks. That usually he would come cater-wauling around her, prodding her temper and stoking her wrath with his irritating snicker, cocky grin, and painfully true words. Oh, how that galled her—stirred the anger in her belly at the very thought and brought a glint of malice to her dark brown eyes.

"Well, well," she said suddenly. "Would you look at that. There's one of the neighborhood girls who used to chase after him. God only knows why…"

"What?" Mariko jerked around toward the wall mirror and saw that a young woman was looking into it. She had long tresses of ebony curls that she had tied back with a blue slip of ribbon. The lids of her brown eyes were covered in a misty blue shadow—the same color that fell upon mountain valleys at dawn—and her dress was a sky blue with white trim around the short sleeves. It was modest and efficient, but very lovely on her form. She had a matching purse in one hand and was staring curiously into the mirror, obviously not seeing those who were staring back at her. Behind her, the two men at the bar were more than a little vocal as they voiced their impressions and opinions about her.

"Ah, would you look at that one. I wonder where her boy-friend is? He wouldn't be happy if he knew she was here advertising. I know I'd be upset…letting something that tasty get away."

"Wouldn't mind one bit if she climbed into my bed."

"Me either."

"Enough!" Mariko barked suddenly, making the men halt their inappropriate banter. She snorted derisively and rolled her eyes. *Why are men always thinking below the waist?*

The young beauty approached the side of their table. "You're that geisha," she said. "The one Kenji Ota always talked about. He came here sometimes late at night." She motioned with her head toward a dimly lit corner. "He would sit right over there…

all alone. I came here once with friends and saw him staring down at a picture of you with the saddest look on his face. I guess I embarrassed him when I asked what was wrong because he put it in his pocket right away and said he was looking at his dream girl."

Mariko was caught completely off guard. She gazed at the lone table, cringing inside. Then she realized Nikki Ota was watching both of them with interest.

"I'm sorry...that was unkind of me," the young woman said. "I heard the terrible news about his murder a few days ago. In spite of what some people might say, I'm sure he'll be missed." Then she walked away to join a handsome young man at the far end of the bar.

Mariko picked up her glass of gin. The few drops she swallowed made her cough and brought tears to her eyes.

Nikki signaled the bartender for another drink then sat back, scrutinizing the woman before her. "If you truly miss my son and want to be near him, I can make that happen. I can bring him back into your life...tonight," she said.

"I don't understand. How?" The words fell out of Mariko's mouth. She watched Nikki as she opened her purse and took out a gold locket on a long, slender chain.

"With this," she said, dangling it before her. "When you wear it, you will feel him deep in your soul. It will be as if you were together again....united as one."

The geisha accepted the gift and stared down at its strange engravings. It had a catch that opened easily, exposing a cutting of dark, silky hair. Her heart skipped a beat. She lifted her wide eyes to Nikki's.

"Yes...that's his hair," she said nonchalantly. "Keep it close to your heart. When you need him most, you'll feel his presence." The odd woman accepted her second drink and tossed it back in seconds flat. She asked for the bill then stood, looking around as though lost in thought. A strange smile played on her lips. "People are threads," she murmured. "When they leave us, we can choose to gather every memory they represent, cherish them to the end of our days, and exist solely for the moment when we can join them. Or we can bury them and move on. Find a new purpose and create a better life for ourselves. Today you've been given that option, Mariko. I advise you to choose the wisest path and never look back."

# 31

Rachel stepped into the shower and leaned her head against the tile wall, letting the water cascade down her back and across her face. The hot water felt good on her tired, aching muscles. She could stay here forever, letting the water massage her body and work its way through the tension. If only there was enough hot water in the world. The notion evoked a sarcastic laugh. In the last seventy-two hours, gangsters, enormous sharks, and mind-bending ghosts had challenged her survival skills and she was worrying about the water temperature? It seemed crazy that after all they'd gone through their mission in coming here would ultimately remain unfinished. She was still perplexed as to how their task in finding the third missing sword could be so easily dismissed along with the trapped souls Shinzo had been determined to free. Were they really expected to fly away and feel gratified for a job well done?

Reluctantly she lifted her head and reached for the shampoo. She squeezed out too much and frowned. After lathering thoroughly, she stuck her head under the faucet again to let the water rinse her hair instead of making the effort herself. She'd been up for far too long, and the past few days had been hectic, to say the least. She was beginning to think things would never calm down—her life would never be normal again. But that's what she'd signed on for with Chase Cohen: the thrill of finding hidden treasures and exploring the unknown while traveling the world together.

The door to the bathroom slid open. Rachel raised her eyebrows. She could have sworn she'd locked the door. "Hello?" she called out. She didn't receive an answer. Instead, she heard the faint rustling of clothing. There was only one person who had the nerve to invade her privacy.

A blond head peeked around the curtain and stared at her lazily. "Can I join you?" Chase asked. Before Rachel could answer, he was already in the shower with her. She smiled weakly at him before turning away. He reached for the soapy washcloth hanging from the hook and scrutinized her minor injury before carefully sliding it up and down her back. Seconds later, she felt his hands snake around her waist, his lips pressed against the top of her shoulder.

"It's a sad day," she remarked idly, reaching her hands around his neck, "when the only privacy we get is in the shower." He breathed into her neck and didn't bother to respond. His energy seemed totally devoted to holding her, and she wasn't complaining. It felt good to be pressed up against him like this, the water running down her body.

"I almost lost you today," he whispered in her ear.

"And I almost lost you." Rachel turned around to face him. The first thing Chase did was capture her mouth in his own. She opened her lips as his tongue flicked across them. He knew her mouth well and could invoke a heated reaction, but her mind was drifting—thinking about the diamonds, Shinzo's disappointment, and Yuki's odd comment. Who was the stranger she had casually mentioned? Did she know more than she was letting on?

Chase released Rachel's mouth and pulled away just enough to look into her eyes. "I know you're worried," he said, as if reading her mind. "But like Yuki said, this fight isn't over yet. Remember the footprints? Someone was in that cave before we got there. If she has any idea who that might have been, then she's probably got a lead on the missing sword."

"You really think so? But what about the diamonds? How do you explain the fact that she took them and said nothing? Surely that makes you question her motives."

"Baby, that hasn't escaped my attention. Whether she keeps them or gives them away, it really doesn't matter at this point, does it? Like you said, they're cursed, whatever that means. Which reminds me...how exactly did you know that?"

"I honestly don't know. It was so strange, Chase. I felt like I was in a children's game of telephone being funneled all these messages...translating what I was hearing."

"What about that ghost you saw? It was like you'd become physic or something."

"I can't explain that either. It just came on like a sudden rush, filling my thoughts, imprinting images on my brain. I've never experienced anything like that in my life."

"Well, I'm just glad you're all right." He lifted her chin and looked deep into her eyes. "Aside from that nasty scrape on your back, you are, aren't you?"

Rachel swallowed hard and nodded. She laid her head back against his chest and listened to his pounding heart as he stroked her hair. They hadn't touched each other since Friday. And it was, what, Sunday? Maybe Monday. Far too long either way. It was amazing how much Rachel missed the feel of his body. He lifted her chin and kissed her again and she wasn't about to stop him—even if her mind was telling her they shouldn't be doing this right now.

With reckless abandonment, she twisted her fingers in his damp hair. He grabbed her rear in retaliation. She smiled into their kiss and let her free hand slide down past his waistline. He groaned in delighted annoyance.

Things were already getting out of hand quickly, she realized. Not only did they not have time for this, she wasn't sure she had the energy for it either. But it felt so nice...so damn sexy.

She turned her head and broke their kiss. Chase descended on her neck again. There was no doubt about it...she was going to have a lovely purple mark later. He was obsessed with hickeys. It would be annoying if not for the fact that she liked being marked as his. Strange? Maybe.

Everyone has their quirks, she told herself. Perhaps secretly she liked being dominated. She just hoped Chase never figured this out.

"Chase, I'm thinking I shouldn't postpone it any longer. I should call Shinzo and get Mariko's number. We should meet at the hotel tomorrow...before we fly out."

"Whatever you think is best," he murmured as he moved to her collarbone. "And maybe we could even finish what we started two nights ago," he said before trailing kisses down to her chest.

Rachel let herself smile, but couldn't formulate a response as he descended to her abdomen.

Damn! They needed to stop this right now. This was so bad....so poorly timed with unfinished matters to think about. But stopping Chase when she was equally hungry would lead to an argument, and that was the last thing she needed right now.

He devoured her mouth, pushing her back against the wall, trapping her body against the cold tiles, and Rachel met his ardor with startling equality. Her breasts were squashed against him, her nipples painfully tight as his hard chest abraded the sensitive tips. His erection pushed into the apex of her thighs, butting against her as they ground their pelvises together. She had a nagging feeling she'd pay for it later, but that was later... not now.

His mouth abruptly left hers and lowered to capture a nipple, a hand moving to the other breast, squeezing, the thumb circling and flicking. She held his head and cried out as he sucked hard and his teeth grazed the tight bud in his mouth. Her body flooded with sensation and she rocked against him, wanting more, wanting to be closer, wanting to be part of him. He lifted her buttocks, lifted her feet off the floor, and anchored her against the wall with his chest. Her legs automatically circled his waist and held on for dear life.

"I want you," he groaned in her ear. Chase entered her with no resistance and rammed into her as the water drummed on his back, mingling with her cries and the desperate need to cleanse away the events of the day and reaffirm life. She finally collapsed into his arms, panting so hard she didn't even realize the water had turned cold until he reached behind her to turn it back to warm.

Chase kissed her gently, holding her up. She felt so tired, but exhilarated too. He leaned his head against hers and let out a long, slow breath.

"Tell me about it," she mumbled.

"I think you need some rest," he told her, stifling a yawn. "Lord knows I do."

"I think I need another shower," she told him.

Chase grinned.

"I suppose they'll both have to wait," she said. "We've got ten miles to drive and a plane to catch in a few hours."

He gave a huge yawn. "Okay. Stop fretting, Rachel. Everything's packed and ready to go. Let's take a nap for thirty minutes. What's the harm?" He kissed her again to stifle her protest then pulled back and gave her a stern look. "You need rest and I need rest. Let's go to sleep. I'll set the alarm. If the end of the world comes before we wake up, at least we'll be together."

Rachel was tempted to say no, if only to have Chase drag her to bed anyway. She didn't, though. She waited as he turned off the shower and handed her a towel. She followed him back to her bedroom where she slipped on boxers and a T-shirt. Chase set the clock, applied more salve on her back, and pulled her into bed. The cool sheets felt nice, and it was easier than it should have been to turn her mind off. The last thing that registered was Chase snuggling up next to her and kissing her bare shoulder.

When she opened her eyes again and glanced at the clock, she was surprised to discover a full hour had slipped by. The alarm hadn't gone off! She rolled over to admonish Chase for letting them sleep so long, but he looked strangely endearing when he slept. His hair was more messed up than it was normally and his mouth hung slightly open. He looked so young— so incredibly peaceful. Rachel ran her finger along the stubble of his constant five o'clock shadow. She leaned over and planted a kiss on his cheek.

"Hmmm..." Chase opened his eyes slightly. "What a nice way to wake up." he told her, stretching. "Just wish we could've slept awhile longer."

"I didn't want to wake you," Rachel told him honestly.

He curled back into her, pulling her close. "Time?" "Quarter after four."

He let out a long-suffering sigh. "We should get up," he whispered, as though Rachel might not hear him and he wouldn't have to move. "You're probably starving by now too."

"You're right," she answered, but neither of them made any effort to move.

"Maybe Yuki's sleeping. Maybe we could just stay in bed." Chase sounded hopeful, leaving Rachel smirking. "Maybe she'll walk in and produce the missing sword and all of this will finally be over."

Rachel rested her head against his chest and gave in to the warm feeling—the need to feel close to another human being.

"I love you," he said.

Rachel smiled softly. "I know." Chase's feelings for her were so open, so genuine and sincere. His heartfelt words came so freely, with absolutely no strings attached. It would be so easy to reciprocate. To tell him what he wanted to hear, but it was a daily battle to know her own mind. To understand her changing emotions and bury her nagging fear of being left behind. So what if Kaito Mitsui was an evil warlord? What if he sent his solders into the local department store and kidnapped every woman in the cosmetic aisle? She probably wouldn't care enough to get out of this bed. In fact, there was probably nothing that could make her leave the warmth and safety of Chase's arms right now. At that moment, it was exactly the way she liked it— exactly the way she wanted it to stay. At least until the phone rang and Shinzo's voice came on the line, shocking her into a sitting position.

"Can you postpone your trip?" he asked. "I'm not talking about Tokyo. I mean back to the States?"

Rachel glanced at Chase, propped on his elbow with a question mark on his face. "Why? What's going on?" she asked Shinzo.

"When Yuki didn't answer her phone, I called the inn, and the hostess said she left with three men an hour ago," Shinzo told her. "I don't know for certain, but I think Mitsui-san's men were sent there and might be pressuring her to find out where the swords are."

"Oh my God," Rachel gasped. "They know about them?"

"Apparently a mysterious journal came into their possession...something Kenji Ota had apparently been keeping. Two men broke into his apartment a few hours ago and took it along with every sword in his collection. Fortunately Mariko wasn't there, but her roommate Tamayo witnessed it all and called me right after it happened." "What is it?" Chase asked. He was sitting up in the bed, looking anxious...preparing to take the phone from Rachel's hands if she didn't answer him.

"Somehow Mitsui's men found out about the swords," she told him. "They broke into Kenji's apartment and...Yuki was taken away."

Chase brows pinched. "From his apartment?"

"No. From here," she answered.

Shinzo was back on the line. "Listen to me carefully," he told her. "We're running out of time. If the tanto isn't found and returned to the Shoten temple by August twenty-first, when the next blue moon occurs, Tokyo will experience the largest earthquake in Japan's history. Millions of homes and buildings will be destroyed within minutes. A multitude of innocent people will die. Contamination and disease will run rampant. The islands and everything on them will be completely wiped out."

"Hold on!" Rachel yelled. "What are you talking about? That's less than forty-eight hours from now."

"I know, Miss Lyons. That's why it's crucial to act quickly. Visions of this horrible disaster came to me last night in a dream.

I know it sounds farfetched and conveniently planned, but I assure you, it's very real."

Rachel glimpsed Chase's vexed expression. "What do you want us to do?" she asked into the phone.

"Leave right now," Shinzo told her. "Go back to your hotel in Tokyo as soon as possible. I'm going to speak to Mitsui-san and explain the whole situation. He lent his support to the families affected by the tsunami after it destroyed their homes and killed more than nineteen thousand people. Hopefully the compassion and decency he demonstrated and once possessed will be strong enough to overcome the hostility between us. With his help, we might be able to bring an end to all of this before it's too late."

# 32

"What happened here?" Mariko asked, walking into Kenji's tossed apartment.

Tamayo ran at her and threw her arms around her waist. "Some men broke in while you were gone," she whimpered. "I was so scared."

Mariko separated herself from Tamayo's embrace. She closed and secured the door then led her to the sofa she had risen from and sat beside her. "Are you all right?"

The maiko nodded, looking younger than her years. All around them drawers had been emptied, cushions had been tossed, and pictures were torn from the walls. "I recognized one of them," Tamayo told her. "He was Hiroshi Mori's driver...the same man I saw in Gion Kobu four days ago waiting outside the Komura teahouse. He smashed a hole through the locked closet in the bedroom and found Kenji's book. One of them flipped through it and then both of them started tearing the place apart looking for something else. When they left, they took his duffel bag and black katana from the closet and told me to keep quiet or they'd come back for me."

Mariko came to her feet and hurried into the bedroom. Items had been cleaned out of the closet and were piled on the bed. The walls had minor damage, including several holes, which appeared to have been made by the hammer she saw lying on the living room floor. The heavy, king-sized mattress was slightly twisted, but fortunately it was still on the frame. She moved to the left side and slid her hand between the mattress and box springs until her arm was buried up to her elbow between them. When she felt two braided handles with her fingertips, she breathed a sigh of relief. She pulled out Kenji's red katana and the diamond-embedded short sword, thankful she had had the foresight to hide them.

Tamayo wandered into the room. "They made a terrible mess, didn't they? Do you have any idea what they were looking for?" she asked.

"This," Mariko answered, extending the butt of the knife toward her. "It's part of a rare imperial set. According to the journal they stole, a man died stealing this from a tomb. Kenji confiscated it from someone else and was intending to give it to his sister, but then he discovered too many people were looking for it and he would only be putting her life at risk."

"Is that why the Americans are here...with Shinzo?" she asked.

"Yes. But you need to be quiet about it. If the purpose of their expedition becomes public knowledge, there's no telling what kind of trouble might follow."

Tamayo's mouth slacked. She searched Mariko's eyes long and hard for understanding. "I hope I didn't make a mistake by calling Shinzo."

"You did what?"

"I turned to him because he always looks after us. I thought he should know about the danger you might be in."

Mariko heaved a heavy breath. "All right, this is what I want you to do. Grab your bag and take my keys and meet me at my apartment. I'm just going to gather my things together and then I'll join you. And make sure to lock the door and don't let anyone in until I get there. Is that understood?"

"But why can't I wait for you? I really don't think it's safe to bring that sword with you...especially by yourself."

"Let me worry about it. Now get going." As Tamayo disappeared around the corner, Mariko pulled her oversized suitcase from under the pile on the bed. She changed into a black silk top and matching capris before folding her kimonos and setting them gently inside. Then she began systematically emptying disheveled drawers and adding them to her belongings. She heard Tamayo announce her departure before closing the door.

After gathering everything from the bathroom, she closed the lid on her suitcase and took a last look around. But suddenly it occurred to her the locket was still in the small purse she'd already packed. The idea of leaving and never coming back to this place left her rummaging through the bag. Her fingers found the chain and pulled it free. She lifted it to her throat and secured it at the back of her neck. Just as Mrs. Ota had instructed, she slid it under the collar of her shirt and felt its coolness against her skin. She pressed it against her heart for only a moment and thought of Kenji and what it might have been like to be here with him. Then she locked the suitcase, tucked the tanto knife into her belt, and gazed down at Kenji's katana.

The air around her changed in an instant. It was hot and putrid, engulfing the room in a blanket of despair. As she watched in strange fascination, it began swirling and spinning around her, picking up speed along with the white feathers from the floor. She was caught in the center of a mini tornado, frozen in place. She had a sense of being encroached upon, overtaken, and devoured. The spirit entered her mouth, filled her belly, twisted around her heart, and covered her eyes in a blinding fog. Exultation lifted her lips into a half smile, as if some power of significant import was now controlling the workings of her body and mind. She felt daring and reckless, confident in her strength. The voice in her head was as seductive as the sea—whispering, clamoring. Inviting her soul to wander for a spell in the abysses of solitude, to lose itself in mazes of inward contemplation.

She stretched her arms out at her sides, and instantly her biceps became hard and defined. Her long, layered hair fell loose around her shoulders, partially covering one eye. She'd become something foreign and alluring, dark and mysterious—a masculine, vengeful spirit trapped in a beautiful, seductive body. She picked up the katana and held it before her, gazing into the full-length mirror. The most sought after geisha in Japan had morphed into a deadly adversary no one would suspect or see coming. With one look at her dark, transfixing eyes and Kenji Ota's enemies would know he was back.

# 33

Rachel and Chase jumped out of the taxi, checked in at the ticket counter, and hurried to the departure gate. Once they were on board and seated for their flight to Tokyo, they stared out of the right and left side of the plane through the windows. Although not a word was shared between them and Rachel's safety was foremost in his mind, Chase knew they shared a growing concern.

What was happening to Yuki...and who was going to rescue her?

As soon as they landed, they exited the plane and headed for the baggage claim area. Everything seemed to be going fine until the moment when Chase left Rachel's side to use the bathroom and returned to find her gone. He walked back and forth, dodging exiting passengers, but he didn't see her anywhere. He opened the door to the women's bathroom, called out for her, and received no response. With his heart racing, he charged up and down the escalator, calling out her name over and over again. Returning to the baggage claim area, he spotted their bags sitting alone next to the rotating belt. He cornered the baggage handler and asked if he'd seen her, describing Rachel the best way he knew how. But it was no use. Whether it was the language barrier or the man's indecipherable answer, he seemed to be getting nowhere. Chase approached several couples he recognized from their flight and was left with the same head-shaking results. He tried Rachel's cell phone but it rang endlessly, and Shinzo wasn't answering his phone either. In a panic, he sought out a security guard, but couldn't find anyone who spoke English. With no ready solution, he picked up their bags and headed outside. After scanning the one-way street and walking throughout the parking lot, he returned to the taxi pickup area and dropped both bags on the sidewalk.

"Where the hell are you?" he yelled into the air. Several people standing in line turned to stare, but Chase didn't care. Embarrassment was the least of his worries.

Soon an MK cab drove up and it was his turn to go somewhere, anywhere. But how could he leave without Rachel? Struggling with the only Japanese he could muster, he instructed the driver to take him to the nearest police station and sat back, hoping it was where they would end up. Four lights and ten turns later, they came to an abrupt stop. Chase paid for the ride before sending the taxi on its way.

As soon as he hurried into the station, a man stepped forward and identified himself as Detective Kobayashi. He listened in silence to Chase's full account. "She would never leave without telling me," Chase assured him.

"Has she been upset lately? Have you had a recent disagreement? Has she been away from you for an extended period of time?"

Chase could answer yes to all of his questions, but he also knew his relationship with Rachel was better than ever. At least he thought so. "What about the men who have been following us?" he asked.

The detective seemed incredulous. He wasn't writing anything down. Instead, he reached into a file cabinet, returned with a folder, and showed him a stack of posters of missing women from the area.

"Is one person doing all of this?" Chase asked.

Kobayashi shrugged. "We're not sure. I've got six men searching…knocking on doors in every neighborhood. I don't have anyone else available to help you."

"But we're Americans. Surely—"

The detective glanced down, shaking his head. "I'm sorry. I can't help you. Please come back to the station if Miss Lyons hasn't returned by Monday. Then I'll see what we can do."

Chase had it in his head that Rachel could be dead by then. He considered going to the American embassy but realized he'd probably get the same answer there. As Kobayashi stepped away to take a call, another detective pulled him aside.

"Here," he said, giving him a business card. "My name is Honda…just like the car. I'll make some inquiries and do whatever I can. In the meantime, if you hear back from Miss Lyons or think of anything else that might be helpful, please call me. I don't want Americans believing Japan isn't a safe place to visit."

Chase walked outside and climbed into the back seat of a cab feeling completely defeated. He tried not to think of the worst-case scenario, but with barbaric hoods running the country and no one doing anything to stop them, his imagination was going wild.

The driver turned back to face him. *"Doko desu ka?"*

Chase released a deep sigh. "Otani hotel," he told him, not knowing where else to go. Maybe he was overreacting and Rachel would show up…walk right into their room as if nothing had happened. He could only hope that was the case.

As the car pulled away from the police station, Chase's phone rang. He recognized Shinzo's number and hoped to God he had good news to share.

"I have no idea where she might be," the monk replied to his question. "But I have a feeling we're going to know soon enough. One thing about the Zakura-kai…they like bargaining chips. If they're after the swords, as all signs are pointing, they'll let Rachel go as soon as I hand them over. However, I still need the missing knife and an opportunity to stop the destruction."

"But you said that—"

"I know…I know. I thought you were leaving, which would have been best under the circumstances. However, with Rachel missing, I thought you should know Yuki has insight into the location of the third sword…even if she's not aware of it yet. With two days left and the clock running, one way or another this matter will be resolved."

"Not at the risk of losing Rachel."

For a few seconds, Shinzo was quiet on the phone then he delivered one of his well-meaning anecdotes in an effort to alleviate Chase's worst fear. "We will all survive this, Cohen-san. Hold onto that belief. Faith enables us to slay our enemies without lifting a sword."

Yeah, right. "So what now? I hope you're not expecting me to sit back and do nothing."

"At the moment, I'm afraid you have no choice. Not until Rachel's abductors make their intent known. As soon as we know what that is, I'll do everything within my power to bring her back safely."

Chase ended the call and stared out the window at the passing traffic. The idea of a Buddhist monk going up against an army of assassins was almost laughable—like something out of a far-fetched television show. But then he realized that in this country anything was possible.

As the cab continued on its way, he spotted a familiar street where Yuki had taken them days earlier. He leaned forward in his seat and told the driver to stop.

"*Koko de?*"

"*Hai.* Drop me off here."

The driver pulled up to the curb and accepted Chase's fare in the palm of his white glove. Then he hit a button, opening the door. Chase jumped out and the door closed behind him. He walked quickly to the corner of the busy intersection as the cab drove away. In his mind, there was only one way to deal with a nest of nasty scorpions: break into their hiding place and take out their leader. And that's just what he intended to do.

# 34

Where are we going? Rachel lifted her chin and stared up at the blue sky and towering buildings overhead. She twisted around to look out the rear window and was jabbed in the side with an elbow.

"Ouch! What was that fo—" She stopped short, interrupted by the gangster's steely glare.

"Stop jumping around," he growled. "We're almost there."

Rachel cowered in her seat. It took a few seconds for her fuzzy brain to digest her predicament. It had happened so quickly. After Chase stepped away, a tall, broad-shouldered man had accosted her, grabbing her by the arm and dragging her toward the exit door as people stood by watching.

"Don't say a word, or you'll regret it," he had threatened.

She'd looked around in desperation as he pulled her outside and shoved her into the back seat of a waiting car. And now she was here, sitting next to this frowning, despicable hoodlum, wondering why he was doing this to her.

"*Migi,*" he told the man in the front seat.

Rachel remained still, staring through the windshield as the car veered sharply to the right. An embroidered gold totem dangled from the car's rearview mirror, reminding her of the charms being sold outside of the temples she'd toured. Both men wore black sunglasses, masking their eyes, but their stiff postures implied their gazes were set resolutely forward.

Rachel stared down at her sweaty hands clenched nervously in her lap but couldn't help occasionally glancing up. They were rolling by mills and textile shops and casually dressed men and women hurrying along on freshly washed sidewalks. From the bundles they were carrying and the familiar streets they were passing, she realized they were in the Nippori Textile Town district next to Ueno in North Tokyo.

Once they were parked, the men exited the car with Rachel pressed between them and proceeded down a side street. Some of the local residents shot them strange looks, but the men she was with kept moving, as if they weren't bothered at all. After walking a few hundred feet, they came to a crossroads. The street curved off to the right in one direction and continued straight in the other. The driver jerked his chin toward a space between two run-down buildings, right where the roads diverged. With no words spoken, they proceeded in that direction. Rachel realized anything could happen. She could be raped and left for dead and no one would help her—no one in this place would care.

She looked up at the driver as they walked. "Please," her voice quavered, "just tell me where we're going."

The man remained silent, staring straight ahead with an unreadable expression on his face.

"Are you going to kill me?" Rachel asked.

His head snapped to the side. "Of course not! What a stupid thing to say."

"Then why are you bringing me here?"

"Be quiet. You'll know soon enough."

Heavy metal music was blaring through an open doorway a short distance ahead. When they reached the source of the obnoxious sound, the driver halted and reached into his pocket to pull out a thin cigar and metal lighter. As he lit up, four twentyish-looking females exited the building with matching cigarettes in hand. They were female gang members dressed in sailor-style school uniforms modified with demon patches and lengthened navy skirts. If not for their cartoonish, brightly dyed hair and colorful striped socks, they would have resembled any of the young girls Rachel had seen walking to and from the schools in the area. However, these women were a curious mixture of innocent and slutty. Their gum-snapping cocky poses teemed with sexuality, narcissism, and a general dissatisfaction with life, just like the story she'd read about.

Standing nearly a foot taller than the rest of them was the sukeban—the equivalent of a yakuza gang leader. She was an attractive young woman with long, pinned-back hair and a black fingerless glove, straight out of a Japanese comic book. While puffing on her cigarette, she flipped a yo-yo, making it seem more like a deadly weapon than a nostalgic toy.

"Takashi!" she called over her shoulder to a person standing in the shadow of the open doorway. Two of her cohorts stepped aside, allowing the approach of the young acne-scarred rebel, still dressed in his signature sharkskin suit. Rachel began edging backward, but the driver stood solidly behind her, blocking any possibility of escape.

"What do you want from me?" she asked him.

The yo-yo queen blew a stream of smoke to the side and rattled off something indecipherable. By her hip resting posture and pursed lips, she seemed none too pleased with the situation.

She motioned Rachel forward with her index finger. When she didn't react fast enough, she was shoved from behind.

"This one's trouble," the woman told Takashi. Her shift to English was an unexpected surprise. Then Rachel realized it was strictly for her benefit. "I'm Chiyo Oshima...the person my cousin reaches out to when he wants something dealt with." She tilted her head to one side and smiled—an eerie quirk of her lips that didn't extend to her hollow eyes. She grabbed Rachel's chin and stared into her face. With her lit cigarette only inches away, she announced, "Be a real shame to mess her up."

Rachel jerked her face away. "Don't touch me!" she yelled.

The group of young women looked at each other before breaking into derisive laughter. Chiyo's reaction was less entertaining. She shoved Rachel hard against the concrete wall, leaving her gasping. Although she was tempted, Rachel didn't take the offensive. Instead, she turned to Takashi. He was standing with his arms crossed, silently observing the female's assault.

"Why am I here?" Rachel demanded.

"I need your help."

Rachel stared at him long and hard before asking, "With what?" She fully expected him to mention Prince Ngami's samurai swords, but apparently there was a more pressing matter on his mind.

"Mitsui-san. He's fond of you. He'll listen to what you say."

Rachel was taken back for a moment. "About what?"

Takashi garbled something in Japanese, sending Chiyo and her gang members back inside the building. Then his eyes returned to Rachel. He lowered his voice. "I need you to tell him I didn't kill Hiroshi Mori."

Unbelievable. "First of all, I have no idea who Mori is. And secondly, how do I know you didn't do it?"

"You don't, Miss Lyons. You only have my word for it. My men have been watching you for days and haven't threatened you once. I have no interest in stealing your swords...only in keeping my head."

"How did you know about the swords?"

"Sake never helped Kenji keep secrets," he assured her.

She considered asking how his dead friend had found out about them in the first place but thought better of it. "Do you know where the diamond sword is?"

"The tanto?" he asked.

She nodded enthusiastically. "Yes. Do you know where I can find it?"

"After Kenji was killed, Mori went to his apartment to find it. When he showed up, someone was waiting for him, and it sure wasn't me." He glanced at his men, talking quietly among themselves. "I was at the club drinking...like the night my keys and phone disappeared. My friends can back me on that, but Mitsui-san won't believe them. He thinks they would say anything to protect me. Especially after what happened to Kenji."

Rachel was losing what little patience she had left. "You haven't answered my question yet. Where's the tanto being kept?"

Takashi glanced at the schoolgirls inside the doorway, still smoking their cigarettes. "Mariko Abe was staying at his place. I'm sure she knows. I'll find out from her when we're through. So do we have a deal?"

"I'm not sure I should help you...especially after your men kidnapped me. Do you realize how worried my boyfriend must be right now?"

"You don't understand. I had no choice."

"Really? You couldn't have just asked for my help?"

"Why would I take that risk? If I'm seen walking around, I'll be turned into ashes...like Kenji."

Rachel noted Takashi's sweaty forehead and the constant movement of his hands. When he wasn't rubbing them together, he was touching his face and hair like someone who had spent his life getting stoned.

"What about Yuki? What have you done with her?"

"Done with her? You're kidding, right? No one messes with Yuki Ota."

"While we were in Kyushu, three men were seen taking her away. How do I know you weren't involved?"

"Are you sure about that? Yuki would drop any man who laid a hand on her. I should know. She's never allowed me within five feet of her."

Rachel looked around at the people standing nearby, half listening to their conversation. "So now what?" she asked.

"My men will take you to see Mitsui-san. Tell him that I had nothing to do with your missing swords...that I followed his orders to keep an eye on you and nothing more."

"Better yet," Rachel said, "why don't you bring the missing sword to my hotel? Then I'll call your boss and tell him how helpful you were."

"This isn't a game, Miss Lyons." He pulled a gun from his pocket and held it loosely in his hand. "If you don't do what I ask, you're good as dead to me." The assurance in his voice sent chills up her spine. From where she stood, the alley was only a short distance away. It was empty aside from a scrawny white cat feeding in the Dumpster. In the opposite direction, the sounds of traffic had grown in volume, but the possibility of reaching the avenue and flagging down a car without being shot seemed unlikely. As she debated her best alternative, Takashi's men moved directly alongside her, one at each arm. They were considerably taller and reeked of sweaty testosterone. From the look in their narrow, shifty eyes, they were prepared to change her mind by whatever means necessary

"Wait!" she said. "I'll go see him."

Takashi studied her for a moment before waving his men away. Then he stepped closer and flashed his crooked yellow teeth. "That's more like it," he said.

Rachel swallowed hard. She'd been waiting for a chance to make her move, and this dolt had just provided it. She lunged forward and grabbed his gun. With her fingers wrapped around the smooth barrel, she rolled onto the ground. One of his men was on top of her in an instant, shoving her cheek against the concrete walkway. But he was too late. The grip was firmly in her hand.

"*Sore wa ore no mono da!*" Takashi yelled. "*Ore no tokoro ni modose!*"

*I'm strong. I have no more fear. I can do this.* Rachel squeezed her eyes shut and pulled the trigger at the same time. She heard the shot as the bullet discharged. When she opened her eyes again, Takashi was on the ground grabbing his balls, screaming at the top of his lungs.

"*Yarareta! Yarareta!*"

Chiyo ran back into the street. With the fight gone out of Rachel and one of Takashi's men still holding her down, Chiyo took the gun away with no effort at all. "*Dete ike!*" She yelled at the startled men. "*Bekku mo turete ike!*"

While Takashi moaned and cursed in a guttural voice, the driver slipped his hands under his arms and the other man lifted his feet. They carried him down the street toward the parked car.

When they were out of range, Chiyo faced the three wide---eyed schoolgirls. "*Onna o tukamaero!*" she yelled.

Two of the female gang members began moving closer. As Rachel crouched down, expecting the worst, the pink-haired girl sprang from the pack. She assaulted one of her cohorts, knocking her to the ground and punching her in the face and chest with both fists. Then the schoolgirl with spiky blue hair joined in and a nasty brawl broke out.

"Run!" the pink---haired instigator screamed.

Rachel took off in a flash with Chiyo yelling profanities in her wake. Miraculously, she pushed aside her exhaustion and headed straight toward the center of town. However, when she glanced over her shoulder, she discovered the schoolgirls hadn't been distracted for long. They were upright, sprinting right behind her, while onlookers stared in stunned disbelief. The women blew past crowds of confused-looking shoppers, and two taxis at the intersection slammed on their brakes after witnessing the strange pursuit.

As Rachel rounded a corner, she nearly collided with the gang member who had aided in her escape. Before she knew it, they were running side by side, parallel to the curb on the narrow adjoining street. After a few minutes, she glanced back again and was relieved to discover no one was following them.

The schoolgirl at her side yelled, "Stop!"

Rachel whipped her head around only to discover the gangster schoolgirls had somehow managed to beat them to the end of the block and were now running directly toward them. She dug the rubber soles of her shoes into the sidewalk and skidded to a stop. Then she quickly turned and headed east toward a housing district.

"Rachel---san, wait!" her running mate yelled.

Rachel slowed down long enough for her to catch up. "How do you know my name?"

The schoolgirl was gasping for breath. "Later. We have to get inside somewhere and fight them off. We can't just run forever!"

"You're right!" Rachel shouted back. "But how am I going to fight them off? I've never hit anyone in my life." As it turned out, they didn't have to wait long to find out. After barreling around another corner and down a back alley, they came face to face with a large delivery van parked outside of a high-rise apartment. With their path now blocked, they turned around and spotted Chiyo and her cohorts standing at the opposite end of the street.

The blue-haired gang member stepped forward. "How stupid you are!" she yelled. "All that running for nothing."

Chiyo raised her leather-knuckled fist in the air. "No chance you're getting away again. This time I'm ready."

Great. With the sense of dread building, Rachel glanced around and realized she was now alone. There was no telling where the pink-haired schoolgirl had run off to, and with her energy spent, she could merely watch as the group headed straight for her.

"I can't believe you shot him!" Chiyo snapped. She shoved Rachel backward into the concrete wall and grabbed her by the throat, cutting off her air supply. She raised her right fist, preparing to strike a blow. But in the nick of time, Rachel's protective instinct awoke. With as much force as she could muster, she pulled back her arm and drove her fist into Chiyo's side.

"Ahhh!" the sukeban yelled. Her hand fell from Rachel's throat. "So you want to play rough, huh?" While still holding her ribs, she swung her right hand, slapping Rachel hard.

"Ow!" The sting brought Rachel's hand to her cheek and tears to her eyes. No one, let alone a schoolgirl street fighter, had ever slapped her before.

Chiyo's left hand was back on her neck, but somehow Rachel struggled out of her grasp. "Someone help me!" she screamed. But only a raspy, choked sound came out. As Chiyo came at her again, anger seized Rachel's logical mind. She delivered a powerful back fist to the gang leader's face, whipping her head to the side. Chiyo pressed her palm against her cheek and spat out blood. She stared at Rachel for a long moment, as if mystified by her ability to fight back. She confirmed her witnesses were still standing close by watching before growling and swinging a wild fist. Rachel was quick, using the side of her arm to deflect her powerful punch. Then Chiyo spun around in place, back sweeping Rachel's legs out from under her. She hit the ground hard, knocking the wind from her lungs. Chiyo stood over her, throwing down punches.

The young pink-haired avenger suddenly came from nowhere, launching her body at Chiyo. Caught unaware, the gang leader fell backward, slamming her head hard against the sidewalk. As Rachel watched in stunned disbelief, Chiyo rolled over moaning, clutching her skull with both hands. Meanwhile her youthful protector swayed slightly on her feet and had to brace herself to keep from falling over.

"Nori, *kattobase!*" Chiyo yelled at the blue-haired schoolgirl. Nori jumped in and lifted a knee. Fortunately Rachel's compatriot had enough wits about her to bounce around like a kangaroo. With a well-timed duck, she averted being struck, and Nori's flying heel hit the wall. She dropped to the ground, clutching her knee and cursing idiotically under her breath. Rachel's ally pulled her yo-yo from her pocket. She glared at the only standing gang member, daring her to attack. But after glimpsing her damaged schoolmates, the challenger turned and ran away.

"That was incredible!" Rachel raved. "Who are you anyway?"

The unlikely hero shook her pink bangs out of her eyes. "Everyone calls me Kimi. I've been hearing about you from people around town. They said you and your boyfriend came here to find treasure."

"Really?" It seemed secrets were in short supply in Japan. "But why would you risk yourself to save me?" Rachel asked.

"I'm sorry, but this wasn't about you. Four days ago, Takashi Bekku gave my friend Suemi sedatives. He had her slip them under her tongue and French kiss some rich kid. He woke up while everyone was partying on his money and pulled a knife from his pocket. One of Takashi's men yanked it away and Suemi stepped in to protect the guy. He ended up getting badly beaten and left in a back alley. Then Chiyo punished my best friend by having her hung."

*Hung? With a rope?* Rachel couldn't believe her ears. After hitting Chiyo in the face and shooting Takashi in the groin, she couldn't imagine what kind of punishment she had earned.

"I've been waiting for a chance to get even," Kimi told her. "Suemi made some mistakes, but she didn't deserve—" Her chin suddenly lifted and Rachel's eyes followed. Chiyo was standing nearby with a piece of rubble clenched in her hand.

"No!" Kimi shrieked. She jumped forward, forcing Rachel out of the way. The spinning chunk of concrete struck her right leg. She screamed in agony and collapsed, whimpering. Without a thought for her own safety, Rachel stepped in front of Chiyo. Never in her lifetime would she have imagined herself caught in a female gang fight with nothing but her fists to protect herself. She drew a deep breath, squared her legs, and lifted her arms. If she could avoid being killed by marauding pirates on Stargazer, she sure as hell could defend herself against a smug, gum-popping schoolgirl.

"Bring it on," she said, sounding remarkably confident. A whirling sound captured her attention. As she turned, Nori's metal yo-yo bashed the side of her head, knocking her unconscious in a matter of seconds.

※

When Rachel opened her eyes again, she had a horrible headache and a painful knot on the side of her head. She looked around and discovered she was on the floor in a small room that was shoddily made out of wood. There weren't any furnishings, aside from a few mismatched chairs, a corner cot, and an electric light bulb hanging overhead on a rafter. Across from her, Kimi lay in a heap, her right leg splayed out at an unnatural angle. In their present condition, Rachel couldn't imagine how they were going to escape, or if it was even possible.

The first entrants into the room came as a great surprise. Instead of delinquent schoolgirls and yakuza gang members, an attractive middle-aged geisha showed up dressed in a light blue kimono followed closely by two old women with backs curved like snails.

"Who are you?" Rachel asked, pushing herself upright.

"Nikki Ota. I believe you know my daughter, Yuki." She stepped closer and extended a damp washcloth. "You're not looking so good."

Rachel took the kind offering and ran it over her forehead and across the back of her neck. She lifted her chin and closed her eyes briefly, relishing the cold against her skin. "Is it over? Did Yuki find the third sword?"

"Not that I know of, but I'm sure she will soon enough. Why did you get involved in all of this anyway?"

Rachel opened her mouth to respond then closed it.

"Never mind," the woman said. "It doesn't really matter. You're in a lot of trouble, you know. Did you really have to shoot Takashi?"

Before Rachel could answer, Kimi awoke and pushed herself upright. She used the back of a broken chair to stand on one foot until the two old women came to her aid. Propped between them, she spoke—her voice clearly strained.

"Konichiwa, Ota---sama."

Nikki glared at Kimi. "You're in a mess too," she said in English, perhaps for her benefit. "But then it was just a matter of time. You're always running off at the mouth, ignoring everyone's orders. At least you'll serve a useful purpose now."

The two women helped Kimi to a small cot in the far corner of the room. As one held out a bowl of water, the other attended to her injured leg.

"I don't understand," Rachel said. "I thought you came here to help us."

"I'm afraid you're beyond help, Miss Lyons. Takashi wanted me to have you buried alive. Fortunately I was able to change his mind."

Rachel stared at her, aghast and completely dumbfounded. "You're working together...with that nutcase?"

Nikki smiled. "He is, isn't he? I never understood what my son saw in him. But it doesn't really matter now. I'm leaving for England in the morning. Bidding farewell to all the misery in this forsaken place."

"What about Yuki?" Rachel asked. "Does she know I'm being kept here?"

"I very much doubt it. My daughter and I seldom speak."

Rachel glanced at the doorway where two enormous men now stood. "So if you have no intention of letting me go," she asked Nikki, "what are you planning to do with me?"

Kimi was quick to answer. "You're going for a ride in an ocean freight container. We're both going to be shipped out tomorrow."

"Actually, later tonight," Nikki corrected. "Right after the dinner party at my okiya. I'm passing the reins to my adopted daughter before I leave."

Rachel looked at Kimi, thoroughly confused. "If you haven't figured it out yet," Kimi told her, "you're talking to the mastermind behind Takashi's prostitution ring. The same woman who's been using the sukeban to lure girls away from their families. She stockpiles them in warehouses and ships them to Thailand. But I don't know why she thinks no one's going to miss you. Americans always rescue their own."

"Not when they think the yakuza disposed of her," Nikki said with a soft smile. "With Mitsui's men hanging around all the time, no one would ever believe I was involved."

Rachel narrowed her eyes. "And to think I admired geishas in this country."

Nikki huffed a laugh. "If you play your cards right, you might even become one. In Thailand, that is."

"I guess now I understand why Yuki kept her distance. Who would want you for a mother?"

Nikki crossed her arms. Her face curled into a dour expression. "How could you think so poorly of me, Miss Lyons?" She shook her head and heaved a sigh. "I'm just a survivor, like everyone else. Doing what I have to in order to get by. You haven't a clue what it's like to be a woman in this country. Bowing down to every man. Holding your tongue until you want to scream. But now you'll have time to figure that out for yourself…with your new occupation."

Rachel glanced at the pink-haired girl shifting uncomfortably on the cot, her leg now fully bandaged. "Why are you doing this to her? She hasn't harmed you."

"My partner would think otherwise. But the fifty thousand dollars she'll bring along with money from all the other girls will ease his pain and suffering considerably."

Before Rachel could respond to Nikki's callous remarks, she crossed the floor to address Kimi. "Why did you have to screw everything up? You and your hoodlum friends were supposed to watch her. That's all."

When Kimi spoke, her voice was hesitant but her words were carefully chosen. "Takashi had other plans for her involving Mitsui-san. He only cares about his own neck, Ota-sama. Anyway, that doesn't matter right now. This woman has nothing to do with your business. Why can't you keep her tied up until you're gone?"

"Because her boyfriend would come looking for me and I'm not about to take that chance."

Rachel took a step toward her. "You don't need to do this, Nikki. Just let us go. I won't say anything about you."

"Somehow I doubt that, Miss Lyons. Your fine morals would get in the way. I don't believe you'd ignore the fact that I'm exporting twenty-two girls against their wishes. And besides, even if I was willing to set everyone free, my partners in Thailand would never agree. There are some people you don't break contracts with...not if you hope to keep breathing."

Rachel glanced at the two men waiting in the doorway. They were standing shoulder to shoulder, wearing dark, solemn expressions—resembling bouncers at a Las Vegas nightclub. She swallowed hard and considered her options, which appeared to be nonexistent without the help of an outsider. For crying out loud, Chase, she thought. Where the hell are you?

"You might have noticed by now that your escorts are here," Nikki said. "As they say in America, it's not polite to keep them waiting."

"You can't do this!" Rachel yelled. "Please...I'm begging you!"

Nikki walked toward the door. She turned and stared back at her, and for an instant Rachel held out hope that she had changed her mind. That somehow compassion had won out over greed. But then Nikki lowered her eyes, turned, and walked away, leaving her minions in charge.

Rachel could hardly breathe. She dropped to her knees, shivering with the truth. With Nikki's menacing plot in full swing and Japan on the verge of destruction, any possibility of Chase finding her would end in a matter of hours.

# 35

The cargo agent sat in his chair, his body glistening with oily sweat. One of his sad female assistants was kneeling before him, rubbing his swollen, gouty foot. Lined up, just inside the warehouse door, was a selection of girls for him to inspect. Without resistance, they arrived one by one in front of him. He stared at their faces from various angles, judging their ages, bone structure, and beauty—or lack of it. Each one was told to lift her garments so he could inspect them as one would cattle. He raised his fingers with indifference, indicating who would bring the highest dollar. The woman across from him gave them a momentary glance then returned to her book, scribbling compulsory notes based on the grumbling noises he made.

Soon it was Rachel's turn. She was shoved forward for a complete inspection, much as she had been with Chiyo. He stared into her face and she returned an angry, defiant look. He stood up and lifted her hair away from her neck. She pulled back, rejecting his touch.

*"Dare desu ka?"* he asked her.

She didn't answer, prompting another prying question.

*"Namea wa?"*

*My name?* "None of your business," she said.

He looked at her in astonishment. It seemed he wasn't prepared for her hostility or the fact that she was American. Either way, he yelled for one of the men who had brought her and appeared to demand an explanation. By the tilt of his chin and the concentration in his thin, cold eyes, Rachel was sure she'd be rejected and directed away from the loading door. But a handful of cash swayed the agent's mind and his assistant's rough hands moved her forward,  allowing space for the next apprehensive girl.

In assembly line fashion, zip ties were cut from their wrists, and fresh clothes and a packet of toiletries were thrust into their hands, along with a boxed bento lunch. Each woman was ushered to a hay-covered area and told to sit down. Looking around, Rachel saw no sign of Kimi and wondered if she'd actually been brought here, regardless of her injury.

When the storage unit had reached full capacity, a woman's scream brought two warehouse workers and the bookkeeper running. Words were exchanged and several captives moved aside, allowing the cargo agent access. He bent over a girl, examining her. With annoyance furrowing his brow, he pushed back her eyelids and looked into her dead eyes. Then he rose to his feet and shook his head at all of them. There was no expression of horror on his face, no words of regret for the curious onlookers. He simply shrugged and whacked off the rope binding the young girl's hands with the slash of a knife and slipped it back into his belt.

Rachel watched with stony-eyed revulsion as her body was carried out with the same disregard as a bag of trash. The door was slid shut, two guards resumed their posts, and a young girl approached Rachel from the side.

"She chose the easy way out," she whispered in her ear. Rachel's breath caught in her throat. She turned and realized it was Kimi...out from wherever she'd been hiding. Although she still favored her injured leg, the pink-haired juvenile delinquent seemed to be none the worse for wear.

"She killed herself?" Rachel asked.

"Most likely," Kimi answered nonchalantly. "Don't see that I blame her. It's tough enough surviving here. I can't imagine what it's going to be like living in the backstreets of Bangkok."

Rachel glanced at all the young girls and women surrounding her—some sobbing, others eating, a few mindlessly staring into space. They represented a range of ages and Asian nationalities, leaving her wondering if they'd been taken from cities and townships throughout Japan. Surely they had family members and friends...places where they all belonged. Communities where they had turned up missing. Someone out there had to be looking for them, wondering if they were dead or alive.

"Half of these women won't last more than three months," Kimi told her. "They'll either die on the way there or be beaten up by the pimps who control them. And once we're on board that ship, there's no going back. None of them will ever see their homes again."

Rachel swallowed hard and made a promise to herself that no matter how many bodies dropped, including her own, she would never cooperate. With twenty--four women against six

guards, there was every reason to believe a rebellion would suc-
ceed. She just had to instill confidence in a group of women who
had been trained since birth to fear their superiors, accept their
status in life, and walk five feet behind men.

One of the guards turned on the television and the confined
group listened quietly to the nine o'clock news reporting tremors and high tides along the coastal towns. Huddled together in
their anxiety, they kept vigil in the cramped room. Through a
small westerly facing window, there was a brilliant red sky unlike
anything Rachel had ever seen. After the sunset, the air cooled
in the room and rain began dumping from the sky. Everywhere
it was quiet and still. Hushed and nervous they waited. By ten
o'clock it was pitch black outside. An unseasonable wind had
risen, making the metal gate outside bang and clatter. At ten
to eleven, one of the guards came into the room to walk three
ladies at a time to the closest bathroom. When he returned,
Rachel raised her hand.

"Bathroom, please," she said. She finished using the facility
and washed her hands in the sink. On the other side of the wall,
the guard's footsteps clumped noisily on the floorboards as he
paced back and forth. Returning to the warehouse, Rachel spotted a dark vehicle gliding slowly up the street and backing into
the loading dock. According to her watch, it was now eleven. The
van that would take them to the shipping container on the water-
front had arrived. One of the guards asked to see the identifica-
tion tags they'd each been given, and then they began to load up
the women and their belongings. Like soldiers in a concentration camp, the armed men directed their female prisoners from

the warehouse to the van. The scene was strangely surreal—the hostages' compliance inconceivable.

*What have I done to deserve this?* Rachel thought. Recollections of her naivety, her insensitivity to news reports involving the blatant disregard for human rights were stupefying. She had heard of forced labor, people who had been shot in the head, boys who had been kneecapped—brutality implemented to squelch unrest and political opposition. Although the catalogue of violence spilled out across the world, she had never realized the gravity of injustice until she was thrust into the middle of it.

Kimi was back at her side. "I tried to find a way out, but it's no use. They've got all the doors locked and the guards never let you out of their sight. So I guess we have no choice but to go along. But don't worry. At least we'll be on the ship together."

One of the guards ushered Rachel to the waiting van. After handing her unused items to him, she climbed into the back, sat down on an inside seat, and waited for the engine to start. The van slowly maneuvered out onto the street and down the main road. She leaned forward, watching through the large windshield as they approached the motorway bridge. Two figures with something clutched in their hands stood side by side in the darkness. She strained her eyes, hoping they were police officers that would demand papers and do a thorough search. But no such luck. The van shot past the dock workers and headed straight for a row of shipping containers and an enormous lit crane loading outgoing vessels. They came to an abrupt stop, and the driver and two guards got out. They circled around to the back doors while the women nervously waited.

Rachel leaned toward Kimi, seated across from her. "I'm going to make a run for it. If we all take off at the same time in different directions, they won't be able to catch most of us."

Kimi nodded. She turned to the woman next to her and whispered Rachel's plan. The women in the van continued the process, passing her message along until everyone's eyes were fixed on Rachel. Some of them were frightened and shook their heads, but the majority appeared to be onboard. There was the sound of a key in the lock and the first door opened. Rachel moved into position next to the exit and waited to pounce. Loud voices outside pulled the attention of one of the guards, but the other two men at the door kept their focus on their nervous cargo.

As word traveled quietly among the women, Rachel learned that one of the dock workers was involved in a scuffle with his boss and angry fists were flying. The only thing she could grasp from the yelling outside were the words police, coming, and now. From her limited view, she was able to see that the fallen supervisor had managed to sit up and the dock workers were jeering at him. Two more suited men appeared and immediately become involved in pushing and shoving matches with the men closest to them.

Five security guards, recognizable by their blue uniforms, suddenly appeared on the scene. These rather hulking figures carried truncheons and began pushing the dock workers toward the other side of the street, separating them from their bosses. Some of the men attempted to resist, and blows from the truncheons began raining down on them. While this violent confrontation grew, word was apparently spreading, as late-night workers began spilling out on the street.

"What should we do?" Rachel asked Kimi.

The girl's pink hair shook back and forth. "Nothing. They're not going to allow anyone out of here. Not now."

*Shit.* Rachel fell back in her seat as the engine sprang to life. The door was slammed shut and locked, and the van sped out of the parking lot. Although the dock uprising had prevented the women's transfer into shipping containers, it had also eliminated the only opportunity for their escape.

As Rachel looked at the mournful faces surrounding her, it seemed all hope had vanished and the few grains of time that remained on this earth were about to be washed away.

# 36

As Chase entered the dimly lit room accompanied by several of Mitsui's men, the yakuza boss patted the floor chair beside him. Then he returned his attention to an ongoing Bunraku puppet show taking place on the portable theater sitting directly before him. The young maiko seated on the opposite side of Mitsui rose gracefully and lowered herself to a kneeling position directly behind Chase. After a brief nod, she proceeded to explain the nature of the main characters in the play, all of which had been damaged in some way by love yet also looked to it in order to heal themselves.

"They are powerless and vulnerable, inescapably bound to their emotions and the mercy of their desires and regrets," she explained, lending weight to the dolls' lifelike movements. Then she smiled sweetly and added softly, "We're privileged and honored to witness the magic of Yoshida-san's creations. He's one of Japan's greatest puppet masters."

Although remarkable and beautiful to watch, Chase had no interest in the puppets or any other form of entertainment. He had come specifically to find Rachel, and his patience was long gone. With a heated sigh, he stole a look in Mitsui's direction. The jovial man was a far cry from the snarling thug he'd previously encountered. As the story before them unfolded, he chuckled and cheered. He nodded in approval and clapped his hands like a child at a birthday party.

Chase gave the room a sweeping look while anxiously waiting to gain Mitsui's attention. The three men who had brought him here stood with their arms crossed near the rear wall, staring straight ahead with stoic expressions. The ticking sound of a wall clock in the sparsely furnished room was a constant reminder that minutes were slipping away and the threat of imminent danger was growing.

A young woman approached from the opposite side of the room, bringing beer from the neighboring kitchen. Without acknowledging her, Mitsui picked up his amber glass and drained it. Then she refilled it and offered a frosty beer-filled glass to Chase.

*"Ketsukodesu,"* he answered, declining politely. He was feeling slightly sick to his stomach from worrying, and the stifling heat in the room wasn't helping.

The play finally came to an end and the lights slowly came up. Without acknowledging Chase's presence, the yakuza boss spoke. "It surprises me that you've come here this evening. I thought you were inspecting my boat...to determine if it's worth saving." He paused before angling a curious look. "Or are you still conducting sight- seeing trips?"

"Neither," Chase answered tersely. "I came here to find out what you did with Rachel."

"Excuse me?" It was Mitsui's turn to lift a brow. "What exactly are you accusing me of?"

His men began to move forward. He waved them back quickly. The maiko seemed to feel the tension between them, as she was now staring down at the floor.

"If she's missing, like you say," Mitsui said, "why would you assume I took her? You must truly think the worst of me, Cohen-san. I have no interest in harming Miss Lyons. In fact, my only interest has been in studying her and knowing her better."

Chase was utterly lost. "What exactly is that supposed to mean?"

"Well, if you haven't figured it out yet, the young lady sitting next to you is my niece. I've looked out for her since my sister's death eight years ago. Her father was an American sea captain who I think you might have known. He was living in California and had been estranged from his wife when he came here. I had my own feelings about that and never believed he had honorable intentions. But my sister had a mind of her own. Tamayo wanted to share this information with Miss Lyons, but I discouraged her from it...until I understood what kind of woman she was dealing with."

Chase absorbed all of this, frowning. Everything Mitsui had said struck him as accurate, yet he had an even stronger impression that this man's agenda, for some reason, was to push him down the wrong path. He had similar thoughts about the maiko in their company, but staring at her pale face and into her steady eyes, he couldn't be sure of anything.

"Why don't you tell me what's going on?" Mitsui asked. "Has someone kidnapped Miss Lyons?"

Chase wasted no time in retelling his story. When he mentioned the police and their lack of support, Mitsui shook his head.

"Kobayashi, huh? That doesn't surprise me. He's just waiting for his day to retire.

*Great.* That's just what Chase needed to hear.

"Anything else?" the old man asked. "Surely you have more to go on."

"Well, the officer did say something about other women missing. He pulled out a file and showed me dozens of pictures." A fresh thought occurred to Chase. "Do you think it's possible the same man took Rachel?"

Mitsui took another sip from his beer glass. "In her case, I think it would have taken several men."

Chase offered a weak smile. There was no doubt about it… Rachel was a dynamo. She was sharp and intuitive, and fully capable of figuring her way out of a jam. But that didn't lessen his concern. Not one tiny bit.

"I'll tell you what," Mitsui said, pulling his cell phone out of his pocket. "Let me make a few calls and see what I can find out. If one of the other families is involved, I'll know soon enough. In the meantime, go back to your hotel and wait. Miss Lyons might call, and it wouldn't be good if you were still here."

Chase stood on the curb with two suitcases in hand, waiting until the light changed. As he searched vainly for an empty cab, his eyes strayed to two Japanese men standing on the opposite side of the street. One was holding what appeared to be a photograph while intermittently glancing in Chase's direction. After a few seconds, he pointed directly at him and the second man nodded in agreement. Fearing that the men were about to cross the street and approach him, Chase gave up trying to hail a cab. He spun on his heel and immediately began to walk quickly toward the imperial gardens, weaving in and out of the sidewalk crowds. Even though Mitsui had surprisingly agreed to help him, he'd never seen these particular individuals and assumed they were from another yakuza family. He had no idea why they would be interested in him and preferred to keep it that way.

As he reached the next busy intersection and prepared to cross the street, he glanced to his left to see if the men had joined the crowd of businessmen, tourists, and female shoppers on the crowded sidewalk. He breathed a sigh of relief at not seeing them and figured the incident was just his worry over Rachel and an overactive imagination. However, after spotting signs for the train station on the opposite street corner, Chase ventured another glance over his shoulder. To his dismay, he saw the same two men skirting around people and heading straight toward him while carrying on a conversation with two men creeping along in a black SUV.

*You've got to be kidding.* As soon as their eyes met, the men responded by upping their speed and breaking off all conversations. Still clutching the two small suitcases he had brought with him, Chase sprinted through the press of people, unsure of which way to go. The stairway entrance to the complicated subway with multiple train lines was like a distant oasis promising safety, but how was he going to get there before being overtaken by the men following him?

Salvation materialized in the next instant when a taxi pulled to the curb and discharged a passenger. Without a second's hesitation, Chase veered through the oncoming pedestrians and leaped into the taxi before the disembarking passenger had both feet on the ground. Out of breath, Chase gasped, "Ginza subway line."

Miffed at getting such a brief fare, the driver made an illegal U-turn, causing Chase to slide against the door he had just managed to close. Once the cab was straightened out, he pushed himself upright and glanced out the back window in time to see the two men stumble to a halt. He didn't know if they'd seen him jump into the taxi, but he was sure they had no idea where he was headed.

Chase made it safely to the underground entrance on Ginzanamiki Street. He hurried down the staircase, through the crowded white tunnel, and managed to pass quickly through the turnstile with his pre-purchased metro ticket in hand. He made his way to the proper track and approached the edge of the concrete platform, watching the mouth of the tunnel in search of his train. Stepping back from the edge, Chase glanced suspiciously at the other passengers, all of whom were avoiding eye contact. The platform rapidly filled as he waited. Commuters read newspapers or played with their cell phones or stared blankly into the middle distance. More people arrived,   pressing everyone closer and closer together. Trains thundered into the station, but always on other tracks.

It was then that Chase saw him—the same man who had held his picture on the other side of town. He was only five or six feet behind him, regarding Chase out of the corner of his piercing black eyes. With a renewed sense of danger, Chase tried to move away from the stranger, but it was difficult with more and more passengers arriving every few seconds. Having managed to move only a few yards, he looked ahead to see what was impeding his progress. The second man was standing ahead of him, pretending to read a paper. He was the same distance away, leaving Chase trapped between the tracks and tiled wall.

As his fear maxed out, the westbound train suddenly arrived, roaring out of the mouth of its tunnel. One second there had been relative quiet, the next a crescendo of ferocious wind, ear-splitting noise, and earthshaking vibration. During this minor maelstrom Chase became aware that the two men were pushing through the waiting crowd, pressing in on him. He was prepared to hit them with his suitcases if either one touched him, but they didn't. All he was aware of was a concussive hiss that he felt more than heard, since the noise was completely drowned out by the arriving train. Simultaneously the ground trembled and the overhead signs began swinging. A dizzy sensation hit him although nothing else seemed to be moving. The incident lasted only a few seconds. Then the sound of a speaker announcement filled the metro station. Chase looked around him and was surprised to see everyone had frozen in place, looking up at the speakers. Waiting for the second announcement to come. When it did, the subway passengers returned to their lives—answering their phones, skimming their newspapers, chatting among themselves. The scene was once again normal. Too normal.

A man touched Chase's arm, startling him and causing him to raise his fist "Are you okay?" It was Detective Honda, the officer he'd met at the police station. The same man who had offered his assistance in finding Rachel when his boss walked away.

"Yeah, I'm fine." As the crowd thinned around them, Chase realized the men who had followed him were now nowhere in sight. Had the detective's presence expedited their departure?

"It was a low-level earthquake," Honda explained. "We get them here all the time. Nothing to worry about. In fact, the subway is probably one of the safest places in the city."

Chase considered Shinzo's warning to Rachel. The tremor was merely the beginning of what would eventually come if the last sword wasn't found. For a second he was tempted to tell the officer about the pending disaster, but then realized it would come off sounding completely crazy.

"That's good to know," Chase said, eyeing him suspiciously. Honda's sudden appearance seemed a bit too coincidental. It was late in the afternoon, the busiest time in downtown

Tokyo—much too early for him to be off duty. "What are you doing here anyway?" Chase asked.

"Actually, I was looking for you. Some of my men saw you heading this way."

"Those were your men? The guys following me?"

Honda nodded.

"Geez...I thought they were gang members," Chase said. "Does everyone in this town wear a suit?"

The detective muffled a laugh. "Mostly, I guess. Anyway, I wanted to find out if you've heard anything out of your girlfriend since we spoke."

Chase shook his head, unsure where his question was leading.

"Then all the more reason we should work together. Takashi Bekku was treated at a hospital last night. My department was called because his injury involved a gun. He was picked up and brought to the station for questioning, but the only thing we got out of him was that Rachel was involved."

"She shot him? With a gun?"

"Yes, sir. The fact that you reported her missing leads me to believe he was responsible for taking her as well. With so many girls missing, including my daughter, I'm hoping he'll lead us to their whereabouts."

"Your daughter?"

"Kimiko. She's only sixteen. I'm ashamed to say she's been out on her own for the last year. But she's made a point of calling me every day. I haven't heard from her for nearly a week, and her friends haven't spoken to her either. I know you've been in close contact with Kaito Mitsui. If you have any influence with him at all, I recommend asking for his assistance in regard to Takashi Bekku. Since this man works for him, Mitsui-san might make a greater impression than any of us."

*Impression? Are you kidding?* "I'll ask him, but from what I understand, Mitsui keeps a tight rein on his men. He has to know by now that you're holding Takashi. Of course I'll do whatever I can to help, but what I'd really like to do is see Takashi. Maybe there's some way I could get him to open up and—"

"No, Mr. Cohen. Bekku is refusing to speak to anyone. I really don't see how your being there is going to make a difference."

"If you want my cooperation," Chase said, "then let me do this. Just give me ten minutes alone with him. I know I can get him to talk."

"Unfortunately, you're not a police officer, Mr. Cohen, and even if you were, you don't have the jurisdiction or rights to interrogate a criminal in this country. Although I would personally like to beat the shit out of this man, the only way we're going to get his cooperation is with Mitsui-san's involvement. So please, I'm asking you kindly...do this not only for my daughter but for the sake of Miss Lyons."

Chase was utterly confused. He was a stranger in a strange land, overcome by extenuating circumstances—a dilemma utterly beyond his control. But through it all, he had clung to the conviction that he needed to appear calm and sophisticated. He couldn't let anyone suspect that he wasn't sure of himself... or something terrible might happen. Of course, he was wrong; something terrible had already happened. He was indeed a total stranger in a strange and confusing land, but he didn't think, in retrospect, that he was capable of making the situation worse by visiting a police station and blurting out his predicament.

With great reluctance, he agreed to speak with Mitsui. However, as he walked away, he was struck by the notion that the police department was at the mercy of a yakuza boss and no one in Japan seemed to mind.

# 37

Mariko stood in the shade of an ancient cherry tree watching through Kenji's eyes as Yuki exited Shinzo's ministry office. Yuki was carrying his red wakizashi and anime mask and had disappointment written all over her face. It seemed with Shinzo's absence that Yuki had missed her opportunity to end another man's life. As she boarded a southbound taxi and headed across town, Mariko followed suit. The cars arrived one after the other in front of the ancient Shoten temple. It was the same place where Shinzo had gone an hour earlier to meet with visiting monks.

Mariko paid her driver and crossed the gravel courtyard behind Yuki with a matching red katana slung high across her back. The sought-after tanto knife was tucked beneath her leather belt, brushing against her thigh with every step. Although she had no intention of using either weapon, Mariko felt compelled to keep them close at hand.

Like their ancestors before them, the women stepped carefully on the crunching stones. However, the ingenious ninja alarm made it impossible to go undetected. Yuki suddenly turned around. Her eyes narrowed at the sight of Mariko, standing on the edge of her shadow.

"I've been hunting all over for you," she claimed.

Mariko silently glared, revealing nothing to this wicked creature—this woman who would betray her own blood for the money the three relics would bring.

Yuki narrowed her eyes and tilted her head to the side, scrutinizing the geisha's disheveled appearance. "Why are you acting so strange?" she asked. "You look like you stepped out of a samurai manga series." Her gaze moved to the top of Kenji's red katana then down to the tanto holstered in Mariko's belt. Her mouth fell open as she stared at the stolen knife, disbelief filling her gaze. "You thief!" Yuki shrieked, dropping the anime mask. She unsheathed her sword and swung it with deadly precision.

Mariko was quick on her feet, rolling under the wakizashi before it could strike. "I don't want to hurt you," she yelled back. She had come there only to ask questions—to discover the truth about the deaths she'd caused. But with Yuki extending her sword and determined to harm her, there was no point in holding back.

"Hurt me?" Yuki chuckled. "That's impossible. You're nothing but a geisha. What could you possibly know about sword fighting?"

"More than you could ever imagine," Mariko answered.

"Really? Somehow I doubt that." Yuki bowed deeply, never taking her eyes off Mariko. "To the death or first blood?" she said like a gallant knight of a bygone era. Before the geisha could respond, Yuki wielded her sword, slicing the air where she had stood seconds earlier.

Unfortunately, Mariko's jump had brought her a foot closer. "Both," she answered. Her lips twisted into a cynical smile. She drew the katana with a flourish and lunged at Yuki but was blocked by the smashing of swords. With no forewarning, Yuki spun around, landing a roundhouse kick to the side of Mariko's face. Dazed by the hit, Mariko was thrown to one knee. She quickly picked up the katana and blocked the wakizashi that was coming straight at her in Yuki's attempt to impale her. She rolled over and regained her footing. Then she quickly raised her katana and charged at Yuki, jumping three feet in the air. With concentrated effort, Mariko kicked her back into the wall, but it stunned her for only a moment. Yuki swung her sword wildly and the geisha ducked to the side as it came. From left to right, she dodged her swipes, showing no sign of slowing.

Yuki gave a short laugh. "I have to admit I'm impressed. Kenji must've taught you well, but you're still no match—"

Mariko halted her boast midsentence with a kick to the side of her head. Although she was sent back to the wall, Yuki still managed to stay on her feet. Mariko watched for an opening and used it to drive a punch into her midsection. She followed it with a hard uppercut to her jaw. Amazingly, there was no stopping Yuki, no way of keeping her down. Instead she sprang effortlessly to her feet, pointed her wakizashi, and charged again.

Mariko raised Kenji's katana, avoiding another strike. She drove Yuki forward and was blocked by her sword. They clashed over and over, both unleashing a flurry of swipes. Then Mariko locked Yuki's weapon and pushed her back hard. She swung Kenji's katana and Yuki ducked, losing a few strands of her hair. She screeched and stepped sideways to dodge another oncoming strike.

Mariko threw a roundhouse kick, sending Yuki flying backward into the air. She raised Kenji's katana and directed a vertical strike but was blocked yet again. They both ran toward each other screaming their battle cries, their long ebony hair flying and their swords swinging above their heads. As they met in the middle, they locked into a stalemate and pushed off each other before slashing at each other again and again.

The battle continued for five more minutes and eventually Mariko grew bored with the evenly matched struggle. She pulled the tanto knife from her belt. Yuki's eyes widened as the diamond shimmered, blinding her at a timely moment. Mariko sliced the air in a wide arc with the katana, crashing violently into Yuki's wakizashi. She drew the knife back with every intention of driving it under Yuki's arm and into her stomach, twisting it to enact her revenge.

"No! Stop it!" The yell came from Shinzo. Mariko's deadly thrust halted at the sound of his voice and the sight of him running straight at them. At the same time, Yuki took advantage of Mariko's distraction to deliver a powerful, sweeping blow. The red katana and diamond tanto flew out of her hands and clattered to the ground. Shinzo hurriedly bent down to pick up the knife. He was about to claim Kenji's sword when Mariko rushed at him, snatching it out from under him.

Eight Zen monks wearing large straw hats had followed Shinzo into the courtyard and were now watching her from the sideline with stony expressions. Shinzo moved slightly, blocking her view. He leaned down to look at her more closely.

"What's wrong with you, Mariko?" he asked. "Why are you acting so strangely?"

The geisha studied his hand, which was holding the tanto in a practiced grip, exhibiting the confidence of a master swordsman. She looked beyond him at Yuki, appearing calm and collected. The vision of her leaving Shinzo's office suddenly came rushing back.

Mariko stiffened her knees and looked deep into Shinzo's eyes. There was something there—a hidden agenda, a reason for barring the truth. He reached out to touch her arm. She jerked away from his grasp. He put his arm around her and tried to draw her close, but she pulled away from him and snarled at him in disgust.

"Don't...ever...touch me," she gritted out. While the monks stared in silence, she slid Kenji's red katana into its scabbard and slung it over her back. She turned to walk away then began running as fast as she could. The cab that had brought her there was still waiting next to the curb. She jumped inside and told the driver her address. Then she rocked back and forth in her seat until the cab came to a stop in front of her apartment building.

After throwing money at the driver, she jumped out of the cab and took the elevator to the sixth floor. She had to try three times before her hand was steady enough to slide the key into the lock. When finally inside, she slammed the door shut and slid to the floor, preventing anyone's entry. By all appearances, Yuki and Shinzo were covering for each other. Whatever their motives, their blind allegiance had led to Kenji's death. The thought was inconceivable, beyond reason...beyond doubt.

I hate them, I hate them, I hate them, her mind screamed. Badly in need of a dulling agent, she climbed to her feet and wandered into the kitchen. She opened the refrigerator, took out the half liter of Oroku sake, unscrewed the cap, and began guzzling it straight from the bottle. Then she dropped into a kitchen chair and set to work plotting the best way to get even— the best way to humiliate and destroy both of them without losing a drop of sweat.

# 38

Chase left the train station at 8:00 p.m. and entered the horde of commuters on the neon-blanketed street, his thoughts scrambled and his heart racing. Rachel had been missing for over six hours and the sense of helplessness was chewing a hole in his gut. Although Mitsui had told him to return to his hotel to await word from her, Honda's concern for his own daughter's safety and the suffocating heat from the sidewalk had raised Chase's panic level to a boiling point. With his common sense quickly evaporating, he scanned the boulevard for an empty taxi to seek out Mitsui's assistance. Miraculously, a green MK taxi pulled up beside him and the door automatically opened.

Without hesitation, he slid inside and directed his destination to the back of the driver's head. "Shinjuku."

The man turned, and his familiar profile caught Chase completely off guard. It was the same driver who had taken him to Shinzo's blind tasting dinner and Mitsui's social club earlier that day. If not for his worries over Rachel and Japan's looming threat, he might have chuckled at seeing the wiry-haired character for a third time.

"Oh, hello...it's you!" the man said into his rearview mirror. "Remember me?"

Chase sniffed a noncommittal laugh. "Looks like you're the only driver in town."

The man flashed him a broad, toothy smile. "You no go to Otani Hotel?"

"Great memory, but no...not this time. I need you to take me back to the Zakura-kai social club. Looks like I'm becoming a regular." He offered a weak smile then stared out the side window, avoiding the man's puzzled stare.

After they arrived, Chase paid his fare and bid the driver farewell. He walked the familiar path through back streets and past alleyways before coming to Mitsui's place of business. Strangely, there were no guards waiting or lights glowing overhead to indicate anyone was milling about. When he tried the side door, he discovered it was locked, and the blinds on the upper windows were fully drawn.

An elderly woman from a neighboring shop stopped sweeping the sidewalk long enough to watch him.

"Do you speak English?" Chase called out to her. She shook her head and returned to her work. "Mitsui-san. He was here." Chase pointed at the building, incorporating a childlike sign language. "Do you know where he is?"

The old woman shook her head, avoiding his eyes.

"*Bushisuke de...shitsurei shimasu,*" he said, carefully enunciating the apology he'd painstakingly practiced during his long plane ride to Japan.

"*Denwa o kake mashitaka?*" she called back.

"*Gomennasai. Wakarimasen.*" He was hoping for clarification while dreading an answer he knew he would never understand.

She pointed to the cell phone bulging from his jean pocket. "Phone. Mitsui-san. You call," she said before turning away. It seemed they were the only words in English she was willing to share.

"I don't know his number!" Chase yelled. "But maybe if you could tell me..."

The woman disappeared inside, taking her broom and frown with her.

"It's an emergency. I have to reach him," he called after her, knowing it was useless to pursue her attention.

*Great. Now what?* Chase looked up and down the street, but the lack of activity gave him no options other than to abide by Mitsui's instructions. He was considering returning to the intersection to get another taxi when suddenly a black limo pulled up alongside the curb. The rear passenger window instantly rolled down and a familiar face came into view.

"Mr. Cohen?" Tamayo said. "I was just coming to your hotel to find you. My uncle spoke with one of Bekku-san's men. Can you please join me? I have news about Miss Lyons."

The limo driver hurried around the back of the car and beckoned to Chase, who followed after him without a second thought. Tamayo's words beat in his ears with a sense of growing excitement. He lowered himself onto the seat then turned to her as the door shut behind him. This doll-like creature seemed to show up everywhere at just the right moment. A true godsend, if ever there was one. However, when she spoke, her voice seemed small and constricted...as if being forced out of her body.

"I'm afraid I have some rather bad news," she said. "This is very...difficult for me, Cohen-san. I have not been properly trained to say such things. I am an entertainer, a singer...a musician. Maikos should never be messengers of sadness." Tamayo looked down thoughtfully. Her brows pinched, emphasizing her worry. "We are trained to take burdens away, not add to them."

Chase closed his eyes and swallowed hard, fearing the news she'd come there to share—the devastating outcome he had been incapable of preventing. She has to be all right, he told himself. How can I live without her? The thought of Rachel being ripped from his life was inconceivable, too horrible to even imagine. How could he go on without her? What purpose would there be for living? Never seeing her again, never sharing her smile…never feeling her touch or hearing her voice. It would be the cruelest punishment of all. He would suffer for the rest of his life knowing he hadn't protected her— hadn't been there when she needed him most. The sad realization filled his eyes with moisture, threatened to break his inner strength. Although his brain was fighting for answers, his heart didn't want him to ask—didn't want to know the terrible truth.

He raked his hands through his hair and gripped the back of his sweaty neck. Then he turned his eyes toward Tamayo, exposing his raw emotions.

"Tell me how it happened." His voice was hoarse. "Did she suffer in the end?"

Tamayo's gaze moved down to his mouth and remained there, as if digesting the meaning of his words. Then she began shaking her head over and over again. "No, no," she said. "That's not what I meant. Rachel's not dead. She's very much alive. We need to hurry before the cargo ship leaves the harbor and she disappears forever." Chase stared at the maiko in stunned disbelief.

"What are you talking about? What ship?"

"The one that's taking her across the ocean," she answered. "Delivering her to the men who bought her."

"Bought her?" he snapped. "How...who...when did this happen? Where is she being held? Does Mitsui-san know these men?" His questions came fast and furious, driving Tamayo into the back of her seat.

She was cowering now, as if being physically struck by his pelting words.

"I'm sorry," Chase said when his senses finally took hold. He rested his hand gently on her arm and looked deep into her eyes. "I didn't mean to frighten you. I should be thankful that you found me...that there's still a chance to rescue Rachel. Please tell me, Tamayo...are we heading to the docks? Is that where your driver is taking us?"

The tension eased in her face. She nodded and a shaky smile lifted the corners of her lips.

"Good," he said. "Where is your uncle? Is he going to help us?"

"He's already there," she said. "But he may be gone when we arrive.

"Gone? I don't understand. Why wouldn't he wait for us to show up?"

"My uncle leaves when there's trouble, Cohen-san. But I assure you, he looks after everyone he cares about."

"Does that include Rachel?"

"I don't know," she answered honestly. "We can only hope that he recognizes her as my sister."

# 39

There it was...Kokoro. The treasured sword everyone wanted and would kill to own. Mariko slipped into the inner sanctuary of the temple where Shinzo had foolishly left it unguarded on an altar table. Its emerald heart shimmered like a lover begging to be touched, while its encasement remained as flawless as the day it was made. She picked it up and pulled the sword from its ebony scabbard to study its exquisite, seamless edge. The weapon felt perfectly balanced in her hands, a true credit to its skilled maker. Beneath her fingers, its braided handle emitted unexpected warmth—a demonic presence unlike any her conjoined soul had experienced. This katana had destroyed many lives throughout history and would soon bring the walls tumbling down, smothering Japan under the ocean without mercy or a deep-winded breath.

Mariko smiled. With Kenji's demise, any loyalties or compassion he'd once felt had been erased. Only his hatred remained—dark, spiteful, and twisted, longing for satisfaction. This tool would serve him well indeed. Mariko's imminent death would leave their souls entwined forever, and despite Shinzo's miraculous powers, there was nothing he could do to prevent it.

In a mindless haze, Mariko held the exposed blade under her chin and visualized standing before Shinzo, drawing it across her throat until a stream of red burst forth like a dam condemning him to hell forever. The sound of footsteps in the hallway halted her thoughts and she quickly hid in the gray, shadowy alcove. From their voices, she was able to ascertain that two temple guards were returning to their duties. Although they were obviously unaware of her presence, leaving with Kokoro would now be impossible without being discovered. She leaned back against the wall while determining her next move. To her amazement, the wall shifted slightly behind her. Holding the sword with one hand, she ran the other along the interior panel and discovered a small metal lever camouflaged inside.

What's this? A way to travel within the temple walls? The possibilities could prove limitless, allowing her to hear and see without being detected. She lifted the lever, which caused a loud click, and the wall turned, revealing a secret passageway.

"Unbelievable," she said aloud. Was Shinzo aware of the hidden access that might have been used for thievery and spying on their religious order? In the recesses of her mind, she had always believed the Butokan monks were a sly, deceptive lot, and this all but confirmed it.

Without a backward glance, she stepped into the narrow corridor, and the alcove swung right back into place. As she traveled through the maze of twists and turns with Kokoro at her side, the mysterious vestibule leading to who knows where intrigued her. Eventually she reached a rock wall housing an inner fireplace. She felt blindly in the dark for a matching lever, but it was no use. This was just a mortared wall, and although the fine cracks in the ceiling provided slits of light, movement from feet passing overhead caused loosened dirt to fall from the sheared walls and ancient wood beams.

Grumbling, she turned and stomped back down the hallway, figuring she must have missed a turn somewhere. Another tunnel took her to the far end of the building where a loud hum could be heard from a gathering in the interior space. She pressed her ear against the wall. Rhythmic chanting was coming from monks who had come together in prayer, giving thanks to the gods for the safe return of the treasured swords and Japan's ultimate salvation.

*Stupid fools!*

As Mariko continued along the wall, she felt cool air coming from the other side. On further inspection, she found a peephole strategically placed across from the doorway where comings and goings in the room could be observed. Another lever had been cleverly mounted directly beneath the catch. She lifted it, and a small section of the panel-covered wall slid away, providing her access into the room. Looking quickly around, she realized she was in the temple library. Hundreds of scrolls and stacks of ancient leather-bound books were stored on crudely made shelves. Three old scholar desks with stiff wooden chairs and dusty, half-filled oil lamps were scattered about.

*This is what being close to god brings you? No wonder they focus on the rewards of heaven.*

On an adjacent wall sat a set of mismatched candlesticks. She approached one and discovered it was firmly attached. However, she could move the other one and gave it a slight twist. It rotated excitingly on its bracket...and popped off. One of the screws fell to the floor with a click, but nothing else happened.

*Dammit.* There had to be another way out of this room. Crouching to examine the fireplace, she soon found a brick slightly different in color than the rest. She tried to pull on it then twist it. But that didn't work either. So she started methodically pushing on every brick in turn. After several minutes, she had gained nothing except a lot of soot all over her hands and clothes. Still brushing herself off, she headed into the hallway and ran straight into Shinzo Yamada.

Grabbing her wrist, he brushed his eyes over the sword she was holding before returning his gaze to her face. His silence and the intensity of his stare confirmed his ability to see through her physical body and recognize the soul manipulating her actions.

"I'm sorry, Kenji," Shinzo said. "I can't let you take Kokoro. I won't let you destroy Mariko or the world we're living in. It's time to go where your soul belongs. Back with the demons waiting to collect you."

Mariko jerked her arm free just as two temple guards approached. She glanced around them, searching for an avenue of escape.

"Hold her," Shinzo ordered the guards. The men stepped forward just as Mariko lifted Kokoro and unsheathed a third of the blade. She glared at Shinzo over its gleaming edge and began speaking in a hoarse, angry voice.

"Touch me and she's dead," the voice threatened.

"Stay strong, Mariko," Shinzo directed, then to Kenji he demanded, "You don't want to do this."

"Oh, but I do," said the voice.

Mariko lengthened the weapon by extracting it. Just as it cleared the scabbard, someone grabbed her waist from behind and pulled her into a crushing embrace. Despite her inability to break free, Mariko managed to raise the katana high in the air. But before she could twist it around and thrust Kokoro through her body and into her captor's thigh, one of the guards grabbed her elbow and ripped the weapon from her hand.

The other guard confiscated it quickly while she remained trapped between Shinzo and her unseen assailant. "Don't move," the beefy guard said, snarling like a temple dog. Mariko went into minor shock as Shinzo's protectors tied her elbows tightly together behind her back. Next they stuck a stout bamboo pole through the crook in her bound elbows and across the middle of her back. She was left grimacing, angry, and completely defenseless. Against her will, she was turned around until she came face-to-face with her unknown captor.

"Yuki." Mariko chuckled softly to herself. "You're tougher than I gave you credit." She noticed blood seeping through a bandage secured to Yuki's side. Although painful in appearance, her wound hadn't hindered her formable strength in the least. "Hmmm...that looks like first blood to me," Mariko continued. "Seems you lost after all, Yuki-chan."

Kenji's sister silently stared into the geisha's eyes as if searching for a familiar soul.

"Traitor." Mariko was compelled to look away. "I should have killed you both when I had the chance," she told Shinzo.

"So why didn't you?" He surveyed her body with his prying eyes then stopped, finding what he had apparently been looking for. His fingers pinched the long gold chain against her skin and lifted it from her neck. As Mariko struggled to pull away, he withdrew its full length and captured the dangling locket that had been secretly hidden beneath her black shirt.

Shinzo's voice dropped to a guttural growl—an alien sound from the mild-mannered monk. "Where did you get this?"

The trinket gifted to her by Nikki Ota rested in his palm and his eyes pierced her brain.

"None of your business," she growled.

Shinzo held it high enough for Yuki to see. Mariko responded by jerking her head back in a fruitless attempt to reclaim it.

"Is it too late?" Yuki asked him. "We have less than an hour. Is that enough time?"

Mariko's eyes bounced back and forth between them. "Time for what?"

Shinzo barely looked at her before answering. "Ending all of this...once and for all." He waved a hand at the guard holding her. "Bring Mariko along. She needs to be bound to the column in the sanctuary before we begin."

"Are you going to sacrifice me to your gods?" Sarcasm dripped from Mariko's words.

Shinzo turned away, deliberately ignoring her. She reacted by kicking out and screeching profanities. The guard holding Kokoro glared at her while the other guard bumped the pole behind her back, unleashing a surge of pain.

"Ow! That hurt!" she cried out.

"That's enough," Shinzo said coolly. He took the katana from the guard and began walking through the long, dark hallway with Yuki at his side. "We need to hurry," he called back. The first guard joined them and the guard behind Mariko urged her forward. However, before taking a single step, she happened to glance to her right and spotted something no one else seemed to have noticed. Behind the peephole, a mysterious eye had taken up residence then vanished before being detected. It seemed someone was traveling through the passageway she'd discovered and was now following their every move.

# 40

Tamayo ended the call to her uncle in the limousine before facing Chase. She dictated his instructions then reminded him that the police could be there in twenty minutes, if he was just willing to wait. But, of course, he wasn't.

"Please be careful, Cohen-san," she called out to him. "It wouldn't be good for anything to happen to you."

Chase glanced back at her and flashed a smile before crossing the parking lot. He passed by two dozing guards and wasn't sure if they'd been sharing a joint but there was a familiar sweet smell in the air, and their incompetence only encouraged him to move faster. After approaching the warehouse, he cautiously made his way inside. The only light in the building emanated from a few busted out painted windows bordering the catwalk above. He couldn't distinguish where the sound of a man's soft voice was coming from, which left him constantly turning in circles as he crossed the warehouse floor. Near the end of the warehouse, he spied a stairwell going down to a lower level. As he neared the stairs, he could see a metal fire door at the bottom, opened just slightly with no light. He looked above and all around, trying to muster the courage to walk down the dark concrete staircase. One by one, he crept down the uneven steps. He braced himself against the wall and prepared to enter the basement, pulling the gun Tamayo's driver had given him close to his shoulder. He placed his boot at the base of the door and gave it a swift kick. The door broke loose and swung wide open. He nearly toppled over from the wall of fear slamming into him. There was a sudden rush of movement and the odor of sweat and sickness, turning his stomach.

It took a few seconds for his eyes to adjust to the dim light, and then he saw them. Japanese women of varying ages and levels of panic crowded together in the room. "Don't scream," Chase rumbled. "I'm not going hurt you. I'm looking for an American woman…long reddish-brown hair, hazel eyes, dressed in tan slacks and a white blouse. She goes by the name of Rachel. Have you seen her?"

The weary teenager shook her head. Chase grunted, letting her go, and moved on, searching further. By the time he had asked six different girls, everyone in the filled warehouse had woken up. Homeless teens and young women were standing everywhere, eyeing him nervously. Chase groaned when the seventh girl also answered in the negative. He stood to his full height and raised his voice. If he drew attention from the men upstairs Tamayo had warned him about, then so be it; he could use a good fight anyway, and if the two characters outside were any indication of what he'd have to deal with, it wouldn't take him long to finish them off.

"Listen to me, everyone," he said. "I'm lookin' for a woman named Rachel Lyons…auburn hair, blue-green eyes. Gets loud when she's mad and might have thrown a fist or two. She was brought here yesterday afternoon. Has anyone seen her? Rachel!" he called out. "If you're here, speak up."

The women around him were silent for a minute. Then one near the center of the room stood and wove between bodies to reach him. "She's this way. But...she's with Kimi...in a bad way, and..." the woman's voice trailed off into silence. Chase nodded slightly and followed the woman to one of the back corners where a single candle was barely burning, on the verge of guttering out. He strained to see a woman lying on a pallet composed of blankets and outer garments. Three other women sat alongside her—one wiping her face with a scrap of filthy cloth. The corner stunk from sweat, filth, and sickness. A moan came from the covered body on the pallet. She turned her face toward Chase, eyelashes fluttering and pink cropped hair covering her head. To his relief, it wasn't Rachel.

A rustling sound drew his attention toward a woman returning with a cup of water. The sight of her dirt- smudged face caused his heart to leap in his chest.

"Chase...it's you." Rachel stood frozen in place, staring at him in disbelief. Then she suddenly came to life, throwing an arm around his neck—half hugging him while holding the sloshing cup in her other hand. "You're really here. How in the world did you find me?"

Before he could answer, her eyes fell on her suffering patient on the ground. She knelt down and the other women stepped away. "I got her," she told them.

Seeing the concern etching their faces, Chase added, "It's all right. If you hurry you can get outta here before anyone notices. Just go up the stairs and be quiet about it." The women thanked him enthusiastically until he growled and sent them away to gather the rest of the women—twenty-two in all. They did as they were told. The one who had been wiping the young girl's sweating brow pressed the rag into his hand before squeezing his shoulder sympathetically. Then she scurried off after the others.

Chase looked Rachel over closely as she lifted the cup and poured small amounts of water between the girl's parted lips. Other than a messy ponytail and dark circles under her eyes, she appeared to be completely intact—unlike the young girl she was caring for. His stomach turned at sight of the bloodstained bandage wound around her small abdomen. He watched Rachel peel it back gingerly and curse under her breath. "In a bad way" was an understatement. Gut wounds were hard enough to heal in a hospital, let alone a filthy warehouse. Rachel rewrapped the bandage the best she could while Chase pulled out his phone.

"I found Rachel," he told Tamayo. "But there's a girl here who's been seriously hurt and left for dead. You wouldn't believe how many women I found in this place. Let your uncle know right away. I'll need his help to get her out of here and your driver to take her to a hospital." He pocketed his cell and looked down at Rachel—a far cry from the spirited woman he knew.

"Kimi, wake up. It's time to go," she said. The young girl stirred with a disgruntled sound and her eyes fluttered open. When she saw who was hovering over her, her whole face lit up with joy and she raised a weak, trembling hand toward Rachel's face. She caught it and laced their fingers together, squeezing lightly.

"Your boyfriend came to save you," she croaked. "Just like I told you he would."

Chase clenched his jaw at the sound of her weak voice. "I've been worried sick about...all of you. If not for Mitsui and his niece, I wouldn't have known where to look."

Rachel's face fell slightly, her beatific expression replaced by a small, wry smile. "Mitsui? He brought you here? Does he know about Takashi...that I shot him?"

"Yeah, I suppose he does. But he didn't bring me here. His niece did. She's waiting a few blocks away in a limousine. There was no need to put her in danger as well."

"I saw the keys...the ones the guard dropped," Kimi said suddenly, as if needing to explain. "I picked them up and he came at me. I pulled the knife from his belt and he slugged me. I got one slash across his leg before I went down." Her smile brightened but dimmed just as quickly. "He got me across the stomach with a katana before Rachel stepped in. She took the knife and stabbed him in the throat. When the other guard saw her standing there, threatening to do the same, he ran away with the keys." Kimi's brow furrowed. It was apparent that she had to concentrate hard in order to form words.

Chase stared hard at Rachel, trying to absorb the scene Kimi had just painted. "I can't believe you actually stabbed him," he said tersely. "And you shot another man too. Here I was thinking you couldn't defend yourself against these guys. Wow...was I wrong."

She lowered her chin and her voice. "Believe me, it's not something I want to repeat."

"I sure hope not."

Rachel looked at him from the top of her eyes. He was reminded of her reaction at hearing him compliment Yuki's warrior skills, only now her look was bordering on hatred. Everything about this barbaric place was changing his partner, and by all accounts and appearances it was for the worse.

"I'm going to get you both out of here and Kimi into a hospital," he told her.

Rachel nodded and put her palm on the young girl's forehead. By the anxious expression on her face, Chase knew her charge was running a high fever. He cursed under his breath and looked around, fearing the intrusion of a guard. He knew he had to get them out of there quickly.

Kimi gasped loudly and fought back a whimper when Chase jostled her torso trying to lift her. He couldn't stand tears, never had been able to when it came to women. So he sat beside her for several minutes while Rachel wiped the sweat from her face with the cloth he'd been given wondering what was taking Mitsui so long to call. Surely he must have gotten his message by now.

Rachel checked Kimi's wound again. He cursed continuously under his breath as she unwound the bandage, which was more stained than it had been just moments earlier. When it finally came free and they both saw the extent of Kimi's wound, his cursing turned to silence. He had seen enough men die from diving and boating accidents to know this young girl didn't have long to live. None of them did if they stayed here much longer.

"Rachel," she whispered, "you have to go without me."

"How can I do that?" she asked, doing her best to smooth Kimi's pink spiky hair with her fingers.

"He came here for you, not me. I might be young, but I'm not stupid."

Rachel frowned for a moment. Then she looked to Chase for the reassurance the dying girl needed.

"Kimi..." he began.

"No," she said, "you both know I'm not going to get out of here alive. So don't tell me otherwise. I only wish I'd made peace with my father...before this."

"Your father?" Rachel asked.

"He's a detective...a good man. My death won't be easy for him." Her words had become slurred and difficult to understand but Chase knew who she was referring to in an instant.

"Maybe there's some way to find him...to get word to him," Rachel said. "What's his name?"

"Honda," Chase answered. He glimpsed the cracks in the ceiling above him. With muffled noise from the women escaping, he was vaguely surprised that the guards hadn't awoken and the men upstairs hadn't responded. But then there was a possibility they'd been overpowered by Mitsui's men. Perhaps it was one of them Chase had heard talking – directing assassins while he entered the warehouse.

Kimi smiled softly. "That's right. You know him?"

Chase clenched his jaw so hard his teeth creaked, but nodded nonetheless.

"I'm glad to know that," she murmured. "But now you should go. Rachel has been through enough."

He knew Kimiko was right. There was no point in staying. But he could also see the attachment Rachel had formed for this girl in the short time they'd spent together. He stood and holstered the borrowed gun in the back of his pants and reached into his pocket to fish out the business card he'd been given. Then he took out his phone and called the number. Just as he feared, the operator rattled off words in Japanese. He was at a loss as to how to respond but tried his best to reach out to the man who had shared his desperation.

"Detective Honda. *Hayakusite kudasai.*"

"*Koko dewa arimasen,*" the woman's voice said. She elaborated with a half dozen more lines, but Chase didn't have a clue what she was saying. He looked back at Kimiko with her eyes shut and her breathing now shallow. The grains in her hourglass were nearly spent.

"I found his daughter," he blurted on the phone. "She's at the end of Sumitomo pier in warehouse forty-nine. Tell him to hurry and get here."

He could only hope the woman understood—that she was capable of relaying his message before it was too late. Kimiko whispered something faintly, and Chase came closer to hear.

"Take care of Rachel…" Her voice trailed off as she gasped for breath. Even though he didn't know this girl, his heart was heavy from the suffering she had to endure. His inability to help her was tearing him up.

"We could still make a run for it," he told Rachel. "It's better than leaving her here to die."

Kimiko let out a long sigh. "Please…go," she breathed, and didn't inhale again. Her eyes opened wide and her arms went slack. Rachel pressed her fingers against the young girl's throat and waited several seconds to verify what had become apparent.

"She's gone."

Kimiko Honda had passed. Her eyes stared into nothingness, void of all life. Just full of darkness and death. Rachel laid the girl's limp arms across her chest and gently closed her eyelids. She looked up at Chase, and in that moment he realized he'd never seen her look so sad, so dark, so breakable. He drew her into his arms and held her tight against his chest and silently thanked God to have her back.

"There was nothing we could do," he assured her. "Believe me, she's in a much better place now."

Shouts and pounding footsteps suddenly erupted outside. Chase held Rachel away from him and pulled the gun free. Knowing a battle was inevitable, a feral grin split his face in two. "Looks like I'll be counting on those new skills you developed after all."

The sound of scraping metal filled the warehouse space and was soon followed by a man's voice calling to them from the corner of the room. "Rachel-san! Cohen-san! Is everything all right?"

That unmistakable voice. Chase stared at the slim silhouette leaning on the frame of the steel door. It wasn't possible...his eyes had to have failed him. And yet...

"Shinzo...?"

# 41

The monk offered a weak smile before stepping aside to allow Detective Honda and his partner access into the warehouse. As Chase and Rachel stood silently watching, they escorted two handcuffed guards through the entry and screamed for them to get down on their knees. His unidentified partner stayed with them while Honda purposefully crossed the room. Arriving in the dimly lit corner, he froze for a moment then crumpled to the ground. He scooped his daughter's lifeless body in his arms and pressed his ear close to her chest. After confirming her absent heartbeat, he squeezed his eyes shut and threw his head back, releasing a mournful cry.

"Noooo!!! *Ika nai de kure! Ima sugu modotte kite,*" he pleaded. *"Yurushite kure."*

Rachel had never heard these words before. Yet from the emotion in his voice and the anguish in his face, she grasped their sorrowful meaning. He was begging her to come back, begging her not to leave. Begging her to forgive him.

"*Yurushite kure!*" he repeated over and over again. Even as he screamed and shook her in his grief, he was trying to wipe his tears from her face. He stroked her hair forcefully and kissed her forehead then sniffed and cried even more.

Rachel's heart melted with pity. She felt the need to reach out to him, but this would mean acknowledging his display of weakness—something Japanese men had been socialized to avoid, and she saw no point in embarrassing him.

Chase, on the other hand, seemed to have no problem in speaking out. "We're so sorry," he said in all sincerity. The man's sobs were now shaking his whole body. "Detective," Chase said more loudly, more insistently. But it was no use. No one in the room seemed capable of consoling him.

Shinzo approached and, as if by magic, produced a wad of tissues in front of the grieving man's face. From Rachel's prospective, it took the detective a few seconds to realize who had offered them. He looked up into the monk's sweet, smiling face and instantly calmed.

"*Arigato*," he said, taking the tissues. He appeared to be ashamed and relieved at the same time.

"I know of your pain," Shinzo said in English, obviously for Chase and Rachel's benefit. "No matter how hard we try, there are never right words at a time like this." He laid his hand on Honda's shoulder and looked deep into his eyes. "Please know you and Kimiko will be in my thoughts and prayers."

The detective sniffed and wiped his nose. Then he turned toward Chase and lowered his head. With his eyes on the ground, he said in a low voice, "I received a personal call from Mitsui-san directing me here. Thank you for finding my daughter and not leaving her...to die alone."

Chase nodded his furrowed brow. He pulled Rachel into a protective embrace and kissed the top of her head, warming her heavy heart.

"Now that you and Miss Lyons are back together, I believe it would be best if you returned to your hotel," Honda said, resuming his official duties. "I would accompany you, but I still need to take care of…" His voice trailed off, but his obligation was obvious.

"No need," Chase answered. "Tamayo is waiting for us. She must be incredibly worried by now."

"I'm afraid she'll be worrying a bit longer," Shinzo said. "I need you to return to the temple with me. We still have unfinished business to take care of." As if hearing his words, the earth began rumbling again. But this time the sound was deep in tone. The quake was under their feet, all around them, causing the metal walls in the warehouse to creak and bend. Rachel and Chase rushed outside in time to see cars in the vast parking lot turning in different directions. Then the ground started rolling like waves on the sea, reaching between one and two feet in height. It was remarkable to see them rise under deserted buildings on the wharf, causing them to sway, lift, and fall. Telephone poles began whipping back and forth along the roadway, and the rumbling turned into a roar.

*Oh my God.* Rachel looked up at Chase and could read the fear in his eyes. As the earthquake continued, some of the people on the street fled in panic, but most froze in their tracks. She wondered if the earth would open up beneath them and swallow them whole. Then, as quickly as it started, it subsided. Rachel lifted her eyes to the heavens. The new moon was peeking out from the clouds, emitting an unearthly glow.

Shinzo pulled the sleeve of his white shirt back and glanced down at his watch. "It's twenty minutes to twelve. This is just the beginning," he said. "We have to hurry before it's too late."

Tamayo's driver pulled up in front of them in the black limousine as if on cue. He raced around to the side door to usher them all inside. Chase made a point of returning his gun then climbed inside with Shinzo. But before joining them, Rachel looked back at Detective Honda and called out to him. "Are you coming?"

He answered with a shake of his head then stood watching from the doorway with his partner nearby as they drove away, traveling at breakneck speed.

Rachel climbed out of the car and was briefly overwhelmed by the Shoten temple's sheer size. The brilliant orange building was nearly a block long and had a massive three-door entry and thick roof covered in ornate ceramic tiles. She lowered her eyes and hurried after Shinzo to keep up. But after arriving inside its glowing sanctuary, she froze in her tracks, stunned by the scene playing out before her. Mariko had been tied to an enormous wooden column with her hands and arms pinned behind her back. Her perfectly coifed hair hung past her shoulders and covered half her face, making her seem more like a wild creature than the beautiful geisha she'd previously met. Her black, haunting eyes locked with Rachel's, and she practically growled at the sight of Shinzo.

*You've got to be kidding me,* Rachel said to herself. In this place, she was far removed from her elements— the comfort of her father's rocking ship, her calm, complacent life in the tidy ocean cottage in San Palo. Despite Shinzo's forewarning, she couldn't have been more ill-prepared for this logistic night-mare or the psychotic woman glaring at her from across the room.

As the men quietly talked in a corner, she took the opportunity to survey their sparse, musty surroundings. The raised wooden platform housed an eight-foot-tall bronze Buddha with a lotus blossom held in one hand and the fingers on the other hand gesturing the circle of perfection. A round glass panel had been installed in the ceiling directly above it and the eerie moon was rapidly approaching its center. Torches burned at the front of the room, intensifying the smell of the sickeningly sweet incense curling above two ash---covered plates. All three swords were now resting on the altar—essential instruments for the ceremony that Shinzo had told her in the limo would soon follow. With six white-hooded monks standing off to the side chanting in deep, guttural tones, the surreal scene brought to mind a satanic ritual instead of a holy exorcism.

Shinzo waved Rachel over and quietly explained the true reason for her involvement. "Although many religions preach against reincarnation, the Buddhist faith focuses on spiritualism and nurturing the awareness gained from our past lives. This might be difficult to understand or believe, but you've lived in Japan many times, Rachel. One of your earliest experiences directly involves what's happening here today. Do you remember how I told you that you were one of the chosen?"

She hesitated before answering, "Yes."

"That's because your name was Noriko Hirata. You were born into a noble family and were loved by many...including two of Japan's greatest leaders. One of them happened to be Prince Ngami and the other General Maeda."

*What?* "Are you saying I was the general's wife? The one he murdered?"

Shinzo nodded. "And Yuki was your husband, which explains her preoccupation with world travel, adventure, and ancient samurai swords."

*My husband?* Rachel glanced at Yuki, who she suddenly noticed standing next to the altar. She was met with a quick, insincere smile.

"One of the reasons you've been drawn to Chase is because he too was involved in this drama," Shinzo continued. "But this time around, fate has been kind and you've been given a second chance with your prince."

Rachel looked at Chase's mouth, quirked in a half smile.

"Yep, that's me," he said. "Prince Charming."

Rachel drew her lips in to prevent a nervous laugh. She'd experienced coincidence more than once in her life, but this was beyond ridiculous—just one step short of the loony bin. She glanced at the meditative monks across the room that had apparently accepted Shinzo's claims and Mariko staring blindly into space. Why, she wondered, was she the only one believing this was crazy? "It's time to get started," Shinzo told them. "I need all of you to approach the altar and pick up your designated sword. Yuki, the wakizashi Rachel, the tanto. And Chase...Kokoro, the Heart of Darkness." Each of them did as they were told. Then Shinzo pointed to the large flower etched on the stone wall. "At my counting," he said, "drive your weapons into the center of the imperial symbol at the same time... burying them to the hilt. No matter what you might hear or see, don't stop. Not for any reason. Even though they're not aware of it at this moment, everyone in Japan is depending on us to save them."

"But there's no slits in the stone," Chase lamented. "How will the swords enter?"

"Remember...the swords you're holding are beyond powerful. The greatest craftsman in the world created them. If put to the test, they could pierce steel with one blow."

Yuki's eyebrows dipped. "After they're imbedded, can they be pulled out again?"

"This isn't a fairy tale from King Arthur," Shinzo told her. "Once they're fused in the stone, no one will be able to retrieve them again. Not without destroying them."

She murmured something under her breath before curling her lips in a prevalent frown.

"It's the price for taking something that doesn't belong to us," Shinzo said.

The sound of a door closing turned Rachel's head.

*"Onegai da kara yamete kudasai,"* Tamayo pleaded. Her voice carried from the back of the room, where she'd been sitting and waiting quietly. They all froze when they saw that a middle-aged man with messy brown hair had pulled her to her feet and was standing behind her with a gun leveled at her head.

Rachel didn't recognize him, but Shinzo knew him immediately. "Put the gun down, Daiichi," he said. "There's no reason to harm Tamayo. She only came here to help us."

Rachel glimpsed the moon almost directly above them. The villain's timing couldn't have been worse.

"Give me Kokoro," Daiichi demanded. *"Ima!"*

"When we're finished here, you can have all three swords."

"You think I'm a fool? I've been hiding in the walls. I heard everything you said. Give it to me or I'll kill her. I mean it!"

"Please," Shinzo begged him. "You have to let her go. You're not a murderer, Daiichi."

"Really? Kenji Ota and Hiroshi Mori might disagree with that."

The crazed woman latched to the column suddenly came to life. "You killed Kenji? But you're just a plumber. How could you—"

"Just? You wouldn't give me the time of day, Mariko...thinking you were better than anyone. But you didn't hesitate to spread your legs for Kenji and Shinzo. What does that make you?"

"Ahhhh!!" she screamed, jerking the ropes wildly. "You're dead! Do you hear me? Dead! Dead! Dead!"

"So are you if you don't shut up!" Daiichi shot back.

Rachel held onto the diamond dagger and waited for him to come close. After knifing one of the guards, shooting Takashi, and slugging Chiyo, she felt confident in handling herself—more confident than anyone in their right mind should be.

"Do as I say, Shinzo," he yelled. "Or I'll kill all of you. Beginning with this ugly, stupid girl."

The sound of a gun clicked and exploded in the room, faster than sound, echoing from every hand-hewn rafter. Rachel dropped to the ground. Chase followed, covering her body with his. Shinzo was nearby with his arm over Yuki, protecting her.

Rachel's mind screamed. *Oh my God! He killed her. I can't believe he killed her!*

The air was filled with unnerving quiet. After a few seconds, Rachel's curiosity got the better of her. She pushed herself upright and looked toward the back of the room. Tamayo was frozen in place with her hands over her ears and her eyes squeezed tight. One look to her left and the reason why quickly became apparent. A bullet had burned through Daiichi's face and splattered his brains against the wall like an abstract painting. Whatever was left of his body was now slumped against a post.

In the doorway, a huge black-suited man stood poised with his gun at half mast. Mitsui stepped forward with satisfaction adorning his lips. He drew Tamayo into his arms and announced for everyone to hear, "No one tries to kill my niece and lives to talk about it."

Chase came to his feet beside Rachel. "Are you okay?" Before she could answer, the ground rumbled its discontent. Lights in the hallway flickered. The walls around them shook. It seemed hell had accepted another evil soul and in a matter of seconds they would be joining him.

"Resume your places!" Shinzo yelled.

Yuki, Chase, and Rachel returned to the altar and took up their swords. Then they waited, looking at Shinzo expectantly.

"After everything you've been through to make this possible, we can only pray this works. Now get ready to follow my count," he said. "One...two...three...now!"

The blue moon shot a steady beam through the center of the glass at the exact moment all three blades hit the wall. At the same time, Shinzo extended his hands before him and belted out Japanese gibberish. The room was lit ablaze with the light of a red orb, growing in intensity and size. Screaming fiends blasted the air and streaming white ghouls circled around them, leaving Rachel dizzy and sick to her stomach. The pain in her ears was so severe she had to grit her teeth to keep from crying out. She held the weapon so tight that her knuckles turned bone white from the effort.

It seemed to go on for an eternity. Then the air stilled. The light dimmed and the monks filed out of the room, one after the other. Rachel felt a warm presence hovering close by and Shinzo's hand resting on her shoulder.

"It's done," he told her. "The nightmare is over. We can all return to our lives and breathe a sigh of relief knowing we survived this day."

Rachel had to force her fingers to release their hold before stepping back with Chase and Yuki. Three sword handles now protruded from the wall in a triangular formation. Just as Shinzo had predicted, the metal plates between the blade bases and grips had melted and fused with the stone, locking them in place forever.

"Would you look at that," came from Mitsui. His new assassin stood protectively at his side equally engrossed in the large panel that had opened in the north-facing wall. Chase and Rachel stood back with Shinzo and Yuki watching as a door to an interior safe sprang open like a pair of angel's wings. Inside stood four tables clothed in black and a set of burnished scales covered in glass. Pearl pliers lay on a tray and filled display cases lined the inner walls.

Yuki rushed inside with Mitsui close on her heels. It took a few seconds for Rachel to brave the entrance, while Chase and Shinzo too lagged behind. On the first table, an enormous pink pearl had been left out on a black porcelain dish. Rachel gazed with rapture at its exquisite beauty and waved Chase over.

"Have you seen anything like that in your life?"

"No. I can't say I have." His hand was on her shoulder. His eyes scoped the room around them.

"Listen to me," Shinzo said loud enough for everyone to hear. "Don't touch anything. I'm not saying this because I don't want you to get rich...to walk out of here with a million dollars in jewels. I'm warning you because things are not what they seem. There's a presence in this room. An evil curse on everything you see."

"Then I must be blind," Yuki said. She lifted one of the stacked bags and showed it to Mitsui, verifying that it was burned with a family crest. Then she plunged her hand deep inside and withdrew a collection of colorful gems. With dollar signs glowing in her eyes, she held them out for Rachel's inspection.

"These beautiful gems belonged to the Ngami family," Yuki informed her. "The long forgotten treasure that accumulated after trading their bronze, silk and porcelain with foreign ships. From everything I've read, no one believes it actually existed. All of these jewels have been sealed away for thousands of years, guarded by the Shoten monks. And now they're ours for the taking. Ours alone to enjoy." She opened mysterious drawers, which shut again with a tight spring, and produced shabby woven baskets holding raw gems of priceless worth. Dangling in a corner were strings of iridescent pearls, gleaming with prismatic hues. There were dazzling diamonds, sparkling with brilliant rays. A ruby worth thousands, a blue topaz fit for a queen's finger, diamonds, garnets, pearls, emeralds, sapphires, and more cats' eyes—all staring back at them.

"Ah...and here's the aristocratic jewel," Yuki said, rolling a black pearl between her fingers. "No one but the rich and famous have ever been able to afford to own one. They should be perfectly round like a marble, pure and spotless. You know, it would take a thousand shells to find one like this. And to think that there's a hundred more filling this place. Unbelievable." She picked up a shimmering emerald and held it before the light. "I want to take all of this with me, but I don't even know where to begin!" she squealed.

"Listen to me!" Shinzo yelled again. "Drop whatever you're holding! You all have to get out of here now...before it's too late."

Yuki wasn't having any of it. "Why? So you can keep all of this yourself? I knew you had secrets, but nothing like this."

Shinzo shook his head in frustration. "If these jewels are real, why wouldn't I have taken advantage of their worth? Why would this temple be in need of repairs and the monks still be asking for contributions? It's not here, I'm telling you. None of this exists. It's a trick...an elaborate illusion. A way for the condemned Shinto priest to buy your souls and replace the ones he's lost."

Rachel looked around at the shimmering stones, at Yuki collecting bags, at Mitsui filling his pockets and Chase rubbing his jaw. She was completely stumped. Trapped in indecision. Wanting to take everything she could get her hands on, yet sensing it was wrong.

"Close your eyes," Shinzo told them. "Trust your instincts, and you'll see what is truly filling this place...the evil that has seeped through the walls. I'm telling you it's the temptation of Dante. There are demons in the air...circling all around you even now."

Rachel stood perfectly still. She closed her eyes and drew long, deep, abdominal breaths, uttering the word "calm" in her mind with every exhalation. She visualized a pathway of relaxation moving down through her face, throat, chest, stomach, thighs, legs, and ankles—all of the tension leaving her body through her toes as dark, curling smoke. She concentrated on clearing her muddled thoughts with every cleansing breath then slowly opened her eyes.

A young girl was standing before her tilting her head to the side and smiling sweetly. Rachel opened her mouth to speak to her then gasped as the creature's skin melted away, leaving behind a ghoulish black-eyed skeleton with a gaping, cavernous mouth. It moved across the room, dragging a leg, and disappeared through the rear wall. Circling in the air above them were greenish-gray misty entities with red bulging eyes, reaching out to touch them with each pass. They were growing even stronger and brighter with Yuki and Mitsui's greed.

Rachel turned to Shinzo with her arms wrapped around herself, sharing the fear in his eyes.

"You see them, don't you?" he asked her. "In the air... everywhere."

Rachel nodded and looked at Chase. His blue eyes were dark, filled with apprehension. "What is it, Rachel? What did you see?"

She opened her mouth, but nothing came out. No words could explain what she was witnessing.

"We're getting out of here," Chase said. He pushed Rachel behind him and began backing toward the door. Yuki and Mitsui were still picking up jewels, holding them to the light and marveling at them—consumed with the trappings of this hellish place.

"What are you going to do?" Rachel called out to Shinzo. "You'll never get them out of here."

"Stay with Cohen-san," he told her. "I'll take care of this."

She watched from the doorway with Chase's arms wrapped around her as Shinzo lowered himself to the floor. He closed his eyes, pressed his palms together, and began rocking back and forth, chanting louder and louder with an unearthly guttural sound. As his body shook violently, the heat from his aura spread from the center of his being, filling the space in a blinding orange light.

All of a sudden, the room ignited with a loud boom in etheric fireworks. Fragments of color drifted from the ceiling— glittering confetti, vaporizing the jewels into dust. Rachel could feel the outtake of air, vacuuming souls into another dimension. The trapped entities inhabiting this place were no longer crystallized on the etheric planes. They had become bigger, brighter, more enlightened spirits capable of existing on higher frequencies—able to cross over to the other side.

The wall lights flickered and darkened once more, returning to their normal, deteriorated state. With Shinzo's miraculous gift, the veil had been dropped along with the dazzling illusion. Yuki stared at the crumbling bags in her hands before dropping them. Mitsui gazed down at his empty palms and yelped. He spun round and round in place with his eyes stretched open wide, howling like a haunted mad man. The empty walls and shelves around them were now covered in dust. The room was in complete shambles—filled with stacked boards, broken tables, and spider webs. Every jewel, priceless stone, and illustrious pearl had vanished into thin air, leaving Yuki and Mitsui gasping in disbelief.

Shinzo stood his ground, silently watching as Mitsui's common sense returned. He walked past the monk and back into the sanctuary with his face lacking any amusement. He seemed to be slightly embarrassed by his foolish outburst.

"*Ikimashou*," he told Yuki. But she wasn't about to be persuaded to leave. Still inside the vault, she stood her ground, leveling her anger at Shinzo.

"Where is it? Bring it back! What have you done with them? Where are my emeralds?" she bellowed.

The muffled sound of shuffling feet pulled Rachel's eyes toward the altar. The six hooded monks had resumed their positions, kneeling before the Buddha. Their hands were pressed together in prayer. Their eyes were fixed on the floor ahead of them. Their chanting began softly then grew in volume, lifting tiny hairs on Rachel's arms.

"We need to close the door, Yuki," Shinzo told her. "Everyone needs to leave. It's time for our prayer vigil to begin."

"No!" Yuki yelled. *"Modotte kite, watashi o tasukete.* Come back and help me! They have to be in here somewhere! I know it!"

"Be grateful you're still alive," Chase told her. "Now come on!"

"You're all crazy! The treasure is in here, I'm telling you. He's hidden it in the walls somewhere. I know it! Don't go, Cohen-san. How can you leave empty-handed?"

"I'm not," Chase told her. He pulled Rachel close against to him. "I've got all I need right here."

At hearing those words, Mariko, forgotten until that moment, lifted her sagging head. She looked around and called out in a panic, "Please...someone help me!"

Shinzo crossed the room quickly and studied her face long and hard. By all appearances, she seemed to have regained her senses. Her brown eyes were soft and kind once more, filled with genuine hurt and confusion.

"What's going on?" she asked. "How did I get here? Shinzo... *doushitano?"*

The monk leaned down and whispered, leaving her staring back at him in astonishment. He untied her bindings and she rewarded him with a heartfelt hug.

Mitsui watched in silence then nodded his approval. He glanced back at Yuki: pushing tables out of her way, tearing down shelves, yelling at no one. *"Burakumin,"* he muttered under his breath. Then he ordered his assassin to end the matter. *"Kerio, tsuke-yoze!"*

Wordlessly the man slammed the door on the safe. The panel closed automatically behind it, sealing Yuki inside.

Rachel stared at Mitsui, aghast. "You can't do that! She'll suffocate in there."

The yakuza boss dismissed her words in lieu of addressing Shinzo. *"Ichi-jikan."*

The monk nodded his approval.

"Shinzo...wh--what did he say?" Rachel asked.

"One hour." His eyes came back to Mitsui. "What about the money I owe you?"

Mitsui glanced at Rachel and Chase before answering. "Yuki left diamonds in her apartment...the one I pay for. They now belong to me. Yamada- san...*yurushimasu desu*. All is forgiven." He bowed his head deeply. Shinzo did the same. After everything that had happened, it seemed that mutual respect and admiration had been restored.

"But the diamonds were in the grave with the wakizashi sword," Rachel told them. "I thought they were cursed."

Shinzo's smile returned. "No, Miss Lyons, they're not. I allowed Yuki to believe they were to keep her from robbing Prince Ngami's tomb. But you can see how little she hears and how slowly she learns."

Rachel huffed a laugh. "So you lied? I didn't think monks could do that."

Shinzo's lips spread into a smile. "You'd be surprised what we can do."

"And what about you?" Mitsui asked Rachel in his unmistakable gruff voice. "Don't you have unfinished business to take care of?" Without waiting for an answer, he walked over to Tamayo, fidgeting nervously with her black prayer beads. He glanced back at Rachel and spoke loud enough for her to hear. "Miss Lyons and Cohen-san will ride back to the hotel with you. In the morning, you will call me with news. *Wakatta?*"

Tamayo nodded her understanding and watched him leave. With a quick wave of his hand, he climbed into the back seat of a black Mercedes sedan with his assassin at his side. The driver pulled away from the curb with a second car following, and both vehicles disappeared into the flow of traffic. Rachel breathed a sigh of relief after realizing the notorious gangster was finally gone. She would never cross paths with him again…at least not in this lifetime. But thanks to Shinzo and the unimaginable experience she'd been through, he would remain forever ingrained in her memory. The man with a thousand eyes…or better yet, five hundred disciples all willing to die for him.

Tamayo rose to her feet and was escorted back to the waiting limousine. Seconds later, her driver returned for Chase and Rachel. After they bid Shinzo and Mariko goodbye, they followed him to the car and slid inside. Tamayo uncorked a chilled bottle of Cristal and poured equal amounts into two fluted glasses. She offered one to each of them, and then Rachel took ownership of the bottle. She poured a third serving—in proper Japanese fashion—and extended it to their accommodating companion.

"I'm honored to officially make your acquaintance, Rachel-san," the maiko said with her eyes downcast. "My name is Aiko Tamayo Lyons and I believe you may be my…sister."

Rachel paused before answering, "No, Tamayo. I don't believe you're my sister at all." The maiko spilled her drink and profusely apologized. Chase glared at Rachel, obviously disappointed, but she knew exactly what she was doing. After learning about Mitsui's confession and witnessing his niece's selfless intent, there was absolutely no doubt in her mind. She lifted her glass and smiled slowly. "I know you are," she said.

# 42

Even with Shinzo's reassurances, it would take a long time for Mariko to master her emotions—to erase the distrust Kenji's spirit had evoked. With that thought fresh in her mind, she reached for the locket fastened around her throat and broke the chain with one pull.

"Maybe you could find a use for this...the next time you pray for lost souls."

Shinzo took the augury necklace and tucked it into his back pocket then reached for her hand. "I will," he assured her. "But I'm afraid there are going to be a lot more souls to worry about if I don't get busy." He squeezed her hand reassuringly. "Will you be all right in your apartment for a few hours?"

"Of course." She wrapped her arms around Shinzo's neck and closed her eyes. She could still hear Kenji's voice, breathe his musky scent...see the wry smile on his face. It was as though a piece of him was still floating around, watching and waiting. Hoping for the chance to crawl under her skin and into her heart again. She could feel something else moving deep within her too. A welling panic that wasn't pushed aside as easily as it had once been. A feeling of danger that she couldn't put her finger on.

The taxi drove up, and as Shinzo held her, Mariko stared into the early evening light. She could still feel it, those eyes watching her, malevolent, filled with an evil promise. There had always been a curtain between her and happiness. It always seemed to be hovering around her, but never touching her, until this moment. Something inside her seemed freer, less contained, but she was terribly afraid that loosening her emotions was also why the memories were rushing back—why the panic was building inside her. She could feel that amplified sense of being watched, being touched by evil. Her shoulders were tight with it, her skin crawled with it. She looked up toward the balcony on the fourth floor where Shinzo's superior was staring down with a smile on his face. Everything was starting to come together. Wickedness was being pushed back to make room for goodness in the world. So why were her fears growing? Why did she feel death reaching out for her, threatening to block any possibility of normality...any chance of happiness in her life?

Mariko glanced off to her right and noticed a large number of birds roosting on the power lines. She could see through the wire fence to the open field where cattle had gathered together and were now lying down. Days earlier, she'd seen a group of turtles crossing the street, nearly being hit by the limo traveling up the mountain. Nature was going crazy with the vibrations in the air. If she didn't stay close to Shinzo and keep her eyes open wide, she might find herself being drawn behind a veil of evil and disappearing forever.

"Right here," Mariko told the taxi driver. She slid across the seat and waited for the door to open.

"Are you sure?" he asked, pushing the door release button. "I don't think it's safe to be here alone at this hour."

"I'll be fine," she said, forcing a smile. After stepping away from the car, she strolled through the dense woods and stopped near the water's edge. Thoughts of how to end the pain touched her mind as she sat in the quiet dark by the lake, her eyes closed to the world. Then she realized she heard someone singing. The notes were soft and melodious and touched a deep part of her soul. Opening her eyes, she searched for the person who years ago had graced her with beautiful, soothing music in a teahouse karaoke room. Standing some yards away from her, a handsome young man stood under a tree at the edge of the lake. The limbs of the willow surrounded him as if he stood in a natural cathedral.

Drawn to the sound of his voice, she walked towards the young man until she was standing only a few feet behind him. She closed her eyes and allowed his music to glide over her and enter every pore. The soft tones filled her with a quiet joy and pushed aside the depression threatening to overtake her mind. The notes played her soul like a harp, stroking her pain away and dropping a veil of comfort over her spirit. She smiled softly as the notes brought a long forgotten tranquility to her spirit.

At peace, they stood beside the lake, he singing his notes of joy and she allowing the music to cleanse her mind and spirit of harsh thoughts. After a time, she realized he had stopped singing. Opening her eyes, she saw he was no longer standing beneath the tree, but was directly in front of her with white feathers at his feet. Surprisingly, she felt no fear when he reached out to her.

His hand rested gently on her cheek, and in a voice warm and full of strength, he told her, "Don't be afraid. You're not alone, Mariko. You have the strength to overcome any obstacle. All you need to do is believe." With those words, he turned and walked away. As he slowly disappeared from her sight, she realized her face was warm and tingled where he had touched her. The soft scent of flowers lingered after he had left and white feathers trailed behind him. A peace had descended upon her and she thought to herself, I needed to be rescued and he came for me. Whole and pure...uncorrupted by the evil in this world.

As she walked back to the waiting car, her thoughts became clearer and her pain lessened. She had received a message from above and felt joy in her heart for the first time in days. Turning her face to the sky, she smiled and murmured a quiet thank you to the universe for the happiness she cradled in her heart and the peace Kenji Ota had finally found.

# 43

While Chase finished packing his belongings in the back bedroom, Rachel pulled out the bundle of postcards Tamayo's mother had cruelly returned. She had hoped for the opportunity to share them with her but respected the maiko's decision to read them in the privacy of her home. The money Sam had left her, however, was a completely different matter. Tamayo refused the gesture several times before finally agreeing to use his "contribution" for the needs of her family.

"I'm sure Okaasan will be very grateful," she told Rachel. "The okiya is very old and has leaks in the roof. This will go a long way in making repairs." After tucking the thick envelope into her drawstring bag, she reached for the bottle of cold sake the hotel's room service had delivered. She filled Rachel's cup and waited for her to do the same before toasting their newfound sisterhood. For the next forty minutes, they talked about every subject under the stars. They shared their beliefs, childhood memories, and time spent with their father, laughing at his foul temper, biting remarks, and annoying habits.

They exchanged womanly advice, shed tears over abandonment issues, and were amazed at how much they had in common.

It was the love fest Rachel never saw coming. "I wish we could stay longer, but we've already postponed our flight twice. We have to leave for the airport in five hours."

Chase came back in the room with his suitcase in tow. "Rachel hasn't slept in days," he told Tamayo. "I was hoping she would lie down for a while."

Disappointed filled the maiko's eyes. "But tonight's the lantern festival...the celebration for the dead. It would be wonderful if we could say goodbye to our father together."

"It's almost one in the morning," Chase reminded her. "You're sure this is a good idea?"

Tamayo nodded eagerly. "I promise you won't be disappointed. It's really remarkable. During this season, our ancestors' spirits return to our families. We write their names and our names on paper lanterns and float them down a river to ease their suffering and guide them back to their resting places. With the orange color from candles burning and the midnight blue sky, it's all very dramatic."

"And so are you."

"Ah, come on, Chase," Rachel said. "It'll be okay." She held his arm like a child and pulled him toward the next room. "I can sleep on the plane. When will we ever have a chance like this again?"

It took him a moment before he finally agreed, and after he did, he was even less keen on borrowing the blue yukatas from the dresser drawer. "I don't think this is what the hotel had in mind," he protested.

Rachel belted her robe around her middle before helping him do the same. Then she stood beside him in the bathroom mirror and flashed a mischievous grin. "If not for that blond mop on your head, we'd blend right in, Cohen-san."

Chase had to admit there was something fun and sexy about wearing cotton pajamas outside and partying with a bunch of strangers in the middle of the night.

"Please hurry," Tamayo called out. "It's almost over. We need to go now."

Chase followed Rachel back into the living room. Her young sister had used the extra time to pin dangling white and orange flowers into her hair—the perfect addition to her brown leaf-printed kimono.

"What about Shinzo and Mariko?" he asked. "Will Yuki be there?"

Tamayo smiled sweetly. "It's a very special holiday. I wouldn't be surprised if they all came."

"Wonderful," he grumbled. "Then they can all see me in this crazy getup."

Rachel chuckled and smoothed the fine hairs at the top of his chest. "Ah, and just think how lucky they'll be."

While Chase paid the fare, Rachel and Tamayo got out of the cab, both practically giddy over joining the partygoers that filled the street leading to one of the largest shrines in Tokyo. All around them bright lanterns were waving in the dark night with bodies moving to a dreamlike Bon Odori dance.

As they walked, Tamayo explained, "This is one of the three greatest fire festivals of summer. Its origins lie in the ancient legend of how the emperor and his entourage, hindered by fog, were received by villagers holding pine torches to illuminate their path."

Before them, thousands of men and women dressed in cotton kimonos and ancient costumes bounced to and fro with lit gold and silver lanterns on their heads singing and lining up for the pine torch procession. Down every street and alleyway, decorations in the shape of shrines and castles were aglow. Overhead, colorful fireworks exploded above the river terrace.

"This way," Tamayo's voice called out. She directed them down a winding path leading to the water's edge. They stopped at a tented booth long enough to purchase three candles and lanterns then waited while she painted each of their names in beautiful Japanese calligraphy. Then they were off again, stepping gingerly on the rocky slope in open toe zoris, trying to find a safe spot on the riverbank.

When Rachel lifted her eyes, she couldn't help but gasp. Never in her life had she witnessed anything so extraordinary, so bewitching and wonderful. The waterway was completely covered with orange flickering lanterns endlessly floating by.

"It's our turn," Tamayo told them.

On bended knees, each of them lit a candle inside their lantern with a long wooden match and set it on the rippling surface. Then they stood and watched the flickering lights join all the other lanterns on their journey.

Tamayo reached for Rachel's hand and squeezed it. "Sayonara, Papa-san," she said into the night.

"Goodbye, Dad," Rachel added.

While the maiko continued to watch the spectacle, Rachel and Chase stepped away. "Somehow I don't think my father will disappear that easily," she told him.

Chase smiled. "Yeah, I agree. But at least he knows you're doing this together."

Rachel felt warmth in her chest—contentment she had never thought possible. With her partner at her side and Tamayo smiling up at her, she realized the broken pieces in her life had been fully restored.

"Are you happy?" Chase asked her. Rachel's face filled with a glowing, impassioned smile. Within her hazel eyes, he saw the light of a million dancing souls. In that moment, he knew the wound in her heart had been healed. The peace she had longed for had finally been found.

"More than I could ever imagine," she answered. Chase pulled her into his arms. They were eye to eye, their noses nearly touching. He began to kiss her, and Rachel sighed contentedly, slipping her arms around his neck.

"And you?" she asked, laughing softly.

He closed his eyes and inhaled the scent of her vanilla hair. "I'll remember this for the rest of my life."

There was something he needed to ask her— something she needed to hear. But he wasn't sure if this was the right time or place. Or how she would react.

Rachel touched his cheek and smiled, sending his heart racing and scattering his doubts.

"Look who's here!" Tamayo said, excitedly breaking into his thoughts.

Shinzo approached them with Mariko on his arm. "I'm glad to see you both decided to come out and play before leaving."

"Me too," Rachel said. Then she turned to Mariko. "I'm so glad you're feeling better."

The beautiful geisha smiled coyly. Then her eyes moved toward a gathering a short distance away. She seemed to recognize a fellow geisha in their midst. "If you don't mind," she told Shinzo, "there's someone I need to speak with. Rachel...Cohen-san, it was nice seeing you again."

Together they nodded a farewell, and she walked away in her elegant crème kimono. Tamayo hurried to catch up and join her then looked back with a beaming white smile.

"Seems Mariko is back to her old self again," Chase told Shinzo.

As the monk's eyes latched onto her, his lips curled into a smile. "Though the flame be put out, the wick remains."

"Which means?"

"I remain forever hopeful."

"What about Yuki?" Rachel asked.

Shinzo straightened his collar. "I believe she's resting comfortably at home this evening."

"Will she have any kind of future? I mean with everything that happened..."

He shook his head and chuckled. "You both worry too much, Cohen-san. But in this case, you needn't do so. Yuki will be just fine. In fact, she's planning another trip overseas...an extended one, as the result of Mitsui-san's advice." His attention shifted to an ice cream stand preparing to close. "Would you look at that? I think they have those red bean Popsicles you like. If you hurry, you just might be able to get one..."

"Do you mind?" Chase asked Rachel. "I'll buy you one too, if you'd like."

She huffed a sweet laugh. "No, go enjoy yourself, silly. Who knows when you'll find one of those again?"

After he was gone Shinzo turned to Rachel and looked at her lovingly. "And what about you? Do you feel you gained anything from this trip?"

"Definitely." She smiled, watching Tamayo interact with other young maikos in the crowd. "I still can't believe I have a sister. You know, that's something I've always wanted."

Shinzo's smile brightened. "I had a feeling that was the case," he said. "You have a lot to look forward to in your life, Rachel. A new relationship with Tamayo, a future with Chase...and now with a child on the way..."

She swallowed hard. "What?"

"Oh yes. You're most blessed. He's going to be a beautiful little boy and look a lot like his father. He's going to be a great leader too. It's in his genes."

"How could you know that? I'm not even sure myself."

"Oh, somehow I think you are. You just don't want to admit it. And I know you don't want him to know either, but sooner or later Chase will find out from you or someone else."

Rachel glanced at Chase counting out his coins. "This isn't the way it's supposed to be. I'm just learning how to be a sister. How can I be a mother when I don't even know how to be a wife?"

Shinzo smiled and laughed softly. "You'll figure it out." For Rachel, there was no humor in the awkward situation...only a sense of panic. She looked into the monk's brown eyes, searching for understanding. "Please...don't say anything in front of Chase. I don't want this to be the reason we stay together."

"You need to relax, Miss Lyons," he said. "I think you know as well as I do the way he feels about you. That's not going to change. Not in the least."

"I'm not so sure about that," she said. "People fall out of love all the time."

Chase returned with his reward, beaming like a kid with a candy bar. "You sure you don't want a bite of this? You never know how good something is unless you try it."

Shinzo tilted his head to one side. "He's right about that, Rachel. Sometimes you just need to have a little faith before you dive in."

"And what if the pool's deep and you can't swim?" she asked.

"Then you learn how to tread water."

Chase quirked a brow. "I haven't got a clue what you two are talking about. Rachel's a great swimmer."

Shinzo's face beamed with his usual smile. "She's always been a natural…just wasn't aware of it."

A weak smile graced her lips when she faced him again. He reacted by pulling her in for a powerful hug. Then he shook hands with Chase and bid them farewell before disappearing into the thick, buzzing crowd. Like the pope in St. Peter's Square, all around him people pressed closer, as if hoping to touch him, to be blessed by his power, to witness the message in his words.

Chase looked down at Rachel and smoothed his hand over her hair. "He's quite a guy, isn't he?"

She nodded. With sad thoughts of Shinzo's last goodbye, she added, "He sure is."

As they strolled back to the hotel hand in hand, Rachel glanced back over her shoulder, hoping for a chance to see him once more—for a final glance at the Buddhist monk who wore prayer beads and a silver cross under his shirt. The man who believed every religion was a piece of the pie and that some people preferred slender portions while others enjoyed the feast. Unfortunately, he was nowhere to be seen. He was either gone or hidden from view. Perhaps back at Mariko's side once more, the way she liked to think of him. But without even realizing it, Rachel's appetite for enlightenment had been whet. Under Shinzo's guidance, she had pierced the veil of the invisible, glimpsed the impossible, and seen into the unknown. Her vision of the world had been forever altered, and through his passion and kind words, a seed of faith had been planted in her nurturing heart.

# 44

As Chase sat in the Tokyo airport waiting to board the flight to Los Angeles, he unzipped the side pocket on his suitcase. He withdrew the blue velvet box he had made a point of hiding throughout the whole trip. After opening the hinged lid, he ran his thumb over the three- carat yellow cushion-cut diamond ring and found himself wondering if he'd made the right choice. Would she like it? Would she have preferred a traditional ring and the opportunity to pick it out together? Shit. What if the answer was no and she didn't want to marry him at all? What was he supposed to do then?

The lantern festival would have been perfect, he told himself. She was so happy and the mood felt exactly right. It would have been romantic to ask her under the shimmering blue moon sky. But then Tamayo had been there and everyone in Japan would have been watching. Or at least it would have seemed that way.

Honestly. For once in his life, why couldn't he be spontaneous like Rachel? As strong and confident as she had become? He pocketed the ring quickly just as she returned from the bathroom, looking flushed and slightly irritable. She had eaten crackers all the way to the airport in the taxi after complaining about breakfast and the unbearable summer heat. Judging from the perspiration on her forehead and her nervous pacing, she seemed to have lost them along with her cheery disposition.

"Are you okay?" he asked, not knowing what else to say.

"Yeah, I'm...fine," she said unconvincingly.

She was as closemouthed as ever. Revealing nothing at all. Over the past four days, they had taken two steps forward in their relationship and now they were falling three steps back.

Rachel sat on the plane next to Chase, studying his profile. She'd read stories about women telling their boyfriends about their pregnancies. At first the guys were happy about the news but then became terribly cold and distant and eventually angry. They would say things like they were overwhelmed and needed space to deal with all of it. One of them even had a superstition that the news of a pregnancy would damage his luck. Conversations between him and his girlfriend became strained, and when asked if he wanted their relationship to be over, he'd walked away saying they needed more time.

Time. That was something she was lacking. By Rachel's best estimate, she was over eight weeks along. She had no idea what was going on in Chase's head or if their relationship would get any better. Then she considered the past...the way he had left her when her father had died. At a time when she needed him most. She stared out the window and wondered if she could find a way to get over him. To walk away from him...the way he had walked away from her four years ago.

"Tamayo is pretty amazing, isn't she?" Chase asked, looking down at the photograph on his iPhone of them standing together near the lake. "It's going to be fun showing her around California when she comes this spring. You know she made me promise we'd take her to Disneyland. I guess she's more of a kid than she lets on."

Chase's trademark smile twisted the corners of his lips, and the sight of it loosened the tears in her eyes. As if on cue, his brow came down and his hand went up, tenderly wiping them away. "Baby, what is it?" he asked.

Rachel drew a deep breath. She looked into his light blue eyes, praying she'd have the strength to get through this…to tell him what he had every right to know. "I'm having a baby and I'm really pleased you're the father," she blurted out. "I'll go it alone even if you won't support me. I don't want you to feel obligated. And if you do contribute, that's great. But what I'd really like is for you to share in it, and if it doesn't work, I won't hold it against you."

Chase blew out a deep breath and stared at her with his mouth agape, as if she'd just spoken a strange new language. He seemed to be grappling with what to do…what to say. Evaluating the dreams and plans for his future she had destroyed in one fell swoop.

"You're…you're pregnant? How? Are you sure? I mean…you didn't think you were before and now—"

Rachel glanced down and shook her head. "I'm sorry. I should have told you. I wasn't sure until this morning and then I didn't really want to believe it. I just thought it would go away and…" She laughed at her own stupidity. At her inability to be honest with herself. "Anyway, I meant what I said. You don't have to be a part of this if you don't want to."

"Are you crazy? Why wouldn't I? I'm in love with you. Don't you know that? And having a child with you is even better. It would be a dream come true. Baby, for once in your life, have a little faith in me...please."

Tears were streaming down her face and her nose was running. She was sniveling like a silly child and couldn't stop no matter how hard she tried. Chase took a box of tissues from the flight attendant and handed them to Rachel. He helped her wipe her face and then tipped her head back and stared into her eyes.

"Rachel, tell me how you feel," he said. "Not what a terrible wife or mother you'd make or the burden that for some God-awful reason you think you would be in my life. All I need to hear...all I need to know...is that you love me."

She hesitated before nodding. "Yes. I love you," she whispered.

"That's it? That's all you can say?"

"I'm afraid our only concern will be this baby. That we'll lose sight of each other and—"

"Goddammit, girl!" he snapped, not caring if anyone in the airplane heard. "I love you, and if you're not going to accept that, then I don't know what else to tell you. Yes, you are carrying my child and that gives me every reason to keep you in my life. If you would just lose this mentality that you have to do everything on your own maybe we can go somewhere with this. Whether it's in my care or your care, our baby is goin' to be taken care of. And damn it, yes. We both have problems and have made our share of mistakes. But can you just put yours aside long enough to tell me you love me and mean it? That's all I wanna know, baby. If you tell me that, I promise you won't have anything else to worry about. You deserve better, I know that. But I'm tellin' you, God sent you to me for this. Just tell me you love me, sweetheart. That's all I really ask."

Rachel stared at him, blinking, amazed by the passion he felt. The same passion she had kept tied up for years, afraid to believe in, afraid to turn loose. She nodded earnestly. Her smile spread wide. Tears of joy streamed down her cheeks. "I love you...I love you...I love you," she said, her voice cracking with emotion.

Chase pulled off his seat belt. He stepped into the aisle and dropped to one knee.

"We're about to take off," a male flight attendant told him. "Everyone in their seat. That includes you, sir."

"Not yet," the pretty blond flight attendant said, holding his shoulder. "I think the captain would make an exception here."

Chase took the ring box out of his pocket and flipped it open. He looked up at Rachel and said, "Then marry me. I offer you my hand, my heart, my world. Marry me, end my torment... and for God's sake, make my life complete."

Rachel was crying so hard she could barely breathe. Could barely get the words out of her mouth. "Yes...yes...yes! I'll marry you. Now get off your knee so we can go home."

The plane erupted in cheers and applause, and for a moment Chase felt a sense of embarrassment for his overly dramatic display. But then he realized as he sat down, fastened his seat belt, and took Rachel's hands in his, that he would drop his drawers in front of the world if it meant keeping this girl.

With a smile plastered on his face, he took the ring from the box and slid it onto her finger. It fit perfectly— as if it was made for her.

Rachel gave him an exuberant kiss. "It's beautiful," she said, admiring her hand.

He leaned over and kissed her then murmured against her lips, "You'll always be my greatest treasure."

She smiled and sat back in her seat. Then she reached into the breast pocket of her white blouse and pulled out a small silk bag. "Even greater than these?"

"And what do we have here?" he asked, taking it from her.

"A little going away gift. It was sent to our room before we left along with a note from Shinzo. After he arranged for one way tickets to Bangkok for Nikki Ota and Takashi Bekku, Mitsui-san contacted Shinzo and told him that he didn't want us to go home empty handed."

Chase tugged open the bag and poured five shimmering diamonds into the palm of his hand. He stared at them without blinking. "I can't even imagine what these are worth."

"More than me?" she asked, looking at him from the top of her eyes.

He chuckled. Then he claimed her mouth and tugged gently on her bottom lip with his teeth, drinking in the little sound of pleasure she made.

She pulled back with a questioning look on her face. "What about my uncle? I know I'm not a child, but he's been my guardian since my father died. We'll need to go to London to ask his permission." She paused before adding, "What if he says no?"

"Now why would he do that? I'm only planning to make an honest woman out of you."

"Honest?" she asked. "Little ol' me?"

"Well, as much as humanly possible anyway." He propped his head on the armrest so he could watch her expression, the happy glint in her eyes.

"If you do, sir, then I shall look forward to you corrupting me all over again." Rachel giggled and watched him try to keep his carefree, devilish grin from spreading.

"It will be my pleasure," Chase said, taking her hand and kissing it. He loved the effect Rachel had on him—the way she could warm his heart with one lingering look. As she showed his ring off to the passengers around her and the smiling blond flight attendant, he found himself fantasizing about all the reactions he could evoke from Rachel while snuggling on board Stargazer in the captain's quarters, traveling for weeks on end...all the way to Europe and back.

# EPILOGUE

*Two months later...*

Mariko stood before a gold framed mirror in the bathroom of a large private home in Minami-Azabu, Tokyo's most expensive residential area. She adjusted the sharp metal chopstick she'd used to secure the twisted bun on top of her head, while allowing loose strands to seductively fall over her shoulders. With a growing sense of dread, she blew out a breath and wiped a finger under her eyes to clear away her tear smudged eyeliner. Then she stepped back to assess her appearance. Her red glossy lips stood out against her fair skin and complemented her black silk dress with its low cut neckline. The expensive skintight creation molded her figure in all the right places and featured a revealing thigh high slit. Exactly what the man ordered.

Waiting in the next room was the Halloween party's guest of honor—a high-ranking statesman in his mid- sixties with secret yakuza connections. He had taken over where Takashi Bekku had left off...shipping homeless girls to China and Thailand.

Only this guy preferred to educate the young ones himself and could be brutal in the process. At least that's what Mitsui-san had told her.

The day after Rachel Lyons and Chase Cohen had flown back to America, the Zakura-kai boss had shown up uninvited at her apartment in Kyoto with two of his men. His frown and cagey demeanor told her that he wasn't there for pleasantries. Without warning, he charged inside, sending her cowering behind the doorway.

"Why did you try to kill me?" Mitsui yelled. "What have I ever done to you?"

Mariko swallowed hard. Her eyes filled with fearful tears that she dared not let leave her eyes. "Kill you? Why would I do that?" she asked, struggling to control her shaking voice. She glanced at his soldiers and realized their faces were etched with contempt, mirroring the expression of the man standing before them.

Mitsui remained ominously silent then angled his head to the side. "So I guess the dishwasher in your okiya was lying when he said he saw you try to poison me and Takashi Bekku. Just before he switched the teacups you used."

Mariko's lips parted. Oh my God. He knows. Her gaze dropped to the carpet...to the top of the three pairs of shoes that remained on their assailants' feet. They had come here to kill her. There was no doubt in her mind. And just when she thought she was in the clear and had a chance for a normal life with Shinzo. At least as normal as it could be after everything she'd been through.

"Well...what do you have to say? Should I cut out his tongue for lying to me?" Mitsui threatened.

It took every ounce of courage for Mariko to lift her eyes and meet his. She shook her head but had no words to offer.

"Are you going to tell me the truth?" he persisted. "Why would you do such a thing? Were you hoping to get caught? Is that it? Do you want to join Kenji that badly?"

She swallowed hard again but didn't look away, although she desperately wanted to. "It was for my father," she murmured. "For ordering his death."

"Your father? How could you know..." He stopped short and looked around. Then he seemed to remember the source of her information. The black journal his men had confiscated. "Despite what Kenji wrote," he told her, "your father's bad judgment caused four of my men to be killed. There's no reason I needed to tell you that or to justify my actions. And whether you believe it or not is of no concern to me. But the fact that you risked your own life to try to take mine disturbs me beyond measure. If Kenji was here, I would order him to handle this with no questions asked. Have him pour poison down your throat and watch you squirm until the job was done." Mitsui shook his head. "No...now that I think about it, that's too easy. Way too quick. I have a far better solution. Something that couldn't be more perfect under the circumstances."

Mitsui's lips curled into an unnatural smile. He glanced back at his men before facing her. Then he presented his ultimatum—the new profession that came with his promise to kill everyone she loved if she ever disobeyed him. It would be a departure from her life as a geisha, a journey over the edge and into a shadowy underworld with no means of escape other than suicide or a vengeful death enacted by another sole survivor.

Weeks passed and Mariko did exactly as she was told. She cut herself off from Shinzo, from everyone she knew or loved. She trained with the other assassins, and after carrying out four murders, she knew there would never be an end to her obligation.

There would never be forgiveness from the Buddhist monk or a way to share in his happiness. Not without being discovered or foolishly putting his life at risk.

Mariko had been condemned to hell on earth. The only road to redemption rested in her afterlife and Shinzo's willingness to pray for her soul—to guide her to the light Kenji had found at the end of his long, dark tunnel. In the meantime, she needed to bury her threads, as Nikki had told her...to distance herself from her memories. There was work to be done tonight—another job to grow her reputation as Mitsui's trained black widow spider.

A pounding fist hit the bathroom door, jarring her thoughts and reminding her to turn off the running water in the sink. With all the guests now gone, she took her time drying her hands on the towel before slipping Kenji's red katana over her shoulder. Then she drew a deep, cleansing breath and mentally rehearsed her actions. As directed by her heartless boss, this one would suffer more than the rest—more than she had ever witnessed before or would ever want to again.

"Damn it, Katsumi," came from her drunken, soon-to-be victim. "Are we going to have that party you promised or not?"

# ABOUT THE AUTHOR

Kaylin McFarren is a California native who has enjoyed traveling around the world. She previously worked as director for a fine art gallery, where she helped foster the careers of various artists before feeling the urge to satisfy her own creative impulses.

Since launching her writing career, McFarren has earned more than a dozen literary awards in addition to a finalist spot in the 2008 RWA Golden Heart Contest. A member of RWA, Rose City Romance Writers, and Willamette Writers, she also lends her participation and support to various charitable and educational organizations in the Pacific Northwest.

McFarren currently lives with her husband in Oregon. They have three children and two grandchildren.

## *Inspiration behind the story*

For more than forty years, Kaylin has been fascinated with the arts and culture of Japan and has been fortunate to travel throughout Asia with her family. Due to her husband's business interests and roots stemming from Japan, she has had the remarkable opportunity to develop personal relationships with Japanese shipping agents, politicians, company executives, religious leaders, and talented geikos and maikos who reside and perform in Kyoto's Gion district.

Her interest in this field, along with her fascination with the Japanese underworld, inspired her to write this erotic, action filled drama, which involved researching Japanese history, the yakuza, geishas, and the natural disasters that befell Japan from the seventeenth to the twenty-first centuries. It is her hope that this story will entertain readers and honor dedicated geikos and their sisters who strive to maintain the true culture and beauty of Japan.

Made in the USA
Middletown, DE
04 April 2016